The Life & Travels of Saint Cuthwin

By

IRVING WARNER

PLEASURE BOAT STUDIO: A LITERARY PRESS

Edited by Jack Estes
Cover and Book Design by Lauren Grosskopf

The image to represent Cwenburh's 'clasp' on the cover,
and metaphorically as a clasp to open the book, is a medieval Anglo-Saxon
Gold belt buckle from the ship-burial at Sutton Hoo:
© The Trustees of the British Museum

Pleasure Boat Studio books are available through your
favorite bookstore and through the following:

SPD (Small Press Distribution) Tel. 800-869-7553
Baker & Taylor 800-775-1100
Ingram Tel 615-793-5000
Amazon.com and bn.com
& through

PLEASURE BOAT STUDIO: A NONPROFIT LITERARY PRESS
NONPROFIT CORPORATION / EIN 82-3128519 / D-U-N-S Number is 080932413 /
UBI 604-179-537 / Business ID#: 001 / Location: 0001 / Seattle, Washington
PLEASUREBOATSTUDIO.COM

Contact *Lauren Grosskopf, Publisher*
Lauren@pleasureboatstudio.com

CuthwinANDCwenburh.COM

Preface

The inclusion of a fictional introduction was done from the very first days of my composition of *The Life & Travels of Saint Cuthwin*. At that time, as I do now, I wanted an Edwardian tone to the text to add the luster of reality to my text, plus make reasonable the full range of our story-teller's language.

Since I was not a specialist in eleventh-century England, but wanted historical accuracy, I had much research to do. I knew I would not deceive the specialist, but wanted to appear that I respected the period, which I do.

The noted exception to historical accuracy is there was never a Cuthwin; he is completely my invention. However, he was real to me at the end, and now. I hope he will be to the reader as well. I do reaffirm that beyond this point, this is a work of historical fiction.

IRVING WARNER, 2018

The wicked in his pride persecutes the poor;
let them be caught in the plots which they have devised.
For the wicked boasts his heart's desire; he blesses
the greedy and renounces the Lord.

Psalm 10, ii-iii.

INTRODUCTION
The Life & Travels of Saint Cuthwin
R. AUBREY RICHARDS

THE TEXT YOU ARE ABOUT TO READ WAS DICTATED TO THE MONKS of St. Kea Monastery in modern Cornwall between about 1105 to 1107 by Cuthwin the Fencebuilder, born Cuthwin-of-Alnwick, around 1015 in the village of that name. He was Saxon and became fluent in reading and writing that language. However, he had ruined his hands after years of arduous work constructing stone fences.

This necessitated his dictating his story between the ages of 85 and 90 years. His stated point—knowing he was venerated and possibly would become acclaimed a Saint on death—was to dash any notion that he become acclaimed a Saint on death. Instead he steadfastly set out to communicate that he was an ordinary Saxon who had seen an entire swath of history and had a unique life and travels. He starts at his earliest memory, and ends—we assume—not too long before his death. All the words are his, *save the summaries of individual books* which were posthumous additions by his devoted followers who, contrary to his wishes, acclaimed him Saint anyway.

Enough said about that—the rest you will glean serendipitously from Cuthwin as he allows his story to unfold.

As for my role, I was contacted by the publishers to revise this translation done directly from Old English to Edwardian-era English—to make it more "comfortable" for the modern reader. The translation was originally done by my grandfather, Edward L. Sutherland, between 1906-1909.

My grandfather's translation, as stated, was made directly from Old English. I advised the current publishers that to revise it would be to alter artistry of a manuscript just for the sake of modern tone and diction. The open translation of Old English's earthier words and expressions no longer hinders publication as they did in 1910.

The provenance of the extant manuscript is excellent. It was sold along with other medieval manuscripts in a revision of all Vatican Library inventory ordered by Pope Pius VII in 1822. It is supposed that the purged manuscripts were sold for containing material negative to the Church, possibly even heretical.

"The Life & Travels of Saint Cuthwin" was one of these manuscripts, and the oldest. It is now—and since 1822 has been—in possession of a private collector in England. This family has generously given me free access throughout this process, as they did my grandfather. Why the manuscript would be felt "negative" by the Church, I will leave to the modern reader.

r.a.r. 2018

The Life & Travels of Saint Cuthwin

Introduction to the
OVERALL PROCEEDINGS

I NARRATE MY LIFE AND TRAVELS IN THIS YEAR 1097 TO GOOD ISWHL-of-Ilchester with modest aims. At onset I remind all that I am Cuthwin the Fencebuilder, who has striven to build and mend fences along the boisterous coast of Kernowec these past thirty-odd years. I am nothing more than most hard-working freedmen, and certainly not a holy man, never having taken tonsure. I am an honest keeper of our Savior's words, like most Saxon folk.

And I am indeed Saxon both in kind and tongue which these last nearly forty years diminishes at court, in market, and croft. Fence-building has ruined my hands for writing or much else; hence Iswhl takes my words spoken, and commits them to writing, but admonishes me to read them over carefully, and I do.

Countrymen throughout the hills and shores come to my hermitage and, due to my travels and age, have sought advice on many topics. Since I have knowledge of letters and words, I do my best to share that God-given fortune. Hence, over the years good people have mistakenly attributed age, experience, perhaps wisdom—for holiness. Too often of late I have heard my name uttered in the context of religious gift.

So I write this to impart to all, for I will soon be gone: That I began life as a poor man who lived honestly, and will be taken by God in the same humble circumstances. This is what I desire to pass on to those reading of my life and travels.

Book 1

St. Cuthwin commences the telling of his early life, including his place of birth, and the circumstances of how he came to Peterborough Abby; his youthful education and subsequent departure from Peterborough to commence his early wanderings.

In the name of the Father, the Son, and the Holy Ghost, I, Cuthwin-of-Alnwick, a simple child subject no more nor less to the baser nature of all men, begin the story of my long travels. I do so on this year of the tragic death of King William Rufus of England and the accession of his brother Henry[1]. I was born a freedman on the Nativity of Saint Mary[2], and thanks to a generous Creator have thus far seen eighty-nine winters. Possessing clear memory and present mind, after long urging from my more learned and reverend brethren, I proceed with the story of my humble but wide-ranging life.

At the beginning of King Cnut's long reign[3], God keep his soul, I was born to a house scull belonging to the Manor of Pilson-of-Withernsea, then an under-tenant to a thane of a Great Lord. There is nothing known of my father, save he was one of many pitiless Danes who ravaged Withernsea. The woman violated was Sarah, keen for the joys of fellowship and good ale, and much less for the hard work of kitchen and hearth. For these trespasses, I was told later, she was oft punished. Because of her ill-balanced humors, I had many brothers and sisters, for I was the eleventh of fourteen. Most of my siblings were rescued in early infancy from this troubled world by merciful God.

It was aired even in my person that my father, the Dane, violated territory oft yielded voluntarily or secured trespass in less-than-bad spirited circumstances. It was some weeks after being delivered of her fourteenth child that my mother departed this earth. I was told she died shriven, for her ways oft had been contrary to one of steady faith. I have only vague memory of this poor woman, my mother, but to this day pray for her soul as any true son would.

---

[1] King of England, 1100-1135

[2] September 9th

[3] King of England, 1016-1035

I was raised at commonality in the Manor of Pilson-of-Withernsea until not yet a stripling. I do remember the Lord of the Manor as a largish Saxon with great strands of red hair. He often drank to excess, falling off his horse onto whatever earthly circumstances lay beneath.

Working at livery, I would greet the animal as it arrived without its besotted rider. Joined by the Master of Horse's boy and others, we would search in all directions until we found our Lord. The lad finding him was rewarded with a ha'pence, after which we struggled at litter returning Pilson-of-Withernsea to the Manor proper. This Manor was meager, unlike Norman manors current, though boards always were sufficient of necessity for keeping body and spirit served.

At about the time a lad begins finding his staff, I and several serfs were transacted to Gilbert-of-Wharram Percy by our previous master to satisfy debt.

Wharram Percy was several leagues[4] from my birthplace and upon soks much different. The Manor House of Gilbert was larger, and I was put in service to one of his trusted housecarls named Alwystle, He was a harsh master for any lad, of loutish nature, quick with cruel hand and foot, a man of colic temper. Thankfully he was slow of wit and easily hooded even by young boys.

Furthermore, he was plagued with badly portioned humors, and given to base excesses common to those not thoroughly of Christian virtue, which he was not. Alwystle was not of Saxon blood or natural tongue, and what little Christian goodness he practiced or espoused was different than most. He mocked the local clerics, refusing them entry upon his lands, and claimed it was because they celebrated Roman Easter rather than of the True Faith. Lastly, he claimed it was because of these Roman blasphemies that beasts and gorgons plagued the country.

Alwystle's household was both of village and field. I was given to the fields, and saw little of the village. Mostly I stayed in a cottage distant and labored for various bondsmen long in Alwystle's service. These all despised him, cheating his offices whenever possible to increase their lot, but if caught were whipped severely at post, summer or winter.

---

[4] League. In 11th century England, a league was 1.4 miles or 2.2 km.

Being of the field, I grew into young manhood with little guidance but what nature and my fellows devised. Hence young and raw boys, as they will, allowed ourselves pleasures as we might follow. For little was at hand that offered respite from hard work, the brutish kick, or the whipping piece.

From older men we were told the ways of pleasure in stable and paddock. We did not question their views, and indeed observed our diverse overseers in such acts. As boys do when learning from men, we followed their example. But when one of Alwystle's head men observed us in such an act, he became angry.

Not understanding the strange contradiction of saying one thing and doing another, we waxed truthful of what we'd seen and heard others do. Both our ill-timed behavior plus revealing what we should not against our elders promised us horrible punishment. Rather than face this, I along with a lad named Pyster ran off. This itself was a grievous offense—then as now—for lads under guardianship or bond were tethered by law to our manorial Lords.

We feared the consequences of our acts. At the very least, Pyster guessed, we would be relieved of those body parts most responsible for bringing the Evil One into the fold of Alwystle Manor.

It was late spring; we were young of body and spirit, as suited to field and copse as young hares, with little more sense than such lame-witted creatures. We spent the days venturing down the River Humber, living by our wits and avoiding people. Any soul seeing such boys at leisure, even the simplest cottar[4], would have deduced our ill-stood status. By catching us and informing Master Alwystle, they would gain considerable reward. Therefore, elusive as young hinds, we made our way down the great river.

After much idle travel, on the morning of the fourth day we observed great amounts of smoke seaward. Since we were far distant from Wharram Percy we became more confident. The smoke caused a vast haze everywhere and smelled of autumn when fields were burned, yet it was not yet summer.

A crone happened by in a wagon drawn by a largish cottar—looking more beast than human. We knew that neither of them could catch us so risked asking her what the meaning of the fire was. She took rest, and said several dragons were loosed in the valley below and had set everything afire, being in great temper after suffering one indignity or another by haughty villagers.

My companion and I were struck with fear and were about to flee inland. She stopped us and said in thoughtful manner that she was knowledgeable about such monsters and was taking a road around the troubles on her way to a copse where she had cottage and croft. She looked us up and down, and said she had need for two lads. Her old bones made work in croft difficult, and gesturing to the lout who pulled her cart, told us, "The dumb beast you see before you is good for nothing but burden, being deficient of mind. So," she allowed, ". . . you decide as you must. I must resume before the worms advance this way."

Prodding the poor lout onward, she continued on her way, passing downhill into a copse of great trees where flowed a stream. We in fact had spent the night there. Pyster and I were shy of her offer, yet knew she could not catch us, so he opined that we could follow along, for smoke was thickening, making eyes smart. Pyster had heard much about dragons and knew them to be clever in pursuing and catching folk. The crone would surely know how to avoid such monsters; otherwise how might she enjoy such a long life?

We caught up with her and she was not surprised. While pulled along, she told us of diverse wonders. She was merry and true to her word, and soon the fires were more behind us and we moved uphill, along more of a path than road, so progress was slow but of good spirit.

At midday we reached the border of a thick forest and aged stone bridge traversing a considerable stream. She ordered the lout to stop and had us help her down from the wagon where she made repast. She shared bread and a kipper with us. Having fed for days on wild fare, we fell on her victuals keenly.

We began to sup when four men appeared from the woods, and the lout for the first time became aware of events, allowed outcry, and ran into the woods like the beast he was. They made no move to pursue but closed in. Seeing his chance Pyster ran, at once pursued by two of the men—but he was so fleet he evaded them and, like the lout, was swallowed up by the thick, shadowy forest. The pursuers returned at once. I never saw Pyster nor lout again.

Two of those remaining—one seemingly in charge—were so near me I knew I would not have the success Pyster had. The crone immediately visited foul words on them, then suddenly all switched to a tongue I could not understand, though I discerned the words were wholly unpleasant.

Drawing a knife, two of the four seized the crone, lifted her up, and despite outcry and protest, threw her kicking off the bridge and into the stream, in the last moment slitting her throat. They murdered her as if doing any minor, bothersome chore.

The cart, however, drew immediate and keen inspection.

These wretches' headman, seeing I had befouled myself in abject fright, laughed and informed me the crone was transporting the two of us to the Danes who were presently harrying. They were part of the host that was burning and looting the countryside for nearly a week.

"Two young men sold into serfdom would have brought a month of high living for the old sow if she knew her trading. Well, one will do us. Demons and fiends will consume the other."

They sat and partook the ill-begotten victuals, offering me none though in truth I could not have eaten. They talked in the foreign tongue and seemed cheered by their new possession, the cart.

"Who was that great gorgon of hers who ran off?" The headman asked, and I told him he drew her cart.

One of them eyed me while they talked, and since I was bound to the cart was at the mercy of the scum. Seeing what they did to the crone and how the lout had fled, I was sorrowful of my future. Though considerable daylight remained, each of them fell asleep, having consumed most the bread, ale, and all the kipper; hence, like stoats filled with ill-begotten food, they slept richly satisfied.

Though I'd been tethered skillfully to the cart, they had used the crone's old, worn lines, which were rotted. With youthful teeth sharp as a hayrake, I soon gnawed my way free and fled into the wood and away from the trail. As night approached, I was afraid and whistled for Pyster until my lips were chaffed. This was the first night I spent in my own company. The creatures that roamed in darkness, their calls and moans, caused me to tremble. This was a long night.

In the morning I awoke with a violent shaking and stout yank by my britches, and I found myself elevated and looking into the eyes of two different brutish cottars[5]. They wrested me about, secured my elbows together and dragged me along as they might a sack of wool. When I cried out, one smote me—knocking me mute and foggy-headed.

My brainpan was just clearing when I found myself half-standing before a towering black horse. From atop this grand mount, the likes of which I had never seen, its imposing rider looked down—a man in black habit, and with his hood back, I saw he was tonsured and despite my youthful ignorance knew him to be a holy man.

My two captors presented me proudly to him, like dogs with a joint of mutton.

But there was no time to think further on this, for I was knocked

---

[5] Farm laborers living in a cottage. Probably free.

down by one of them with the other brute shouting, "On your belly when you're before His Reverence, you little toad!"

One informed how they had found me in the woods having cleverly tracked me there. With this information, the Reverend thought some time, then asked, "What do they call you—who do you belong to? Now, if you lie to me, I'll know and have your tongue cut out and fed to the rooks."

I believed him and told him everything save the reason for my fleeing Alwystle's manor. Even at this early age, craft of mind was my guardian, though later it also became my demon. But at this moment I sensed this cleric's authority, and kept mute regards reasons for running off.

This sent him into another rumination, and when my captors spoke, he ordered them silent, still considering me. Finally, "And why did you abandon rightful board which was God's place for you?"

"I unwittingly saw acts there, ungodly; also yesterday witnessed the murder of an old woman, Your Reverence, and was afraid for life and soul."

He maintained his gaze. Finally taking a great draught of air he shook his head. "So it seems your running away led to witnessing the murder of a hag—so you have not improved your lot."

From behind, a pair of horsemen approached. They too rode fine animals and, unlike the pair who caught me these were housecarls[6], so armed and dressed.

One cast a glance back, then looked with weariness to me. "Shall we hang this creature too, Your Reverence? The other four are quite cold now," he laughed and added, ". . . but will be warmer soon enough."

Subcellarer[7] Eadsige—for indeed this was that holy man who later arose to great success and fame—was then young but already sure of office. In the following half-dozen years, I was to learn much indirectly from his words and ways.

Without paying any notice to his attendants' suggestion, he held up his hand—for the others had laughed. They ceased at once.

---

[6] A member of household/manor troops or bodyguard.

[7] A monk a step below the cellarer who is an officer or obedienciary in the monastery responsible for supplying food and drink. In Benedictine monasteries the cellarer's duties were expanded greatly.

"He's young and strong, and our Gardener has work on the fens. Take him back with us. Feed him, but watch he doesn't escape."

So began my first long journey. In truth I'd never been more than twenty leagues from my birthplace at Withernsea, or indeed south of the Humbria. During our way south, I was kept tethered and watched by that brace of vultures who'd captured me; I was fed and treated tolerably, as I recall. During the second day I was told I was now in Bond of Default to the Abbey at Peterborough.

So this is how I first heard of such monastic offices. Furthermore, I only had vague knowledge of the great center at Peterborough, and nothing of abbeys save they were the havens of great men.

From the sun and stars, I reckoned we continued directly south. We were a large party all the time on the alert. Mammoth carts under burden were each towed by four braces of mighty burgundy oxen, the finest and strongest I ever saw.

All were in rich, bold array: The housecarls, a dozen of them, and several additional monks like Eadsige. These latter reverences stayed apart from the rest, but without doubt in overall command was Eadsige who devised and directed business each day.

In the party was one named Gilbert, a stableman, who was a good person. He attended the many horses and mules of our procession. On the third or fourth day he was kind enough to attend to wounds developed in my bindings—and the one upon my head where I had been smitten. Gilbert so attended despite mocking words from the cottars: "He'll make fine sport for our Lord Gardener."

This and many other taunts they visited on me. Yet my youthful mind was nimble—equal to the task of perceiving 'which fowl pecked who,' as they said in the farmyard. These cottars were of the lowest sort—not armed, and of rough garb. They hoped for great profit for my capture when they reached Peterborough.

Gilbert used few words, for he was a Welshman and not comfortable in our language, though skilled enough. Finally while attending my head wound, he said to them, "You two cotsets[8] strike him any harder, and

---

[8] Lowest sort of cottar, without land and frequently bonded.

Father Abbot will have nothing but a corpse."

Words were visited on Gilbert, the two taking exception to being called cotsets. But Gilbert ignored them. They did not press the matter further, and remained quiet if sullen.

This was the first night I spent in some peace, for Gilbert moved me to the makeshift animal shelter. He slept near his animals, and as if I were one, kept a keen eye on my head wound, which took an ill turn. While freshening a thick, pasty unguent upon the wound, he asked, "Do you know where you are being taken?"

"Peterborough."

"Yes. But do you know what such a place is and what they do?"

"It is an abbey. They pray?"

He smiled in a manner which I learned was about the droll man's most extreme of humor.

"No. Prayer is not all of it. So, Young Cuthwin, speak when spoken to, volunteer nothing, and know well to keep your place."

That evening was warm for spring, and listening to the wild creatures at their songs and cries, I considered Gilbert's words. They confused and kept me musing during the warm, strange night.

It is only frail memory and God's grace after the passage of four-score circuits that informs me of that time so long ago. I came to the great Abbey of Peterborough; if not precise, only a little short of Abbot Elsin's twenty-fifth year in that high office.

As our now-considerable procession trailed out upon the East Anglia fenland, our number had increased to many carts and animals destined for the Abbey at Peterborough. We had converged with other provisioning parties, and Subcellarer Eadsige rode before them on his grand animal, both as black as a raven's mantle.

With us was a substantial group of housecarls who guarded, all owing service to the Abbey. These traveled with His Reverence Eadsige. My wounds were better thanks to Gilbert and the vigor of youth. Distant from familiar land, to attempt my escape would be folly; also, when re-captured, the result would be even more painful than the first. The same cottars who had caught me still followed closely, for I was of considerable worth to them. They bragged about their accomplishment to any who might listen.

"A healthy, well-fed boy with so much hard work in him! He would have been the very devil to ferret from wood and hollow without the likes of us."

When the time for their reward drew closer, they became friendlier with he who represented their increase in life. And since we traveled exclusively through hundreds or sokes[9] belonging to the Abbey, foresters in our procession took wild game, so all ate well.

I applied Gilbert's advice, and despite growing familiarity, answered only when asked. In fresh possession of youthful wit and cunning, I listened and measured each weave of my circumstances. At Peterborough, instruction and advice were rarely offered and never repeated.

As we approached the walls of Peterborough, it seemed to me that we were entering a county and town from great sagas—the Monastery and Cathedral in the center and surrounding houses inside and outside the walls were imposing to me. In the days when the hosts frequently plagued common folk, walls were a balm, for it was better to be walled in than out.

Upon our arrival within the sanctuary of Peterborough Abbey, I stood enthralled at the sight of all the activity. For the major provisions and supplies we had carried involved all non-tonsured and tonsured in the Abbey to unload, and distribute.

I knew we would not see Cellarer Dagobert, for I learned he was grievously indisposed and not expected to survive long. His great office and all our procession's efforts and material were ultimately subject to Father Abbot Elsin's of Peterborough Abbey, the greatest man in all the country.

When Cellarer Dagobert fell deathly sick, his office was filled by Eadsige. It was assumed that Abbot Elsin would select Eadsige as the new Cellarer upon his return. Like so many great personages, the Reverend Abbot often traveled to far places on important holy missions.

---

[9] Hundred or soke. A large administrative unit of land, each having its own representative body from local villages. The right of local jurisdiction of a particular territory.

So it was this day that began my almost eight years of residence at Peterborough Abbey and its adjoining manors. I was to learn much between my eighth and seventeenth year that would benefit me in the travels this account will bring forth. To learn monastic ways and the Rule of St. Benedict benefited me for the entirety of my life by providing knowledge and skills. May God forgive me for applying some of that for purposes that met the afflictions of the immediate, though ignoring the consequences of the eternal.

Though my story is not of cloister, details of monastic life I should describe, however modestly. The Monastery was an ordered yet secure place as of which I had not benefit earlier. As the sages observe, you learn by what you do not have in contrast to that you come by.

A youth born and raised in meager holdings saw much to gape at in Peterborough and adjacent manors. Just the numbers of souls astounded, for I never saw so many in one place any time. On this first morning I saw over a hundred people at the Monastery within the walls and without— the two gates were maws belching people in and out. It was spring and much business was being conducted and haying was growing close. The arrival of our train carrying a bounty of feorms[10] beholden to the Abbey resulted much bustle by the diverse responsibilities receiving cartage.

My anxious captors ignored this work, intent on my person, though they did offer—for the first time—an opinion of our Superior's proven skills: "When this Subcellarer Eadsige goes afield, he milks the very trees of pith for his beloved Abbot."

These two creatures remained at my elbows until their audience was finally at hand. I was pushed before them—presented for the second time to Eadsige and another tonsured cleric, Gardener Dundage, a Saxon of a dour nature. He looked me over, and opined aloud that I would run off at

---

[10] In kind payment, such as honey or grain, etc.

first opportunity, seeing I was a "Godless runaway born and likely bred."

As one might barter horse or ox, the greedy cottars began to reckon the years at labor my youthful person would offer Father Abbot. Gardener Dundage cut them short with a surprising curse, causing Eadsige to hold out his hand for peace.

"See the Bursar for your coin, then leave this place."

They frowned—the price not up to their expectations. But with a swinish glance at one another, and under the terrible eyes of Gardener Dundage, they left without further word.

"Think you, Brother, would not this lad be good for the weirs at the lake. An eel fisher?" And he offered a smile at Dundage who I was to learn never smiled.

"Perhaps. But one ill-step and the others will crack him open like a clam, even if he has cost Father Abbot coin."

"Good!" Eadsige gestured for me to go, adding, "Wait outside for Gardener Dundage. And oh, young Cuthwin, add Father Abbot in your prayers, for you owe him your life."

As I backed out, Gardener Dundage traced me with those baleful eyes, surmounted by vast black eyebrows, like clumps of tarry moss. The door closed behind me. For the first time since my capture, I was alone.

It was indeed a stout building; I was to learn that it served as the Cellarer's residence. Monastery officers did not live cloistered but without for their business was with common folk. The smells of the cellar were such I never encountered: wines, cheeses, smoked and salted meats and fishes—and so many other things mixed in that my stomach growled with hunger.

I was not alone for long, for two cellar doors pivoted open, pushed by one worker in time to greet two others burdened with recently arrived goods. They descended, legs bent, carrying goods into capacious cellars beneath.

But that was not all.

Abruptly, to the opposing side of the hall, a great harangue of invective and outcry burst from within—not in the cellars, nor in the room where subcellarer Eadsige and Gardener Dundage still conferred, but yet another room. And despite the closed door of this room, the outcries grew louder, until the door burst open violently and allowed me view of a sight still vivid and shocking this three-quarter century later: By the outcry I expected a scene of torture, but instead a massive enormity of a man—tonsured, wearing a vastness of ill-stained habit—was being held from the front by two bordars. From the rear, another unfortunate held up his robe, exposing a wide vista of bare buttocks, yet a fourth and fifth manned a stave tub into which this great leviathan of a monk was defecating.

"If you two dogs drop me again, I swear upon our Savior that it'll be the whipping house for you!!"

The two that held their tormentor in a position to best empty his bowels struggled to support his massive bulk, and yet there was a sixth man—this sad self having thrown the door open—bent over at the waist and then standing upright, he took in a vast draught of air. He looked out and to no one in particular cried, "Oh, by Saint Oswald, this stench is the devil's work."

"Get back in here, you pile of turds, and help hold me. And by Saint Cuthbert, close the goddamned door."

And this he did—the thick, wood door closing, pushing out some of the fetid air of which the man had so recently complained. I was not unused to the smells of nature's call, yet was taken unsuspecting how horridly foul a creature's innards might become close to a time of death. I braced my arm against the wall, but at the moment caught sight of a tall heron of a man, who to the left and right of him was escorted by two monks.

This stern, stiff-necked man saw what I did within. He gazed at me, his lips curled—his two escorts covered their noses against the diminishing stench. With a gesture towards the closed door he said with a grim, almost satisfied, smile, "See you Cellarer Dagobert—and how pride and gluttony brings low the sinner. Now, who are you?"

And this was my first sight of Prior Denewulf who in absence of Father Abbot commanded all Peterborough, its demesne and soks. His two escorts were Whipmen, his enforcers. They saw I was new and didn't know how to respond, so one strode forward and kicked me.

"Down, you mooncalf, show respect before Prior Denewulf!"

"He is Cuthwin, Brother Prior, and with us just arrived from the north."

Subcellarer Eadsige and Gardener Dundage had opened the door and stood, bowing momentarily to Prior Denewulf. As we stood there the ruckus within not only did not cease, but increased—following a loud report of something very large meeting the floor—which I assumed was the unfortunate Cellarer Dagobert.

Reverend Eadsige described the most subtle of head motions towards Gardener Dundage who at once beckoned me to follow. We left there, me rubbing hard the place recently kicked. Frankly, despite my fright and the strangeness of everything, I was a sturdy lad used to hard goings, and had the urge to kick the blackguard back.

In a dirt-covered quadrangle yard, carts were still being unloaded—in this case, the very largest with wheels taller than a man. It carried massive barrels being so handled that I knew them empty. Gardener Dundage stopped, pointing to them.

"We will be filling those with fat, salted eels soon enough. Which will be your work, and you will serve under the master eelman Ordgar who will instruct you in the craft."

"I'll do my best, but if he kicks me, I'll kick him back."

He looked me up and down; a hand, gnarled by arthritis and rough use, pointed at me, its forefinger a warped branch.

"You will address me by my office, or I'll kick you. Those two hounds traveling with Lord Prior are henchmen whose job it is to kick. Anyway, where you're going, no need to worry about the likes of Brother Prior or his hounds."

Then we turned and left the yard, and in fact the Monastery gate. Down a narrow cart road, I followed. Beyond everywhere stretched the fens, to the rim of the sky, they extended. Being spring, great flocks of ducks and geese rose and fell from the watery land in all directions.

This limitless expanse and the creatures above and on the fens became my benign taskmaster. This was a new land, one that still lives fondly within me to the time of this telling.

Whatever was to stay dry and above the spring-flooded fens either was built upon a natural sand and pebble rise in the otherwise soggy plain or had been by labor and craft elevated on same material. Some buildings and outbuildings were even raised on wooden piles. Pathways led in several directions, and we followed along one of those that led off from the wider, more substantial cart road.

We soon came to a tiny fishing settlement, an island of houses and other such structures. It was made mostly of materials gleaned from the fens—reed houses, with thick, thatched roof—clever designs where considerable skills went into their making.

Outside the largest of these, a woman emptied a basket of leavings for pigs. They nosed them up with deep grunting, the greedy creatures begrudging nearby barn fowl food, yet who darted in stealing bits for themselves. Seeing Gardener Dundage, she bowed low—a flaxen-haired woman of some age who spoke our language with the accent of a foreigner. After her greeting Gardener Dundage directed her to speak with her husband Ordgar, explaining I was a new bondsman intended to learn the fisherman's trade.

"I'm sorry, Master Gardener, Ordgar is within and very ill this day with the fen ague."

There was a moment of thought, and Gardener Dundage looked back at me, giving me over to the eelman's wife and admonished to do what she bid. Saying he would speak to Ordgar at a better time, he was gone. It was a sudden turn of circumstances from the day before.

"I am Esa, wife of Ordgar, who is your new master. You will sleep there."

She pointed to a long, narrow building on piles, separate from our present isle. I was impressed, seeing goats upon its roof. The animals, I later learned, grazed upon grasses sprouting from the thatch. For the moment they had settled upon their hocks with full bellies.

"In fact, Ordgar is within with the apprentices and other sorts. Have you eaten?"

I was to learn good Esa's ways, for they always hewed to the simpler things of life, for as the wife of Ordgar, hers was not easy. Inside their house I took bread and ale, then ventured to the building where Esa earlier pointed.

Entering I saw scattered in disarray nearly a dozen fellows, most snoring or grunting to besotted sleep. Propped against the wall sprawled

Eelmaster Ordgar. Though his eyes were open, he looked blankly at the floor. Mistress Esa had not gone in. I looked from Ordgar to the others—all fishermen, watermen, or eelmen—his wards. There was not a soul of them in steady mind nor awake.

The stench of spilled and sour ale prevailed, and though just a boy, I knew well the sight of men suffering the murky wake of heavy cupping. The 'fen ague' this day was the sturdy brand of barley ale favored upon the fens—stronger than most.

So, here were my master and new fellows.

I was as I stood—owning and carrying nothing, close to a hundred leagues from my birthplace, in possession of my life by the grace of God. Finding voice, I announced myself Cuthwin-of-Withernsea, but no one took note—least of all my new master.

Hearing a great gnashing of teeth against bone, I looked over—and in the far corner was a hound chewing a bone, the size of which looked to be from a late but great ox. Seeing me staring at his fare, the hound showed teeth, offered a low growl and continued—clearly meaning not to share his windfall.

Slipping into the opposite corner—stepping over sleeping cottars—I lowered myself to the floor. What sort of place had I come to? Outside the fens stretched towards land and sea. To run off from here was a different matter than running off from Alwystle's croft at Wharram Percy. No copse or field offered substance here, and even the water was slow and dark.

I recall the hollowness I felt—how dark my future appeared in this new, watery land. Life at least had been providing me dry land and warm shelter. Now, I feared, I would follow the ways of stoats and water rats.

5

I spent a half-dozen change-of-seasons, close to two years, on the fens with Eelman Ordgar, learning the way of fisher folk. It was a life reckoned in seasons and rains, then, seaward on the River Nene, the ebbs and flows of tides. Ordgar was fair enough with his bondsmen, being himself a coilbert[11]. He had spent his life on the fens, mostly along the River Nene as a fisherman. Now he was Father Abbot's master eelman, the eel being a prized trade good to the Abbey then as now. But all fisher folk being his wards fell into Master Ordgar's duties.

Dwelling in Ordgar's house, I lived and worked outside the walls of the Abbey except for visits on holy days and such. Yet by listening, much asking, and remembering better, I learned about Peterborough Abbey and monastery ways.

Despite being a simple eelman, I began to learn the troubled ways of great men.

Soon after my arrival at the Abbey, Cellarer Dagobert joined the souls in heaven, his excesses of food and drink hopefully forgiven. And true to prediction, Subcellarer Eadsige became Cellarer, yet Gardener Dundage declined to become Subcellarer, which caused talk.

The two fellows whom I worked with most, Efen and Siegluf, were uncomplicated eelmen of good humor and, praise God, slow to curse or kick.

Since they were keen on their ale and this loosed their tongues, I learned more than just the ways of fish and fishing. And even this early, I was curious about the ways of cloister.

I learned tonsured holders of offices of Peterborough Monastery commanded the everyday functions of the Monastery and stood in high authority over their designated domain. Father Abbot looked to these officers to oversee concerns in Monastery business. He was often quest-

---

[11] A freedman, a former slave given a bit of land.

ing in far lands for sainted bones and other holy remains for which the Abbey was famed everywhere.

Most held that save for the Prior, the Cellarer was the most important office. He enjoyed his own residence outside cloister, and responsibility for sub-officers under him, including Gardener Dundage who in turn was holy overseer of fishing. Fisher folk licensed by Father Abbot were ordinary bordars or coilberts and owed a portion of their catch to Father Abbot, that share subject to his whim. If, however, fisher folk plied waters and marshes in sok strictly for Father Abbot, they fell under the protective cover of the Monastery proper. This was Master Ordgar's lot.

Still living in cloister yet overseeing all and with the real power was Prior Denewulf, almost always accompanied by his brace of Whipmen. Both my fellows, even in front of Ordgar, freely opined these two souls were excessive in seeing to their duty: "Those two tonsured gut-piles aren't shy with whips, nor is Lord Prior light in seeing to its use."

So the Prior was feared, though even Ordgar, and especially wife Esa, would call for silence if any of his wards, free *or* bonded, waxed averse regards Reverend Prior. Doing this was poor business.

Because of my first meeting with Reverend Prior—remembering his Whipman's kick sending me to the floor—I made a special effort to stay clear of him and them.

Going afoot and using bog craft, I was learning enough to check the traps each summer evening alone. Days of great heat and low water saw few fish in the traps, and Ordgar and the others fell early to their cups and saw little gain in leaving.

So one such evening I was returning with a few skinny pike in my basket. I had tied my bog craft secure and was walking the road leading to a treadway that branched off to Ordgar's. On the road I overtook a tiny, elderly man who limped along with an old donkey loaded to its maximum behind—and the obstinate beast was tired, so sat and refused to go on.

The elderly man was a monk, tonsured, and was lecturing the animal in a tongue I recognized as that of the Church. The beast wasn't interested and remained sitting. I asked for His Reverence's blessing; he gave it and then said in clear, unaccented Saxon, "This creature has given up.

Her name is Waddles," and smiling widely, he turned to his companion and ordered, "Waddles, I beseech you in the name of God to get up!"

Getting behind Waddles, I put down my basket and got my back under the donkey's rear while His Reverence pulled from the front, and with outlandish complaints, the creature rose. But move, she would not.

I pointed out to his Reverence my basket was light, almost empty, and that if I took some of the load, Waddles might decide a night in the stable was an improvement to being here on the fens. It being the beginning of summer, the biting flies swarmed about her.

I did this with his help; he was careful what I took from the animal, helping me putting it in my basket.

"You fish for Ordgar?"

"Yes, Your Reverence, I do."

So we secured things—even His Reverence taking some of the load, so much I protested in view of his age and small size. Then Waddles decided to continue—to the stern admonishment of His Reverence in yet another language.

As we moved towards the Abbey, he asked my name and how fishing went, then looked about him—pointing with his wooden staff. "Living on the fens under the rule of Saint Benedict is the joy of my life, young Cuthwin. I have missed these six months. Have you thought of such a life yourself?"

I said it seemed too grand a design for me, but he replied indeed it was not. At this point, I wondered what purpose he served at the Monastery, but knew it too bold to ask. With such an inferior animal and plain garb, I knew it must be some unknown sub-office, for he was not in cloister as an ordinary monk must be.

By the time we reached the walls of Peterborough, the night watch was closing the doors, and swallows and swifts had roosted for the night. But when the pair of watchman saw us, they gave out a shout, which at once was relayed throughout. The evening peace ended with the Monastery bell ringing loud and often. From within, I heard the cry, "Look to it. It is Father Abbot. Our Father Abbot has returned at last!"

They fell down before him; he blessed them, and I felt a mixture of confusion and youthful awe. I'd never seen an Abbot nor any such great personage. He looked at me and sighed, "Well, seems our visit is over, young Cuthwin. I thank you for your help. Now rise."

And he helped me up, for I'd gone to my knees, basket and all. Waddles, not caring about the formalities of greetings, just continued past everyone towards the stable. For her, the journey was over and, if her cargo was needed, we could come fetch it. She was pursued by two monks, one hanging onto her tail, the other her lead, causing great braying.

When others, plus myself, unloaded Father Abbot's freight from my basket, many tonsured monks busied themselves about his person; mostly they spoke in the Church language. Their words were of bountiful cheer; several wept, and many went to their knees for a blessing. Taking my basket, and assuming I had leave, I had just turned when I saw Prior Denewulf and his two Whipmen coming at fast pace.

I received baleful stares from them, perceived by myself at that last moment when I turned back to Ordgar's stead. The Prior's eyes closed blade-narrow and his fine, parchment-like skin that clung tightly to his large head gave further meanness to an already ill-omened gaze.

My feet carried me and my two pike home, more than nimbly.

My lateness was noticed by Esa, for the others were in the eelhouse and time was passing them by in good fellowship.

"Where have you been? The fish might have spoiled you've been so long."

I at once described my encounter with Father Abbot; Esa slapped hand to her mouth then rushed out instructing me to stay where I was.

She returned at once, Ordgar staggering behind, rubbing his face, clearly alarmed and struggling against the ale. Esa pointed at me.

"Now tell your master what you told me."

While I did so, Esa boiled water with some spices, a brew to put sense back in Ordgar.

Ordgar's anger was a mixture—but in it was fear.

"Fool boy, did you not know it was Father Abbot? The whole sok knows of that stupid donkey and how Father Abbot goes about like a cottar or such."

"Too late for that, Husband. He did not. He must go. At once."

While Esa hastily packed things in a basket, Ordgar went to the door. By now it was dark. Since even this late he was fearing who might approach, I knew this threat must be grim. Darkness on the fens is the blackest of nights, so only those who could afford torches—on the grandest errands—did travel.

Husband and wife exchanged a look, and when he reported that no one approached, Esa whispered, "Praise Lord Jesus, we have time."

"I must be here to answer. Take him to the traps on the flats; I'll say he's there repairing weirs prior to season. Go!"

While she did thus, pushing me before her, Ordgar saw my confusion and managed to say, "Father Abbot is one who sees good in everyone and bad in none. By Prior Dundage's sternest rule, if ordinary folk see Father Abbot, you must drop all, and run to the Abbey with the news. The Prior fears what by chance might be mentioned before Father Abbot without his presence. So you are in peril, young Cuthwin."

I had no time; I was beckoned to follow Esa's stout figure down the pathway, and just before reaching the cart road, we saw a lantern in the distance.

"Lord Jesus! There come the Whipmen. Hurry. God help us, I fear for Ordgar."

At the River Nene we stopped at a dock where diverse fishing craft were tied. Hurrying me into one, Esa cast a look back; she was torn between two responsibilities.

"You have been to the weirs on the flats?"

"I have."

"Can you get downriver and find them or your own?"

Though only there a few times, I felt I could navigate to them and told her so; though at night, I had great fear. She quickly gave me directions to the Weirman's cottage in the flats.

"I believe you, but not at dark. Pole downriver, then into the weeds, wrap yourself in the blanket I've put in the basket, pass the night until first light. Understand me?"

At that point, eager to apologize for the wrong I did, I pled her forgiveness for trespass by helping Father Abbot with his donkey. Since my eyes had adjusted to the light of the stars on this moonless night, I made out her wide forehead, straw-colored hair and the wrinkles from the hard work and years on the fens.

"Young Cuthwin, there is much you don't know about the Abbey, and I have no time. Enough to remember that when the cat is away the mice will play. Now, hurry. Remember, go downriver and hide in the rushes and sleep until light."

And she turned and was gone, only the vaguest suggestion of her becoming smaller under the flimsy light of the heavens. Then I was alone. I pushed off and poled my way down the River Nene that ran slowly through the fens. Its channels and sloughs were clogged with the summer growth of rushes and lush water plants.

Pushing my way into a tall island of them, they closed around me until my craft was enclosed like a weaver bird in his basket. I tried to make sense out of events. It was easy to understand that my master, his wife, and myself were in danger; however, the extreme of this situation seemed confusing in view of how simple and kindly Father Abbot was.

Though a warm evening, I took up the blanket and recognized the strange smell it emitted from the previous summer, my first on the fens. It was characteristic of an ointment applied to give relief from the hordes of biting flies that abounded. I understood a blanket so treated would repel at least some of the demons, for swarms had already found me.

I bedded in the bottom of the boat—perhaps even dosed—when I heard an uproar of a single voice from the landing, for I was still close. Then several voices joined the one—perhaps as many as three or four exchanging harsh words.

Then, one great angry shout—understandable even from where I hid: "YOU SONS-OF-WHORES. GO SCREW A PIG AND LEAVE ME BE!"

This was repeated—and other strong invective. In fact, whoever's fierce soul launched such language I could discern was coming closer, which meant they traveled by boat.

Then I heard pole against boat as its pilot maneuvered the Nene adjacent to my lair. If possible I would have stilled my heart, for though hearing nothing more, I knew someone was near. Then, I heard rushes, gathered together to make fast a line.

I did not breathe.

"You! Within! The turds are gone. It is good for you that Lord Prior's minions are stupid, or they would have seen there's a boat short."

Throughout the fens, the creatures became silent, for such a clatter had disturbed the night. But now, group by group, they resumed, and soon all plied their unordered conversations. But I knew well that who-ever spoke was less than two boat-lengths distant. *Only*, thought I, *could a wizard or demon know I'm within. For the reeds absolutely conceal.*

Then I heard someone make water—a gasp, followed by, "Ah, Jesu! God pity me! Hell itself could burn my vitals no hotter. A great curse on that slattern!" Then, after a moment to regain breath, "You fool! I know you are hidden within! Only a blind man, even in this light, could not see the vast path you've furrowed. So pole you out and tell me why I was besieged with the Prior's dogs who should be at Matins, the fucks."

Seeing that hiding had failed, I did as beckoned, and this is how I met Frog, for such was his name, a name I had heard mentioned and never in good spirit. After introducing himself, he explained his naming: "I guess," he said, ". . . it is because I catch them and sell or trade them, along with anything else that swims, flies or hops."

He had me replace the boat at the landing, ". . . in the event someone thinks to count returns."

He decided to guide me to the weir on the tidal flats. I thanked him, telling him of that day's doings. He listened, standing up on a small box, and winding his way down the tortuous Nene. A somber half-moon rose, casting light over this plain of reed and water that was the fens. God could not have created a more wonderful sight.

Here and there Frog checked his traps, or in truth, someone else's. With this transgression, he would leer saying he meant not to steal, but was simply satisfying his curiosity. Still, his curiosity several times overcame him, and he took the catch for later inspection. Instead of responding to my problems, Frog moved on to other matters.

"I venture Ordgar has talked of me?" Then he made an even wider smile, ". . . or maybe not?"

"No, he has not, but his wards have."

"And how do the years treat Esa. She is a good woman, and such are rare."

'The Frog' was never spoken of in Ordgar's hearing. But my fellows, left to their own, often declared: "The Frog be a great thief, liar, fornicator, and heretic who is cursed in manor and cloister." Even though a freedman, he would be hanged if they ever caught him at his work.

In the fast-rising moon, he followed the Nene onto the wide expanse of tidal flats where countless channels gleamed in the white glow, flaring in every direction. At once I wondered at my folly telling Esa I could find the weir cottage. Yet Frog came to it without a missed left or right.

"The tide is falling and I have work."

He put me, my basket, and a half-stick[12] of frogs on an elevated landing platform. He instructed to make free with the frogs, and he would return with a few cockles on his way to market.

"I'm reckoning you'll be here for several days, if not a week, young Cuthwin."

Since he had not responded to the issue of my story, I finally asked, "Did I indeed create so much misery by helping Father Abbot?"

"Prior Denewulf is corrupt. So, even unwitting talk to his Lordship might set the bats free before dark."

I learned it was Frog's manner never to speak directly, and he left me to parse this, which I did quickly enough.

So a few weeks short of my fourteenth year, I stood on this unsteady platform, the tidal stretches seamless and infinite spreading in all directions, the moon climbing above me. And, once again, even if I wished to bolt, where would I go?

I looked to the hapless frogs wriggling on the stick. They were surely grand fare for the likes of a cottar. But I knew them purloined, each

---

[12] Stick. Unit of measure for eels, fish and frogs. Equal to 25 attached by head to a stick or cord.

a sentence of approbation—each a transgression against God's Commandments. In the gloaming I could still distinguish Frog, polling away towards the cockle beds. It was the first time I saw a soul free from care, and it set off sinful curiosity.

As my aged memory serves, it was months not weeks that necessity required me to stay on the fens, secure from punishment of great men. My companion and teacher remained mostly Frog, wise in the ways of fish and fowl, though shunned by all folk in sok and manor.

Ordgar I saw infrequently, yet Esa more, and my fellow eelmen, both old and young—for they would sometimes join me in tasks. Yet when any visited, Frog would absent himself. None asked after him, though all knew he was near. However, kind Esa did ask after Frog, and this only once, with the hesitancy understandable from such a Godly woman: "How fares Edbert, young Cuthwin?"

"Edbert?"

"'Frog,' they call him now. But he was born Edbert. How fares he, rogue that he is?"

"He is healthy and fit."

She handed me a basket of victuals from their hearth and larder, a weekly favor towards Ordgar's eelmen outposted on the fens. Looking off over the fens, she nodded. Work had made her body thick. Ordgar and she had many children, though most left earthly circumstances ascending early to better places.

Sometime later when Frog and I were repairing a weir (I was never fully informed about whose weir we worked on), I told him of Esa's inquiry.

He never showed sign of how the water flowed within his breast, so he grunted a bit. While Frog and I were looking over our work, he said, "We often don't get what we want, but I think more so what we deserve. Such is God's way."

I regularly recall his wisdom, and as were his knowledge of creatures, those words were indeed accurate. They made rising sense as I grew older.

Frog was not a soul without a sense of leisure. He was always sober—with keen senses—on the fens. However, he occasionally set off on great ruttings, and ventured to outer villages indulging in notable liberties with drink and such.

"That asshole Frog with a snoot full is not of good cheer."

A visiting eelman offered this one evening. He sported a dressing across his gnarled old brainpan illustrating his declaration about Frog. He picked up a half dozen sticks of eels—bargained to him by Frog—and after rough talk towards my person, poled off.

Days later, when Frog made an appearance, he was also harnessed in dressings on limb and head. But he seemed unconcerned about such, and lived each day as the previous.

Such was Frog and his ways, yet I learned much from him, for God was generous in allowing us to meet.

One day a great change arrived simply and abruptly, as they mostly do. Ordgar poled to my watery hutch, instructing me to fetch my few carryings and come with him.

"Father Abbot wants you at the Monastery. In speaking privately with Father Abbot, you've either encountered good fortune or bad, depending on fate and God. Be careful inside Peterborough."

As we approached the landing, I saw a single monk waiting, and knew—acutely well—that if I were to see my adopted fens again, I must be careful, especially if I wanted to return of sound body and limb.

The monk was Osfer, Father Abbot's clerk—equal in years to Father Abbot himself, who was approaching the half-century mark. He greeted Ordgar with a silent bow, and beckoned me to follow. That luxuriant morning on the fens was unforgettable: The sun was gathering strength in the east, tossing nourishing light over the watery expanses. It was late summer, and all was life itself—the countless fowl took wing everywhere, heavy-bodied from their layer of belly fat—a life-giving result from this expanse of richness.

Osfer stopped, opened a small basket and took out bread and bottle, sat at a ditch intersect with its system of gates, and gazed out over this wonder.

"I tell you, God has blessed us. Eat. Drink. There is good issue in simple bread and beer."

It was late summer and swallows were thick, their young having taken wing—they and their parents darted over the fens, taking their fill of the cursed biting flies. They would swirl, and it seemed to me that Osfer watched each, smiling a bit as he pushed bread into his near toothless mouth. He spoke around this: "Young Cuthwin, Father Abbot liked your sense of kindness and thoughtfulness for Waddles' welfare. That animal is a curse to all of us, but God help him, Father Abbot is devoted to her."

Osfer's old grey eyes gleamed with presence of mind and not a little kindness. He looked me over and I kept silent—Master Odgar's caution close in mind. To say nothing would befriend me best.

Osfer favored this silence, and me his, and we finished our repast in peace. Then we continued on to the walls of Peterborough. Behind those stout barriers were the only safety for folk when invading hosts harried. The village within again addled me with so many people. The fens did little to prepare me for its ways. From the village was a brief passing into the Monastery itself.

Osfer halted at its gate—not the main gate, I was to learn. He began to say something—an instruction—but thought better of whatever it was, and instead directed to me, "We are going to Father Abbot's quarters. Speak when spoken to; answer what's asked. And you will see this day through soundly."

"Yes, Your Reverence."

"'Yes *Brother Osfer!*' I was never ordained priest."

He allowed a chuckle as we entered a separate large building. There I was confronted with the sight of vast rooms such I had never seen. Despite my inexperience, I judged the rooms inappropriately provided. Large rooms, even to an unwitting youth, presage grand contents. But this wasn't their state.

Brother Osfer gave a look around, sniffed a bit, and sighed. "Father Abbot keeps rich furnishings and such stored unless grand men visit, forgetting he is a grand personage."

I was startled by a snort! I looked quickly towards it, and saw a large hound—aged beyond belief. It lay sleeping, barely showing life save for that struggled utterance.

My eyes traced this and more emptiness, and when we entered another room, it was the same.

We stopped—for behind the next thick door, which was partially open, there was talking. I craned my neck towards a great brightness. Despite the emptiness, shutter boards were open. The light of the day shone to every corner—high and low—and the room was immaculate. I never saw such a clean yet unused room.

Osfer gently took my head, and straightened it—towards the door.

"Look thee! Prior is within. When he leaves, you bow low, Cuthwin, and hold until he gives you leave to straighten."

And true to his word, Prior left—without his Whipmen. Seeing me—though I at once bowed low—I heard his leather-bound feet stop.

"And what may this creature's purpose be within, Brother Osfer?"

"I know not, Reverend Prior. Save that Father Abbot bade me summon him."

Under my chin I felt a hand take strong grip, lifting my head. I found myself staring into the angry eyes of Reverend Prior. He held—I tried to avert, but the hand gripped me hard.

Then he let go, at the moment pushing my head down. And he was gone—his stride long and purposeful. Then, without pause, Brother Osfer's kinder voice, "Follow. And do as I do."

We entered another room—once again, this as bare and plain as those previous. Behind a simple but wide table sat Father Abbot, but I only glimpsed this for the moment, when Osfer pushed me down beside him, and he knelt. Though his head was up, he held mine down—I eyed the plain, wooden floor. Its grain was outstanding in cleanliness; even at that strange moment, I marveled at its wear from hard scrubbing.

"Young Cuthwin is here, Father Abbot."

"For the love of Jesus and St. Peter, get up! I'm beginning to think everyone pegs about on their knees."

Doing so I saw an Abbot Elsin far different from the cheerful monk

I'd seen on the fens struggling with Waddles. His features were worn, haggard. He looked years older, and though the smile was the same, I was too young to know what might cause such wear in just a few months.

Now on my feet, I moved my eyes down, not knowing what was proper. Brother Osfer's voice hinted at the peevish.

"Have you eaten, Father Abbot?"

Osfer interrupted Abbot Elsin in mid-word; he looked annoyed in a mild way, shook his head and began again, but Osfer wouldn't have it.

"Then you'll perish. And then what shall we do, your children who love you? Let me at least fetch cold broth."

He glared at Osfer—in good spirit—smiled and looked to me, shaking his head.

"Well, young Cuthwin, seems I must take broth, or we can't get on with our visit," and he nodded and Osfer went out, for the door was still open a crack, but only momentarily. Then another showed walking behind, carrying broth—evidently he had stood at ready with it. I didn't know then that oblates stood by always for any possible wish or need of Father Abbot.

Father Abbot got to his feet—which did not elevate him much—he being a very short man. He rubbed the top of his tonsured head and made a face, "I have just gotten even with events and business herein, and now I must to France, perhaps even Rome, yet I have not forgotten you, young Cuthwin. Do you know—well of course you don't—that I had a beloved brother also named Cuthwin. Oh, he was a great one for his traps."

"And not necessarily his own," Osfer offered.

Then both Father Abbot and Osfer shared a great laugh—breaking into a strange tongue which wasn't of Rome, which brought increase to their laughter. The unfortunate young oblate stood balancing a cup of broth.

Instantly, Father Abbot became stern, and began quizzing the poor wretch in the language of Rome—while Osfer retrieved the broth before he spilt it.

At each fired question, the lad—who was several years younger than I—responded, while his fearful eyes looked floorward. Then Father

Abbot laughed aloud and broke into what I immediately recognized as the Norman tongue, for even then I knew some of it. With great relief, the lad—evidently having responded successfully—thanked Father Abbot and scurried out.

Osfer wasn't about to forget the object of the lad's visit, and extended the cup.

"This is for you, Father Abbot. I broke my fast."

He took it, sipped, then drank deeply, sitting back down. Unmonk-like—or what I thought to be unmonklike—he smacked his lips and burped.

"Cuthwin! Have you thought of becoming one of us—living under the Rule. I avow, it is a life of many blessings and peace, as long as you avoid offices and keep to simplicity."

"He is too old, Father Abbot. Plus, he is unschooled and wild as a hare."

"True. But we've taken oblates his age before. And for all that—we were *both* once wild as hares, Osfer, make no doubt of that."

They were about to argufy—like Ordgar so did over ale with his contrary eelmen. I learned even in those first minutes that Osfer and Father Abbot had been cronies—raised together in adjoined croft.

Father Abbot drank again—to pull himself from discussion—then, looking up, enjoyed another belch, and looked kindly at me.

"Well? You thought of that, Young Cuthwin?"

"It is too great for one like me, Father Abbot. But please, your Reverence, I do enjoy my lot as eelman, at learning so much, God be praised."

He and Osfer exchanged looks—hints of smiles, perhaps. Osfer gestured towards the cup, now empty.

"And some bread, Father Abbot? That would round you for the day and allow your innards to function."

Father Abbot sighed, and Osfer without pause for 'yes' or 'no' went to the door, and while briefly absent, His Reverence added, "Osfer worries about my innards, which God Himself protects." Then he glanced hopefully into the cup, now empty; then quick as a swallow's turn looked up at me, "And how be Frog? Have you seen Frog, one of God's unruly creatures?"

Osfer re-entered at the moment, leaving me scrambling—for I didn't want to inform on my teacher. I knew Frog to be outlawed by every soul—and especially Father Abbot who ruled all—water, lands, and people in every direction.

My tongue, nimbler then, managed, "I have seen one called Edbert, Father Abbot, but on the fens I work mostly alone."

Osfer brought his foot back to kick me, while Father Abbot shook his head and intercepted the same oblate who carried in a trencher of bread. "Why, the young stoat has even learned to lie like Frog, and Father Abbot sounds *him* about living the blessed Rule!"

But Osfer lowered his foot, and they both enjoyed the confusion of the oblate who held the trencher—quaking a bit, thinking him to witness violence right in Father Abbot's presence.

His Holy Reverence relieved him of the trencher, thought to quiz him again—but with nod, found the boy instead kneeling. And understanding his wish, Father Abbot gripped his shoulder and made the sign over him, giving blessing.

The boy left, content for blessing given by such a great man. Father Abbot broke off a piece of trencher and—his hunger having been primed—stuffed it in his mouth and chewed with pleasure. Osfer motioned to me.

"Let us dispose of this little rogue, Father Abbot. Turn him over to the Prior's Whipmen for lying to you, of all people. Only through such a trial will God forgive him."

Abbot Elsin sat down, but I now was aware enough to know the two were making sport with me. Instead, Father Abbot broke off another piece, offering me some, which I dared not take.

"I shall correct my course then, young Cuthwin: How be this Edbert you saw? I baptized him some thirty years ago."

"He is very well, Father Abbot."

"Good. It is well to hang only healthy souls."

Osfer added this and taking my hand, opened it and put in the offered chuck of trencher—and I could smell its richness at the once, and he had no need to close my hand.

They both chortled a bit over this business about Frog. I saw that both—though aware of his ill-chosen ways—didn't condemn, or at the least harbor ill-will.

"Now, to business: Recall me, Brother Osfer, how much we paid those cotsets for this lad?"

"It was all of ten shillings, Father Abbot."

He shook his head sadly, said something in the language of Rome, then looked at me with grave concern.

"So, Young Cuthwin, your labor as eelman has not consumed much of your debt. Yet I have another route—a faster one for meeting this responsibility."

"Yes, Father Abbot."

"At livery. Our liveryman Gilbert thought well of you, and also our Scriptorium. Know this term—'Scriptorium'?"

"A place of books, Father Abbot."

"Correct. They have rats and other vermin that must be controlled, and our brothers need help."

"Much of it, indeed, Father Abbot! God does not mean us to have learned vermin."

"Mercy of Our Savior, are you sure, Osfer?!"

And once more they enjoyed hearty chortle, while I slid into despair. How might I—in my lifetime—ever compensate Father Abbot *ten shillings*? Twelve stick of eels weren't worth a single shilling. And *ten shillings!* It seemed a fantastic sum.

"So! Osfer, show him to Liveryman Gilbert," and he came around his plain but massive table, beckoning to us both, "…now come thee."

And at that, following Osfer's guiding hand, we knelt before Father Abbot, and he then placed his hand on our heads and made sign over us. I still, these nigh four generations gone, remember the compassion conveyed in that single, simple touch.

When we stood and extended our thanks, I saw sadly that at once Father Abbot returned to the worn, worried state of mind I had noticed upon entering.

Outside we entered a small closet at rear of which was a portal. Osfer gestured around—considering all directions.

"In good time, Cuthwin, you'll learn this rabbit warren we call our cloister—follow."

Exiting a rear entrance from Father Abbot's single, massive residence, we entered a short covered archway leading to the main monastery. Along this, we turned into a narrow hallway spanned with dozens of wooden arches. I followed in Osfer's rapid paces when suddenly he stopped and, palm outward, leaned against the stone wall.

He had gone white—and clapped a fist to his chest. Looking, he saw a low shelf near a tiny alcove and sat.

"I will fetch water, Brother Osfer."

"Stay! It passes."

His body was old, small; he shuddered once, and closed his eyes. The fist on his chest opened and its old, gnarled fingers outspread—each pressed into his frail chest, the pads pushing his habit down.

Though in pain, he opened his eyes—and in them gleamed the self-possession of before. And a smile.

"It passes. Now… sit on the floor here. This moment God has given for a purpose."

At his feet I saw bare calluses through rents in his trods' old leather. He lifted the hand away from his chest—at first doubtful—then gestured inward—towards cloister.

"Now observe these principals in these walls, even as one without tonsure or commitment. Understand me, Cuthwin?"

"Yes."

"'Yes, Brother Osfer'."

"Yes, Brother Osfer."

"That is firstly—be content with your place, and to know your place—and most importantly that of others, and to respect it always. Secondly, do not gossip—with anyone—about anyone. You see everything, know less, and say nothing. Follow me?"

"Yes, Brother Osfer."

"And do all duties with obedience. *Always* be obedient. Lastly, keep to yourself, say your prayers, and eat what is given you with thanks to God."

"Yes, Brother Osfer."

He was silent—his words done. Standing, he took breath and continued; I followed and soon he encountered the smell of stables. We exited that building, and entered a long stable—built from ground up of stout plank and beam. Each paddock could be occupied by one or two animals.

But above all I heard the braying first.

Osfer shook his head as we moved into view of a larger paddock. The livery workplace held all sorts of strange tackle for horses and wagon. In there was Gilbert. But it was not livery occupying him; instead he held the head of a youngster under water in a stout bucket— but that moment pulled him clear. Pushing him, he sent the lad—far younger than myself—headlong followed with an authoritative kick to his buttocks.

"Now do as I told, you worthless suckling. No one cares about your wounds. Feed and groom her, damn you!"

Brother Osfer turned away—feigning not hearing such language in a holy place. The young boy—an oblate, whose garb was full sodden— scrambled away down the straw-strewn floor of the stables in the direction of his onerous noisy task.

Seeing Osfer, Gilbert drew himself up somewhat in the manner of regret. "My apologies, Brother Osfer. There is much trouble here. Waddles' fiendish nature provided her with foreknowledge that Father Abbot will to France and leave her. And when she rouses, all beasts follow." He looked towards the paddocks and held his hands outward. "Dumb beasts are like people—when one is disobedient, others so emboldened follow suit."

Osfer nodded in understanding while taking hold of me and moving me before him. Gilbert was not done.

"Why Father Abbot loves that terrible creature…. It is like keeping a fire-breathing worm in stable."

But raised voices were needed to be heard over the angry braying of Waddles. Being with animals of pasture and livery for my first dozen years, I experienced some exchanges with donkeys. I knew them as cross-tempered beasts. Further, a donkey was clever using tooth and hoof—more so than the most evil-intended stallion.

"Here is Cuthwin, who I understand you met on his journey here."

"Yes. Months ago. How fare you, Cuthwin?"

"Well, Master Liveryman."

The two exchanged satisfied looks and moved closer to a smoldering forge where a rough-dented pot heated water. Gilbert took down a basket and tossed a pinch of a special herbal essence into the pot, and without voice, invited Osfer to sit on nearby bench—rough made, lower on one end than the other.

"Ah surely, Gilbert, your Welshman's good brew will bolster old bones and repair unbalanced humors."

He pushed the pot closer to the fire's heart, and it began to steam at once. Gilbert took a stick from a pocket on his ox-hide apron and gave the pot a stir, tapping it thoughtfully on its edge.

"How long will Father Abbot be gone?"

"Months."

There was great thinking between the two during the process of straining out two wooden cups of this brew with a muslin cloth. Gilbert served Osfer—then, suddenly remembering me, fetched a third cup, and I too was served.

Its exotic aroma promised me, young and unstudied in such potions, little pleasure. An entire conversation took place without words. Gilbert's brows raised—held—there was a single shake of his head as he prepared our cups.

Osfer stared into the forge, as if gazing into better times. He knocked on the lower end of the bench with bare knuckle, inviting me to sit.

They drank with deliberation and nods of their heads. I sipped cautiously, and its taste, though not bad, neither was good.

Through this all, Waddles' awful braying continued—joined here and there by her fellow animals—an occasional whinny, another lowing of oxen. It seemed to me, that even the livery-yard cocks, ubiquitous fowl in all such places, crowed more frequently and louder. In all it was a grand bit of noise.

But the two old friends—for that's what Gilbert and Osfer were—enjoyed their brew in contentment, ruminating over things I could not guess.

God had mercy on us, and Waddles' braying stopped—Gilbert smiled, put his cup aside and nodded. "The soaking did its work. He has managed it. The awful creature is hungry. We have that advantage."

"And now she will allow grooming?"

"Yes, but quickly while she eats. No time to spare either, for Father Abbot will look in on her soon. And she must look her best. God spare Father Abbot and all of us."

Pigeons cooed overhead, rustled about as they prepared to roost from a day in the fields, for it was approaching Vespers[13]. I noticed at once the birds' sleekness and full flesh. Unmerciful thoughts crowded my mind when of a sudden Gilbert said with a sigh, "So, Cuthwin. You have traded the smell of the fens for horseshit?"

"And for that of ink and the infernal Italian miasmas of Brother Cassartorius in his beloved Scriptorium." Osfer followed this with a chuckle while rising, handing the cup back to Gilbert with a nod of thanks, "...now I to Vespers, in advance of our cracked bell."

He looked me up and over, nodded, and bade, "Do well, Cuthwin, and God will keep you."

Though boys were not supposed to weep, I was close to that watching Osfer leave. My days on the free-living fens were done, and I was behind walls with those who practiced severe ways. Such persons as Whipmen and livery keepers who hold boys' heads in buckets promised ill.

Worse, I owed a sum never repayable in my lifetime, and I did not want a life within monastic confines. Watching Osfer prepare to leave, and always of a practical mind, I knew I must run away at first opportunity and join those like Frog on the fens. A life of a rogue and outlaw seemed far better, despite the likelihood of a gibbet or hangman's noose awaiting.

When the young oblate burdened with caring for Waddles rounded the stall, he met Gilbert. Hurriedly putting the bucket aside, bowing to the master liveryman, he rushed to Vespers, perhaps fearing another dunking.

"That was oblate Alswyn—this is his week in stables," Gilbert told me as he stepped around the bucket and bade me to follow. He strode

<hr />

[13] Vespers. Evening/sunset prayer. Part of the *liturgy of the hours* in a Benedictine Monastery.

with the deliberate and steady way of a master craftsman. I saw most stalls were empty. Stables at Peterborough Monastery were the largest I'd seen, with accommodation for all sorts of animals.

"It is Summer so our beasts are on demesne leaving us the infirm and such." And precisely then we came within range of Waddles' stall—larger than most. She wheeled and faced off with Gilbert. They both stared for the shortest of pauses.

He walked on. "Waddles and I have borne each other these twenty-odd years, and neither of us the better, I would guess."

I felt Waddles stare on my back, for being long resident she knew a newcomer was in stable. Only God could sound what she might be thinking, and I vowed not to try, for my plan had begun to unfurl.

He led me to a stall nearest the west-facing doorway; it was shielded off with blankets and a few boards, and within was a bedding area. In a strong beam of setting sun passing between boards, I saw fleas hopping about, and ruefully I knew this forlorn space was for me.

Then Gilbert made more speech than I had heard him use previous: "You sleep and do repast here. You are now Stableman. The post has been absented for months. But," he extended a hand, dropping it suddenly to his side, ". . . such as it is. You get your food from the back of the refectory from Brother Ostand and eat it where you will. I have duties elsewhere now. You have watch from sunset to Matins when Alswyn will begin. Fire and sick animals are the watch's burden. Napping or neglect of duty, and it'll be the Whipmen for you, and those two will not leave an unflayed piece of hide on you." He pointed to a strip of iron with a wooden striker hanging close by. "If there is fire, raise clatter with that, then attend. If there is a sick animal you cannot deal with, fetch me."

Questions about where to fetch him, or when I might rest between my duties as stableman—plus catching rats in the Scriptorium—I held. Sunrise would not find me in Peterborough Monastery, so I had no need for such information.

He walked out the stall, taking off his apron while moving away. When he was out of sight, I sat on a low stool—the only furniture in the quarters. In a corner was a wooden cup, its rim worn down from use.

Between midnight and Lauds[14] I knew would be the best time to get away—few would be about, and my watch—whatever that required—would be done.

I was a little older than when I bolted from Wharram with Pyster, and wiser. I resolved not to follow the word of a devious crone, or in fact anyone. I had begun to learn the ways and life on the fens. Upon them were God-given virtual plains of thick grasses and tall reeds over-growing and lining meandering sloughs fed by the River Nene, all swept by the inevitable flow of tides.

To a stripling this was plan enough.

◈ 8 ◈

I struck out to discover and claim my meal at the aforementioned back door. The future held uncertain days of nourishment, and it was wise to take present opportunity.

Like the vast stable, I had never seen a kitchen the size of the refectory at Peterborough Monastery. It bellowed heat and the smells of foods.

Brother Ostand was a smallish fellow, round of belly yet quick as an asp with kick and backhand. Oblates flew from the back door like bats from eaves while he filled the air with a brutish language unknown to me.

These hard-pressed souls fetched blocks of peat, fuel for the massive hearths.

In an open square behind the kitchen, working folk—bondsmen, or cottars like myself who worked inside the Monastery—stood or sat eating from wooden bowls.

An oblate half my age ladled soup and handed out pulls of bread at the rear step. We confronted each other—for I had no bowl. Pushing around him, Ostand looked down—then vented in his strange tongue. I struggled to make sense of it.

Seeing I was mystified of his meaning, he switched to Saxon, though

---

[14] Lauds. Around 3:00 a.m. in the *liturgy of the hours* in a Benedictine Monastery.

making a terrible mash of it, worse than a Dane or Pict: "You bowl?! Where? Pour in his mouth maybe you want—what you bowl, you shit worm?"

Thankfully beyond foot range, I made explanation. In frustration he cuffed the oblate, who ducked most of its force.

"No bowl. No food! This refectory! Forbid me God to give fair bowl to every oink and snort pig."

Brother Ostand stormed off inside to attend kitchen hustling, switching back to yelling in his language. The oblate then handed me a great handful of bread, took a bowl and broken spoon off a nearby shelf. "This was Myslyn's who God took from us."

Though an old vessel almost worn through, it held well enough. And at once was filled with a rich stew with lusty aroma of barley and spelt. At center was dropped a portion of cured eel.

It took my breath away, for I never ate such in all my fourteen years.

Meat of any beast was rare, but of eel never, unless we filched one on the fens, a terrible offence.

I sat with my stout meal, securing the bowl in my lap, and fell to it. The bread was Peterborough cheat bread, the sort usually seen not eaten, for cotsets usually ate coarser sorts. I had eyes for my food, yet ears heard soft voices. Next to me two women whispered; I was their intended audience.

"So they've given you Myslyn's bowl and spoon. Poor soul, he was. Always fair."

When I looked to them, one put fingers to her lips. "No talking at repast, so speak low. We are sisters who work for Reverend Sacrist at weave—I am Sara, she is Menda. Working our obligation due Father Abbot."

Though not elderly, both were without teeth and chewed away at the soup and bread. Checking nervously the kitchen door for sign of Ostand, they offered, "In cloister, they eat well on ordinary days."

I nodded, said my name—as softly as possible—and ate. I had a dozen questions but asked none, remembering Osfer's warning and my coming intentions.

"Poor Myslyn died sudden when demons inhabited him."

"Yes. Demons."

I knew they expected questions, but I would not be drawn out. If there were demons in an unlikely place as Peterborough cloister, they weren't in my bowl or bread.

"Demons are terri—"

They stopped inside a word, their toothless mouths gaped. The unfortunates might have actually seen the coming of said demons, judging by their eyes. Instead it was the Whipmen.

Their habits, unlike all other monks, had red sashes which secured their badge and implement of office—black, ugly things with the knotted tentacles of pig leather.

"So, you old bags of shit, eat and talk, do you?"

The heel of one's hand went to the butt of his whip, and I recoiled against the wooden wall. The women sat, virtual stones—mouths still agape. Yet the weapon stayed in its place, and instead both turned towards me. "We're looking for you, and have no time for these old squints. Cuthwin is your name?"

My bladder loosened, but I assented—watching the butt of his hairy paw on the whip-end. They both loomed—so close I knew they had no room to swing their weapons.

Their little round eyes were red from the smoke and fire of monastery life. They were not great- or young-aged if they were any age at all. By God and Our Savior, they made ready truth from the sisters' words about demons.

"You went against Prior's rules once and got away with it, but you won't again, you little bastard. Understand you are in cloister now and we have rules, and those rules are our concern."

"Our concern is The Rule, you fuck!" The second Whipman smiled reaffirming his fellow—for indeed, they were tonsured. Unlike monks in cloister, those with duties out of cloister, like themselves, went about as necessity bade, which meant on any business for Reverend Prior.

One was short and solidly stout—built like a smith; his fellow was tall, a snout like a fisher bird, with eyes set closer together like a lizard.

The two sisters, seeing I was center of unpleasantness, used the moment for getaway, but the leaner of the two Whipmen swiveled like a jackdaw, pointing. "And you two old slatterns will get apt treatment if we see you yakking again at repast."

The terrified women's move to seek safety was a mistake. Both Whipmen faced them. The burley muscled arm of the first removed his whip, its mean ends falling loose at his side.

"Sit down until you're told otherwise!" And he looked up to the taller and muttered, ". . . we ought to give them a taste, Brother, for their great wagging tongues."

The women clutched their bowl and cup to their aprons—attempted to speak, but I supposed, without leave, that too would be contrary.

Finally: "What transpires, dear Brothers?"

Both sisters reclined against the wall—eyes closing, as if an angel descended. Behind us approached a tall monk with a golden sash about his middle, rather than usual plain brown. Both Whipmen stopped their business; their huntsman features lightened.

"Reverend Sacrist, our intent was to convey rules of silence to these two hags. They incessantly gossip, as you know. Reverend Prior is adamant against such."

The Sacrist replied in the Roman tongue, and they bowed, the one putting away his whip and then both going off without further word.

The grateful souls went down, kneeling before the Sacrist, allowing him to scowl first to one, then the other, shaking his head.

"Oh, thank you Reverend Sacrist, Brother Aethyl, that is. Oh, Lord Jesus bless you. We were only making a few words in Christian kindness as we are taught."

"Ah! Even now you chatter like rooks. You left Father Abbot's weave pending. Return to it until Compline[15]. One day I'll not come along and you will both feel the bite of their instruments. **Go!**"

They shuttled off like mud crabs fearing marooning on the outgoing tide. Brother Aethyl's look became less stern; indeed, his eyes glowed in an unfamiliar way.

"And who are you, young man?"

"Cuthwin. I work in the stable."

---

[15] Compline. Around 9:00 p.m.

"Gilbert's new fellow?"

"Yes."

"A lucky stroke for Gilbert; I hope he applies you aptly."

And with a smile, he turned and was gone. My food had gone cold—or rather I had. All events built a strong case for not letting the door strike my backsides at Peterborough Monastery.

Good had turned bad and was fast becoming built into worse. Unless God himself gave sign, I would hasten westward until many leagues were between me and Peterborough before the passing of another day.

I hid the portion of bread in my blouse; I would have keener need of it in hours to come.

This first watch after Compline, which would be my last, was a confusing time. No one explained further about watches, only Gilbert's alerts of 'fire and sick animal' being guide. I strode about avoiding Waddles' stall in fear she commence braying—but with the sun down, she rested, praise God.

Unnecessary attention brought to the stables was not good for me now. I avoided the stall assigned to me in fear of sleep. That day began early on the fens. The space in spirit and place my life covered since dawn was dizzying.

My travels had just begun, for I must put vast distance between me and my pursuers—angry for my abandoned debt.

Escape now would be far more prudently done for I knew the needs of travel. My modest sack of carryings contained everything God had conveyed to me since birth—an old knife, a sliver of flint and striker, a tiny cross made from bones of fowl—the only remaining I had of my mother. Then odds and ends of leather and cloth picked up here and there. These snippets were good for snares and such, including generous turns of reed twine used to choke the bag shut and to serve as spare lengths.

Then there were the clothes I wore, including the old sash at my middle. Also, there were the cracked, worn turnshoes usually kept in my sack instead of wearing. These carryings and the sense and guile God gave me were what I possessed. They seemed to promise saner escape.

Furthermore, I had a few more preparations in mind.

When peace settled over the stables after Compline, I took a leather strip to fashion jesses. Agile as a stoat, I climbed into the overhang, sidled down an old beam, and confronted a row of roosting pigeons—those same plump fowl seen earlier.

The following day would be entirely taken with pursuit, and like all lads born in country I was expert at killing, plucking, and cooking small fowl in a nod and wink—ideal rations for a fleeing boy.

I selected two of the dumb birds—so amply fleshed both my hands barely spanned their midsections. Being in the torpor of roost, they hardly struggled—portable yet hearty fare, a vital cog of my plan.

And compounding wrong with such theft? I thought little of this—compared to owing Father Abbot an enormous sum, two plump monastery pigeons would add negligible sin to that already shouldered. Plus, how might they know? Did they count pigeons?

Adding the bread held back from mealtime, I tied off my sack, hid it within my paddock, and sat astride a post fence.

In the near-distance I saw the walls of Peterborough, the old gates shut and outer watches posted. Since the watches, such as they were, scrutinized out rather than in, and stealthy as I was—walls and watches would cast no problems to surmount without notice.

It was the last few weeks of summer, and I had two months of warm weather for flight. I considered the world ahead; great imaginings and adventures passed through my head, helping me while away hours.

Flitting right by me flew bats nabbing hordes of insects in stable. I didn't fear the creatures, hardly believing the stories told about them. Darting about in their erratic way, they hunted the fens until dawn devouring biting flies and gnats with devotion; hence even these ugly little creatures I viewed as God's gift to man.

The evening winds carried to me the aromas of field—and even with it, tinges of the fens. I saw a whitish streak of a passing owl before the stable, when a voice nearly made me fall headlong.

"It is time, Brother Cuthwin, God be praised."

Behind me tiny Alswyn stared up, and I was momentarily out of temper.

"You but scared the shit out of me, little brother!"

"Oh, I'm sorry."

He was a kindly tot, and for the moment—and I recall this well—I was of a mind to offer him to accompany me. Yet I suspected he had taken holy vow to God so he would be sworn to report my ill intentions.

I told him all was quiet, made my 'good-night,' then slipped over to my stall, secured my sack at my sash, and, seeing him sit and looking the other way, I made nimbly for the walls. I crept along the shadowy edges of the outer yard, passing near to the Refectory where hours before the Whipmen menaced.

There was a space needs covered by my last dash between the Refectory and the building—low, massive, yet of single story. This was Father Abbot's residence and greeting hall. Checking well, I started across when—like a dash of cold water—words tumbled over me: "Young Cuthwin, out so late?"

There I was planted looking into the shadows at Father Abbot sitting on a low bench with that great, ancient hound a few feet away, his old nose to the ground, his partially bald tail flopping weakly right and left.

"It is Erthwin's greatest joy in life and mine, his nightly outing. Poor brute served me well these fifteen years. Ah, he was a great hound in bone and flesh when young."

So here was the most powerful and grand man in all the lands and waters—for dozens of hundreds[16] in all directions. I owed him more money than I could imagine, and there he sat witnessing me fleeing responsible debt after his kindnesses.

I paused, waiting for him to call the watch, but he held the tether of his hound. He had unloosed Erthwin, so it hung loosely in his hand. It occurred to me it would give him a handy whipping strap, though I was a half dozen paces off.

Yet I reckoned to be fast enough to still escape, even if he gave the alarm, such was my cocksureness of youth.

There was a half-moon above. My eyes adjusted to what light there was, and I saw Father Abbot was leaning against the wall with a sad gaze as he looked at Erthwin nosing about.

The old animal was weak in the legs, but like all hounds, at peace with sniffing and being off leash or out of pen. He sidled up to a trough attempting to raise his leg, but instead nearly fell over. Father Abbot shook his head. "He can barely make water, and this will be the last night, I fear, we will share together. Tomorrow I'm gone, and God will claim old Erthwin before my return. God's unstoppable will can be very difficult for those we love."

At once I saw an absence of my situation in Father Abbot's mind. He looked upon his old dog with sadness. As I had witnessed with Waddles, he loved the animal. I reckoned, knowing hounds—and frankly being fond of them—Erthwin had not been of practical use for years now.

"I don't believe I've seen such an old hound, Father Abbot."

He smiled as the dog hobbled up, leaning against Father Abbot, and receiving a fond scratching of a tattered ear, evidence of past battles.

"Erthwin fought always, but God has forgiven him, dumb beast that he is. Yet even a hound should not give injury." He looked keenly for the first time at me, nodded, and motioned to the edge of the trough, and I understood he wanted me to sit, and I did.

I could not help myself, but curiosity flows as rapidly and unpredictably in the young as does every other notion.

"Do such beasts go to heaven, Father Abbot?"

"Oh, yes. Though most thoughtful canons would decry me. I believe by the spirits of the Father, Son, and Holy Ghost that Erthwin and I shall walk the fields honored with God's love for eternity. And you, Cuthwin?"

His question jolted, for no one had asked me anything other than for some immediate item, and certainly never for anything I thought. I had reflected on many such things myself—but only to myself. But up to this moment, I was never questioned by another mortal, and never dreamed I might by a great personage as an Abbot.

My mouth dropped, but I kept my wits, and to this day, almost eight decades later, I remain proud of my honest response: "I never, I'm afraid, wondered about beasts, Father Abbot, but very often after my mother. Though I barely recall her."

"Her name?"

"Sarah-of-Alnwick, Father Abbot."

There was much to explain about my mother—the things I'd heard about her: Many were not altogether Christ's desired praises. Through my rough rearing, when ill-behaved, I was told I risked joining her in hell if I maintained such behavior.

Yet I did remember my mother before the grand fire at Withernsea Manor: She had an infant at breast, for as memory serves—she always had an infant in one arm, and worked with the other.

She was a stout woman, of round Saxon stock, and good in every way of manner with glib tongue. My clearest memory was her stories of diverse beasts: *"Great worms carouse countrysides devouring here and there, thrashing grand tails, sending sharp, leathery scales flying off in all direction—the size of flagstones,"* she had told me.

And it was that moment, remembering her—and especially the mean words attached to such a good woman—that unaccountably I began weeping. For why couldn't God allow me to know her better? I believed they lied about her and she was in heaven, not hell.

And indeed, if she owed such a sum as I, Sarah-of-Alnwick would not have flown to field and woods.

Father Abbot patted Erthwin then held up his hand, as if to pat me, though I was some distance away.

"During my trip, I shall say prayers daily for good Sarah-of-Alnwick. Know this, souls who say bad things about people sin and need absolve themselves of such. Only God can sit in judgment."

I was embarrassed to have wept, and while gathering myself, Father Abbot pointed at my waist. "Whatever you do, Cuthwin, I would ask you to free those two innocent birds in sack. They are creatures of Peterborough Monastery, and deserve not to have blood shed through their protector's inactivity. Promise me that." And he stood and beckoned me once again forth. "Now come. Who knows if this might be the last blessing God will allow me to confer on you."

And kneeling before him, I again felt him put that most peaceful and kindly hand on my head. His blessing done, he looped the tether around Erthwin's old neck, but the dog had lain down, weary from his outing.

"Come, rise, old hound. We must retire."

Erthwin steeled himself, uprighted with front legs, allowed a groan, then completed the labor with his rear legs. Alongside Father Abbot, he tottered off towards a tiny rear door to the Residence.

Feeling the fowl's movement at my waist, I returned to the stables, untied the sack, and climbing back up, placed the dimwitted but fortunate birds on a beam.

Back on the floor of the stable, I looked briefly for Alswyn. I did not see him, and when I returned to my stall I discovered him curled up in the flea-infested sacking. He slept, thumb in mouth.

Sleep did not seem close, and I returned to the fence, climbed up and sat, watching and listening for things unknown.

And this, reckoning by the Venerable Bede's measure, was how I, Cuthwin-of-Alnwick came to reside in Peterborough Monastery, beginning the late summer of the year of our Savior, 1029.

My half-dozen years at Peterborough Monastery serving Abbot Elsin are the most worthwhile education a youth could receive in preparation for a world harsh and fickle to those of us who labor for their keep.

I thank God, the Son, and the Holy Ghost—a poor cottar's only protector—for guiding me to Peterborough and allowing me rare learning and privilege. Yet in truth I witnessed how even some of His own servants fall from earthly and even eternal grace.

And this was the keenest lesson learned at Peterborough and from Abbot Elsin, though I saw him so pitifully rare those six years. To wit, the world inside cloister and walls of a burh[16] are no more cursed or blessed than the world outside.

Practical advantage was my work in stable and Scriptorium—for Gilbert was not a bad sort despite his moods. Also, Provisioner Cassartorius was peculiar, but his manners were the same with all, from myself to Father Abbot. Yet he was vastly learned though cautious in sharing it with lesser sorts.

---

[16] Burh. A fortified settlement via roads, rivers and walls in defense against invasions.

So the two labors—one inside with books and their makings, the other outside with animals and their necessities—offered me respite from each other. However, I slept and kept watch in the stables, and time-wise I was more a part there than the Scriptorium.

Being expert in trapping and wise to ways of smaller creatures, I brought sudden decrease to vermin who gnawed and constructed safe warrens in the Scriptorium. Those furred trespassers of holy books incurred sad fate to skills learned in woods and pasture. My skills snaring and trapping creatures also offered a source and opportunity that supplemented refectory fare.

God forgive me, but I used my victims as fodder for trade and gift, for they were fat from easy living. I thought, since The Rule did not apply to those not taking tonsure and since the beasts were unwanted, that God and Father Abbot would give leave.

Truth was, many who worked required hours inside cloister enjoyed a roasted morsel. Most surely Gilbert was master at preparing them over the fire in forge, adding to restful times along with his dire Welsh brew. However, he urged caution: "Mind oblates do not see this fare, Cuthwin; the wretches will inform Prior Denewulf at once, desperate to gain his good office."

He did not fear Prior Denewulf, for Prior would not cross Gilbert because he maintained peace in the stables and was unequalled master of his trade. Since most oblates were from great houses and families, we who worked outside tonsure, such as Gilbert, were of common cloth.

Gilbert harbored sparse love for oblates. He was harsh with them and was the poorer for it, I thought even then, may God forgive the good man.

In my hours at the Scriptorium, usually between nones and vespers, my other master—Brother Cassartorius—was not lacking at delivering kick or backhand, yet thank God, he was sparing with these skills.

Far worse dread for ordinary and tonsured souls were Prior Denewulf and his Whipmen, Reverend Prior above all. His severity was intensified by Father Abbott's frequent absences. During them Prior Denewulf was head of cloister, demesne, and lands held under charter to Peterborough Monastery. Obedience without hesitation was required above all others under The Rule by those in cloister, and to violate it brought painful punishment. This Reverend Prior observed with keen scrutiny making no exceptions.

From Prior on down all the people in Peterborough Monastery and town had their own peculiar God-given traits, including being inhabited during evil times by demons and fiends. But through the six years, I faithfully observed Brother Osfer's advice to 'be content with your place, to not gossip, and to *always* be obedient.'

It served me well. I'm sure Brother Osfer had more such wisdom to impart, but he departed us not too long after I was taken in, God having sent his soul to a better place, surely.

"This is a drearier place without him," Gilbert reflected, for Gilbert missed him almost equal to the absences of Father Abbott. Our kindly shepherd learned of Brother Osfer's passing upon return after traveling, and was out of spirit for some days subsequent—speaking little, despite being gone so long, usually when he was at most conversant.

So numerous are the people and events that they fill my mind, urging me to impart here what I learned and saw at Peterborough Monastery. Sadly, if I did, there would be few surfaces made from plant or hide left to write upon anywhere. Instead, I needs hasten to the most significant event for me: Learning letters in my own Saxon tongue, and, to a lesser degree, in Latin, as the language of Rome is rightly called. Letters became my surest friend then and in years ahead.

Even now, I am grateful for God's sure hand in guiding me to the Peterborough Scriptorium. While trapping rats, I needed to move and work through costly books—both whole and partial—and at once I saw they were beautiful indeed.

I was taught how to handle them—a process sped up when brothers delivered vigorous cuffings whenever oblates or myself were too rough in handling tomes which took uncountable hours to complete.

I learned faster than most—enough to receive few such blows, may God forgive my pride. At the same time, the letters—the words they formed—attracted my youthful eyes like a row of fatted doves. I would put my finger at their base, tracing them along, like one might intricacies of a spider's web, woven overnight in solitary corner.

In the labyrinth of places where I trapped, only the leanest brothers could follow me, and I had much time. Like any youth, I would take my leisure, using the times to open the books and examine them in detail. Since I knew by heart many of the holy psalms in my own tongue, I was able to associate the spoken word with those written in Saxon Psalters. The written word in Saxon I would then associate in ear and tongue with those letters on the page.

Since the vermin were quick and easy to catch, I spent more and more time doing this, and soon was able to recognize the simplest words. Yet progress was too slow this way, and it annoyed me. But even at that earliest stage, I knew the Saxon tongue was more appropriate than Latin. Who had I ever heard speak Latin in field and village? Most spoke Saxon as their preferred tongue, as I did.

To write it was akin to learning a special secret, as indeed it virtually was for a cotset. Yet I know my learning would have continued very slowly if it hadn't been for a most memorable incident. Through the providence of God, my life diverted into a direction unforeseen. It made both possible and necessary my life of travels which brought me many curiosities and places which offer me fodder for current telling.

After the passing of my second Christmastide, a somewhat warmer season than in my northern home, I was finding fewer vermin in the Scriptorium. So I busied myself aiming to keep out of the monks' sight, yet necessity required I pass through the working area of the Scriptorium where dozens of manuscripts, writs, and other such works were arduously crafted. By now, I knew Brother Cassatorius was a severe taskmaster. I often noticed looks of anger and mockery exchanged behind his back by both brothers and oblates.

One day, emerging from one of two cavernous rooms where all great writings were kept, I heard a wicked commotion: Foremost was the sound of the whip, then painful outcry, and Prior Denewulf speaking calmly through it all, as if in sermon or lecture. His deep voice penetrated every corner: "Witness! To mock one's superior violates The Rule."

I was caught by my collar by the Whipman presently not involved, and pointed within: "Watch closely, Cuthwin. Clever or not, one day will be your time."

Brother Cassatorius stood next to Prior with head down horrified as I—only occasionally glancing at the Brother—for it was no oblate being whipped, as was usually the case, but a Brother, no longer youthful. Worse, the rare whipping of a Brother was supposed done in a special place, but not on this occasion.

Held at Prior's side was a large drawing—for most of the brother monks' at work in the Scriptorium were wonderful draughtsman at catching likenesses. I'd learned this skill was thought to be sinful idleness, and forbidden. This transgressor sadly had a hand recognized by all. He had drawn an expert likeness of Brother Cassatorius, with the Saxon words, "God Curse This Lombard Devil," beneath it. Recognizing a few of the words, I drew away in shock at its scandalous intent. I never thought such blasphemy would be attached to a tonsured brother in a holy place.

At that moment, since he had averted his eyes from the gore, Master Cassatorius saw me and understood at once I'd comprehended those words, or some of them. And when I looked back his gaze was fixed upon me.

At the same time, Prior held out his arm, stopping the Whipman in mid-stroke. The victim's habit had been thrown over head and shoulder; his tattered undergarment had blood soaking through. It was beginning to run down his buttocks and onto his legs.

Prior held aloft the derisive drawing, turning it this way and that, making sure we all saw it: "See this blasphemy!" Then to the wretchedly maimed Brother, "And you will atone further, Brother Shawn, and may God forgive."

All in Scriptorium were compelled to watch, and like me appalled at the sight of blood. I had seen a few whippings but none like this.

I returned to stable soon, seeking my place. But already Gilbert heard of events, for in the Monastery news traveled seemingly through the ether. I had first watch, and Gilbert informed I might well end up with all watches, for there would likely be a special chapter meeting and oblates' routines could be affected.

"And Father Abbot is gone, God help Brother Shawn. It is outposting for him, surely."

Peterborough Monastery had outlying priories; some were little more than nooks where living was rough. In fact, an oblate just tonsured into Brotherhood often spent their first years in such holy places.

These offered opportunity to Prior Denewulf for extending punishment. Brother Shawn's skills in Scriptorium notwithstanding, his future appeared grim if the guilt remained upon him.

He would be examined in chapter and long outposted by the time of Father Abbot's return. All knew if Father Abbot was present his punishment would be less severe and, in God's name, fairer.

But God forgive me, on that eve my fate was my concern, not that of my fellow man. I knew Brother Cassatorius had seen me attempt to read, a serious violation of place.

At the serving door of the refectory untonsured workers were especially silent that night. We passed the winter solstice just weeks before; it was still dark at Vespers, and darkness swept over my inner spirit as well.

For Brother Osfer's forewarnings on that first day was central to all others: *In Monastery to always know one's place.* A mere cotset learning letters, I feared, upset that order almost more than crafting blasphemous drawings.

After meal time, this fear was confirmed when I returned to the stable and instead of finding only the watch-lantern lit, I saw two lanterns alight. This use of candle was a rare indulgence. Worse, sitting before them was Gilbert and—God help me—Brother Ithamar.

Gilbert's eyes were sad, and seeing me, he pointed at a spot before them both—to stand, not sit.

"Brother Ithamar needs question you, and mind you be straight, Cuthwin. None of your sly word play."

Brother Ithamar was Master Cassatorius' assistant, with more than usual responsibilities. This was required because Brother Cassatorius was extreme of application of the Rule of Silence. Though silence was required of the tonsured during meals, many had leave outside that time. But never Brother Cassatorius, who practiced otherwise.

However, the other language of cloister—a hundred different signs, long held and understood—were practiced in rapid and nimble order by our silent Provisioner. Yet when speech was necessary, especially for dealing with those outside of the Scriptorium, it fell to Brother Ithamar to make office.

He was a massive, dark-countenanced Saxon, completely grey and without cheer, uncommonly skilled in all matters and crafts of the Scriptorium.

"Cuthwin, how did you come to know letters in your brutish tongue?"

When Ithamar spoke, it was assumed—unless he said otherwise—to be in the voice of Master Cassatorius, a strange situation.

For that disparaging view of things Saxon was Brother Cassatorius' opinion. Being a Lombard, and common to them, he held longstanding arrogance towards what they viewed as savage tongues; this surely included Saxon.

Gilbert intervened, and, in his way, allowed me time or room to answer.

"He's a clever lad, Brother. Good at things."

"Allow Cuthwin to respond, good Gilbert. He has tongue."

There was no good path. Answering truthful meant, at least, trouble. Unlike Brother Shawn, I was a freedman and deeply in debt. My lot seemed even uglier.

"I know only a few from working with books and such, Brother Ithamar."

"And how might you have done that? Through your skin, as if you were a frog or a prune?"

Gilbert averted his eyes—finding need to adjust the frontpiece on the closest lantern. Familiar with his every move, I saw my response was less than good. But it was my experience that day that truth was unwise when speaking with a cloistered monk.

I simply stopped speaking and looked down—resigned to my lot. I was now fifteen, of fair size, still confident in my ability—if no other choice remained—to flee onto the fens. I would not allow myself to be whipped as a thick-headed drover might a beast; surely Our Savior did not condone such.

"It could be, young Cuthwin, that the letters have come to you by possession of a demon. If such, this grievous situation falls heavily to Reverend Prior's offices, especially during absence of Father Abbot."

To be possessed of a demon moved matters beyond whippings, or indeed debt. Being possessed was a plague. Demons infected all souls who chanced proximity to those so possessed.

There is nothing more harmful or evil than to be demon possessed, as demons do the bidding of the Archfiend Himself.

Brother Ithamar removed a small leather sack from under his sash, took out a smallish book—beautiful in binding and print. Opening it carefully, he turned it towards me and ordered, "Read me what you see writ there, otherwise I needs go direct to Prior Denewulf."

Holding my arms behind me, I tilted forward and saw at once it was a few simple words of a morning prayer. Gilbert's gaze met mine, and I knew I must reveal myself. So I read the passage, and in doing so forever changed my life. How strange such moments are in the lives of ordinary men and women.

"Now, tell me how you came by reading our Saxon letters."

So I explained my process—and while I responded, he closed the tiny book, and returned it to sash. He and Gilbert shared lengthy reverie. I felt my bladder weakening and fear rising.

Ithamar stood, and nodding in something of resolve, said, "Enough of this. Tomorrow is Sabbath. Monday I am guessing events will return to center, including the Scriptorium." He gave thanks to Gilbert and was gone.

Gilbert extinguished lamps and returned them to a shelf with his various ointments. He moved slowly, with deliberation. I knew he had much to say and possibly do. I brought trouble to him from the Scriptorium, besmirching the stables by forgetting my place.

True to his ways, possibly putting off the unpleasant, Gilbert said nothing, but left me to thoughts, as wild and hectic as they were.

While I stood first watch, I prayed God would forgive and intercede in what consequences might follow. Additionally, I prayed Gilbert and his stables would be spared whatever might be visited on me. In truth, despite his often morose ways, I was fond of Gilbert. Though already clever in all ways of animals, I was learning still more. He never laid hand to me as he did sometimes oblates, for we were both of common cloth, with a life of work ahead of us.

Contrary to what was later credited to me, I was never one for great amounts of prayer—no more or less than person of croft and craft. But that night, I indulged in prayer more than at any other time, not anticipating anything but a dismal outcome.

In the morning Gilbert woke me with a nudge of his foot, informed me without explanation—though none was needed—I would no more to the Scriptorium.

"Keep low, Cuthwin. I will design a task to outpost you soon, if there is time."

This gave me hope, like the time of my escape when I was eelman and the Whipmen came looking. Master Ordgar found work for me at once upon the fens—distant from Monastery, and, even better, not accessible by path or road.

Now I lived moment to moment upon the chance Prior Denewulf would remain uninformed concerning my violation of place—helping myself to knowledge beyond God's place and function.

Yet in the absolute order of obedience, Brother Cassartorius was required by The Rule to report my violation to his superior. However promptly might Brother Cassartorius's sense of responsibility be realized? It was not yet Sext when Gilbert had only the briefest opportunity to round the corner of paddock and warn, "Cuthwin, brace yourself, trouble is near. Get up into the main beam, now."

I threw down my work and sprang to the top of the paddock, then at next leap into the massive center rafter—the pride of support for the entire stable. Precisely then the Whipmen strode arrogantly in. Gilbert looked to them with feigned surprise. They gestured everywhere, the taller, grislier of the two was spokesman. He was puffed up with the dark nature of their mission.

"Where is Cuthwin? We call on Prior's business."

"On errand outside the walls."

"After what he did!?"

"I only know the stables, God have mercy. All else is gossip. Cuthwin will return by Compline, for his belly will be talking."

"Where is he?! Reverend Prior orders him fetched directly."

"En route to Wilfrid-of-Loe."

And they turned and were gone, the shorter—the knottier of the two turning to instruct, "If he returns earlier, hold him. Reverend Prior must reckon him at once."

Gilbert picked up the spade I had cast aside, for its careless placement might have betrayed my recent departure if the creatures had sense enough to so perceive.

While putting the tool carefully in its place—and knowing I gazed downward—he spoke to me without looking: "Stay up there until I tell you otherwise. Presently, events have me at odds."

I understood that the worst happened. The best I could expect would be a whipping for violating the Scriptorium's properties by prideful prying—and the worst clapped in confinement for holy trial for any one of a dozen demonic heresies.

The memory of this time aloft in the stable has lingered through the decades. Numberless thoughts of despair raced through my stripling's mind.

Escape to the fens was ten times more difficult than the year before when summer was still at hand. But if suspected of being possessed, escape was impossible. Word of my possession would precede and even the humblest cottar or cotset would have mortal fear of me. Demons took one's soul and must always be feared.

No door would be open nor croft available. Dogs would look ceaselessly until I was dug out of whatever nook I had availed myself.

Gilbert was taking grievous risk, for Wilfred-of-Loe was a dreng who held land far distant; however, the Whipmen would discover they were on a fool's search. Then Gilbert, having lied, would be himself in trouble.

At fifteen years plus months, I was just old enough to be a soldier in dozens of conflicts I heard talk of daily. Other lads ran off to such military struggles. Such sagas of conflict, the ensuing booty and wanton activity, greatly attract foolish striplings. Though not of that mind, I believed such a sinful fate would be far better than being whipped flesh-less. Yet even the most savage armies would not take one possessed unless I were successful enough to flee far away where word had not traveled.

In the midst of such dismal ruminations, the peace was fractured with raucous braying, then report of a violent kick visited against her paddock—and other outlandish disorder. Waddles had broke into her own demonic possession.

Now too old to accompany her beloved Father Abbot anywhere—even within country—she convinced all in Peterborough Monastery that she had uncommon sense about Father Abbot's proximity. And when-ever he stepped off the boat returning from oversea, even though still leagues distant, she knew at the second. And then she would make unholy demonstration to see him. Her simple mind informed that treats of fresh carrot or ones from cellar should commence at the precise moment of his return.

It was decreed by Father Abbot that such vegetables would be denied him in refectory, thereby freeing him to provide such choice fare to a simple donkey. Such was his love for that creature.

None could fathom how Waddles' senses worked, but instead of fear-ing whatever demon enabled her, all utilized her alarm for advantage with early warning. Indeed, upon hearing her commotion, everyone began making preparation for the return of Father Abbot. From that moment on, all would be abustle in preparation for him.

So I knew, clinging to the beam like some furred or feathered crea-ture, that within a day—at most—Father Abbot would arrive and at least I would get fair trial. I was not possessed of a demon, and trusted him to know that.

I did not trust Prior for anything but harshness and coldness of heart and soul. May God forgive me, yet even after so long I never budged in such opinion of him and those like him.

On that day God looked to me and made certain I would stand fair hearing before one of His finest. Waddles was harbinger of reprieve from harsh judgment, thereby requiring forgiveness for her many mean acts when cleaning her stall.

In the cloister of a Monastery, the return of any brother from a long trip, and especially foreign places, meant fresh infusion with news of the times. This itself made the ensuing days after return nearly equal that of holy days in feeling if not fact.

So upon commencement of Waddles' outpourings, Gilbert called me down and I carried on in stable normally. The rough-hewn Saxon said nothing and seemed unworried at gulling the Whipmen.

I learned later Wilfred-of-Loe was Gilbert's kinsman. So when someone was sent by Gilbert, Wilfred at once spun a series of deceptions. He was of boundless mischief, disdaining all holy men from Monastery.

The Whipmen were then sent even farther afield by Wilfred-of-Loe. In the end, they did not even know of Waddles' antics—nor of Father Abbott's arrival—until they returned.

I knew, however, that reckoning must be at hand for me, for violation of place and trust needs be addressed formally. When the waiting became too much, I asked Gilbert, and all he said was, "Be patient, and don't yearn for bad. Know well Prior Denewulf has much sway with Father Abbot."

When the hour came, I was attending Waddles' paddock. The Whipmen loomed upon me. The taller of the duo had his whip out from sash, tapping it on his open palm, the weapon's tendrils hanging down like spiders' legs. "Now Cuthwin, come at once. Prior has need of your arrogant presence."

My bowels loosened. Would there be no fair hearing? I was no oblate, but nearly a full-grown freedman due a rightful hearing. I looked— holding a shovel at my side.

"Are you moonstruck, Cuthwin?! Come at once!" It was the shorter, gnarlier of the two whose brows suddenly furrowed, all grave. "You think of using that shovel, and you'll learn even tonsured brothers know where to shove a thing where it will hurt most, you whore's fuck."

I was not thinking such a thing. I never struck another human nor intended to. But I dropped it and followed. When one took me by the arm—hard—I do admit anger at hearing my mother so brutalized.

"Reverend Brothers, will I have fair hearing?"

"Shut up. That's your hearing."

And they walked faster, and perhaps my bowels would have indeed let go if the legged menaces did not turn at Refectory, and instead went directly into Father Abbot's residence.

Passing through the same rooms again, this time I found them richly furnished, with tapestries finely woven everywhere in doorway and window. Brothers worked, though, taking these down, for Father Abbot would have no finery when resident but rather have it stored.

But when he was absent from Peterborough Monastery, hosting of great persons, including those from court, all—sometimes even the King—fell to Prior Denewulf. As was proper, great men would be received with full regalia adorning the Abbot's residence. In these duties, Prior Denewulf was considered the wiser, for Father Abbot was notorious in plain living and being too extreme in devotion to The Rule. Even Gilbert would allow that "great parties need prideful cloying," though I sensed in his heart he agreed with Father Abbot.

So brothers were busy taking down great weavings and moving stout, finely carved furniture away. The Whipmen walked me between and around this. Entering Father Abbot's room, they pushed me to the floor before Prior Denewulf and Father Abbot. Prior Denewulf intoned, "In the name of the Father, Son, and the Holy Ghost, may God find justice in these proceedings with this wretched sinner."

I was allowed to hear this first in Saxon, then it was repeated by all in Latin. Since the Whipmen held my head down, I heard all but saw nothing. Then I heard the voice of Father Abbot, and it was a vast balm: "Brothers, let him look up and attend us."

Discussion began in Latin and remained that way, allowing me to look at Father Abbot not with a little concern. He was far thinner, his left eye swollen shut, and a dressing about wounds on his head. If he were not a man of endless peace, one might guess involvement in a brawl with him getting the worse of it. I had seen Frog so adorned more than once.

But Father Abbot, God knows, was not Frog. Finally, they settled what discussion they required. Prior Denewulf looked at me directly; his looks were always, it seemed, severe.

"What say you of this sin of pride, Cuthwin? To strive beyond your God-ordained place—that position God has seen fit to bless you with. It is a transgression requiring great penance in the eyes of the Creator."

If this was a fair hearing, I was at a loss how to be heard. I knew little about the sin of pride, save it was always bad. I never intended to do such a thing. But this was one of the few occasions no timely words came to me.

Father Abbot saw this, and then I noticed his keen eyes move left and right—to each Whipman, hovering at my elbows like rooks at the leavings.

"Brothers, give leave to Prior and me, and withdraw momentarily."

I drew breath easier when they obeyed. All the while Prior Denewulf didn't remove his baleful eye lock from me.

"I asked a question, so what say you, Cuthwin?"

"I did not mean—did not intend anything prideful, Prior Denewulf."

"That makes it almost worse, does it not, Father Abbot?"

"Indeed, Cuthwin. You must always be aware and knowledgeable about the sin of false pride, and how the Archfiend baits Innocents with his false attractions."

A dullness drew over me. Even Father Abbot seemed to have turned; he put both his hands to his jaw, and tested it—pressing a bit left and right. Reassured, perhaps, that it still worked, he looked ceiling-ward and mused, "Oh, but Prior Denewulf! If only I had your education at Church Law in Boulogne—ah, what an honor. But allow me: Wasn't it our blessed Saxon King Alfred, Shepherd of the English, who urged our tongue upon his people, both of church and lay?"

"It was, Father Abbot."

"And didn't Himself translate much Latin writing into that tongue and have it distributed? And he suggested school for all in our Saxon tongue. An extraordinary idea!"

"Yes, Father Abbot, but it went for naught."

"So, Cuthwin, in the Latin language, what are your skills?"

"None, Father Abbot."

"So: You see where my thoughts direct, do you not, Brother Denewulf?"

"Indeed. That it is his own tongue, not that of the Church, the former urged upon its people by King Alfred, by both his word and act."

"Precisely. So, since the boy wasn't striving to elevate his station by learning a language that was not his—not his place, like Latin—there is possible mitigation here. Perhaps our Lord knows he was not partaking in false pride. It might be construed that Cuthwin, though unwittingly, followed the wishes of our venerated King Alfred, the most Holy Shepherd of the English. It is, in the writs of holy scholars, the intent of an act, save in cases of possession, that intensifies a transgression against the order of Our Lord. And certainly, we know young Cuthwin is not possessed. What do you say, Brother?"

"Father Abbot is not himself at a loss in Canon Law, or indeed law in general. But there remains the matter of obedience. Permission or leave was needed to be asked of Brother Cassartorius, or at least Brother Ithamar."

I never knew what true opinions existed between Father Abbot and Prior Denewulf. At this point, however, I felt renewal of hope.

"Excellent point. And for fairness sakes, I would in turn, Brother Prior, ask to speak to either, but there is much upset over blood being spilt in Scriptorium. Best to let them be. Especially Brother Cassartorius—he is not himself."

At once, a darker issue settled over the room, one evidently ongoing in cloister. Prior Denewulf turned at the shoulders, noticing Father Abbot shoving irritatingly at his dressing which was coming loose.

"Father Abbot, for the sake of those who love you, allow me to call Brother Callow and have him properly dress those wounds again. He made hasty work of it, weeping as he was."

Noticing me listening and looking on, Brother Prior swept his hand impatiently doorward. "Back to stable, Cuthwin! You will learn of your penance there. And hereafter mind your work and none but your work."

I was intercepted outside by the Whipmen, who oozed chagrin since there was not call for their offices regards myself.

"I tell you Cuthwin, you little stoat, your day will arrive."

I remembered the words they visited on my mother not an hour before. I had not heard such foulness bestowed on another soul by those tonsured—our Savior's servants. Within me was sinful unforgiving anger towards them, may God forgive me.

I was escorted out at double speed. I swore that whatever God's will deemed best for my fate would, by His Grace, be different than desolate corrupt souls like Whipmen.

It was after Vespers Gilbert called me, and going there I found Brother Ithamar sipping my master's strange tea in his workshop. It was the first time I saw Brother Ithamar at rest, for he was a somber and reserved scholar greatly respected by all.

Gilbert looked me over more sternly than usual, and gestured to me with the hand that held his ancient, stained cup.

"On your knees, Cuthwin; Brother Ithamar has honored us with conveying Prior's penance to both of us in his holy person."

When Gilbert put his cup aside to follow suit, Ithamar stopped him by reaching out—and he was such a large man that putting hand to his shoulder stopped Gilbert shortly at once.

I, however, was on my knees when he began: "In the name of the Father, Son, and the Holy Ghost, this is your most forgiving and generous penance, Cuthwin-of-Alnwick."

While he recited I held breath for mention of the whip. There was of course an elaboration of penitent prayer, duty, and enforced fasts, all of it endurable. But I was surprised when Brother Ithamar concluded with, ". . . and so your responsibilities in Brother Cassatorius' Scriptorium are reduced from its former to that of twice weekly, during which you are required to attend lessons in writing and reading our mother tongue on top of your other duties. Further, Prior admonishes you to observe humility and Our Lord's blessed order of things."

He had put his cup aside, made the sign over me, and then looked to Gilbert and added, "And you, Master Stabler, Father Abbot specified your penance—you are to personally accompany our generous and forgiving Cellarer Eadsige to collect Wilfred-of-Loe's rents, tardy as they be."

Gilbert shifted on his stool uncomfortably. And though Ithamar was a cheerless soul, I thought to see movement at the corners of his mouth—the start of a smile, soon stifled.

Then he put a hand to my head, made gesture to Gilbert—and both of us recited our holy contrition. It was by receiving penance and forgiveness from him, I learned Brother Ithamar was ordained—most monks were not, but a few were.

After Brother retired, Gilbert stood—using unusual deliberation while removing his stout stableman's apron. He eyed me—their light gray color always shrewd. He assigned me extra watch and was about to turn, but stopped and, in a rare abundance of words, added, "And you will precede me by several days to Wilfred-of-Loe's, Cuthwin. You will give him alert. As a stableman, you have right to share in Father Abbot's merciful mission of penance."

I had heard of Wilfred-of-Loe so knew this part of my penance would be bad. It would not be pleasant to remind Wilfred-of-Loe his overdue rent to Father Abbot—for all fees of village and field were due under name of Father Abbot.

Yet even facing this tight-fisted Saxon was better than a whipping. And certainly I felt fortunate to still have duty in Scriptorium. But the addendum of having lessons in Saxon excited me, for I never had lessons in anything.

Who would teach such?

For a fast-growing youth, the most severe part of my penance though was fasting for a week from Prime through None, missing always the largest daily meal. I was fond of my bowl and meal. For an entire week to miss my victuals at Sext seemed almost harsher than the whip.

I heard a bit of scuffle come from the direction of Waddles' confines. Attending this, I encountered Father Abbot and a Brother I did not know—the former actually in with Waddles, scratching the inside of one of her vast ears, Father Abbot's attendant, however, kept several arms' distant holding a sack of carrots.

At once I went to my knees, but was told to rise and attend.

"Cuthwin, relieve Brother here this task so he might return to duties for Matins."

Though propriety meant a blessing before dismissal from Father Abbot's presence, the poor soul dreaded being in range of tooth or hoof of Waddles. He swayed back and forth, like a head of wheat in country breeze.

Father Abbot had mercy—nodded, said the necessaries of leave, I supposed, in Latin—and the Brother ran off. So I took the sack and, not so fearful of Waddles, stood closer. Father Abbot spoke to Waddles in Norman—for such was her country of origin.

"She was a Norman-born foal left to die, which explains much. God forgive them for their severe ways with His creatures."

I heard him say this often—perhaps explaining away her crossness. Regards Norman, it was as extreme an opinion he visited on any soul, typical of a man who loved our Savior's creatures.

Watching her enjoyment at eating a carrot and getting an ear rub, I marveled at the love such a troubled animal had for a mortal man, even gentle Father Abbot. There Father Abbot sat, the beast as happy as such a whimsical creature might be.

On this evening—for it was nearly Matins—he explained the dressing applied to injuries about his head.

"Oversea evil men prey on travelers, no matter their business."

"Father Abbot, don't you travel with escort? I've heard a traveler might be slain, otherwise."

"No," he allotted Waddles another carrot, and looked me over. "Do you enjoy your lessons in our mother tongue?"

"Yes, Father Abbot."

"And do well?"

"Yes, Father Abbot."

He nodded in satisfaction, leaned back a bit on his stool and surprised me by chuckling. "You will experience how stingy and of ill nature a Saxon thane may be when you go to Wilfred-of-Loe's informing of rent past due. I guess this will be your duty."

"Yes, Father Abbot."

"Cuthwin! Now hear me: Always be obedient, and learn well. It will not satisfy you to live out life in Peterborough Monastery, and one day you will move on. But no matter where or how, be obedient, kind and always remember the poor. . . . I will now spend time alone with my venerable friend, talking of our great travels of old. Now, come."

And at his gesture, I didn't fear Waddles enough to not kneel directly next to him, feeling his hand and to enjoy his Holy Blessing.

So it was within two meager weeks—long ago—out of all years God has given me, that my life's fortune would be so surely directed. For within the very next week, my years would be further adorned with His blessing.

During all following years I kept close to heart the words of Father Abbot.

Gilbert was not slow in his resolve, for within a few days I trekked to Wilfred-of-Loe's. I carried repaired tackle promised to his kinsman. Also, and most ill, information that the Cellarer would soon to call.

It was late January and plowing time was upon field. As I moved along I remember well the strong, honest smell of dank clay-bound soil stoutly tilled with the heavy blade. High-shouldered mottled oxen bent low, pulling mightily before the ploughman, and his fellow treading close alongside, coaxing the massive beasts with his guiding stick. These were the sights of late winter during those old times when only a Saxon's plain tongue and free-born souls moved oxen and plough along.

Within Peterborough, and moreso inside the Monastery, I missed the feel of open country. So on that morning, despite the daunt of facing Wilfred-of-Loe, my heart rose with cheer by walking free, feeling cold air tingling my skin.

A morning wind recently warmed by a risen sun still cut smartly; furthermore, frosts were not rare, though the more frequent rains were cold and unfriendly. To a plainly clad traveler passing through fen and pasture, weather was harsh.

I promised that if I could complete my task at Loe early, I would divert to Ordgar's and visit with the eelmen, catching fresh news of the fens, including Frog.

When I arrived at Wilfred-of-Loe's, news of my business preceded, as is often the case—carried by elves or wood gnomes? I do not know. Hence the stout Saxon—who had fists and arms like oak limbs—was in temper.

"So, they come out to fleece a miserable coilbert, the holy-bound bastards. I would prefer dealing with a fiend than those swine."

He stormed about, refusing to deal with me. He kicked things left and right, and two elderly women serfs, on guard in event of flying object, greeted me at the doorway. They relieved me of burden, inviting me into a residence built between the fashion of a manor and cottage.

It was a large central room—fire in the middle, the smoke rising through an outlet designed through inner and outer roof. In larger cottages this smoky narrow space was used to store goods and food items smoked and kept stored.

Outside, poultry exploded in cackles and quackings as if a storm moved through their midst; a young woman's voice pierced the walls, as angry rejoinder to Wilfred: "Shut up, you old boar, and by Holy God don't you touch me."

Such was the outburst aimed at Master Wilfred. And there followed hotter and more bitter exchanges—avowing keen damage to one another. The young woman's voice reflected no fear and less respect for Wilfred.

Inside the elderly women spoke in a Danish sort of tongue, laughing a bit, enjoying Wilfred's upset. Still they maintained a modest eye to their work. Outside the great uproar continued: "You demon-child, what disrespect escapes your misshapen mouth. I'll sell you to the salt pedlar for his sport, you cotset's cunt."

Then the women serfs laughed openly, but shut up at once when, as a storm might, the young combatant burst inward. She swept past the woven hanging threshold, wheeled, and responded—hurling her response through the still, swaying cloth: "I would be better off with him than you, who so willingly sired me, you great rutting prick."

Both women implored her in their Danish language, I assumed, to cease. She wheeled again, and seeing me sitting, switched as cleverly as a rook to their Danish tongue, but I readily grasped she was also visiting wrath on me.

Desiring to spread her ire, she switched back to Saxon and gestured outside to Wilfred while holding her angry gaze on me: "So you are the one who brought this storm here. Why doesn't he kick you instead of helpless women?"

And these were the first words aimed at me from Cwenburh-of-Loe's sadly altered mouth—her burden-by-birth. Of a sudden, a third woman—tall and fine-boned—emerged regally from a hut adjoining into the manor-hall. At once all became somber. In calm and routine movement, this imposing Saxon woman fetched a narrow switch and delivered a loud whack across Cwenburh's back who didn't even flinch. This Mistress of the manor, for indeed that is who she was, then gestured to me, scolding mildly. "This is our visitor, Cwenburh, and you are rude. Now make amends or by the Creator I'll give you more of these."

She tossed her implement aside, and went to the tackle I'd brought, looking it over. Cwenburh made a face at her, then, mocking a tiny knee bend towards me, allowed, "Welcome to the hearth of Wilfred-of-Loe, and God Protect you, Traveler."

And that moment, Wilfred himself pushed through the doorway, and was about to continue his demonstration, but came eye upon eye with the Saxon woman who I soon learned was Gytha-of-Loe, his mistress in all respects save Holy Matrimony.

She stood straighter as they braced off. He cast a challenging eye to everyone, then from behind one of the elderly women moved out a heavy bench. Without checking if it were there or not, he sat. He cooled—or at least became calmer, "The visitor will join us at meal."

Gytha shook her head—a lament.

"By now, he thinks us savages, that we likely fly at our food like jackdaws."

But at the order, the board was moved in from the side, set up, and a table prepared. Except for Wilfred, the others stood, sat on the floor, or accommodated at any place makeshift.

I knew no one here would have knowledge of my penance; when bowl and trencher were put before me, I began at once. Directly in center of the vegetable broth-filled bowl was a wondrous hunk of meat, an item completely absent in refectory fare.

It was a generous table, better than Monastery, and in fact better than most places I had eaten, save for the fens where fresh fish and fowl were had by our own hands.

A large pot was loaded with more fare, and covered by cloth. It was then taken out by one of the women for those working in field. Indeed, Wilfred had a dozen cottars and cotsets and families who minded his soke—a good two hides[17]. He claimed it far smaller thereby owing less tax—sorely contested between Monastery and Wilfred.

Such matters were absent from mind as Cwenburh and I studied each other while at our fare. She possessed piercing grey eyes—pale and large; these foretold intelligence and cunning in all things around her. She was a diminutive girl, but mature in all visible ways of a woman.

Taking a massive bite from his trencher, Wilfred gestured to the ploughman's tackle repaired by Gilbert—closing his eyes in wonder.

"I tell you, God Himself couldn't do better repair of harness-work as Gilbert. That kinsman of mine is a wonder."

To which Gytha responded, "You blasphemy as easily as a pig grunts."

I shrunk down, fearful, yet he saw humor in what Gytha offered—and in fact both did—though his eyes moved severely to Cwenburh when she too laughed.

Silence returned. He aimed at me with his spoon then followed it with a gesture outside. "And they will all come—their holy hands out demanding chunks of my skin. When, did Gilbert say?"

"Directly after coming Sabbath Day, Master Wilfred."

He sat up straighter, pleased—gestured to me more fervently, and to Gytha observed, "See how respectful this youth is? Unlike this creature of yours whose misshapen mouth is home to vileness and such." His mistress held back comment, quickly raising hand for her daughter's forbearance, though Cwenburh visited a hot glare towards him. Wilfred cared little about any look or thought beyond his own. "This deformed creature please you, Cuthwin? I see you have wit enough not to have cast in with that collection of greedy sodomites. So you'll need a wife soon. And as plagued as Cwenburh is, she'll come cheap enough on your end.

---

[17] Hide. Roughly 120 acres, though not standardized.

Plus, strong of legs and middle. That's the thing!"

I was taken fearfully embarrassed, for he'd dumbly struck close to my thoughts. Cwenburh put her bowl aside with a clatter and rushed out without saying anything.

Gytha-of-Loe looked sadly towards her exit and added, "Cuthwin, we often suffer at the remarks of Master Wilfred, who uses language unfairly."

"I speak truth. God saw her birthed like that—for a sin? I don't know. But it knocked the bride price quite ill, plus I have her merchet[18] hanging about my neck."

I remember asking excuse from table, and going outside looking about the croft that I might see Cwenburh, but did not. Her eyes had taken hold of me and her fearless spirit had drawn fascination and admiration. And in truth her tiny body opened awareness within. I wanted to see far more of Cwenburh-of-Loe.

On my return to Peterborough and the Monastery, I think I stopped by the eelmen, but on this day I marveled at the miracle God visited on my life inside of just those few days.

For in that short time, he rewarded me with the skill and knowledge that was to provide for me and those around me for the next four-fold decades. And even more providently, joined me with a woman who changed me for the better on every day he allotted.

The time elapsed between inadvertently revealing my knowledge of letters to Brother Cassatorius and my penitential errand to Wilfred-of-Loe's was less than a fortnight. And within them, my path became for-ever diverted from the ordinary by God's will and a working person's choices of necessity.

---

[18] Merchet. A fine paid by a peasant to his lord for allowing the marriage of his daughter.

The following changes of seasons spent at Peterborough Monastery blend as seamlessly as master weavers do in great tapestries. I cannot explain the threads, but can the patterns formed. I do recall the strength, drive, and wit of my youth, which, in God's unknowable will, was in great supply.

My lessons in letters proceeded swiftly, for I possessed curiosity about the nature of the written Saxon tongue. Brother Ithamar became by far my most skilled teacher, though always stern.

But I kept a weather eye on market days. I was there every hour whenever possible. And on the second market day following my sight of her at Loe, Gytha and Cwenburh attended.

I offered to escort them, carrying large a basket and enjoying every move and inflection of the fierce Cwenburh. She bargained as severely as any Saxon woman might, yet remain honest in God's eye.

When they left, and Cwenburh and her mother were putting shoulder to basket, she came close and said, "I go to Loe's old mill next Sabbath to collect pigeon eggs and squabs."

And so we began.

In the stable, Gilbert taught me his trade. He did caution me in his indirect manner about my widening activities, and especially matters pertaining to ways of ordinary folk.

One day he offered, "Know that little is confidential in Peterborough, Cuthwin," and nothing further. For the master of stable and harness believed less said was enough, and too much was wasted on any mind that required it.

I needed no further warning.

I was foolish to think my growing connection and affections for Cwenburh-of-Loe might continue privately. They did not. Our increasing cleverness in meeting flattered our youthful pride. We thought our situation would itself work out a solution, winding a natural way through the complex lacings of property and earthly concerns.

I had not learned yet that in matters of great men, wealth takes precedence over the cares of ordinary people. This is a hard lesson for some and it was for me.

Even today when formerly great Saxon Lords lament over losing their lands to the Normans, one fact never changed: To Saxons, no more or less greedy than Normans, the value of coin and hideage was higher than the sinew and bone of those who toiled for a living.

So, Wilfred-of-Loe would rather suffer toothache than yield a silver penny. And since Cwenburh's mother was a bonded serf to an adjoining soke—not in Father Abbott's realm—the network of the owed, owing and onward, stupefied.

I raised Gilbert's kindly alarm at our next meeting, but Cwenburh was always more brazen than I.

"My mother knows we meet. And that pig father of mine dare not rudely touch or treat Gytha, for she is equal to him in roughness. She once took a great pestle to Wilfred, beating the demon in him until it jumped out his hind end and wept."

She and her mother were—as God and nature intended—bound in heart and soul. But unlike the somber Gytha-of-Loe, Cwenburh loved wordplay and hilarity, spoke diverse tongues with the readiness of a rook, and, God-help-her, used that gift to partake in the vanity of gossip.

"I will speak of whom I wish," she said, when I cautioned against it. "I live in croft not cloister."

At this time I learned I would be going on my first journey from Peterborough on the business of Father Abbott. I was excited about prospects of returning north, and this time with position. It promised future benefice for an ambitious young freedman clever in ways of reading and writing.

Hence I was filled with news about my upcoming mission at my next meeting with Cwenburh.

She had preceded me to the old haycroft we often used, and as was her loving practice, set out our meal of bread and fish. When I arrived bursting with news, Cwenburh deftly cut it short, informing of a far more vital item: She was with child.

I stood flatfooted, stunned. My silence gave her time to observe that my upcoming journey was indeed beneficial, adding, "I'm guessing the babe will be along in early winter. And you'll be back well before then."

When she noted my shock, I explained the ominous warren of complications her news surely promised. For this, she had no more concern than a young doe—pointing out, "Why Cuthwin, with great sport there are consequences. You work at livery!"

Yet she was not free, nor was she a creature-of-livery such as a mare or cow. Wilfred-of-Loe would own our child, or whoever the bond-holder of Gytha was. Information on Cwenburh's standing was craftily couched by Wilfred. When I continued parsing these muddied issues—trying to convince her how cruel the outcome might be, an argument ensued. She flew into a great fury, saying, "I needs live with God's will, but you it seems, will not!"

Then after raining profuse invective on me, she left.

That is how this memorable meeting ended. This news and our fight set a terrible damper over the weeks preceding my progress north. During this time, many preparations begged completion and my mind remained clouded.

During this journey I would be attached as liveryman to the train making up the accounts collections of Cellarer Eadsige and Subcellarer Edgar. These personages survey to distant sokes meant profuse income. They were chartered to Peterborough Abbey, hence Father Abbott's undoubted dominion though not contiguous to Peterborough.

Over all these lands Cellarer Eadsige carried Father Abbott's mantle of authority. Unlike the kindly Father Abbott, our Cellarer would extract the last ha'pence even if it meant bitter response before law.

Furthermore, since the sokes were scattered in so many directions, several of Cellarer Eadsige's appointed factors would make smaller forays to less significant holdings—but not so insignificant that coin was not owed Peterborough Monastery.

Gilbert and I this year would both attend these activities. I would be attached to Subcellarer Edgar's train almost exclusively.

This vital and lavish effort gave me opportunity to establish my worth.

A dozen housecarls under arms would guard these imposing processions. This included armed action when confronting landholders and debtors of various stripe who simply hid in copse or forest to avoid payment. Knowing our train was temporary, they sought the advantage of time to wait things out.

This was harmful thinking.

Cellarer Eadsige would send these housecarls and their caparisoned mounts through the severest of tangles to uproot those owing, if necessary, no matter the trouble involved.

"And there is good sport in this," I overheard one knobby old dreng tell his son while equipping their mounts with repaired harness. "We fetch in some squealing like young pigs. Peeing and shitting themselves most grandly."

Though my excitement should have been high, instead my heart was misery itself. Cwenburh would not meet with me. As the day for departure approached, I grew desperate to see her despite the press of diverse business.

The requirements of duties and the anxiety of Cwenburh's absence rendered me less aware of inauspicious stirrings. If more alert I might have anticipated a gate of retribution closing behind me.

But I did not and within minutes my future changed.

On the evening prior to the departure I rounded the corner of Gilbert's work quarters and found none other than Prior Denewulf, Wilfred-of-Loe, and Gilbert all waiting. At Prior's back the Whipmen lurked, and there I was, stopped cold center. Wilfred pointed with his staff.

"There he is who has violated my trust, had sport with my daughter, and cost me much money."

Prior Denewulf looked at me and, motioning for the Whipmen to back away, gestured to Wilfred with a single finger, then pointed to me. "And what say you, Cuthwin? If it is so, then you have besmirched the good trust of Peterborough Monastery. Is Cwenburh-of-Loe carrying your child?"

"Yes, Reverend Prior, she is."

"By her consent, without profit?"

"Yes, Reverend Prior."

"What has consent to do with the cost?" Wilfred croaked.

Prior Denewulf was not to be questioned. He looked down his nose at the greedy Wilfred as if hearing the bleating of a sheep. Treating him with an especially weary gaze, he looked to Gilbert. "Master Liveryman, this is all too proximate to the spring rounds of Peterborough Monastery. I want Cuthwin to fulfill his duties on this coming progress. During his absence I shall do more to illuminate matters, but time is too short now. Then, when he returns, we will address this in office proper."

"And meanwhile, she pips and debt is owed!" Wilfred blurted out.

Reverend Prior, so harried, lost patience.

"Wilfred-of-Loe, are you questioning Father Abbott's unending care and compassion for all his people, or his sense of justice and Holy Union with God's Will?"

Though as godless as Wilfred-of-Loe was, he lacked courage to visit further outrage before Reverend Prior. He instead mumbled 'no' and left, but not without casting an ugly glance at me.

I knew matters at Loe would turn even uglier for Cwenburh, and possibly even Gytha.

Prior waited until Wilfred withdrew, then without word he too left— but the silence he left in his wake was as loud as the northeastern storms. Close behind him, both Whipmen straggled; one glanced back at me, and offered a smug pat on the butt of his whip.

Gilbert sat with a clear sense of resolve—or resignation. He had stood by at the ready, and now he reached for the old pot that sat on the edge of the forge.

My legs seemed filled with meal flour; Gilbert saw this, motioned me to sit, and brewed his pungent drink. During preparation of his beverage he enjoyed the silence. Indeed, it enabled my mind to steady. Taking the old broken cup offered, I sipped and steeled myself. Surely Gilbert might be my only friend, if indeed he still was.

"Gytha in wrath over my kinsman's greed has taken Cwenburh and gone back to Tilton-of-Lynn Regis, to her original master. Wilfred has lopped off his nose despite his face, for he fancies Gytha in his doltish way. So he is faced with double deficit. I cannot see a good outcome,

Cuthwin, for either you or Cwenburh."

This struck me with exceeding despair: We both contemplated the nature of my plight. Eventually Gilbert left, telling me to stay put, assuring he would see to the evening rounds with the animals.

I realized Cwenburh and her grim situation, which was ours, was upon my shoulders for the next move. If I had acted, anticipated with keenness—anything, I should have at least been better prepared for this hour instead of impaled on this cruel gibbet.

I could not venture on the Cellarer's progress in pursuit of my own ambitions abandoning the woman I loved and allowing her to drift towards uncertain fate. Cwenburh was my responsibility; she carried our child and lost her home, a loss due to our acts together. With her mother they fled to strange lands that might, for all I knew, not offer kind welcome.

The trueness of my path was painful but clear.

My time at Peterborough Monastery had come to an end.

There was little material difference between the night of my first intended escape when I arrived from the fens, to the evening of my last stealthy departure from Peterborough Monastery. On the first I was still a boy, had nothing other than a few items in a sack and plump pigeons taken from the livery eaves for provision.

Now I was of age to serve at arms with hosts anywhere and had skills. Fortunately, I owned a few more items than I did those years back. I procured honestly items needed to ply the liveryman's trade, but not many more clothes and certainly no money.

As far as I knew, I still owed the Monastery for the sum to repay the reward for my capture, though I was not sure.

Lynn Regis was about fourteen leagues from Peterborough Monastery, to me a world distant. Further, I knew nothing of Tilton-of-Lynn Regis, the hides of land he might hold, indeed if the tenant was a man, for a man could be long dead and his widow manage all lands.

One item sure was Tilton-of-Lynn Regis was not owing to Father Abbot at Peterborough, but instead the Monastery at Ely. Ownership was not my concern on this evening. Speed and suddenness were now pressing necessity.

If I left after Matins and well before Lauds, even if pursuit began at the start of the work day, I would have good lead. No longer a stripling, I would reach Lynn Regis hours before pursuers. Afoot—over any tangle of obstacles—I would make rapid time opposed to mounted pursuers or a train of hounds and their handlers.

If anything Cwenburh, though tiny, was as agile as I if not moreso. If she wished, I might chase her through an entire day and not catch her, she laughing back at me at length or so ahead. She could cross field and stream, kirtle on or held aloft, with no more thought than a doe hare— under burden or not. Hence, our progress once joined would become no slower, God be praised.

Once together I planned to flee northwest, skirting the sokes of Peterborough and Ely, possibly even hastening towards the western marshes with Wales.

I felt awful guilt about abandoning my Monastery posts. The greatest towards Gilbert who trusted me and imparted skills and advice over my apprenticeship. But lastly, and more than all, Father Abbott, even though I saw and talked with him only a small fraction compared to Gilbert.

Whenever he returned—for he was at present long-absented on duty to the King—I knew Cwenburh and I would have his quiet blessings, forgiveness, and prayers for our child.

But it would show Godless ingratitude to skulk off without farewell and expressing lifelong gratitude to Gilbert. I knew he would not give out alarm and deprive my only advantage in retreat.

I knew no father, and he came closest to it.

I was stuffing diverse items into my leather wallet—things I did acquire during my time—trying to think of everything. At my back I heard Gilbert approach my quarter. He carried several items.

"I suppose you will to Lynn Regis. What do you know of it?"

"Nothing, except its direction."

While telling me what he knew, which was much, he laid out things: An extra wallet to pack more things, some dried food, an ale sack, more tools for leather and harness, and most crucial, a small purse with twenty silver pennies, a sum unimagined.

"In the morning, when all convene, you will of course be missed. So, strike a fast pace."

I stood before him, to whom I owed so much, and found no words, only thickly managing a simple 'thank you,' for I held back considerable tears. He nodded, said he must return to his 'Old Woman,' and they would both pray for me. This was the first time he mentioned his wife other than in most indirect manner, and certainly the only time he mentioned prayer.

He clasped me powerfully in farewell, turned and was gone. I never saw Gilbert again, but know I will in the unknown but peaceful precincts of heaven, God willing. Even to this day, sixty-five years later, I pray regularly for kindly rest of Gilbert's soul.

When I turned up missing it would take little sense to assume I was headed to wherever Cwenburh was. Prior Denewulf certainly would know to where she and Gytha had withdrawn. Mounted housecarls knowledge-able of roads and byways could readily intercept me—cut me short.

I had to take these certainties into consideration.

Through God's good graces, the late spring night was clear, and casting my glance overhead and using the sound knowledge of a coun-tryman, I struck course upon kind Polaris's aspect. Around me, land and water were littered with thousands of glowworms casting their uncan-ny light. They were one of many reasons to avoid walking in country at night. These were sure familiars of pixies and water spirits who inhabited the ceaseless tangles of reeds and grasses on the nighttime fens. Together with the din of frog and diverse night creatures, all cast an imposing strangeness.

These however, frightened me less than being caught, whipped, and no longer able to help Cwenburh. I took heart and kept on.

Young and in perfect flesh, I continued at a steady trot—keeping up through matins and prime. Sometime towards first light, the sun was preceded by a fragile sliver of the waning moon. It cast so much light, compared to the bare heavens and surrounding fens, I increased pace, so once again God struck on our sides. By the time the sun broached the eastern horizon, I had so much road to my back I could not possibly be intercepted.

In fact, I had made eight full leagues.

Thirsty, hungry, and my entire body begging for respite, I stopped behind a dikework and looked out over the River Ouse while partaking of ale and a portion of trencher.

The swallows and swifts had returned to the fens sometimes around the Festival of St. Patrick. In full numbers, they winged every which way at dawn, hunting the wealth of bugs who swarmed with the strengthening sun.

I took God-given peace by sight of this new life: the Mighty Ouse draining the spreading fens, and the flatness of the land; the sea joining along the shore of The Wash, that basin where all rivers pour.

I cast eye on the River Ouse on just a few occasions; however, on this morning, it was a special view. I knew that somehow both Cwenburh-of-Loe and I would be free upon it. Casting a look around at land, sea, and the skies—especially now with the rising sun for precise reference—I knew that Lynn Regis was close and appreciated the good progress made.

Every hour was gold for Cwenburh and me. No one at Lynn Regis would know facts pertaining to my presence. Setting out at a trot, I laced back and forth across courses of dike works and narrow paths. Within an hour I came across an elderly Saxon towing a cart with two fine milk goats bedded in rich straw. These two gazed out at the passing of land and water as might an Empress or Queen in sedan chair.

"God speed, Uncle! Your milk goats are fine creatures, but surely you spoil them. Do you have knowledge of the whereabouts of Tilton-of-Lynn Regis? I am from Peterborough and carry good tidings for them."

He set down the wooden traces, stretched, and cast his remaining good eye on his animals. His face, neck, and shoulders were deeply scarred—one eye completely closed. Indeed, his old wounds testified to a youth occupied at arms. Arrayed along the bottom of the cart on pegs were containers into which he milked his animals. Like so many elders, hard work had twisted him about like a knot of thick beech. He gestured an outstretched hand towards them, proud.

"These two are my finest, God bless them. You cannot indulge too much what brings you a living, and both these creatures know it." He pondered my question, and when I offered him a strip of dried eels, he motioned northeast.

"Tilton-of-Lynn Regis has salt pans. It is run by that old squint Marvis-of-Tilton, a widow whose husband by the Grace of God escaped her through death."

Over ale and dried eel, he provided a bounty of gossip. I learned Tilton-of-Lynn Regis was a fortunate place for a young Gytha to have escaped by sale. Work in salt pans is unforgiving labor—out upon the open shore, swept of wind and sun. Upon these, serfs labored harvesting salt or doing one of a hundred duties required. Then the salt would be crafted into plugs for sale to wandering pedlars.

Furthermore, Marvis-of-Tilton was tighter than Wilfred-of-Loe. I surmised without doubt the two were ideally suited to cheat each other negotiating over serfs, and the contracts therein.

Having the lead on searchers from Peterborough, and with this wealth of information, I offered labor of towing the cart for the ancient. He chatted on about Lynn Regis with even more detail regards Marvis-of-Tilton.

"Tilton be actually where the manor stand. There it squats, perched, with the pans all about it, like a kirtle on a fat woman. The old bag Marvis consumes serfs faster than the weasel does rats. Buries them unshriven on those tufts of soil by the dozen, but she can afford such. Ah, she's a rich old patch of leather, she is."

He knew the smallest of items about Lynn Regis. In fact, he was the equal of Cwenburh—herself devoted to gossip about diverse sins and follies everywhere, God forgive. Meeting this milk pedlar was indeed Our Savior's blessing.

Reaching a single pathway extending towards the pans, he pointed the way and warned, "Unless your good tidings have silver attached, you'll not be given anything for repast there. And who are you? I am Syth-of-Lynn Regis."

"And I Cuthwin-of-Alnwick, Liveryman. My thanks to you."

It had not occurred to lie about my name, for dissembling was not my natural way. Later necessity altered this.

The directed path met the shallow, tide-worn shore of The Wash, and along it salt pans formed a checkerboard. There were dozens, and in the morning progress I saw many workers laboring.

Some looked landward at me as I trekked past; others worked on, bent from the work. Finally, one came into view who was a mounted overseer, his steed, a donkey. Whipping the hapless animal, he led it trotting over to me. The fellow pointed a worn thornwood switch at me.

"State your business, Stranger. You are upon my Mistress's soke."

I at once disdained this devil; his bristled countenance, gap-toothed leer, and watery eyes repulsed. At the moment it occurred I had no plan whatsoever—so operated on the spur.

"I am from Peterborough, and carry profitable tidings for your Mistress."

"And who are you?"

"Cuthwin-of-Alnwick, messenger and factor."

"She is ill abed. Tell your tidings to me, and I shall carry them to her."

"I cannot. My sworn duty is to deal with Good Mistress directly. With God's grace, I hope she is not too ill."

He turned his switch inward, giving himself a good scratching on his buttocks. I thought he might offer to show me to the croft or manor where this creature maintained her lair. Instead he directed me to wait so he might ride for proper instruction. But just when he set off, he turned about, asking, "You say you're Cuthwin-of-Peterborough?"

"No, Cuthwin-of-Alnwick. I am messenger and factor from Peterborough."

Whatever crude trick that bespoke, or if he was simply brain-worn through imbibing vastnesses of ale and beer, I did not know. But the time waiting gave me opportunity to finish crafting a precise weave of a plan.

As experience in life taught, wit was my surer ally rather than a strong arm. And thanks to my gossipy acquaintance, my foreknowledge yielded more than enough material to manufacture 'good tidings.'

While my thoughts so stirred, two serfs passed, back-borne hoppers laden with dearly priced salt. The Unfortunates struggled but managed to look up from under their burdens. I raised a greeting.

"God's tidings to you."

Yet the wretched souls threaded on only managing to respond with toneless murmur. So harshly were they used by work that save for their wearing tattered kirtles, I could not have distinguished man from woman. Their plight raised even uglier fears, for did this life await Cwenburh and Gytha and indeed our child?

This despondent portrait at once raised desperation, even boldness, to access immediate ingenuity of story. I became absolute in my urgency to free Cwenburh—and indeed Gytha—any way short of violence.

When the doltish overseer returned, he brought a pair of house-carls of a sort, along with his mistresses' response. Each housecarl was mounted on a horse with ribs and hide prominent and worn, themselves four-legged victims of the pans. A trot would be all they might manage.

One of these gnarled squints carried a massive cudgel, and I supposed him to be headman. The Saxon he managed was broken and rasped by some foreign tongue.

"Mistress Marvis bid you follow us in peace."

"In God's truth, brothers, peace is what I bear."

One fell behind, the headman preceded, and we followed the wide rim of The Wash. It began to angle northerly when we encountered what my chatty milkman termed 'the tuft of dry land.'

And upon it was a hodgepodge composing burh and manor. As we passed through the stout wall, I saw all the inner structures. Those attached to manor and those outside were built of matter and beam of the type I had never seen. Instead of board and diverse thatch, and other common stuff of construct, all instead appeared to have been pushed and stacked together by giants or massive gnomes.

Their aspect was singular because their origins were apparently diverse sorts of wood drifted in from the sea—grounded over the years along vast tidal flats of The Wash, the larger and more substantial, the better.

But on second glance, all the structures were not of drift. Everywhere apparent were included pieces of ship and cart in the construct. For The Wash was a grand place for arrival and retreat of invading hosts of Danes, and indeed anyone landing on this coast.

All wall and buildings were put together piecemeal—like wasps would a nest.

The gate was left open during these times of comparative peace. But at any hint of trouble, it would be clapped shut and the Archfiend Himself would be challenged to break into the Manor. Likewise it could trap a mere mortal inside.

From within carried on a seat mounted on a carrying platform entered Marvis-of-Tilton. Each end was carried by a stout serf. These two had light burden, for their mistress was an ancient, shrunken to a knot of skin and sinew. If not for a pair of burning, dark eyes that shone like those of a pitiless dragon, their burden might be mistaken for a corpse.

As a wand of office, she carried a stout stick that I guessed rightly was not ceremonial. Dressed in old tatters, these contrasted vastly to a brilliant Norman mantle, a singular sign of wealth. The sight of her struck in me fear—yet desperation and love for Cwenburh rendered me stouthearted.

"I bring you greetings from Wilfred-of-Loe, Mistress. I am Cuthwin-of-Alnwick."

"Fuck him and his greetings. I expected as much seeing his serf mistress with her whelp recently returned to me because of some outrage. Well, she still is my serf. He is owing me remainder and has for years, which has accrued interest."

"Indeed, as hired factor I am here to negotiate that debt and bring fair settlement to this old proceeding. He misses daughter and mother greatly."

She looked me over, raised her switch and swatted a girl who approached with a cup.

"Not now, stupid bitch!" Then shifted to one side adding, "You are young for a factor."

"Thank you, Mistress. I have been factor with my father and uncle these two years now."

"Well, Cuthwin-of-Wherever, Wilfred-of-Loe will require two pound fifteen shillings King's silver for each to clear debt. You see I have what he wants, the stupid shit."

I nearly collapsed at mention of such a sum, but plowed on.

"I cannot negotiate price yet, Mistress. First, I'm under strict instruction to make sure the souls are in same health as when they ran off from Master Wilfred."

At a sudden she spat, and by gesture with the same talon that clung to her switch, beckoned. In a moment, a brutish cottar pushed Gytha from one of the out-huts, but not without words from her, in fact making him jump away when she raised an arm: "Keep your hands from me, you whoreson."

"This be Gytha-of-Loe. And you can see she is of healthy limb and voice."

Her presence of mind was such that Gytha gave not a wink of recognition or disconcertion at my presence.

"And her daughter? My commission for both is clear."

When Cwenburh came into view, my heart leapt wildly. She indeed looked fuller, and if anything more beautiful to my eyes. So possessed was I by her, my legs weakened. Unlike Gytha, she eyed me such I feared the old fiend might perceive a connection. At once Cwenburh returned to a countenance equal to her mother. They stood together.

"There they are. Two-pound fifteen and you can have them. Only silver is acceptable."

"Wilfred-of-Loe could purchase three-hide more of land for so great a price, Mistress. With such news, I doubt he would even pay me my fee. Surely, I cannot, as his factor, make contract thusly. No factor would."

"He can purchase what he may. But for these two he compensates with merchet and interest for his wife and her daughter. That is what the price is. I don't bargain save with salt pedlars who are lowborn shitheads to a cursed man of them."

"Then, with the price set so, and not wishing to return all the way, especially in view you charge interest, I've been instructed by Wilfred to seek appeal from the Hundred or Father Abbot of Ely himself. There is much complication here of previous agreement."

All matters from Peterborough were easily dismissed by this ancient menace; however, an appeal instead at the local Hundred for justice, or worse, the Monastery at Ely, was another. As landholder, she must have favor and permit from Father Abbot of Ely to operate her pans, and to sell their produce, and to pay geld on each. But her last claim, that of charging interest was usury—a sin.

I guessed—on the fly—that such a troubled crone would have made enemies there by such practices, and in fact before the Hundred.

She bristled—drew back her head a notch, and described a circle in the air with her, wand of authority, as it were: "So it is. Now get off my lands, return to that fornicator Wilfred and tell him Marvis-of-Tilton tells him to get himself to hell." She then looked to her bearers and up she was hefted, and made to return within.

"You old worm! What is going on here!?"

A youngish man—or years younger than Mistress—astride a towering mule trotted in. The rider was rotund of belly, and a servant slid up a platform enabling him to dismount. Afoot he confronted Mistress Marvis. The moment between them gave me opportunity to cast a desperate look at Cwenburh who at once shook her head briskly and mouthed, I thought, 'Go!'

I stood my ground while this new arrival confronted the Mistress; he broke off with her, glanced to me, then back.

"Who is this? And Aunt, what foulness are you up to? I have a big enough mass of enemies when you die, let alone you adding to it daily without my knowledge."

"And *until* I die, Nephew, you possess shit!"

They squared off like rams—the nephew, a stout thane with bald pate. He came closer, circling her by half. Mistress Marvis' bearers lowered her to the ground, clearly preparing to fly for cover in the event of a great clash.

Gytha took Cwenburh by her hand and drew her closer. It was strange that I noted a smile upon Gytha, but it was this that gave me momentary heart. I struggled to continue weaving my false story.

Finally he desisted the eye-to-eye battle and looked to me: "I am Alric, nephew to Mistress and manager here. Who are you, and what is your business that has caused my Aunt's uproar?"

I told him, and he at once pieced everything together—for he appeared sly—not of mind that allowed greed for immediate money to cloud a longer, more profitable direction.

"It is late in Gytha's life to agree to merchet, Factor Cuthwin."

"My commissions are frequently made late; nonetheless, Wilfred-of-Loe desires to make fair merchet, and then wedding contract. And price is two-pound fifteen!"

With a deep breath of patience, Alric thought a moment.

"My Aunt and I must speak of this within." He motioned to a servant woman. "Fetch a repast for this factor. Our bread and beer is less apt to sour in your gut opposed to what you would buy in Lynn, and here at no price."

And while Mistress Marvis squalled and argued, they both withdrew; from inside manor, I heard Alaric's voice rise.

I was shown to a side-yard where I sat on remnants of a broken-down cart. I hoped to avail a private moment with Gytha and hopefully Cwenburh.

My nerves ate at me—virtual granary rats—for every hour taken with my risky dissembling, thanes from Peterborough were closing league by league.

There was the sweetest joy possible by a foolish youth to see Cwenburh. At the same moment I feared I was entangled in a situation to which I was not equal. I had no further plan at the ready on how to continue.

Under orders to prevent talk between this stubborn Peterborough factor and the two souls under negotiation, the two housecarls—still mounted on their dilapidated steeds—kept a weather eye on Gytha and Cwenburh. I was served by an elderly serf. When she bent low, carrying watery beer, she said in careful voice, "I bring these words from Gytha: Watch George the great mule, and be at ready with wallets and yourself. You have little time. God's grace and speed to you both, Cuthwin, and do not worry about Gytha but only Cwenburh and the child."

When my eyes moved to the great mule, I saw Gytha let go of Cwenburh who walked towards the out-hut from where she emerged. The brute who carried the cudgel motioned her back.

"You stay put! If Mistress wanted you to return inside, she would have directed."

"I must pee."

"What!? Pee here."

But in a style so aptly hers, Cwenburh ignored him and went inside. He and his assistant—faced with her disobedience, and she being new to them—knotted their stupid brows. Another servant, this one also young and fetching, emerged with ale for both the housecarls.

"Here, you two. This is good stout ale rather than watery beer."

They eyed both her and the capacious wooden cups with pleasure. The one with cudgel laid it before him, reached down, and relayed the first draught to his companion, then took the second in both paws. And this was the moment evidently awaited.

Cwenburh emerged—walking rapidly, carrying a small sack, and now shod rather than barefoot, putting me on alert at once. With cups to their maws, eyes hidden, the two were still in mid-draught. Indeed, Cwenburh not only kept swiftly on, but after exchanging the briefest of touch with her mother, burst forth—hopped as brazenly as a robin up to the wooden step, and in a wink upon George the Mule.

"Cuthwin! Hurry!"

Realizing their outlandish plan in a rush, I charged across the yard, then with a half-step leaped astride George behind Cwenburh. The animal bolted off sending clods of dirt flying behind him—out the gate— in such a gallop that I clung to its diminutive rider to keep astride. Cwenburh shouted out words. Her legs were hooked into the girth line: "The King's mount himself couldn't catch George!"

It was a ride whose memory would last a lifetime, the act launching us on our new life. The salt-pans whipped by, George charged by everyone—most unstooped themselves to watch us so grandly proceed. None of the hacks mounted by the housecarls would ever catch George unless God himself gave them wings.

And may God strike me lifeless if I tell a lie, but atop George, Cwenburh laughed and found great adventure in this. Like all her actions and whims, it never occurred to the elf that stealing the Mistresses' mule would get us hanged, then impaled upon gibbets or otherwise mortally outraged.

It was all of two or three leagues of such retreat when anything pursuing had long since been left behind. After several vain attempts, I managed to wrestle controls from her, and stop the madness.

"God help us, Cwenburh! Astride such an expensive beast, two such as we stand out like a pair of oxen wearing monks' habits. We must free this animal to return, and for us continue afoot cross country."

"You would think of freeing a mule, but what about me and your child? And I have abandoned my mother, poor soul. This escape was her idea. We planned it ages before your belated arrival."

She thus beset me with various admonishments while I allowed George to go free; instead he just looked at us, offering a nibble or such at nearby tufts of spring growth.

"You see, not even a beast desires to return there."

She removed her shoes, as was her custom—saving them, she maintained, for more important occasions. We walked in line—she ahead, ignoring me. I reminded her—in truth insisted—we direct west, away from The Wash, Ely, and all we knew, towards the western hill country, keeping to thickets and marshes or forests.

"I am indeed going west, Cuthwin. Or do you think an illiterate woman does not know where the sun sets?"

At a loss to touch her, she would pull away at my reach, keeping ahead. And we did proceed west, setting out by as complicated a way across the fens as possible. She, throughout that singular day, refused my touch. Also, she did not offer simple compliment for my wit or resource, instead visiting curtness and sharp word. As I recall, there were several arguments over changes of direction and which distant points to aim for.

But with all young people in love, there was affection, always the strong center of God's blessing that brings them together. For I have come to believe over the subsequent years that coin and station are a curse to man and woman. When riches and manners intrude, the chances to enjoy the wisdom God intended—given in that original wilderness between Adam and Eve—go forever.

Book 2

Here begin the wanderings of St. Cuthwin commencing during the troubled co-reigns of Kings Harold Harefoot and Harthacnut[19]; the many counties he traversed and the extraordinary people and places visited, including many God-ordained occasions related here. Lastly, the taking and mastery of his trade which was to sustain him.

---

[19] King Harold Harefoot, reigned 1035-1040; King Harthacanut, reigned 1040-42. Sons of King Cnut, (or Canute) and half brothers.

We ventured away from the sea hence all places we both knew.
Our escape took us west up the Great River Ouse. We traveled like
muskrats limiting our movements to early morning and late evening. I
was sure of pursuit. Cwenburh fought against these precautions and we
argued. She would have proceeded without nearly the caution, for after
going west twenty leagues or so, she was confident we were beyond the
reach of Marvis-of-Tilton or her housecarls and of any potential for
pursuit from Peterborough.

"Look at the River, and how it has narrowed."

And she marveled at these changes. For Cwenburh had never traveled
any distance at all in her sixteen years, save her and her mother's recent
retreat to Marvis-of-Tilton at Lynn Regis.

Instead of occupying ourselves with the God-given bounty youthful
couples enjoyed since Adam and Eve, we wasted time arguing.

Fortunately, our flight occurred during the bounty of late spring.
Further I had skills and experience to make advantage of the season,
having a skilled teacher in wildcraft and gleaning such as Frog. I was
more knowledgeable of worldly matters, having witnessed powerful men
wield authority over matters of coin and property.

Even in those early days, my way was to take on issues slyly, with
craft rather than more sprightly methods. Also, my background at
Peterborough Abbey, and not least my own personal feelings of God's
Word and teachings of our Holy Savior, meant I observed the Commandments always.

But I learned that Cwenburh, especially with our child each day
growing, had no more scruple-of-Commandment than an auburn-muz-
zled vixen. This meant theft came as natural to her as it did a jackdaw,
and this visited troubles between us.

"If up to you and your Commandments, Cuthwin, you'll christen two
corpses by Christmas."

And at this point I discovered the woman carrying our child was without benefit of our Savior's Holy Waters. She was as heathen as the Dane of legend who plagued our land for foulness and gain.

I fell into a terrible sadness knowing—without her explaining as much—why this would be. This was the doing of her wretched father, that miser Wilfred-of-Loe. His rat-like reasoning was easily seen.

To begin with, Cwenburh's malformed feature would be proof positive of a demon's presence, or punishment for unholy conduct by one or both parents. No one would think Gytha-of-Loe would be the guilty one. If there was sin, all knew Wilfred could supply ample quantity.

Also, he found duel benefit in keeping Cwenburh on croft. It would save Baptism fees and keep him free of possible suspect from monastery clerics—meaning Father Abbot and Prior Denewulf, his disdained landlords.

Yet he knew the deformation of poor Cwenburh's mouth would eventually harm his purse: Any merchet for her would be tiny. But now, with this development, he was greedy for it. With the benefice of our youthful pairing, he feigned outrage to dip deep into the Abbey coffers, for I was their ward and responsibility.

Despite all our arguments, we never brought up this disfigurement, though I knew—despite her strong spirit—it struck her deep. Now this lack of Holy Water made her already difficult path even more troubled.

During a peaceful time between us, which enjoyed increase, in the cover of early summer rushes and flowering thickets along the Great River Ouse, I told her of my fears: "Cwenburh, we must get you Christened by the Holy Waters—it is ordained by God. I worry for both your souls."

"And how shall we do that, and keep low as thieves?"

"We must find out if we are pursued. And to do this, like the fox, we must double back and wait—to see if anyone appears."

By now, I reckoned we'd traveled forty leagues upriver, and I was beginning to agree with Cwenburh that pursuit might have ceased. If so we had vital matters that would be easier to attend.

With a decision to find the truth, we retraced our path downriver a league or two, made hidden camp on high ground—with oversight of the main routes coming upriver on either bank.

Along the opposing side of the Great Ouse was the road bedded and marked with giant rocks, which Cwenburh claimed was the work of gnomes or dwarfs, or even ogres. However long ago its origins, God meant it to benefit all travelers, including those with carts.

I avoided this byway, instead traversing the opposite bank, following narrower paths and wends. But thanks be to God as events developed, I chose to ford back over and make watch by this old road.

I took opportunity of time to fashion and set out better traps. I selected a great chestnut tree and designed an aerie atop. From this I was able to see leagues in all directions, the best view being downriver.

We at once argued about Cwenburh joining me aloft, me absolutely banning such, for she was now mounded in girth. But I no longer would wrestle her to make my point. Such struggles often ended in sport, and the issue or whim of the moment would be forgotten. But her situation had changed.

Cwenburh remained strong as a she-badger losing none of her strength; yet I feared jostling our child within. Cwenburh, true to her nature, once forbidden only prodded her on more. Hence, she was soon perched beside me in the tree's top, and in truth we enjoyed it there.

The view from such lofty point during the early beauty of summer bore witness to the sweetness of God's natural gifts. All the great birds from the south were there making commotion along the river marshes and lands.

Their colors, as they flew across the green and bounty of the land, were a greatness to our young lives. All the creatures of air and croft thrived in this weather. No matter how much age has overtaken me, I can never cease marveling at God's unfathomable mystery giving mankind such richness, then allowing the meanness and cruelty of winter to follow, doing this every year.

By late in the third day, Cwenburh had grown bored in our platform aloft and was attending breakfast below when I saw the two men at far distance making their way up the Great Ouse.

There were two housecarls mounted and begun as mere specks. At first I allowed they could be traveling upriver for many purposes—for in fact, they weren't the first travelers we had seen on our watch.

But these two wended their way upriver on the bank opposite of the road where the travelers usually traversed—on the bank we had originally taken. And as they grew close enough to see detail, I saw they followed our former path almost precise. When closer yet, I saw what made my marrow chill: Before them, nosing along slowly but with keen purpose, was a great meat hound.

It still being early, the housecarls—if such they were—half dozed astride, keeping an eye on the hound's progress. The beast's reddish color and large size caught the eye even more than the housecarls' mounts. I tossed a branch below, signaling alarm. Fast as a hen-grouse, Cwenburh folded up all, ready to fly. She was next to me in moments— having equaled me in ability to scramble upwards through the stout limbs of the chestnut.

The lush-leafed tree offered complete cover at this awful moment, plus we had the Great Ouse between us and them. Neither of us spoke as they came upriver; moreover, this closing distance enabled me to see their poor livery, still poorer mounts, and the overall appearance of want.

These were not housecarls, but cotsets or coilberts—landless freed-men who lived by their wits, involved in any business for gain. Their wealth was tied up in even those poor mounts, and certainly that meat hound—if indeed they had come by any of those honestly.

I often heard of such men over the years. These were rootless from any soke or manor, and pursued souls free or otherwise who fled owing money and had significant value attached. This made it worthwhile for an Abbot or Prior, or indeed a Lord or his subtenant—to put a price sufficient to make lengthy pursuit of potential value.

Such vultures were called *coinmen* in our dialect and were held in low-est esteem. But I never heard of coinmen with a fine dog like this, a hound invariably in the keep of great men finely liveried.

"They stole that hound, certainly."

Cwenburh guessed what I had, but as they came abreast on the oppo-site bank, we looked over and down at them as they paused at the river's edge. They were now half a furlong distant.

One made water from atop his mount, causing us a bit of mirth, while the second talked on, but we could not quite hear what language.

The hound flopped down at the once, his great hide rolling about him as he sought comfort. Prominent above all was his large moist, black nose—it thrust out before all.

When they resumed, the hound did not rise, and when they shouted at it, both of us recognized the out a Norman tongue at once. The creature responded, but with hesitancy, until one brought a morsel from his pack. He was stopped by his fellow who instead snatched it away, ate it himself, and cursed the hound.

These were surely the worst sorts of Norman curses, and when they made to use a knotted strap to prosecute their order, the hound slunk off and resumed, or appeared to, for indeed he went off askance.

This was an alliance that did not sit well with the hound.

They would proceed, I knew, upriver about four leagues, until they came across the trail when we crossed over to this bank. Then they would know our ploy and set out faster, without doubt. Also, they would have guessed—if they had wit enough—that we had seen them pass us and knew they used a hound.

So, with their slow progress and the hound's uncertain application, we had time to decide a reaction to this grim news. With such a hound, these two might pursue us for weeks more, an unexpected situation.

"How much value did they put on me to pursue so?" I asked myself.

It was bitter explaining to Cwenburh the diverse price of poor souls such as we. It was worse for serfs both afoot and unborn—and how a hefty sum of money resulted in this effort. Best to avoid figures.

"There is the both of us, Cwenburh, no telling how much remained on my debt at Peterborough, save it was considerable. So there it is."

Reward for us loomed. With all the game and fish we consumed, it could be more. No matter how small or inconsequential—these were the property of the tenant or undertenant of whatever lands and waters we passed. At the best, we were just common freebooters, stealing rightful property.

By now on our journey, I had completed fashioning a fine limb of elm into a sleek cudgel—great enough weight and design to have stunned an ox, but light enough to wield smartly. Extending her hand onto it,

Cwenburh, now in a temper, suggested an act that, even to this day, astounds me in reflecting on womankind.

"Then since they don't know we follow yet, we shall lay in wait until the swine are abed, then knock their brain pans loose, and be done with it. It is us and our child, or them, Cuthwin."

"Jesus our Savior! Then you would have us be murderers as well!"

I added, as I ought, that by committing such a sacrilege against God, how might we ever take Holy Sacrament of Baptism or Marriage. If she thought I would commit such a sacrilege against God, what sort of woman had I fallen in with? And we fell into our worse squall, soon followed by a sulk.

The seriousness, however, was no longer the stuff of young people arguing, but life and death or at least freedom and serfdom. I found steadying resource in necessity, doing what I might to cool Cwenburh, for I knew the plan we must follow to keep our immortal souls. To bring peace I aired it at once.

"You are right. They don't know we follow for the time. And if we can, we will steal that hound; if we cannot, we will kill it. For without it, the men are useless. And a hound, even a fine one, is not a person before God. And to steal something that is stolen, the Lord and His Son will forgive."

At this, Cwenburh gave me the strangest look, held for a moment, then broke off while we descended, and I began packing the last of our few things. This complete, she looked at me as someone pondering a riddle. Then, as if satisfying herself to some inner answer, she nodded and we moved on. Cautiously, we retraced our tracks upriver.

In previous days and weeks, we gave habitation wide berth. These coin-men did not, but instead were partial to company and ale; hence, they halted at a mill we had avoided days before. Yet before going in, they tethered the hound distant, gave it a bare bone, and crossed the river paying visit to the mill without it.

By now our eyes were locked on the hound, and Cwenburh most of all, for she pitied the creature's lot.

"They well know anyone would realize they stole it, so the sly wretches keep it out of sight."

This far upriver in early summer, the Great Ouse ran low and narrow. It was a ribbon of water—an annoying barrier between them and the hound.

And us. I regretted that aspect.

"Ah! We should have crossed."

But Cwenburh did not further my own criticism, but watched the two wretches barter with the mill workers, this time in our language. She—mink that she was—lay close to my ear and said, "You are a keen one, Cuthwin. Be patient. I know, if it weren't for the river, you would charge forth and smash that poor hound's head with your mighty cudgel."

And seeing our two tormentors dismounted to take a repast and exchange fellowship with the mill workers—notoriously lonely souls—Cwenburh lay over on her back. She placed her tiny hand atop her swollen belly and smiled, for her mood changed. I was learning her mind better each day and in truth she mine.

I was angry at once.

"So, you tease me to be unable to kill a hound, yet advise me to kill the men. You are surely one of God's unending mysteries."

Without adding argument to opportunity already wasted, we picked up, held our things high, waded across out of view of the mill. Now we were on the same side of the river as the hound.

Then, God forbid, it set up an awful howl; its mighty hound's voice could be heard for furlongs. In a bolt of despair, I realized that with the river crossing, the light summer wind was now at our backs, carrying our scent towards the beast.

It was, I might have known, nothing else but scent driven, and especially our scent.

"Oh Jesus, Cuthwin, it's taken scent of us."

That hound was audible out to creation, and I knew at the once the blunder I'd made, and that I must rush forward and stop it, for our freedom was on the verge of ceasing. The hound must perish; there was no holding back now.

Pushing Cwenburh into cover, I sprinted with my cudgel through the dense thickets and brambles, arriving too late at the edge of the clearing proximate to where our pursuers crossed over to the mill. One of them had forded back and was confronting the hound.

I was within a half-courtyard of them, and the beast jumped at his lanyard; but instead of wanting free on scent, he begged for a hunk of marrowbone held aloft by the cruel bastard.

He laughed at it, spoke in Norman—teasing it by tasting the meat himself, waving it in the air—the hound's great eyes following every hair's width the bone traveled in mid-air.

Then in our language, "Here, the fat oaf of a mill worker took kindness—and such a lazy bitch as yourself."

And she fell on it before it struck ground. When the coinman turned to wade back over, I saw he was already in his cups, for he half fell— emitted a curse—recovered and went on.

"Oh, dear me, Cuthwin! The poor creature is a bitch. Look at the wretched animal!"

Typically, Cwenburh had not stayed safe. Her words reflected a croft person's horror at seeing any fine animal so maltreated, especially a female who had a life of birth ahead. And indeed I had never seen such a fine-blooded hound, nor one in such horrendous condition, a victim, clearly, of heavy cruelty.

Since the coinman was no longer in view, and without a thought or word, Cwenburh emerged and strode over as boldly as if it were a pup rather than a stout-boned hound a stone or two heavier than she.

"God forbid! Use caution, Cwenburh! It has meat."

And the bitch did growl—she would never yield this rare treasure—her eyes menaced, but only for a moment. For in the way of God's creatures, it sensed at once Cwenburh meant no harm. Though keeping an eye on her, it resumed its meal.

Following with our carryings, I stooped next to Cwenburh and took assessment. Vermin crawled over it, and her hide and fur were spoilt in many places, and in a few she had chewed or licked her sores even rawer. She was kept not far from starvation, and every one of her ribs and back joints poked out.

One eye was badly sore, and surely was of no use for some time. Yet she was a great reddish hound with ears the size I had not seen, and a great muzzle and a vast, black nose—both which bespoke a keenness of scent unmatchable.

Her legs and feet were as stout as a pony, and the teeth that worked the joint were fine and white, and I guessed this was a young bitch—possibly had never whelped—for her dugs remained tiny.

We'd been privileged to spend almost three days in one place, and, with better traps, instead of snaring scrawny hares, we had caught robust rabbits. Once skinned, they dripped with fat. In a night, I would snare two or three. By this time, we carried nearly four heavy quarters in sack, for despite eating to our youthful content, we cooked surplus.

Of one mind, I handed Cwenburh the sack with victals, including a dozen duck eggs wrapped in cool bank moss and eel grass. She took out a forequarter of rabbit and held it out.

The bitch caught sight of that fat forequarter as one might a holy relic, and stood—straining against the line that held her to post.

On youthful impulse, I simply untied it and we moved quickly upriver, it following—not forgetting its joint.

And so it was that we came in temporary care of a fine hound, although one in great need of medicines.

Behind us, the vile coinmen capered at board and cup with the millmen, and at the moment thought of little else.

By the following morning, we were at least a dozen leagues up river. We had, with good sense, moved quickly—even using a sliver of a waning moon to thread our way along through half the night.

By late morning Cwenburh and 'Hilla,' so Herself named it, were as thick as sisters. She began tending to the poor animal's wounds at once. Taught well at such skills by Gytha-of-Loe, Cwenburh was knowledgeable in the ways of wild-crafting. She fashioned elixirs and potions from woody leaf and stem, this being the best season for it. By midday, Cwenburh claimed Hilla to be ours forever, fool-at-heart that she was.

I reminded her of the truth about our dubious standing.

"Cwenburh, I saw last summer on Peter and Paul's Fair at Peterborough Market a finely bred bitch not half Hilla's noble blood fetch four shilling—paid by a rich thane, tenant to Father Abbot. If a Lord or histhane finds poor folk like us, especially wanderers, in possession of such as Hilla, his men would hang me and enserf you for theft without pause. To grand men we are nothing. A fine bitch, however, is a vital part of sport and chase enjoyed by those who need not toil or spend hours in prayer, but serve in arms to Lord or King." I refrained from adding how I also saw female and male serfs in wretched flesh brought from far north in chains who sold for less than a fine hound. This sad business, though approved by the King, was forbidden by Father Abbot; yet such evil business persisted outside the walls.

"Why is it that great Lords get their way with beast and soul under the approving gaze of God, Cuthwin?"

She was sad, and talked of tending Hilla—it had been weeks since she and her mother Gytha fled from Wilfred-of-Loe's lands, and I knew she missed her duties. At Loe these extended to care for all creatures of croft. Cwenburh's gentle and compassionate nature, despite her cutting use of word and action, knew only affection for animals over her nearly seventeen years.

The miserable Wilfred-of-Loe rarely allowed her to fair or market, nor allowed her to village church, save at Gytha's insistence on Holy Days. How could Cwenburh know of such as Hilla or grand but ruthless men who put higher worth on sword than they did woman or man born to commonality?

"It is not our place to question if God approves or disapproves of things mortal. Nor might we question the place of his great men, Cwenburh. At Peterborough you could have been whipped for such question."

She puckered her lips, offered a bit of squint with her mischievous eyes, and tended, "Shit on Peterborough Abbey and your great men."

And at that—proving again herself incurably blasphemous and plain of speech—we both set to laughter. This prompted great tail-flopping from the hound, who had clearly been long gone from good will or laughter.

Our retreat west had dual purpose, for now there was Hilla's presence to deal with. Wit must be used.

Climbing aloft an occasional great tree to set direction, we left the river Ouse at a smaller water course. We resolved (at risk of false pride, it was at my initial insistence) that we turn over the hound at Abbey or Priory. These holy places were independent by royal charter from Lord, thane—or any townspeople or tenant; also any King's Sheriff, Undersheriff, or any hundred owing to them. There the Abbot or Prior held sole justice. Through their high office, each ruled and decided on matters of *manor a demesne*, and able to give sanctuary.

Unlike the untamable Cwenburh, I had my years at a renowned monastery as Peterborough to expose me to diverse talk about brother and sister houses. This talk included those owing allegiance to our Lord Abbot, but also to other abbots and priors of different charter.

And some of these great men were good and others not so good, and frequently, as kind Gilbert would say in his thoughtful way, "Some are bad of soul and dishonest in deed." And for him, that was the start and end of talk about such holy offices.

I told Cwenburh it would be dimwitted to stride into an unknown holy place leading such a fine creature as Hilla. It would be equally unwise doing same in a village or town church where almost certainly the priest would be relative or owing benefice to the Lord or Manor born, not unusually a higher churchman.

The only sanctuary granted at a town church was through one's ample wallet or purse.

And we were united in purpose as we continued traveling upstream along this small running creek until it coursed proximate to a walled village.

I then put a plan into order: While she and Hilla kept under cover outside the walls, I would go in and seek word about a nearby Abbey or Priory with honest reputation.

Weeks before, we established our story in event we encountered people: I was a young liveryman traveling west to Hereford to my eldest brother's stables where I was to start my tradesman's life.

I had the rudimentary tools with me, the knowledge if asked to show skill, and the wit to keep to that story without contradiction—as did Cwenburh, who was my young wife with child.

And my story would continue that we were from King's Lynn where I had served my time with an uncle. Cwenburh knew enough about that town to seem genuine.

But when it was time to leave and announce myself outside the walls, Cwenburh's resolve became weak.

"Why don't I tie up Hilla, leave her with good bone, and go in with you. Then, before their own eyes, your story is whole. For it is mostly truth."

Her eyes were sad and fearful. She knew that Hilla would not enjoy solitude—bone or no bone—and her great baying and howling would be heard back to The Wash.

I sat and made fireless breakfast with her, for that day no one came outside the walls. We had timed this plan to take place on the Sabbath. These were days when travelers most commonly came into walled village to attend church service and refresh their wallets.

We had been together without break for a month. Though often at contention—for we dealt with grave troubles and responsibility growing within her—the tether holding us together grew surer and stronger with each day.

Indeed, God keep us, it would always remain so—and it was those first anguished weeks in flight that wove us together forever.

We ate cold hindquarter of rabbit while Hilla enjoyed both forequarters in a wink. Then, taking prayer together, Cwenburh gave me her blessing and I set off for the walls.

I was young, knowledgeable of more than one craft, had coin and cudgel—certainly a purpose, and had much waiting for me outside the walls. Though never of great brawn, I had my wits and remained vigilant as a rook for anything amiss.

The village was one Wixamtree, and like most villages had walls of wood and stonecraft. But these had been peaceful times free from the hosts for many years. Oldsters remembered violent times, however, and somberly reminded those who now allowed gates to remain open.

Inside, I at once sought the liveryman. This was a traveler's customary act—a stranger wandering would properly seek a man of like trade. And this custom served well.

His name has left me now these many decades later, but he was a great, thoughtful Saxon who welcomed me and admired some little work I carried. After midday repast, he thought towards my question.

"I would approach Elstow Abbey with unfearful heart, for the Prior is fair, if rough in his ways with the common sort. But, God help him, he is same with those of finer cloth."

He further informed that the Abbot of Elstow had long ago turned fish-minded because of advancing age. Therefore, by practicality, the Prior functioned in that office for several years.

At evening I returned to Cwenburh with new potables and story, and our reunion was joyful. By this time, love and care resulted in allowing Hilla's appetite to return. Both of us wished elves would turn her into horse or ox; then she could satisfy herself with grass and browse.

But God in his wisdom made her a great hound—so great, that when she lay over on either of us for a good ear-and-paunch rub, we came close to being crushed. I made humor about her—for she made remarkable time in vanquishing a rabbit—a tidbit to her.

The Abbey of Elstow was within a few leagues of Wixamtree and we reached it within a day but hesitated to make entry. On an elevated hill thick with cover, we allowed two days to pass, watching.

"Once they see us and Hilla, Cuthwin, the cat is freed from the sack."

Being near to diverse croft and hideage, the area was fertile and well-peopled. My snaring—even of small creatures—was not as fruitful and at more risk.

For a poor person, even this simple gleaning for victual was theft. For ones seeking solution and sanctuary, theft was the worst sort of introduction of character.

Yet Hilla kept us poor-of-food, for she would eat every scrap offered, and beg with pitiless skill for more.

"Cuthwin, I see why only rich people have such blooded creatures as Hilla. She could devour an ox in a week, simple beast that she is."

So, bracing ourselves, making Hilla fast between us with strong tether, we entered the Abbey at Elstow at midweek just before Sext, giving us time to escape if the worm turned sour.

With these long summer days, we could make a half dozen leagues by dark. And to make sure of our escape, I readied my cudgel—for freedom had become powerful nectar to me, and would remain so, and to Cwenburh, no less. We discussed that morning how best to continue.

"If we needs run, I had better not be shod. Running with these is poorly done." She tidied up her kirtle, took out her headrail and both our turnshoes from bundle fretting how she might appear to strangers. But in addition to garb, I knew her flaw-of-nature was foremost in mind, as it was to me. I feared the unlucky presence of demon-fearing zealots, who possess little sense and less heart.

Her point of being shod or unshod was practical and keen.

In truth, Cwenburh was not much tamer than a hind, and when running—even great with child—she remained barefooted, like I.

Elstow's outer barrier had evolved into a tangle of thatch and brush, some now even taken root and growing. Two poor travelers such as we lacked a calling horn to announce our approach, so upon entry we were looked over with caution, until they saw Hilla. Her appearance and standing was such that their curiosity replaced all else, and all marveled at such a beast.

I sought out the liveryman, a compact Saxon, gnarled from heavy work. Welcoming us to his shop, I saw some of his fine crafting, and he was surely near equal to Gilbert. He examined my meager work, and from our discussions and my knowledge, knew me to be as I said.

He made us welcome—chased off children and such from marveling at Hilla. I told him about passing through Wixamtree, and he knew well this fellow tradesman.

Soon, he had sent off for a Brother within cloister.

"I do all their tackle work for animals, as they are a modest monastery and have no full-time liveryman within."

Soon the Abbey Subcellarer arrived with a young oblate—this official was a Norman named Paul, who was a happy fellow, and stood flat admiring Hilla. His Saxon was clear, having surely been in country for many years.

"In our Savior's Grace and Mysteries, how did you come by such a grand animal?"

And, as I do when slyness and truth are needed, I stuck as much to the latter as possible, omitting our origins. He would, I hoped, accept without question this explanation.

And he did, asking nothing further beyond the story of how we came across Hilla and the coinman at the mill.

The Subcellarer sent the oblate back into cloister, and sat at repast provided by the wife of the liveryman. His position—as with any Cellarer of Monastery—called for daily commerce beyond the confines of cloister, an exception to The Rule.

And indeed, this tonsured officer took joy in this society. He and the liveryman opined about Hilla while Cwenburh and I sat next to this hound, both of us feeling relieved at benign developments.

When the Cellarer himself arrived with the same oblate, the tone took a business-like direction. He was a tall, straight-spined Brother named Loef—a Welshman whose Saxon was bent and awkward, as Welshman will do with it. He declined repast—or even a seat—and indeed the Subcellarer stood as well, folding his hands and arms before him, assuming a somber air. The Cellarer regarded Hilla from head to tail, and decided,

"I must consult Prior; he will want to know of this."

They made the mistake of trying to escort Hilla off, but she would not go, instead whining and pulling away—seeking out Cwenburh's flank. Finally, the Subcellarer suggested, "This great animal regards highly this young wife, Brother Loef, Praise God's wisdom to send such a kind soul to rescue it."

The Cellarer nodded a sour sort of agreement, and he and his oblate left, and the Subcellarer gladly returned to his repast of beer and talk with the liveryman. Two urchins, grandchildren of the Liveryman, were invited by Cwenburh to stroke Hilla, for the hound appreciated admiration almost equal to food.

Villagers were leaving confines of the crofts for the fields, for it was haying time and work was underway in earnest. I took it as trust we were left alone outside the liveryman's shop under an outer roof to wait events.

The heat of the day was coming on, and shade and open air was a kindness. Passing by us with tackle over shoulder, the liveryman looked back, smiling, "Brother Paul is discussing the best manner of ridding flour of weevils with my wife, and both can so talk for hours," but then he glanced towards the monastery walls and added, "Father Prior is often not well in the morning. But he is a fair Brother."

And left us wondering what affliction gripped Prior on a morning so warm and fair. What the liveryman forewarned was accurate, for we in fact dozed alternately through the morning. It was approaching Sext when Prior Everux arrived with the Cellarer and a single Whipman, without whip, and two young oblates following.

The Subcellarer left table, and attended—both he and the Cellarer standing at each of Prior's elbow. The wife came in behind Prior with stool, and he sat, sighing with relief as his great stature was so relieved, for he was a towering man.

And I saw at once Prior was suffering from the identical morning affliction I observed so many times years before at Ordgar's. When he and his eelmen had exceeded modesty in imbibing ale and boisterous society the previous evening, events of the new day were grim and slow to commence.

Prior's eyes were bleary, his jowls weighted, and he turned away a hot herbal brew with a weak toss of hand. He looked, I feared, resentfully, at us, then at Hilla. He marked Hilla with as keen a look as possible, considering his temporary lapse in health. Under those afflicted brows were not eyes of an eelman.

We all waited for Prior to renew questioning, but he maintained silence. In turn nobody spoke, understanding the great man's present desire for silence. On the road passing from the village, cart noises and people taking repast out to field marked the passing of midday.

Then of a sudden, a very old Brother hobbled in, helped by a heavy staff—further aided by an oblate. For a moment, I thought the ailing Father Abbot had risen from his sick bed. But this was an ordinary Brother, also a Norman. After Prior motioned to Hilla, the ancient withdrew a step marveling at the beast. He made the sign and all present took note with respectful nods. I saw at once this Brother was particularly venerated.

He bent a little to Hilla; he was very short, and spoke soft Norman to her, as if asking her permission. Then, taking her massive right ear, turned it outwards, and looking up at Prior indicated deep inside the ear, an inked mark—a holy mark it surely was.

Prior closed his eyes momentarily, then stood at once, and speaking a bit of the Rome language, bade the elder to sit in his stead—almost pushing him down over his objections.

Finally, when Prior spoke, he revealed a Norman heritage, and to guess, I would put him not long in this country.

"Do you swear before Jesus Christ Our Savior that the story of how you came by this animal is true? Be careful, boy. This hound is a *Chien de Saint-Hubert*, its breeding is from the Great Abbey of St. Hubert in France. It is property of Father Abbot there—a most powerful kindly man of God. She has surely been stolen—which is blasphemy."

"Yes, Brother Prior, it is as I have said. At the mill with such men as we saw. And, in truth, your Reverence, this animal would have perished without the expert care of my wife."

"Do not show pride in extending plain Christian charity!"

"I cannot see why not; we could have been murdered, your Holiness, in rescuing this animal from such savage men," Cwenburh rejoined.

All shot a look of shock toward Cwenburh for such talk; my very bowels moved, and the Subcellarer turned away, as if in embarrassment, and the liveryman's wife disappeared within, like a cony into burrow when sighting a hawk.

"What sort of harridan have you married, boy!"

The Whipman's instrument was concealed up his sleeve; but now, a knotted leather line sprang quickly to hand. It was the venerable ancient who raised his hand, restraining him.

"The girl is not used to the ways of things, Prior. And in God's name she has done a great deed for the Church."

Thank God, the whip disappeared as rapidly as it appeared when Prior too raised a hand and thankfully drew a breath of forbearance.

Cwenburh, seeing the way of things, looked sullenly to earth—probably to avert herself and hopefully conceal her confounding intemperate ways.

Without need of word, all of the Brothers went off with Prior; this time the ancient—with the help of two oblates—pushed and dragged Hilla along, the elderly Brother coaxing her in Norman, patting her as she moved.

Within a brief time another oblate came, sold us a few provisions for the road, and led us to a small waddle-slatted shelter immediately adjoining the wall of the Monastery proper.

"You are to stay within our travelers' shelter until Prior sends you notice. Repast is laid out in the corner, God be Praised."

And we were left alone. I struggled to understand how Cwenburh could have committed such a leather-headed blunder. Cwenburh, instead of blessing our luck for having our hides intact, was not in a grateful frame of mind.

"There is no guard. We should fly, Cuthwin. Our story will not stand without further questions from the powers that be."

I was of such anger with her—having so many times in previous days instructed her how to behave in such circumstances—that I did not care to fly anywhere. If it were not for my child within, I would, for that moment, have no more of her. I should have kept silent, but youthful temper burns fiercely.

"For all I care, you can fly by yourself, Cwenburh. You should have at least taken into account our host, the liveryman and his wife."

And she shot past, picking up sack, to do precisely that, but God forgive me, I grabbed her—and child or no child, sent her back onto her hind end—stood over her and shook my cudgel in her face. She stared hatefully up—the cudgel was nothing to her anger.

"Oh, Brave Cuthwin! Now you act like Wilfred-of-Loe, who also fancied me, and when I came of womanhood would have sired many a halfwit on me if not for Gytha."

Then threw herself into a corner, gathered into a furious ball, and covered up her head with edge of her kirtle.

Never before—and never afterwards—did she refer to her father, Wilfred-of-Loe's, bestial ways.

I slumped to the floor, casting my cudgel away. Inwardly, I long suspected such foulness. Wilfred was a pig, and that was the best he was. I looked at Cwenburh, and I don't think she wept under cover, for I never saw her weep before, or in fact ever.

But I did.

We sat in the lengthening shadows of the afternoon, and it was late, towards Compline when Prior reappeared—this time he just walked in, with only the briefest of knock on the threshold.

Bidding us rise I saw at once his features, especially his eyes, had cleared and in doing so bespoke a monk of an even judicial temper. The hut was so small he bent slightly to fit inside.

"Good news, God be praised. I sent an oblate to the mill, a good soul swift of foot, but sadly denied wit. Indeed those thieving blackguards are still there, now drinking great lament over the untoward loss of their animal," and here he let slip a smile. "Good fortune, the mill is ours, and the miller and his two boys are advised to keep them sodden for the interim. Please stay the night here and then continue to your destination in the morning. Please take show of our gratitude—for ours is a poor, small monastery. But in rescuing the fine animal, you have done God's work for Father Abbot of Saint Hubert, and us here."

He handed back the coin paid for the provision, and included a travelers' loaf of rich monastery bread wrapped in cloth with the Monastery emblem dyed atop it.

"It is humbly baked, but even when it becomes stale, it soaks up well. Now kneel, and I shall give you blessing for your travels. Is there anything else I might provide you, good children?"

Kneeling side by side, we exchanged poorly hooded looks: Indeed, there was much he could do. He saw our eyes' furtive language, despite our silence. He put a powerful hand to each of our shoulders, having us rise from kneeling.

"There is? What is it? If it is mine to do, tell me."

Prudence should have directed me to go on as we were. But within the breadth of the moments, I risked truth—one thing was needed over anything else, and it was his to give: "Reverend Prior, through circumstances of her birth and background, my wife Cwenburh lacks the Holy Waters, even though of great belief and prayer."

I saw Cwenburh take her lip between teeth, and, cautiously, she looked up. Prior Evreux took no unusual note of this situation. He nodded and slapped his hands together lightly. At once a lanky oblate entered—his eyes large, innocent; his teeth set poorly in his mouth. This surely was Prior's speedy oblate, for his legs and habit—even his face—were covered with trail mud and tiny slivers of reed and pieces of leaf.

"Go fetch an available Brother to come with my kit. He will know."

Oddly, the oblate repeated this word for word, then vanished. Prior looked to me, gesturing outside.

"Now, I need to be alone with Cwenburh to take confession."

And something so vital to both of us happened in less than the half-hour: Confession was taken, and the oblate returned with another Brother who carried a small leather purse.

In it was the Holy Water, and before us all, Prior anointed Cwenburh in the name of our Savior, Jesus Christ. Such was that God ordained ease in providing so holy a moment by the hands of a kindly man and priest.

No two trusting souls ever spent a night in such joyful anticipation of the new day. As I tell my story nearly eight decades later, I lived to see events—such as with that purloined hound—yield favorable outcomes, but infrequently.

God forgive me, but many times I wished I had foreknowledge that evening concerning how times proceeded for the poor and landless who labored, free or bonded. As years tumbled away, one by one, I learned that such folk as we were pebbles and dirt under heavy merciless wheels of great men and women.

If I possessed such clear truths of the future, without a doubt, I would have taken Cwenburh by the hand, knelt, and prayed to God we stay in Elstow forever, finding any honest work to sustain us.

Having given up Hilla, we changed our travel methods, leaving the river and heading westerly opting to make faster progress towards Hereford. As with many lies, if said often enough, even their manufacturers start to believe them, and it was this way with us both.

What began as a fabrication now came to be hard truth.

"If only I did, Cwenburh, have a brother in Hereford who owned a stable and livery!"

And we found grand adventure in our change of heart. For we knew that Hereford was as good a destination as any for runaways. By now we had a hundred and a half hundred leagues at our rear. It was a month since we high-graded George the mule and fled Lynn Regis.

But without the river or streams, the way increased in difficulty, for hills began to be not only more numerous, but steeper. Both of us were creatures of the fens—the lowlands. But we were young, and traversed what was before us.

Yet in dales and valleys nestling between richly forested domes were settlements and cultivated fields. And trapping small game and wild crafting in general became sparser and called for increase in caution.

Like before, we kept to ourselves strictly. Our way of looking and dealing with events greatly contrasted, and always did: Cwenburh operated by her instincts and feelings of heart while I remained prone to thought and carefully wrought a plan.

"Ah, Cuthwin! You think too much."

Yet in fact we began to agree more—to argue less. It seemed to me, though I said nothing, that after taking Holy Water, Cwenburh became more anxious about her behavior. She cursed less—certainly aired fewer blasphemies at events, though still gossiped if I did not raise objection.

"Oh, piss on all those who look down on healthy gossiping. I find tremendous pleasure in it; it is how poor people carry truth place to place."

She had grand laughter in that and, despite my objections, would carry on about someone or another back in the demesne of Peterborough.

We were thus involved early one morning when we came across a reasonably good trail—even road—which followed the course of a small river. And where there is a river I can catch fish.

But we had not gone far, at somewhat past Sext, when we can across a large encampment of extraordinary make-up. Further, it was very early for travelers—no matter how heavily burdened they traveled—to make camp. But this troop had indeed.

At the center of their camp were two of the largest carts I had seen in my nearly nineteen years. As liveryman with a half-dozen years of work at Peterborough Monastery, I saw many carts, for it was an important crossroads where many travelers pass or are destined.

Each great wheel of both carts, had spokes a dozen or so hand-lengths, meeting in hubs locked to massive axels. Camp awnings extended from the sides of one, and the opposing side of the other. But on the second—on the side facing us, a half-dozen people stood—some with small articles in hand I could not distinguish; a tall, elderly man holding a staff bellowed,

"Oh, not that, you great ox! The *other* words are said just at that point! Goddamn you, your minds are like suet."

Then those alongside the wagon resumed speaking words I recognized from the Holy Book. The elderly man, whose lips passed profanity, listened intently while holding a hand upright, as if testing the wind.

This strange scene peopled by such extraordinary sorts was just a small part of this party. In the midst was a grand makeshift hearth where large iron cookery squatted, and on a nearby spit, a great joint of meat. There, tending each, a half-dozen women worked—a few older, but most young.

And beyond them, along a running line, were two well-fleshed horses and four fine oxen—the latter nearly red, and of healthy frame. All were attended by a man and two boys.

At leisure around a camp awning were two housecarls. Light armor lay nearby, and a young woman worked washing and attending their feet. They drank ale at fine leisure while being so cared for.

And seeing yet another more shocking scene—Cwenburh and I went flat to our bellies like vixen and fox. To the side of the camp was a half roebuck hanging from a tree.

"God help us, Cwenburh, but they have stolen a roebuck. They will all hang if found—yet look at their boldness."

Two small children sat beneath the carcass—one using the folded, green hide for stool. Both waved limbs with thick leaves at the carcass, keeping flies from it. Or rather one—the second having lost interest, now tracing figures into the dirt from its imaginings.

Perhaps at that instant, we should have turned tail and gotten away, for such delicious beasts as roebucks are only for the palates of great men. But, the fickle breeze reversed, turning contrary from us to them, and a dog at once caught wind of us. It was the size, at most, of a small badger—and it bounded up hill towards us, barking the alert.

We turned to retreat, me grabbing the cudgel hard—for now, we prized freedom and would maintain it as we needed. At once the elderly man—evidently the camp's leader—shouted: "Whoever is up there, come out! Do not fear us. We are friends."

The two housecarls rose and, grabbing short swords, sent the girl to her backside in their alarm.

The elder man shouted at the dog.

"Get back! One day you will get yourself killed and eaten."

We smelled the food cooking. On second sight the group did not appear menacing. There were women and children, a sight itself lacking menace. The roasting roebuck emanated robust enticement to our noses.

Cwenburh, taking her own mind, stopped, then I followed her lead.

After a glance and shrug, we move into view.

"Well come on down, take repast with us."

The dog came back—though reluctantly. The housecarls returned to their leisure and drink, but all watched as we came in. The women, when they saw Cwenburh's girth, marveled that she be wandering in the woods like a hind.

"Ah! Your man would have you drop the baby in a wolf den somewhere."

And it was this way that we met Alfred-of-Aylesbury, Master of Train.

Two of the women explained proudly that Alfred-of-Aylesbury was known by name countywide—even beyond. Mostly, they said, it was for his company's presentations about the Holy Martyrs and Saints of the Church at Rome.

"We have done three fairs since spring rains, and now make to Shrewsbury for Lammastide Festival[20], there will be prosperous doing for us."

Like travelers everywhere, they imposed few questions, yet greeted our destination of Hereford with bitter looks—followed by a sorrowful shake of their heads. They motioned to Alfred-of-Aylesbury, who still drilled his troop—alternately screaming blasphemy and holy words.

"Himself says that Hereford is a great sty; invested Holy men root around like pigs, scooping up anything of value—begrudging common folk a ha'penny if they could."

Gertyn, Alfred's wife, ruled everyday management of this train, and especially the women. She applied firm oversight and was given to sharpened words. When seeing the girl still providing for the housecarls' feet, she ordered, "Their feet are too fine—get to the wares."

She assigned us places under the most distant wagon—Cwenburh could nearly stand beneath this behemoth that was our shelter. I felt and tested the joining of the axel and wheel with amazement.

Flapping from a staff on our cart a yellow pennant of fine cloth with noble's insignia waved lively.

---

[20] August 1. It is a festival to mark the annual wheat harvest, and is the first harvest festival of the year.

"Ah, Cwenburh—see! That fine pennant represents the Lord of the Manor's safe passage extended to this grand a party. So this explains the roebuck."

And we rested more comfortably—smelled the great meal with easier anticipation. The rest of the day—hour by hour—was a keen curiosity. Most interestingly, a family of dark-featured individuals traveled with Alfred speaking a language neither of us had ever heard.

One of Gertyn's girls laughed, explaining, "Oh, those are Lombards! Clever with the pantomime for children, always yielding good numbers of ha'pennies and pennies. They are new here in this land—but Alfred is sly that way, offering poor folk new things. Draws folk in from every-where."

This young woman—one of over a half dozen—was part of the eager society that gathered around Cwenburh, talking and questioning all in a bustle of her coming occasion.

I wandered off, inspecting the animals, and met the carpenter, a Norwich man—but one who learned his trade in Normandy. Normans produced grand carts, more akin to ship than a vehicle of land.

"Takes us a entire year to make just one of these," and he gestured to both, ". . . and the rest of your life to keep it going, especially over these shitty English roads."

His two sons were his assistants—and he was rough with them, for necessity required he also functioned as liveryman, a role he had little skill for. Hearing my skills, he suggested I offer up to Alfred to exchange my skills for accompanying them to Shrewsbury with shelter and food provided.

"I tell you, you'll put the flesh on with the victuals they set."

Towards Compline—heavy with meat and bread—we lay in cover, content. Cwenburh told of how she learned that her time was closer than she thought.

"The women here—most have children, as you can see—they think our baby is closer to us than we realize."

And soon, the large fire had burned down to smolders, and we slept the first unguarded sleep in a human shelter since Elstow Abbey.

Feeling Cwenburh asleep next to me, I thought about talking to Alfred about the carpenter's suggestion—especially if Cwenburh's time was closer. With so many knowledgeable women nearby, plus healthy food, such work would be wise. And Shrewsbury?! I had often heard of it in the grandest way.

There was much to sleep on, though, even if we could only know the half of it.

Cwenburh woke me, for her need to make water at night was frequent. I was trying to adjust to her stirrings—when I felt her elbow, and heard her whisper—the tone used when menace was at hand.

"Look! Rats leaving the granary after they let loose the cat."

The two housecarls—each with a squire—were moving. They had muffled their animals' hooves with hides, and were leading them out, their stealth extraordinary considering there were four men with two stout horses.

The darkness swallowed them whole while they sneaked away. All this without a sound. At once, the little hound picked up scent, and charged up into the darkness barking, there was a mortal yelp, and then silence—its end violent.

What more was needed? We scrambled, picking up our things, and were moving when great shouts were heard, and a dozen torches set alight.

"All rise! Get your arses up, you bastards. God's justice is at hand."

Into the camp charged housecarls afoot—each with a squire at his side carrying a torch burning so bright our eyes were blinded. There was continued screaming for all to rise, and the din was so—children began weeping and carrying on—sleeping figures were kicked by the housecarls and squires. Amongst them rode their spokesmen on a sleek roan caparisoned with handsome layers of hand-designed leather and strapping.

"Shut up! You! Silence these bitches. This infernal bleating."

But the chaos continued. Alfred had arisen, and appealed to the mounted man: "Good master, we have full permission of the Lord to pass. What is this great disturbance, Sir?"

"You lying prick, you have no one's permission. I mean to have silence or goddamn all of you."

One of the invaders grabbed an older women who was running past him crying out hysterically. The mounted man—their Master of Horse as it was—gestured to the two men who seized her, and they slit her throat—tossing her down to die.

The others, seeing this horror, found silence at once.

"Yes! Look on! I will order them to kill every one of you whores and thieves if you don't do what I ask."

Another grabbed a child as one might a chicken, and tossed it up to the horseman, who drew a knife,

"And I'll start with this harlot's offspring if you don't obey at once."

The mother of the child rushed him, and since now there was not a sound being made—he just tossed the child down to her, and scowled in every direction.

They made us all sit in a line facing the fire ordering our hands placed on each knee. At that, squires led all the horses in, and torches were put in place—there was even more light, though sunup was close.

Their work began. Belongings were sought and sorted—different types of property put into separate piles. Seeing how these men were equipped and commanded, I knew this was no troop of robbers or free-booters, but those with money and many hides of land were behind them.

And riding into camp astride the grandest horses I ever saw were three men—holy men. Two of them were very stout, and puffed from the labor of riding roughly. These were helped from their horse by squires carrying small stools—each holy man being carefully guided to the ground.

But not the rider in the middle—the most elaborately mounted and clothed of them all. His mantle was rich—headgear of brilliant scarlet and purple—and hanging before him was a massive gold crucifix on a similar chain bejeweled so heavily it glittered in the torch light like a scattering of ruby-colored stars.

He fairly leaped from horse, hit the ground nimbly, and when he cast back his head gear, a full head of red hair fell about his shoulders. Behind me, the Master of Horse—for in fact, that is who led the invasion of the camp, shouted, "All kneel before his Grace, the Bishop of Ludlow. Kneel!"

We now had to take hands from knees, and shift onto our knees—awkward for those older ones.

The Bishop had fierce eyes—looked around at the piles of property, ignoring those kneeling. He took no time for a blessing. Instead he proceeded to tour the camp, looking first at the large carts. When he put a hand to each wheel, I caught glimpse of gold rings on two of his fingers—bejeweled as well.

Then he went to the running lines. He stepped back to admire the four oxen, slapping them on their ample, fat buttocks. He strode back to the fire, slapped one gloved hand into the other, then locked terrible eyes on Alfred. He stepped over towards him—raising a hand and pointing.

"So there you are, Alfred-of-Aylesbury. You have prospered, you wandering dog. You fled owing His Eminence the Archbishop of Hereford money. Where is it?!"

"I did not know his Grace had received the pallium[21]—though of course he deserves such lofty holy office, in the name of our Savior, Jesus Christ."

"His Grace asked a question, you prick-with-ears! Where is the money owed?"

The Master of Horse—still mounted—towered above Alfred. The accused gazed up with dignity at the rider, then returned his eye to His Grace, the Bishop of Ludlow.

"In truth, Your Grace, I did not realize I owed your brother, His Eminence, money."

"Do not trifle with God's messenger. Where is it? If you don't have it, it will be taken in kind."

---

[21] Pallium. A woolen vestment conferred on an archbishop by the Pope.

"In truth, if I do owe a small sum, I was not aware, Your Grace."

"You owe His Eminence five pounds eight shillings. Now where is it?"

Not just Alfred gasped at this unheard of sum, but others as well.

"For the mercy of God, your Grace, I have never seen such a sum, let alone owed it."

Then an official—a little man on a small horse appeared, dismounted, and at once I recognized the emblem about his neck—he was a High Reeve, and bowing short to His Grace, a squire set up a table before the fire. His Grace and the Reeve were within just a few feet of the wretched dead woman, her life's blood drained out in a network of rivulets before all. His Grace still held deathly eyelock on Alfred. His voice fell heavy on each word: "Where is His Eminence's money?"

The Bishop sat, confident that a fine wooden chair had been readied behind him. He extended a hand, and a cup of ale was thrust in it. He gestured to the Reeve.

"Tell him what's writ, Master Reeve."

The Reeve opened a box, took out a scroll, and pinning it open on the table, squinted down. A squire took a torch and held it over him, immediately causing him to cry out, "Not too close, you fool—you will set me afire."

The Bishop smiled, took a drink—and I saw he and Alfred had not taken eyes from one another. The Reeve began to read in his reedy, peevish voice, "Three years interest on one pound twelve shilling." Then he mumbled a bit, finishing with, ". . . this being the amount filched by Alfred of-Ayreshire in fairgeld[22] from His Eminence after slipping off in the night—that Lammastide, and so forth."

"Interest! By Christians?!"

Alfred blurted that out before thinking, causing the Master of Horse to draw and use its massive hilt to club Alfred in the head, sending him down in a heap.

His wife cried out and attended. To bide time, His Grace asked the Master, "Have you found the ready coin?"

He somberly shook his head, reached down and grabbed the old

_____

[22] Fairgeld. A tax paid by those to set up business at a fair.

woman by the hair—reefing her up off the ground. "Worry less about Alfred and more about you, who I know to be his whoremonger. Now His Grace asked where your ready coin is kept, so tell him, or I shall start slitting throats, you old pig."

With Alfred on the ground, bloodied, and the slain woman not far away, Gertyn knew better than to trifle. It wasn't long before a small chest was retrieved and set before the Reeve. Opening it, he shrugged—and droned, "There is only ten shilling here. He has another. This is a dupe to fend off greedy road thieves or stupid creditors."

Having returned to his senses, Alfred—as much as Gertyn—realized there would be no limit to the slaying until satisfied. With a hand, for he still could not speak, he gestured towards the woods. And soon another box—larger—was fetched, and in this the Reeve was more impressed.

"And, yes, here is far more. Over a pound silver, Your Grace."

The Bishop nodded, drew off his drink and passed it back.

"There remains four pounds. Now, if you do not have it, the rest His Eminence will gain by impounding all your property." He turned to the Reeve. "Is there enough?"

The Reeve took a weary appraising look around—now the sun had begun to come up, so there was more light.

"Possibly, Your Grace—close. There are children and young women here, which should help. I need to first complete the initial inventory for accuracy."

"Good. Hang this dog Alfred for making His Eminence go to this expense to collect. The property and others, bring to Ludlow. Give me the box, for I will return to Hereford. My brother, His Eminence, is soon to depart for great honors in Rome."

He rose—for this entire time we all had remained kneeling—and just before he and the two holy men remounted, the carpenter dived into the clearing, just missing the dead woman, and in desperate supplication cried out, "Your Grace! I am an honest carpenter just joined Alfred this spring. My family and I know nothing of any but honest dealing these past two months. I implore, we are God-fearing Saxons—I am here solely to keep these great carts on the road."

"So noted."

And His Grace mounted, nodded to the Master of Horse and Reeve, and rode off at a high canter, his two clerics lagging behind, somewhat akimbo in saddle.

Even though young, I was a keen student of men's language by features and body sign. And I noted this Master of Horse did not overly abide His Grace's words. He closed his eyes momentarily—opening them, he exchanged poorly hooded glances with several of his men and looked on as Alfred was hustled towards a tree. The poor man appealed to all: "Would you allow me to die unshriven?"

His wife—and a few others, bent their head in prayer. In the decades to come, I saw many hangings, but I was never to see one so fast and unceremonious as Alfred's. He was hanging dead within a few minutes.

The body was still swinging when the Reeve began his tedious inventory. He took out more paper, prepared his implements—pinning paper flat against his table and ordering all of us to be lined up before him.

We were allowed to sit in line again; all of our things were taken and we were sure never to be returned. Anyone young and strong enough for work would become property of His Grace to sell into serfdom, and the rest would either be turned loose to die on the road, or possibly hanged. His Grace, the Bishop of Ludlow, did not impress with his compassion.

I cursed the moment Alfred's dog came up for us—and the other, when we turned and came down into their camp. Cwenburh kept silent—she too lamenting inward about this ghastly turn of luck.

We looked at each other—of one mind.

If we had the tiniest opportunity and were able to make the thickets, we could flee uphill into thickets where horses would be useless. And at this stage of our wildness, none of them would catch us afoot.

But that tiny opportunity drew even further away when our wrists were bound—mine in back, Cwenburh's in front. A sharp eye was kept on all, for we were so many shilling on-the-foot, and each of these men would get fair share of all property.

The day grew hot; the Reeve called for water as he interviewed and inventoried each captive's property—if they had any. He worked aloud, asking each their name and function. If they hesitated, a dreng[23] or his squire would give them a whack, and conversation would resume on a straighter course.

Threats and terrible invectives were the rule of the day.

And all was recorded for eventual oversight by either His Grace or His Grace's brother, The Archbishop of Hereford. During it all no one was allowed freedom to relieve themselves, for we were no longer humans, but grist for trade.

Finally—and it seemed hours—when it came time for Cwenburh and me, we were lifted from our own foulness and stood before the Reeve. He now had taken off most outer clothing; flies abounded in the heat. The dead woman had long before been dragged away at his order for drawing so many of these tormenters.

Holding his quill with one hand, he called for us to speak. I gave him our names, and our two sacks of belongings were thrown before him. His squire removed things one by one, watched carefully by the Master of Horse—jealous as a jackdaw over a carcass of fresh-killed hare.

I knew my words must be right.

"I am Cuthwin-of-Alnwick, liveryman, and this is my wife, Cwenburh-of-Loe. We are not of this party, but were received yesterday. We are travelers bound for Hereford, your Honor."

The Reeve's little snout twisted into a grin. "Well, boy, you joined the wrong party. Repeat what you said—you spoke too fast."

He wrote slowly and unskillfully, though his use of Roman numbers was sure and fast. Before he finished, the Master of Horse, who sat on a stool overseeing things, suddenly stood—pushing the Reeve's squire aside. He reached into our few belongings and took out the folded cloth that had held the bread given us by Prior Evreux at Elstow Abbey. Cwenburh, of course, had great plans for such cloth.

He held it in front of the Reeve, looked to each of us, then unfolded it, examining the holy emblem. The Reeve stopped writing at once, staring at it. Another dreng close by asked what it was. "It is the sign of Elstow Abbey, and could not have been stolen."

---

[23] Dreng. A free tenant especially in ancient Northumbria who held partly military and servile form of tenure.

"An Abbey? I have not heard of it."

The Master of Horse drew a resigned breath, saying, "Of course you have not, you stupid turd."

And everyone laughed at the once, save the Reeve who took the cloth—laying it flat above his paper. "The dye is not yet faded. This is recent. How did you get this, boy?"

I told him, including details.

This put a stop to the procedure—and silence. The Reeve and Master of Horse ruminated. The housecarls close by groaned, saying, "She is heavy with child, young and strong. So what if she has a piece of cloth?"

The Reeve looked keenly to them, then to the Master of Horse—and tapped his inventory list.

"I will need to record it—as property."

"Do you?"

"Yes, I do."

Perhaps even the housecarls did not know, but I did. So listed, it would be read by either His Grace, or worse—His Eminence. And the emblem on the cloth was of the Abbot of Elstow. Anything given by the Prior was equal in stature to being given by Father Abbot.

These protocols were second nature to me. If the Reeve would not list it, which was wrongful, the great men would not know, not on record. But thanks to God and our Savior, we had before us an honest Reeve.

"Untie them. They will go to Hereford under guard for audience before His Eminence's court. These two have enjoyed shelter and reward by Father Abbot of Elstow and not part of Alfred's party, God be praised."

Though rough about it, we were freed and escorted to the cart, and shoved under it. I looked up at our guard—a young squire appointed to watch us.

"Could we please have water?"

He provided it in the form of a half-full bucket, thank God. He tied each of our ankles to the wheel, though a knife's thrust would free us in an instant, if I had a knife. But our belongings were held elsewhere of course.

We huddled into one another despite the heat of the day. And we sat without word until I heard Cwenburh almost voicelessly praying. Recognizing the psalm, I joined. At that moment we thanked God and Our Savior for that piece of cloth, knowing full well how much good fortune Prior's loaf of bread had done us.

Subdued weeping prevailed through the night, despite harsh calls for silence. The housecarls and their squires camped close around the fire. The Reeve departed for Hereford with two guards. The Master of Horse, as I thought, retained a minimum of care about the Bishop of Ludlow's wishes.

For in fact, he was a wealthy Saxon Lord and Tenant who owed service to His Eminence through having vast holdings south of us, and only a few in demesne from the Bishop of Ludlow. This Saxon Lord, in fact, provided all the housecarls, drengs, and squires for this action.

He was called Sidroc-the-Old. Sidroc was attended by two squires, talked to no one, staying aloof, quickly becoming sullen in his cups. With that number of men, they ate the remaining half of the roebuck, giving none of Alfred's former train anything but water.

Cwenburh and I were close to them at the fire. During and after Compline, his men talked within earshot, especially the squires. Though the Lombards were closer than us, those poor souls spoke not a word of any language in camp.

Cwenburh was as keen of hearing as I, and we learned via his men's gossip that Sidroc-the-Old did not wish to proceed to Ludlow, and ". . . didn't care a bit if His Grace, the 'Bishop of Thievery' wished him to go north or south. Sidroc-the-Old will go as he wishes."

All other talk pertained to the sharing of money and property, and there was bitter mention that His Grace of Ludlow had departed with the ready coin.

"We won't see a chip of that, the bloody-haired bastard."

There were furtive looks around the fire towards Sidroc, but he was slumped against a pile of hides—occasionally taking swings at the bugs that rose in hordes as the sun sank.

"More smoke! Drive these demons off me."

And squires fed more green wood into the fire—and volumes of white smoke poured through the camp, the wind being unsteady in any direction, making the entirety seem dreamlike, not part of us.

And we finally slept—not knowing what direction our train would go, no better or worse than the others in party. The answer lay in the begrudging mind of Sidroc-the-Old, and like all great men, he would reveal plans when he wished.

At first light, we were jolted awake with a bellow that if its volume were an indicator, might have been the death cry of a dragon: "Up! Up you worthless pissants! What is this shit? Up!"

Sidroc stood before the fire pissing into it and bellowing orders.

Lying at his feet, his face badly bloodied, was a squire. The wretched soul's clothing was torn, one shoe on, the other off. Sidroc hurled a ges-ture at him: "See this fuck! Sleeping on watch. Where in God's name do you think we are?! This pig could've gotten us all killed, but instead got his teeth kicked in." He allowed himself a great, menacing laugh, packed himself up in his breeches and pointed to his dreng: "He is your squire, Edfel. Slit his throat and be done with it. I could have been a Welsh vanguard. Goddamn if I will pay for this rank stupidity."

He was in the most fearsome mood I ever saw a man, and he with great power and wealth to do as he wished. We drew back, fearing another awful murder, yet the squire's dreng, instead of slaying him, motioned for his man to get up and be gone, and kicked him several times while he did so.

Sidroc's order, thank God and Our Savior, was made in anger and not in earnest. His squire dressed and armed him preparing Sidroc for the day while a second readied his horse. All during it he cursed every-one: First those before him—then his man who suggested cutting the dead Alfred down. This brought to his mind they would leave the rope, and he admonished anyone using costly length of braided rope to hang such as Alfred.

Then, in overall resentment, he launched into diatribe about holy men, which I found a rare scandal for anyone to air, let alone a rich, powerful owner.

His men warmed ale for him, a preparation I had not heard of—and this seemed to settle Sidroc. Drinking, he looked up at the sky, as if summoning a direction from the heavens. Returning his attentions back to earth, Sidroc scowled at the carpenter who was shoved forward into his presence, and I was grabbed and pushed along, not far behind.

"You help me get this catch-all to Hereford and your arse can go free along with your family, if His Eminence's court so agrees with my wish. Him behind you, too, for your livery and tackle couldn't last a damned league with most breaking."

There was no agree or disagree. Though the carpenter tried to bend down in thanks, we were half pushed, half led off by squires without further hearing.

The carpenter looked at me when we were back at the animals, and gesturing to the tackle—and it was a mess—warned, "I see you have the beginnings of a family, and I already have one. In our Savior's name, I pray to live on as a born freedman to enjoy them."

We began work most earnestly.

I knew that Cwenburh would be all in readiness for escape, but we were not with fools. She was tethered to the wagon, though I was free to move around. Worse, armed men were everywhere, and all was in great preparation and a hurry. In truth Alfred's train was no insignificant undertaking, and the day was not yet hot—but would become so.

Himself sat on his horse, now partaking in bread and meat. He resumed his usual silence—his ranting finally over. Instead he watched all with the scrutiny of a peregrine.

Several of his men were key sergeants and they oversaw details of the train—no conversation seemed needed until it came to matters of the captives. At this time, Sidroc was close to me, watching the great oxen be readied for burden.

"If the captives ride in the wagons, Sidroc, we will make better time. We could make Ludlow in less than two days that way."

"Fine, but we are not going to Ludlow. We are going to where His Eminence would want us—Hereford."

"That is at least a week."

"Jesus Christ our Savior! You don't think I know that. But I also know that if Alfred's two shitheads betrayed him for money, they would His Grace of Buggery too—and me—to the Welsh, the greedy pricks. We have a fortune here, sparsely guarded."

Our troubles were such it wasn't until that moment that the Marches of Wales became significant to me. I knew we were close, and all talk was rife with accounts of the Welshmen's cruel raids upon the Marches. The King fought with difficulty against Welsh hosts—even moreso than years before against the Danes.

This news moved about us causing much talk amongst his men. Sidroc took a breath and groaned a lament: "I have with me fools and gut buckets! Use your brain pans. If Welshmen lurk between here and Ludlow, and we go opposite to Hereford, that is keen advantage if there has been betrayal. If no, then it doesn't make any fucking difference does it? Save we get full share—cutting out that greedy brother of His Eminence's who has already taken Alfred's coin!"

This was Sidroc's longest speech of the morning—he shouted it, wheeling his horse in all directions. While speaking he gestured all around, towards the west, the east—then south.

"Does it? You stupid oafs. Now get to it, goddamn you. The heat of the day is coming and it grows late."

Loading enough water was hard—and the women made to do it, and so Cwenburh was cut free. The thirsty souls made advantage of this, drinking their fill—and asking for food. Realizing the need for haste—and their help—the housecarls and all others said nothing in reprisal, though no food was given.

The carpenter and I faced many problems. We could have employed a half-dozen carpenter sons in addition to his two. These extraordinarily ponderous carts being loaded with baggage and people created impossible problems.

I felt Sidroc must know. I urged the carpenter to so inform: "This tackle won't stand the heft of loads."

"The carts will not either—over these so-called roads?!"

"Then he must be told."

"Will you, then?"

And me being the junior member, I could not, and we worked on. If the tackle snapped—and it would—I would repair it on the spot; same with the carts.

I had learned at a young age how great men swept aside a powerless man or woman's life and freedom. The horrible day of Alfred's reckoning via Sidroc-the-Old and His Grace, Bishop of Ludlow, provided fresh and grim reaffirmation. Life was opening an all-consuming maw before Cwenburh and me.

The women and children riding in the carts lasted briefly—themselves begging to walk, the path so cursedly rough. They were allowed such but the adults were tied neck-to-neck like animals. The children were left to wander between them, their mothers crying out to keep free of the unmerciful turn of those great cart wheels.

Housecarls followed behind and in front, and for the first time I noted one had a longbow and arrows. Even a child knew it was impossible to out run an arrow. Escape was not an option.

My opinion of the carpenter rose when two of the housecarls began to whip the oxen, who struggled up hills over difficult ground. He at once stood between them and the poor animals—fine-fleshed oxen.

"Stop that. These are beasts not used to such treatment, and if you keep that up, we will get never get to Hereford?! Leave us to the coaxing."

And when they whipped him instead of the oxen, the Norwich man grabbed the whip, despite the pain, and would have pulled the dreng off horse, if not a cooler head—one of Sidroc's sergeants—had not interceded.

"Leave off! Do as the carpenter asks."

And he went on—the carpenter bleeding from his wound, one eye half closed. We said nothing to one another—but drove the oxen sternly though thoughtfully.

The yokes strained and worked around the great animals' necks, and his boys trotted along beside, greasing the joints of the carts and yokes. I followed the lead yoke with switch, urging them on with taps on their vast butts. And as it approached Sext, we made temporary camp to rest through the sun's highest passage.

Seeing we all were due a long trip, the women were allowed to bring out bread for everyone—who had not eaten in a long time. The children nearly choked when wolfing down food.

Spare moments for us tradesmen were spent repairing—for even without people, the carts were hard pressed and needed attention, the tackle and livery as well. To be stopped was to allow at least some serious work on them.

For us, there was no rest.

On the second day of travel—in the settling coolness between Vespers and Compline—a mounted messenger from His Eminence of Hereford overtook us, or actually, encountered us unexpected.

He carried a letter from His Eminence to Sidroc. The messenger jumped from his horse—the poor beast foaming from hard riding—and both man and beast buried their heads in buckets of water. The heat of such a day might kill a horse by its being ridden so—only drastic business would cause it to be thus driven.

Finally, the messenger's thirst slaked—it was I who attended his poor animal—he stood before Sidroc, who held the letter.

"Is this it? What is in it? His Eminence knows I don't read—none of us here do. He thinks my son is with me, but God help me, he is not. Now tell me the drift of what's in this."

"I don't know, Sire, save His Eminence's Secretary thought you would be on route to Ludlow, I did not expect you here, though I thank the Almighty you were."

Sidroc appealed silently to the heavens—then raised his hand with the letter in that direction, bellowing, "Does any man present read—even if by hit and miss?"

None did. Cwenburh moved around into my line-of-sight and, putting a bucket down before a group of children, shook her head discreetly. I became confused. We encountered so many reversals since escaping that I feared encountering my own ghost under each rock.

I thought she would be for a gamble here. The poor girl had seen such mayhem at the hands of Sidroc and his housecarls that the fear had also struck her.

Sidroc, being ill-tempered and under such threat as he was, switched his wrath to the messenger.

"You useless shit! If His Eminence did not trust you, then why don't I just slit your throat right here and now and keep your horse. We have need of a good horse. By our Savior's grace, you *can* trust a good horse."

This resulted in laughter the group 'round—even a few of Alfred's party followed. This time, all knew it was frustration that did the venting, one of Sidroc's harmless privileges.

I made my decision. Yes, I regretted coming into Alfred's camp for comfort of food and shelter, and barely survived it. However, the advantage of reading might well negate a disregard of keeping one's place and flaunting prideful behavior.

People of power and position fear poor folk who transgress the order of God. It portents unseemly ambitions and possibly the workings of demons. But, it was a combination of despair and craft that overcame fear.

In as low a voice as possible, though I knew all would learn, I said, "I do, Sire. I read."

Cwenburh put down the bucket, causing a bit of a splash, and dug her hand in her back, her eyes opening.

Sidroc made to shout, then stopped—looked around, and nodded. There was a thoughtful way about him that rendered his carrying-on deceptive. He sensed that the confidentiality of the letter's contents was more important for that moment than why a liveryman might read.

He led his horse off well out of earshot, handed me down the letter, and ordered me to read.

The message's essence was that he was betrayed: Dozens of well-equipped men under sway of an infamous Welsh Lord were on their way. Knowing we transported a fortune of goods and serfs, they intended to intercept us on our way to Ludlow. Further, they held his brother, His Grace, hostage, for he was betrayed as well. And lastly, His Eminence ordered Sidroc to immediately re-direct to Hereford.

He ordered confidential response by the same messenger.

Having been a day and a half already headed for Hereford, Sidroc might have viewed his decision with pride, but he was somber. He frowned while his mind turned steadily on the situation. He shouted for water, took the letter from me—turned it over—saw it blank on the back.

"You can write as well as read?"

"Yes, Sire. I will need goose feather some stain and ash. They will serve."

At that, he ordered camp made—surprising most, but pleasing all—the heat being awful. Immediately he ordered pickets out to high ground, and brambles and rods to be cut for a surrounding barricade that night.

Housecarls and squires exchanged glances, learning the general drift of the letter from his action. Our armed group was such that they knew only an equal number of brigands—or more—could necessitate such action.

They could not know the force was threefold our number—even more.

Faux angel wings from Alfred's show properties were a good source of fine feathers, and several men, Sidroc and I included, knew the making of crude ink. The stain was blood, in fact his own.

While the messenger waited—a fresh horse exchanged for the spent—Sidroc sat impatiently as I sharpened several quills. We then got down to it—I had not written anything in some time. But they had drilled me so often, and I was so young with hands nimble, I was sure of my strokes.

He was brief—and the only sign he made of his thoughts behind his answer was just before beginning; he disparaged the word 'hostage' to describe His Eminence's brother's situation, and there was no smile in the saying of it.

Then he told His Eminence he needed a dozen or more housecarls or whoever sent as fast as possible. By changing directions early, he had two or two-and-a-half unhindered days, but they would then be overtaken up by the Welshmen when they realized the change.

"What does that say? I did not say that."

He pointed to my large penned words at the beginning, and I reminded him it was customary to begin messages to fine figures by invoking our Savior, His Father, and the Holy Spirit.

I restrained a gasp—for Sidroc was anything but joking, and sent off the messenger with a warning not to get caught, and the consequences if it happened: "Your uncle is my undertenant, and if you ride off and get your throat slit, I'll take it out on him."

And the man was off, taking a grim hold of his leads. Sidroc meant no overstatement but a promise, and the messenger knew it.

Then when I moved to return to duties—he stopped me by reaching out with his foot. He sat on his stool and drank only a light beer, and pulled me back roughly: "Now by hanging you, I would assure confidentiality. No one here knows that we surely are pursued, or how many there are. And who! If so . . . ," and he trailed off, and looked at the spreading camp grimly, and I knew what he meant. Most of his men would flee, for Welshman would kill everyone not fit for the serf merchant. Horse, liveryman, and arms of all those slain were valuable of themselves. Further, the Welsh would enjoy slaughtering Saxons or Saxon adherents, perhaps even prolonging its doing.

"I will say nothing but do my job, Sire."

"Of course you will say nothing, and you will do your job. Especially say nothing to that woman of yours. Otherwise I will have you, your wife, and the whelp in her belly flayed alive. Now get to it, you upstart little turd. I will know the moment you leaked word that a host of Welsh are on our ass."

It was best I avoided talking to anyone. For all noticed that Sidroc stayed away from ale, on alert, and remained surly. He would have slain someone asleep on watch—in fact, said it—and his eyes were everywhere.

The livery—traces and all tackle—were a frayed mess each day. The oxen were driven too hard, as were most of the animals. The carpenter and his sons did what they could, but the massive carts—buildings on wheels, in fact—were coming apart in joint and coupling.

No one asked what the letter said—nor did I give them opportunity to ask. The bugs arose from a nearby wetland by the bushel-weight, and the fires were made to smoke more—itself not a good thing.

"I want your pickets on the highest places. I want them to look sharp for fires during the night."

I do not remember the name of Sidroc's two sergeants, but they had fought together for the King and Archbishop frequently and knew their business—even if the others remained inexperienced.

In fact, I was sure Sidroc had informed his two sergeants what His Eminence had warned. For those two needed no urging from Sidroc.

I made my decision, however. When I lay next to Cwenburh that night, I took her close and told her she—in the event of coming chaos—should keep enough close at hand to survive in the bush, and to escape in the confusion. We very likely would be apart if the fray were to begin.

"I can say no more. But you and the child must survive. Could you find your way back to Elstow?"

"Without you, Cuthwin? Not on my spirit's posterior. I won't find my way anywhere. We go where each other goes."

We were not that far removed from others—we could not argue the matter. I told her life was better than death. It was not just hers but the child as well. Also, that she should not blaspheme, especially now.

I felt in my breast her resolve. Cwenburh was of a nature—and remained so—making me wonder if she were possessed of the same demons that dwelled inside the thorny presence of Waddles, the donkey, who Father Abbot loved so.

Cwenburh's mind was bright—brighter than the best of us—but her bones, sinews, and God-given stubbornness were soulmates of Waddles. And God forgive me for saying this, even nearly these eighty years hence. But that is part of my purpose herein; no saint, you see, could ever state such trespass on so good a soul as Cwenburh-of-Loe.

In recalling those years along the Marches of Wales I cannot say I ever met a Welshman any greedier or crueler than a Saxon, for they are both God's creations. However, I was young, having just turned my nineteenth year. I was not yet knowledgeable how brother will betray brother; furthermore, that great Holy Men and ordinary folk when possessed by greed will stoop to any foulness of deed.

But youth is a vulnerable period of life, for a young man's knowledge is small but opinion of his own abilities large. This is the age that is the sinew—the backbone of armies and brigands who visit violence upon others by the design of Great Men.

So, Sidroc-the-Old—though corrupt of soul—benefited by four-plus decades, much of it in violent struggle. He knew by events His Grace sold out His Eminence, his brother, in hopes of gaining the sale of all our train. This was much more of a sum than I even vaguely appreciated, especially calculating horse, tackle, and weaponry of those killed.

Sidroc-the-Old oversaw us negotiating the remnant of a road to Hereford, urging us along with as much haste as possible. Those first two days after receiving the letter, he even worked us all through the heat of the day. He was more knowledgeable than all of us in tricks to accomplish this. The most valued art was the manner to keep the oxen cool enough to pull; he had them covered with cloth, and a train of the women and boys to haul buckets of water, tossing it over the cloth spread across the great backs of the beasts, and ordering extra rations to the keep them fed and happy.

So doing, they pulled as if it were much cooler.

And nobody, including him, could ride; but tackle was removed or loosened from all horses, and all were given as much water as possible. This was more than the humans, especially the wretches of Alfred's train.

Several dropped—especially the older women. One of the few elderly men was just left, despite the howls of protest. Most knew—certainly I did—that when one of the housecarls went back after we'd proceeded a way, it was to end it for the poor soul—dead he would be unable to inform about our vulnerabilities.

And at frequent turn and rise of the road, our pair of rear observers would arrive, report, water themselves, exchange horses, then ride out.

Sidroc all the while noting everything.

Then, in God's unknowing Grace, on the third day—towards None— it was from before us that we heard great horses. At once the alarm was sounded. Weapons were drawn, horses were mounted. We without weapons experienced our innards stretching tighter than drum-tops; children and women dived under the wagons. Hence it was with immeasurable relief and prayers of thanks when the horsemen turned out to be more than a dozen mounted housecarls led by Lenoc, Sidroc's son.

Sidroc nodded seeing them, asked if they had come by the way of Jerusalem. I remember well his son's response: "No, father, but we did stop to make fine sport in several of your favorite places."

It was not only a vast relief to see them, but to learn that Lenoc was just the opposite of his father—optimistic, and joyful of nature and word.

He announced at once that they'd come to kill Welshmen, and looked forward to it. Furthermore, without bothering to keep the fact unsaid, this would include "His Betrayalship," who he heaped scandalous words upon.

"I will have his red hair in a wad and wipe my arse with it."

And this resulted in the first laughter heard in days—even from bound, troubled people. For he mimed this act while voicing it—rising high in his stirrups. He criticized his father for allowing Alfred's women being used so thoughtlessly, claiming he and his housecarls pick of the best.

He ended his sporting words by advising we camp at once—then his father to lead all armed men back trail and kill every Welshman found.

"We look forward to the sale of stout Welsh horse and equipment, Father. I consider the profit for sale of looted equipment all ours for coming here in such damned Lammastide heat."

Sidroc groused at his son's behavior, but all became of an easier mood, not only because we were now powerfully defended. We also sensed that Sidroc was helpless against his son's mirth and impulse, so high was his regard for him. We all benefited that the elder's surly moods were watered down by Lenoc's nature.

Lenoc was indeed of a randy, sacrilegious way. He showed this again, by remembering aloud several of the women from Alfred's last visit three years before. Finally, even Cwenburh had to recognize that Alfred-of-Aylesbury offered more than Saint's mummings and children's amusements by foreigners during his stops at fair and festival.

It was then I told her a bit about Frog, those years back, and his sinful debaucheries, ballyhooed by others, if only mentioned in lament by their doer.

"I thought, Cuthwin, harlots were all warty, filthy hags with pestilence about them," she replied.

For she made friends of some. Such was her spirit that she viewed them with no less kindness or sisterhood. It was God's gift with people given her, for Cwenburh always kept profuse kindness and love for any-one who did not visit pain and violence on others, no matter their place.

Our lot continued to improve.

At Compline just before, Sidroc-the-Younger arrived—the elder son— and with him were four of his housecarls and squires. His men were powerfully and richly armed; Sidroc-the-Younger was unlike his junior sibling, Lenoc—more like his father, save of even fewer words, and never allowing outburst of temper.

Now we were a formidable army in my view, and there was great comfort, though the night fires were kept going and barricades peopled. Spirited talk—actually gossip—was more common with the presence of Lenoc and his men. Sidroc-the-Younger had no more luck in dampening Lenoc than his father. During the evening, rear-guards brought in a hind and roebuck for meat.

Lenoc celebrated this. He spoke of fattening up the women, giving them back strength. So it was hoped that some of the wild beast's meat— if only bones—would be given to us. It was at Matins, for indeed we now had a young priest with us, that Sidroc-the-Younger's squire fetched me.

Himself sat before a station fire, stirring it thoughtfully with a stick, studying the glow of it while talking.

"My father says you read and write?"

"Yes, Sire."

"I do too. They taught me in the Monastery which is where you learned. I know how I left, my father owns a half-dozen hundreds and the Holy Brothers owe him. But how did you?"

"I'm a freedman; my apprenticeship was served, Sire."

"You lie."

"I am a freedman, Sire. A liveryman."

"If I was given a pound of silver for every liveryman in this entire land who read and wrote, I would have nothing."

"But, Sire, fact is, I am a liveryman, and an able one, surely you've seen."

"I have. I see much, including some things unseen. You even use monks' wordcraft."

He stirred away and thought. It occurred to me that his mistrustful heart suspected I was part of some distant threat sent into Hereford to apprise things. I might, perhaps, be in league with the Welsh or others powerful.

My suspicions were sound, for in the next breath, he said, "We have few friends in the direction of Elstow Abbey, which is a Norman outpost, in my thinking."

So the cloth with its holy emblem that saved us a few days before—or bought us time—now functioned in the reverse by indicating dark allegiance.

I repeated how we came by the cloth and bread. He removed the stick from the fire, and put it aside.

"What I can do is get that woman of yours with the deformed mouth, stand her by, and threaten to slit your throat until she tells me the truth, you dissembling toad. So tell me the truth and perhaps save yourself. This land crawls with enemies of His Eminence, and so enemies of my father."

So I did. I would rather that, than risk what he had promised, for like his father, Sidroc-the-Younger did not employ empty threats. At the very least, I could beg for Cwenburh's life—and the child.

His thoughts—other than giving a toss of his head—he kept to himself. "Return and do your work. I will consider this on our way to Hereford."

It was with absolute resolve I would keep this interview from Cwenburh. But such was her eye this would be difficult. Returning to our shelter under the wagon, she had questions, and I emphasized how he had quizzed me about my ability in written Saxon.

"He seemed satisfied enough," I told her, and I believed it.

"He seems a serious, suspicious sort."

Whether she was sounding me or not, I feigned sleep, and held her to me, which always put her to sleep. Hopefully, by morning her thoughts would be drawn elsewhere. How, I always wondered, at these close, quiet times, could such a tiny bit of humanity contain such ferocity and energy?

For certain, any escape attempt now would be self-destructive—acting as a positive indictment of bad purpose. It was Hereford for us, and there I must use every bit of thoughtful craft God gave me to try and resolve our uncertain situation.

Book 3

The venerable Cuthwin tells the beginning of his innovative vocation in Hereford and how his wanderings began. Also, he speaks of dastardly events experienced by him and his worthy wife, Cwenburh. His account continues, by the Grace of God, including his encounters with strange and gifted souls. Lastly, he describes those of the Devil's craft, and how their ways create misery and evil for Godly men and women.

◇ 1

The City of Hereford in those Saxon days was much simpler than that of today. Now there is a Cathedral and Priory—plus castle and stout fortifications built by the wealthy Normans who take no chances with Welshmen, preferring to keeping them suppressed. Before them the Saxons' imperfect guard caused them losing Hereford to the ruthless Welshman, and many were killed, with property and persons ending up burned or as spoils.

But when Sidroc-the-Old's party and train arrived, it was Lammastide to the day, and there was great relief when we crossed the Wye Bridge and passed over the row ditch[24] and through the gated walls.

While passing the ditch and wall, we encountered busy Lammastide markets and fairs both in and out. I had never seen so many people in one place, even at Peterborough. Cwenburh's mouth gaped open at the sight of this wonder, for she and I were now allowed to walk together.

With our arrival, a great send-up and sport resulted from the clear evidence and outcome of Alfred-of-Aylesbury's train. Children followed, marveling at the massive wheeled carts—and adults hooted and made catcalls after us. They shouted curses at Alfred's dead soul, for news of his end preceded us—and his wife Gertyn stood inside the leading cart. (Women and children chose to ride the last mile into Hereford.) Gertyn heaped severe curses back, and she was joined in like spirit and behavior by the other women of our train.

It was a most formidable arrival.

These abominations exchanged left no doubt that residents of Hereford, low or high born, did not pity Alfred or his kindred. Sidroc-the-Old was joined by Sidroc-the-Younger riding in front, noses held up—whereas Lenoc made great sport of it all, a natural showman before a crowd.

---

[24] Row ditch. A security design surrounding a town or village. A mote when filled with water.

Lenoc, on his fine horse, cavorted north and south along the train. He enjoyed causing laughter, and for every coarse word and expression given, he made return threefold—his better and wittier than theirs. He picked up children, and tossed them on the back of his mount to their vast joy, until the poor horse crawled with them.

Then, well inside the gates, standing on an elevated platform, I recognized the Reeve whom I had encountered before and appeared as a vast man of imposing girth and height. He was dressed entirely in rich, black cloth, with a cross and chain coiled round his neck. On his head he wore a cleric's hat. He was unsmiling and greeted Sidroc-the-Old with a sober nod.

I guessed it was His Eminence, but my inexperience in city matters and great men could be forgiven at that point in life, for of course it was His Eminence's Chief Secretary. It was a three-sided courtyard where he and his Reeve stood, and we all rode in. The noise and outburst of arrival now gone, the crowds absented themselves, understandably reticent from appearing before this powerful officer.

This was a somber setting, and the grim nature of the Secretary sustained that ambience and nature of things.

"Sidroc-the-Old, may God bless you. We prayed for you, hearing of the desperate situation."

"Any word of His Grace, the Holy Bishop of Ludlow? Have the Welshmen skinned him alive, perhaps?"

That set the Secretary into a great frown. Sidroc-the-Younger made no gesture or sign, but glanced curtly at his sibling Lenoc who was about to laugh, instead forcing himself to render a somber face, though he did so poorly.

The Secretary allowed himself a long pause, perhaps thinking the comment's sarcastic aim might diffuse into air,

"We pray for His Eminence's beloved brother, and safe ransom."

Sidroc and his sons dismounted and followed the Reeve and Secretary into the massive stone-structured Bishop's House—actually, more a castle in today's sense, including iron gates, a rare and expensive attachment during these early times.

The train was left in the square, and the sergeants ordered us to stay around the carts, and to avoid any nonsense. They then showed the women where to get the necessities of water and such.

The carpenter, myself, and his sons, however, were escorted—under guard—to taking the oxen and tackle to His Eminence's livery. The rich and powerful man had an extensive stable and several workmen to attend, all overseen by a gnarled old Saxon liveryman. His apprentices greedily took in hand the fine oxen, though harshly criticized the tackle and diverse riggings: "Looks like ignorant cotsets did this work!"

The carpenter bristled, but we were pushed about by guards to be returned to the now-chocked carts. Several of the livery apprentices called out to our backs: "It's His Eminence's auction block for you dogs!"

Added to this were hooting and mean-spirited laughter.

Upon return we sat upon the stone and dirt in dismal mood, for it appeared promises made under duress on way to Hereford were forgotten. Alfred-of-Ayelesbury's train were all as one—grist for negotiation.

Families came together in knots, the remorse of their anticipated bondage causing sadness—even weeping. Cwenburh was becoming pale, and I wondered if her time was getting close. She leaned against me, and I held her up.

"God help us, Cuthwin. I am closer than I thought. The women were right. I couldn't escape now."

And indeed, Cwenburh was massive and walked with difficulty. It was even hotter inside this stone court—away from even a vagrant breeze. The stench of the city was overpowering—even to those used to the smells of croft and village. Flies gathered everywhere, for with Lammastide, chores of His Eminence's people went begging.

Though allowed to haul wellwater, when the children begged for food and the parents naturally asked the guards for it, we discovered a change at once: Guards were no longer squires, or those under employ of housecarls—these had gone. These guards were dark, knobby sorts equipped with a stout club or staff—not any accoutrement of metal—a poor man wields nothing requiring mail or breastplate.

So these beasts struck or hit those begging for food, causing blood wounds and even bones breaking. Immediately, requests for anything ceased.

Now atop the heat, stench, and all else, we were subject to immediate physical harm if complaint were made. It was difficult to keep the children silent—and these guards would strike a child—and did.

Finally, an apparent sergeant-guard yelled at his underlings in mid-stroke: "Be easy, you turd! Make blood and splinters of them, and you'll have His Eminence's Secretary up our arses."

Then he shouted to us all that we'd be fed soon enough, and to keep still or it would go even worse for us. "You're just a miserable lot of harlots and criminals who are not deserving of honest food and shelter."

Despite this awfulness and cruelty, life did not pause. Cwenburh became increasingly distressed. Several women, plus even the dour Gertyn, made something of a decent bed platform under one of the wagons.

In fact, it was Gertyn who shoved me away.

"Cuthwin, do not attend anymore. Let my daughters. Time is close for her. Thank God the sun is going and this heat will lift."

Through the night I prayed fervently to our Savior for Cwenburh's safe delivery and the well-being of the child we had waited so long for—whose coming would be changing our lives so drastically.

I was of croft and paddock and knew well birth and birthing. I was familiar how a ewe can be made to miscarry by even a minor mishap of treatment. And for the past ten days, poor Cwenburh experienced great violations of proper treatment, she no more than a girl—less in weight to a stout ewe.

My expectations were dismal—for I knew if I lost her I would come adrift in this world. Alone I would no longer want to occupy ground or purpose. I hope God has forgiven me for those selfish thoughts. Because it was those prayers I believe that brought punishment down.

Close to Prime of the second day of our coming to Hereford, the carpenter's wife solemnly took me aside and told me our child had never breathed, and that Cwenburh remained in trouble; but with prayer and the help of our Savior, "She could survive. So pray, Cuthwin."

I remained in prayer that day, and one of Alfred's daughters, Matilda, would bring me news how Cwenburh progressed and, though no better, was not worse: "If only a healing woman might be paid, or fresh medicines be bought—but they took all our money and whatever potions and herbs we kept with us. The poor thing is left with prayers, though always a good thing."

For with Lammastide being celebrated just a few furlongs distant, there would be herbalists and healing women of all skills plying their crafts and wares in their niches and pavilions. Wondrous elixirs, potions, and salves were had by the dozens; and of course hands-on services. All these medicines and applications took much knowledge and came dear. Celebrations during fairs and markets to mark holy and saint's days increased chances of great healings, of course, through God's grace.

But these miracles began with the paying of King's silver.

Not only were we without money but branded by Alfred's previous sinful acts. At that time, I did not know that scorn resulting from sin indicated possible advantage for business people. I was to soon learn this was the way of Saxons and, certainly of Normans, God help us.

Even at my prayers, my day became more wrought with despair: A hand on my shoulder, harsh and firm, called me to an interview with Sidroc-the-Younger. Its owner did not care I was at prayer or the purpose of it.

"Up you! Sidroc wants to see you. Now."

I was shoved ahead of a guard—kept moving fast. We went into His Eminence's residence—a warren of passages and courts, past them into St. Guthlac's Church, composed of just a simple transept and apse.

At the end of St. Guthlac's sat Sidroc-the-Younger in contemplation on a fine carved family seat and rail. He wore a plain tunic and shoes, was bareheaded and unarmed. I was left alone with him—in fact, we were entirely alone in the church.

It was a strange—even irreligious place I thought then—to discuss non-holy business.

"My father promised you something, is this right? He told me that."

"Yes. To maintain our freedom and right of travel, with the approval of His Eminence's court."

"His Eminence's court is otherwise occupied and will remain so for a long time."

His sighed and looked up at a carving—very old and fine—of St. Guthlac. He was a much-revered holy man on the fens, and I felt sad even at that terrible time for abandoning the fens.

Sidroc seemed to be—perhaps was—different than before.

"A promise made is kept, even if one of the parties is tainted by Norman monks. You take your wife and go where you will." Then he turned to me, and, raising a finger, pointed at the ceiling, "But you misstep here, and I will hang you, Liveryman."

"Sir, I cannot go at once. My wife lost a child the previous evening and is gravely ill in the courtyard."

"I have lost two wives and many children. Such is God's will."

I was emboldened—if such a promise was being kept—to risk more, for Cwenburh was risking her life: "My items, our items. I have simple but needed tools with them—to get by."

"You have your lives. Stop whining and go."

The same guard came in—by what signal, I cannot say, but it was on the mark. He shoved me out the way I came, and I was struggling with the good news amongst the bad when he took me hard by the shoulder, and pulled me into a small archway. He looked about cautiously, then drew me towards himself, but somewhat more gently. It was with relief I saw him put aside his staff.

"I have heard you can write our language."

"I can."

"My wife is desperate to tell her mother plain things of family, and in her village—many leagues south. I get no peace. My wife says there are priests there who read. I know a way to get the message to her mother. If you write it, I can see you are rewarded, for I heard your plight."

He was ready for my answer, although truly I did not have any choice.

When I consented, he at once led me inside. In a tiny nook with a single candle he had gathered paper, goose feather, and ink—from where I cannot say, but they were of good quality.

His brutishness hid a schemer.

The guard's information was what a daughter would want to tell her mother not seen in over a decade—of children, home, and such. It took an hour, at most. Drying the ink, he rolled it up and put it in a small round case.

"Now follow."

He knew the warrens of the residence well, and we came to a doorway where lay two guards so besotted with ale, they were asleep. A bucket lay on its side, and the companionway reeked unmistakably of strong, barley ale—not the cheap sort.

On the fens, such Saxon ambrosia was rarely afforded, and when it was, the eelmen could not attend work for two days after.

He kicked one's leg aside that blocked the doorway, and once inside a single window admitted light to see. There upon a platform were numerous stacks of plundered items, the responsibility of the guards.

My escort took me, turned me as one might a stubborn animal, and pointed at the lot, "Take two things. Quickly. This is your pay. Say anything, and you will suffer triple what I do, and I promise that."

In fact, he pushed me forward and there was so many items, my head spun around—desperate as I was with Cwenburh's awful plight. But though never of warrior's brawn or imposing looks, God in his kindness gave me plain wit to make up for it.

Knowing I was being paid in items not his, in fact we were taking part in a theft, God forgive, though, I did not hesitate. I choose a beautiful Saxon knife in a sewn pig-leather case and a wrought metal clasp, an item of plenty value. He looked to the ceiling in disgust when I took the clasp.

"Greedy dog!"

He was about to renege, but a sound of laughter outside the window caused him to bolt. He shoved me out—again kicked aside the guard's leg—with a bit more force than needed—and told me to make sure I hid the items; then he turned me on a heel, and warned, "And you keep that clasp hidden until gone from here, goddamn you. Now as Sidroc has directed, I will tell the sergeant of your freedom. But you and I? We have never spoken."

With a parting shove, I was sent into the courtyard—hot and reeking again with the rising heat. I was told at once that Cwenburh still lived, but Matilda, herself having just recently given birth, cautioned, "The girl has the stamina of a mare; if it were me, I would have joined God. None of us have seen the likes of it. Surely it is your prayers. Our prayers."

"I am free now, and will fetch her what quickly I can at market. Tell me exactly what I must get."

"How might you pay, God help us, with thin air?"

In ten days, Cwenburh came to trust Matilda more than anyone else, and indeed the two had similar spirits, though the latter was experienced in so many more ways than Cwenburh and myself. With Alfred and Gertyn, who sullied the word 'Mother' by calling the train's women 'daughters,' Matilda led a difficult and sordid life.

I showed Matilda the clasp and knife.

"These are a long ways from thin air, Matilda. The clasp is worth much."

She gasped, reached out, and, grabbing my hand and the clasp, closed my hand with her two around it.

"Are you mad?! That adorned the kirtle of a rich woman, certainly slain! In the market, you would be set on like fleas upon an old dog when you show that to barter. People will ask what is this poor bedraggled devil doing with it? How did he come by it? All would ask that first, and word would fly about like a flock of rooks. Jesus, save us, Cuthwin. Use good sense. Bartering that will take time and the right place."

She begged me to hide it, and I knew she was right. With no time for thought, when my eye set on such a fine clasp, I allowed my greed to rule. Surely, the clasp was a lesser version of that great meathound: poor people do not come by finery honestly.

That left the knife—the one item I could use for making dozens of items to survive in field and hills. But though well wrought, a freedman having possession of it would arouse no suspicion.

Matilda indicated it.

"Sell it! It should bring three shillings, if you hold your price. Now go! But keep that clasp hidden, Cuthwin, or you and it will be seized by the undersheriff, who in Hereford, as with most places, is as rotten a soul as Satan might ever create."

I left Matilda—who repeated her warning and told me again the potions needed. It was difficult to set the price of such a fine knife as this. In daily tasks, especially when making one's way overland, it was a necessity, a lifetime companion.

Yet I needed help for Cwenburh, and the knife and clasp were a windfall—God reaching down to help her. After a momentary confrontation with the guards about my new freedom—I walked around them and out, reversing my path upon arrival.

I would to the fair and market. Desperate as I was, I did not care about the risk.

It was a somber irony that the previous year's Lammastide fair and market I had spent at Peterborough. It was there when Cwenburh and I kept company together for the first time, and it was a joyful time. I was given the day free by both Brother Cassartorius and Gilbert, the latter knowing the reason for my increased exuberance over market days.

It was a grand day spent following Cwenburh and her mother Gytha from stall to shop, hearing them arguing—trading and bartering—for a year's worth of diverse items needed.

I was their attendant, carrying this—fetching that—sharing in indignation when price was too high, or too low. And the endless joy experiencing all these different peoples and hundreds of items never seen.

And all the time, as I scolded her later, Cwenburh wove her clever women's web about me, capturing me forever.

Though Lammastide at Hereford was distant, it was not dissimilar to that at Peterborough, itself a great place. Yet my feelings and necessity for this one could hardly be more starkly different in spirit.

I felt no joy now, threading my way through the crowds and arrays—keeping alert for the dozens of thieves and such who populate these events. For working in livery at Peterborough Monastery, I experienced many fairs, markets, and holy day festivals during my seven years.

On any Lammastide fair, pitfalls and advantages accompanied such occasions when money, property, and business all came into one. Bad people swarmed and it was for their presence the undersheriff had wardens circulating, their tassels of office dangling prominently from their waist. And as with all fairs and markets, there were stop-boards at the gates and other entries to the town.

At these stop-boards, taxes and tariffs were collected. The first geld was collected on arrival, and the second leaving—by whoever's authority presided over fair or market, which in Hereford's case was the beneficial grace of His Eminence. These many decades gone by, I can say Normans conduct such affairs with a far greedier and more severe hand. If Normans find one avoiding or holding out fees and such, or sniff out thieves, he is hanged or executed at once.

In Saxon times, if criminals were apprehended doing bad deed, they would not necessarily be hanged. Saxons altogether kept a looser weave on things: Some minor officials at gate could be bribed; also, bold truants could slip out at night without paying, evidently as Alfred-of-Aylesbury had done—or was said to have done.

In years prior to Norman conquest, Saxons all took risks and short cuts, for if caught, often got off with nothing but a drubbing by rod or staff.

It occurred to me the knife might be easily identified as stolen—as it surely was—because the case was finely sewn pig-leather and could identify an owner. Such work had its own design and to those familiar would identify it. The knife, however, was of sound craftsmanship; but dozens of such were around countrywide. When bought, they often came without a case.

Being caught would not help Cwenburh, so I removed the case and put it with the clasp for later bargain. I anticipated a need of it.

When coming out of the inner gate, I was paid little mind by the wardens. I suppose this was because I was poor in appearance and empty-handed. But when I approached the outside wall—inside which the most expensive and privileged pavilions were arranged—a warden came up, looked me up and down, and pointed, half in jest, and half otherwise. "A cotset like you must have something to sell, or you are a thief, or both."

The dog was half in his cups, for wardens often were favored at every shop selling drink and food. This one had made a day of it and it wasn't yet Sext. I said I was a livery worker in need of repast. I asked him the best shop for a good heavy slab of lammasloaf and strong barley ale, and as I guessed he was a walking advocate for one. His favorite was his brother-in-law's which was outside of the walls.

What I sought indeed was outside the walls and row-ditch for inside the walls were rich traders and merchants with finery such as fabrics and metals, beyond a poor person's means.

It being summer and long dry, the row-ditch itself was the place of livestock markets—where temporary paddocks were easily made, and paths and temporary steps were worn or installed. For there, a herdsman was at his keenest and most vociferous. A great collection of voices came from there from both creatures and men.

Vendors were also down there selling wares held before them on trays—knowing that where there is trading, silver pennies and shillings might part from a usually tightly closed purse.

As I passed over the row-ditch, flies and smells nearly lifted me up, and I hurried beyond. I surveyed vendors' boards and pavilions outside the row-ditch and immediately encountered the neighborhood I required.

My feelings of guilt were on increase.

I endured anguish knowing that Cwenburh's ordeal was, in the end, my doing. She had been willing to stay at Loe while I traipsed about on Monastery circuit throughout their holdings in duty to the Subcellarer and Father Abbot.

Now we were a hundred leagues and half again distant from our homes. With dismal determination, I got on with it.

Along the shops in the wide middle row demarked with cloth partitions were carved wooden signs common to specific trades and business. I looked for a buckler-sized pence, for this indicated a goods and money trader. Soon I was looking up at such a sign hung from a post by woven line and painted a bright silver, the largest of the group.

I noted this pence had the previous king's portrait on it, so it had been a business established for some time—one who believed a keen wood-carving worthy of its craft, even if out-of-date.

This was, like all of them, businesses that exchanged in money and bought things for same. It was common then for one merchant to do both.

Indeed, there were a half-dozen of them. Not getting proper price at one, I could go to another. At Peterborough, I never entered one of these, but waited outside for a Brother who collected tariffs from them— and they always spoke with disdain for their proprietors.

"They are cheats and demon-worshipers, worldly, ill-spoken London-ers," one Brother always told tell me while putting Father Abbot's fee in one of the great Cellarers' embossed wallets. Indeed my responsibility was to carry it for the Brother, which made me unseemly proud.

But I hesitated now; which one of these half-dozen should I select? What were they like inside? Were all run by Londoners, notorious sorts from any part of the world? They spoke Saxon with a harsh accent, annoying to the ear. And it was said they always did so rapidly, especially in trading, to confuse.

But it was the place with the grand wooden sign I entered.

Inside was partitioned by hangings of ordinary cloth made to improve the look of the place. Items were placed here and there, but not strewn—in rows by type.

Sitting on a stool manipulating stones upon a strange flat board was a small Saxon wearing a high-peaked hat of red cloth decorated with a partridge tail feather. Seeing me, he covered the board with a cloth. My distraction had somehow delayed me spotting, to my left, sitting cross-legged on the floor, the largest human creature I'd ever seen. He polished metal implements, including ware and pots to a good shine—his lower lip held between his teeth as he labored. He wore plain leather breeches, tunic, and turnshoes.

At once fear took me: A half-dozen wardens with staffs couldn't con-tain such a beast if he got loose, or set out with violence on his mind. The proprietor said proudly, "That is Cyrus, whom many call 'The Great.'"

When Cyrus looked up—a gaze like an ox distracted at his trough—his brows straightened, and I saw eyes that reflected more than the sense of an ox, yet thankfully like an ox did not contain an evil gleam in them—which gave me balm. He pointed at himself and admitted, "Yes. 'The Great.' This is true."

Then he chuckled and returned to work.

"And I am Ahulf, owner here, a benefice given me by God's kind grace. What do you desire: To sell, buy, trade, or some combination? I do all of that, fairly, of course. Cyrus can vouch for that."

Cyrus grunted, put aside a pot—took up another far larger one.

Ahulf looked as capable of sniffing out a lie as a rat might a bit of suet. I decided nothing would be gained in couching the truth.

"My wife is within the city. She lost a child this day, and remains at death's door, and I need to sell my knife for medicines."

And I took out the knife and placed it on the cloth covering his device. He at once held both palms out, gesturing his helplessness.

"I am sorry for you and wish you and your wife God's Mercy. But I cannot give more money for an item than it is worth, or I would myself be at death's door. Would we not, Cyrus?"

He grunted again—but now looked up at me, then to the knife. He started to say something, but did not. At that point I did not know Cyrus's other skill nor how he had come by his epithet.

"Then, it is worth nothing?"

"I did not say that. By the way, what is your name?"

"Cuthwin."

"So, Cuthwin. I did not say that. What I said was that it is a plain knife. I see many and have many. So it is not worth but, at most, two pence."

Since it was worth seven or eight times that, I struggled down wrath. By such cruel dealings, no wonder he needed someone of Cyrus's mass about to prevent having harm done him.

I picked up the knife to go elsewhere, and was too angry to consider that a wall with two legs like Cyrus could prevent me from going anywhere—or indeed, just take the knife from me and kick or throw me from the door.

Ahulf put his hand out and took me by the sleeve, admitting he might do better, considering the circumstances, reminding me he was a man given to our Savior's example of giving pity to those troubled,

He asked Cyrus if that were not the case, to which—as he always did—Cyrus grunted an assent.

Cyrus the Great betrayed a trace of a smile, and thanks be to God, I understood I had begun the path of bartering, and as such must wrestle on. It was my first trading.

After all, it was what Gytha did often at market—many times both she and daughter rained bad words upon their opponent and received them in turn. And this was done a half-dozen times in a day without bad feelings afterward.

During our bargaining, Ahulf swept away the cloth covering his numbers device and attacked its stones like a crazed baker—checking and re-checking numbers that he tossed about. Always finding Cyrus in agreement with his calculations. He would point at the board, and accuse, "Do you, a liveryman," for by now, he knew most of me, "doubt the numbers from this ancient, venerable device? My profits are just not there."

In the end, I could get no more than one schilling, three pence, which was just enough for the medicines, but I didn't know what sum—if any-thing—might remain.

I was tired—had I taken so long that Cwenburh might have died, or grown beyond help? It was so hot I was drenched in sweat, angry, and still possessed of that awful sense of guilt.

So, I took the money.

I now had to shop for medicines, get them and perhaps even fetch a healing woman. Cyrus stood with the ease of a smaller man, but his size made his action appear like a mountain sprouting from earth.

"I suppose you now need medicines? I often have need of them, and know one of the best."

While putting on his wide-brimmed hat, he looked at Ahulf who nod-ded back in agreement, "You will do well with Cyrus, God bless him. Cyrus knows his medicine people."

I followed as he bent low, emerging into the hot midday air reeking with animal smells and thick with ubiquitous swarms of flies. He swept absently at the air, and gestured me to come alongside him.

Everyone, or so it seemed, looked at Cyrus as he loped along, and most greeted him and he them—sometimes with a high wave of his hand. They asked him about fights—praising past and asking about future struggles. He saw my confusion, for fighting was strictly forbidden, and despite size, he seemed a peaceful sort. He stopped—removed his hat and mopped his thick head of hair while smiling and looking down at me.

"On the day before each festival Sabbath, I wrestle all comers in the outer arena. These matches are popular and make money. I am bitten and gouged always. Potions and salves of Mistress Braugh have saved me many a miserable fester, and she is true in price."

I was—even at that urgent moment—flummoxed with such a notion.

"God forbid! Who would pay to see men harm one another?"

Cyrus looked down, hesitating a step; his brows knitted up, and he sighed. "Young Cuthwin, there are many strange doings in this world and people will pay to see them, God forgive us all."

Then he resumed, but once more was intercepted by children wanting him to heft them up, and he did so on the move giving good sport. In a few more furlongs, we arrived where healers were set up. There were nearly a dozen pavilions, each belong to different sort of practitioners.

Those with signs used a diverse array of carved symbols to inform passersby of their skills and crafts. Most carved images were inspired by images from the heavens or garden, some both. For all understood healing to be in concert with the heavens, and gardens a source of strong potion and salve.

Cyrus stopped before one with a carving of a man holding a splinter of a waning moon—it was very weathered.

"Mistress Braugh is sharp with words but expert in craft, no doubt. At one time, she was a York beauty, with great men beating on the doors at her quarters."

When he entered her pavilion, I saw an elderly woman, dressed in mostly white cloth but garnished with deep blue cloth, and further enhanced with patches of many colors.

Her hair was long and grey—almost white, and left unbound flowing down her shoulders. Her features were like a hawk—her nose as long as any Saxon woman might have. Her height and frame was so slender, she seemed an angle with movement. No doubt, Mistress Braugh cast an imposing, unique figure.

She was castigating her assistant in an even but severe voice. Her assistant was the first black-skinned human I had seen, blacker than a moonless night. I stood flat while Mistress Braugh cast a gaze on Cyrus, closed her eyes and moaned, "Gouged and bitten again, Cyrus, you great oaf? Someday you will fail in the cure, and they'll lop off your leg or arm. Who is that green-around-the-gills boy with you—did you break his arm? His eyes are popping out! Has he never seen an African? Or a girl? Which is it? If I am to be a show for simpletons, I want King's silver."

"My wife just lost a child and is close to death and needs medicines," I blurted out. And I repeated the three sorts of herbs Matilda said I must get. Idle talk ended.

"It will take three pence for the medicines, and I'll attend and apply them for one shilling two. That is my fee and I do not barter. I am not dealing in sheep."

"I have one shilling three, good lady, and no more, so I must just get the medicines and let Alfred's daughters apply them."

With no bartering or nonsense, I would get back all the sooner with medicines in hand.

She looked to Cyrus and they held upon each other for a moment—his eyes asked for what I didn't. She slapped the African girl on her tiny buttocks and scolded, "Eavesdropping! Get to work! You don't understand Saxon anyway, you twerp."

"I do."

"No, you don't."

She glared at Cyrus, then extended her arm to me. "Then give the coin to me, and we will be off. If she is dead, then I'll just charge a ha'penny for the walk through all this Lammastide filth and heat."

She preceded me, guessing out loud where she was bound, mentioning several of Alfred's girls by name, including kindly mention for good Matilda, lamenting her present trials. The news of Alfred's demise and the seizure of his train were high news at Lammastide in Hereford.

"The old squint Gertyn should have talked Alfred from traveling anywhere close to Hereford. She is lucky not be hanged herself. Alfred was a stubborn one for his money, and she just as greedy."

Two wardens blocked her path—though they rested a leery eye on Cyrus, who decided to follow us within the walls. Braugh carried a staff to help her walk, and no doubt she had other skills with it—for the wardens kept their distance when she raised it.

"What do you two coupling dogs want?"

"Want?! Tariff, you old bag. You enter on business."

"You two wager wisely on me. Will you again?" Cyrus interceded.

They looked at Cyrus who said this cheerfully. I was so distraught, I just wanted on with it. Later I found they let us pass without collecting a tariff and the why of it: They wagered on wrestling, declared contrary to God's Will by His Eminence. Great dispensation could be had, though, if His Eminence's Secretary or Reeve got geld from all players' winnings. Only, of course, if these personages *knew* of such gambling. Few, including these two, wanted to risk sharing past good fortune with His Eminence.

When we reached the wagons, Matilda greeted us with less sadness, for Cwenburh was holding steady, and making, if anything, a harder fight of it. They knew Braugh at once—impressed I fetched the finest healing woman.

Matilda embraced me of a sudden, very bold and hard, and told me that now Cwenburh had great skill on her side, in addition to God's grace. And, furthermore, that I should go within and pray to Our Savior, for certainly it was up to the powers of him and the Father.

I lost at once the companionship of Cyrus. He was surrounded by Alfred's daughters who he knew by name. The carpenter and his sons— and especially the Lombards—attended him. To these foreigners even ordinary-sized Saxons were impressed—they were dumbfounded by Cyrus.

Matilda had good advice—I had much to pray and make contrition for. I moved wearily through various inner warrens and found St. Guthlac Church, where I had received my freedom from Sidroc-the-Younger.

I avoided that end of the church, knelt, and made prayer. About me was the silence and smell of incense and candles. It was too long since I prayed in one of God's great houses, and I felt peace settle over me.

I heard a few people coming and going in old St. Guthlac Church. Long ago, but years after this moment, Guthlac's house of worship was burned to the ground by cruel Welshman. These hard men, like so many, practiced the blasphemy of returning violence with violence, a wheel that turned relentlessly, a bane to Our Savior.

At the time of my youth, it was a quiet salubrious shelter where even an ordinary soul could pray in the sure presence of the Lord.

The holy building's aged wood took sounds and sent them from one side to the other, creating haunting echoes, as if you prayed in a giant wooden cup. I heard steps approaching from behind and a clearing of the throat. I looked back, for I hoped for news of Cwenburh. It was a young priest.

He had a sickly pallor and reddishness around the eyes, and he held a tiny box as if it were inordinately heavy. He said his name and God has graced me by allowing it to have left my memory. He extended the box in my direction—holding it in both palms.

"This holds your stillborn child and needs burial in consecrated ground with all the honor given any Innocent in death. The days are hot and time brings corruption."

My selfish omission in thinking after my stillborn child, and the physical and holy treatment of its mortal remains, struck me hard.

"This church's good Deacon has given me this holy task, but we must at once, I am afraid."

I rose, possibly to take the box which held the child. But he withdrew it slightly, dropped his eyes and said there was the cost of the box, made of cedar, and then the burial tariff: "His Eminence's people do much for all the surrounding souls in both town and field. Such fees, God help us, despite talk of coin being harsh at this sad time, is the way of things, Cuthwin-of-Loe."

"I have no money, Father."

"Nothing of worth, my Son?"

I at once thought of the clasp, but certainly it was worth ten-times what His Eminence might charge for the burial of a tiny box, which meant I would have to sell it. That would take expedience, so I was again pressed. In my pause he assumed I was withholding and his eyes rested on me—questioning, "There is a clasp, my Son."

This, as well as the error in my village-of-origin, raised suspicions. Matilda would never tell anyone of it—which is how he must have mis-learned my name. She knew the risk of having the clasp—it was she who had implored me to keep it hidden. A Secret.

Seeing my confusion, he added kindly, "One of the harlots told me of it, my Son."

My mind caught up with events: Only three souls knew of the clasp, Matilda and the guard who paid me with pillage. And I remembered his angry words at my choice.

In the end I would pay anything to prevent our child's unshriven soul to be cast off without proper Christian burial. So the guard's plan, in league with this priest, had gotten the clasp back—for themselves, of course.

Of the moment I had a physical feeling of absence, and like many such sensations, one is not aware until it comes to mind. I no longer could feel the gentle push of the metal clasp secured between my waist band and skin. My hand went there anyway, confirming what my senses told me: It was not there!

"Father, God forbid, but the clasp is gone!"

Like the rise of a sudden squall over the fens, his face soured. He stooped, put the box on the floor, and announced, "Then I needs keep this box, and you do with the remains what you will. God help its poor, unshriven soul because of your parsimony."

Stooping, he opened the box, removed a piece of cloth, and perfunctorily put it on the flagstone, then stood and stalked off.

Anyone with the God-given stuff of saintliness within would not have become possessed of thoughts seizing me at that moment. I was just a boy, and blood runs hot—prone to harsh decision and action. Yet I was in sanctuary of St. Guthlac, which made the guard's and priest's sins and my unpardonable urges more a travesty upon our Savior's teaching.

As I make witness here—almost eighty years hence—I say that no person thought of as a potential Saint, as I am now by some, might have generated such wild desires for the death by his own hand of other souls, and one—a priest—ordained by God.

But it was God's ceaseless mercy and sure hand that had brought me to sell the knife and not the clasp.

At that most cynical and dark moment, I learned later, I ran—a raving lunatic—from within into the courtyard frothing and ranting, as if possessed of a fiend. Worse, I seized one of the few heavy implements—a great lever for putting the yoke on oxen. At that moment, the brave souls, God bless them—the carpenter and his sons—tackled and sat atop me, the only way they could contain me; beneath them, the carpenter said later, "You flopped like a giant pike, Cuthwin. God forbid. You scared the shit out of us."

Also I carried the limp cloth holding what I thought held our dead child, placing it upon the cart before scrambling for a weapon.

Matilda was called, and trying to prevent the guard overhearing, stuffed an edge of her kirtle into my mouth to stop my murderous ravings. In my eighteen years I had seen only a few rave, taken by madness, a demon—or both. I thank God I had never experienced it myself until then, and never to repeat.

"Cuthwin, for Love of God. Stop!"

Thus I remember Matilda (for my memory was returning) shouting into my ear only moments after a tiny flask in the hands of a hastily called Braugh forced some foul elixir in my flapping mouth. The carpenter held me until I swallowed it. It had a bitter, awful taste that wafted up through my passages, smarting terribly. Braugh lamented, "And who will pay for that!? God bless me for my stupid heart."

And Braugh peered close into my eye as one might into a knothole looking for a squirrel's horde. Over the Healing Woman's shoulder, Matilda looked at me. A great pressure was kept on me by the carpenter's two boys until I felt a strange wave of heaviness take me from the inside, and my limbs went slack.

Braugh disappeared from my view—vision which was fast becoming dream-like. Matilda made scornful noises and scolded, her kind voice watery—each word writ large on my demented mind: "Cuthwin! Don't you know how corrupt these town priests are? It wasn't even the remains of your child—or any child. Remember this, those bastards do this all the time. You nearly spoilt everything—and Cwenburh gaining ground on her affliction."

Whatever plants or dark substances were key to Braugh's potion, they were the stuff of demons, certainly not God's. I sank away—only remembering Matilda's scolding me.

What followed wasn't a sleep; then again it was.

I remember only vaguely dreams that possessed me then, but surely they were borne by demons carrying arrays of evil pleasure. They sang sweet calls of melodies that made all seem to be swathed in innocence and honesty. What might any of us do when so skillfully harkened by the darkest angel of all? Indeed, had not the severest want been put on Our Savior in the harsh desert, testing even Him.

I would only tell events in those dreams to a confessor, never to the light of day.

The matter of my soul and mind returned with the encroachment of light and the sound of voices. I made out the vague face of good Matilda, then others. Soon, I could see sufficiently to understand. I had been moved inside to lie next to Cwenburh. Her eyes were open and she looked at me as I perceived dimensions of my shelter—first the floor of the cart above us. My head felt as if a massive turnip had replaced it.

But Cwenburh was alive—though white as a mushroom and sapped utterly. Even then, her eyes—the love and care in them—brought a wash of balm over me.

"Cuthwin, you've made a great madness. Matilda here told me—hard to believe, God be served."

Matilda and another sister moved in fast, for I was at once sick—experiencing an ague equal to that of the foulest hog cholera.

"Oh, I'm dying. Jesus help me. I was poisoned."

Between the various retching of this foulness, I was told by Matilda—who had little sympathy—that I had fallen into a stupor for over a day. "And you pissed yourself like a geezer in his cups."

Matilda and her sister shared a great laugh about that—and Cwenburh, so very weak, reached out and took my wrist, holding tight. That she lived and was next to me was three times the good of any elixir on earth.

Struggling to full awareness, I was informed of events during my madness—and how I was in the debt of Braugh. Matilda sat between Cwenburh and me, lecturing me about how grateful I should be to the Healing Woman. Then feigning stern countenance, she looked with mock admonishment upon Cwenburh.

"You must order this mulish Cwenburh to give over that clasp, Cuthwin. Seeing it was the draw prompting the old woman to work on strength of future payment. The Healing Woman is beyond anything we might trade."

Cwenburh opened her hand that lay weakly across her bosom, and there the clasp was—and she looked down at it, then over to me, ignoring my shock. It was a God-ordained miracle to see it again.

"Tell Matilda I will keep this always, Cuthwin. It is your bride price, and I ask our Savior's forgiveness for false pride, but I deserve it. I will be buried with it."

A look to me, then Matilda—who was giving suck to her child—conveyed the immutability of her declaration: no one would ever have possession of that clasp while Cwenburh lived. Scurrying into the makeshift sick room, another of her sisters looked at the clasp. Cwenburh handed it to her to examine fondly.

In fact, over the last two days it became a great attraction in the train. One of the sisters was Norman and said something quick in her tongue, pushing Matilda roguishly on her forehead.

"Cuthwin, this creature here in her foul tongue says to learn another thing: Do not let an evil woman embrace you firmly. As girls under direction from Gertyn, we learn the art of lifting men's purses and wallets for survival in this harsh world. When tits and quim are pressed close, men forget their possibles."

Two of the sisters shared a chuckle on that. Their mirth provided explanation for the mystery of the clasp's voyage, for it began with Matilda's sudden embrace of me.

My ills were slight compared to Cwenburh's, so I recovered strength quickly. My concerns were the disposition of our stillborn child and the new debt. Since I was senseless, and Cwenburh yet very ill, Matilda instructed the carpenter's two sons to simply scale the fence on Hereford's outermost cemetery and bury it in a careful grave, marking it so Cwenburh and I could attend when well. This solved the issue over whether our dear soul could be put to rest in consecrated ground. Later I learned this is how the sisters of Alfred's train buried one of their own, knowing that permission would never be granted.

"This way, God will make the decision," Matilda explained, which to us sounded right. For did not the teachings of Our Savior condemn no one?

The clasp was a less sad topic but practically raised a thorny, hard-to-reckon situation.

The clasp was no longer an asset, and that left me to confront Mistress Braugh with an awkward and contrary piece of information regards debt.

Walking up and down the courtyard, regaining my legs, gave me opportunity for thought.

These contemplations were cut short by the carpenter who gently informed that I bit and gouged his sons in my madness. So in addition to other service, the Healing Woman treated them to prevent the foulness, for bites are the nastiest of wounds.

Yet this was not his concern—gouged and bitten sons were of no importance to the carpenter now. He and his family were of great cheer with the news: Alfred's entire train—people, properties and all, had been sold to a Saxon merchant from York as a great investment. He was a cousin to His Eminence and had been visiting the great man for Lammastide.

"And he will put us all to work as it was before, with Gertyn managing things. She has a keener eye for coin than Alfred, who was prone to shortcuts regards money. This rich Saxon summoned his Secretary here, and he and His Eminence's Secretary are learned businessmen, no doubt."

So all the criminal and immoral doings attached to the late Alfred-of-Aylesbury's train were either forgiven or absolved in a holy vapor of silver coin.

Also, sale to His Eminence's kinsman would extend contrition for individuals in Alfred's train burdened with sin. Powerful churchmen had long-reaching powers to forgive and extend God's mercy.

The carpenter at once detected my hesitancy.

"So dour, Cuthwin? It is God's will and good fortune all in one, do you not see?! There is a place for you. I gave him my best word about you. For this clever Secretary has sold the ox and purchased horses! Think of what that change will require! He also sold both of these wheeled giants, and bought four smaller."

He went on while I sank into difficult thinking on top of simple debt.

There is advantage to anticipating trouble, but the disadvantage is worry. I knew disagreements were coming between Cwenburh and me—especially as she regained strength, though her rate of healing was yet unknown.

Gossip being one of her favorite idles when well, convalescing under the wagon gave her vast exposure to it. She would hear of these business changes the carpenter spoke of—indeed, would have already heard of them. Along with that would be word of my chance at employ.

Had we not ventured to Hereford for work?

This would be as far as Cwenburh would take contemplations. She had of course grown to love her sisters, and in fact owed her life to them. Grateful to even a simple hen for such bounty as an egg, Cwenburh would remain true for life to those unfortunate women.

I had been of far less use than they, and I owed them, too.

But my seven years at Peterborough Monastery taught me strict religious tenets. A poor person, unlike those rich and powerful with their own confessors at hand daily, had to show adherence to the teachings of God for fear of one's immortal soul.

Though I was not a Brother—not a clerk of any sort—my main source in learning to read and write was the venerable King Alfred's Bible in our language, amongst other religious works.

The seven deadly sins were an unyielding center of the holy teaching. Each dominated the lessons and sermons of the prophets. They prepared common people for lurking dangers. And certainly, central to these were Lust and Greed.

Even a forgiving soul like Father Abbot knew Satan inhabited a train such as Alfred-of-Aylesbury and that I must quit it even if it meant begging for trenchers at door stops.

However, Cwenburh was of a simple belief that God did not condemn those who did no violence or harm to others, especially by design. And the sisters, she would claim, did not do that, or ever would.

That would be the surface of her thinking and the end of it.

Venturing outside the walls, I thanked God for Cwenburh's life, but this struggle did poorly in overcoming the selfishness over my own troubles. The primary issue was the need in confronting Braugh with the truth, and she was not a charitable woman.

It was a bright Herefordshire summer morning. Rooks and other birds scurried and fought bitterly over the bounty of grisly pickings down in the animal markets.

Swooping through the scourge of flies, hordes of jeweled swallows dived. Chirring their feeding song, stopping, turning in mid-wing, they twirled back through their masses of prey, filling their bellies. All this was a simple cycle of God's ways.

At the market's conclusion, city officers would just open up the gates to the adjacent River Wye, allowing it to flood through one end of the ditch, and out the other—washing clean the animal market refuse in a single pass. These creatures sensed the end of their bounty was near and were intense in their business.

I ached for breakfast. Driving other odors aside, I smelled food everywhere. Proximate were dozens of nooks and shops selling all sorts of victuals. I arrived at Braugh's pavilion with hunger plaguing me and not feeling optimistic.

I found her like before, sitting on a low stool, but now sorting various herbs and such into tidy small piles on a square-cut piece of leather. The black girl sat near by laboring at mortar and pestle while humming a strange tune and grinding a pile of dried berries to a powder.

"So, Cuthwin, you have my money? It is three pence."

I explained why the clasp would not be sold but how I was good for the money, "as God is my witness." She did not alter her work, or look up while I tended my news.

I missed Cyrus awfully—fearing she might leap up and administer one of those horrible potions by some magical way.

She left me standing. The black girl stopped her work—looked up, perhaps to appeal for patience, instead suggesting, "We could call Cyrus, and he would gladly pulverize this fellow, Mistress."

"Shut up, you little ebony pissant! Mind your craft—you are poor enough at it."

But a customer entered before matters became grimmer—before I could plead further. Braugh found me in the way, so pointed at the floor, and I sat. The elderly Saxon was showing signs of a good burden of beer and ale even this early. He delivered a hefty slap to his vast gut and chest, and announced his business.

"I am randy enough. But I need powder to strengthen the pith in my old ram—he has trouble tupping the ewes, but he is of great stock, and I need his line for the lambs."

They went eye to eye—two chickens confronting over a morsel— perhaps it was the strength found in his cups that enabled him to hold. Braugh looked him over—beginning at his bare feet, then stopped at the tip of his small hat.

"Six pence."

"God's Mercy on me, Mistress!"

And they began—contentions I'd heard before in Peterborough market and now here.

When he paid for his powder—handed to him in a small bark cylinder—I made accurate guess Cyrus would not harm me over the debt. Braugh passed coins to the black girl who put them in a clay pot. Her eye returned to me.

"It is said you are clever in the way of reading and writing our language and not that gibberish priests mutter?"

"I am, thanks be to God."

"Then, in exchange for money owed, I would have you write down many of my mixings and powders, for my memory is growing shifty. I can read, but cannot write, not without slowness with the simplest letters. I have tried only too often."

The black girl and I exchanged looks. She made something of a face and put a tiny leaf in her mouth and chewed happily.

"Don't look at her, Cuthwin-of-Alnwick. That creature would be pagan still, if it were not for my intervention."

"Yes, Mistress, I have a piece of the true cross."

While Braugh and the girl eyed each other over her claim, I recognized my decision was clear so agreed at once. She had paper and ink with many goose quills, and said I would start after Sabbath, today being the day preceding.

"Your wife will take a month to repair, and you are to keep your husbandly hands off her for that long, if not more" and she made a resentful look while her assistant enjoyed a chuckle around her wad of leaf. "Young husbands care more for themselves than their wives." She thought a moment, and drawing breath while filling and sealing up a tiny cylinder, added, "So be off with you now—but you need coin to buy her hefty bone for broth and some lammasbread. I will get the money out of you, no doubt. Remember well your ill wife, and don't waste it. Cyrus will fight a bear again at the pit around Vespers. Men folk enjoy that sort of gawk, but do not bet, the bear and Cyrus are long friends."

She extended her hand, and the African girl opened the pot with coin, and handed me five silver pennies, the King's face freshly struck in their middle.

A renewed spirit took hold.

Meandering a return, I mused on this being the third time in two weeks my skills learned at Peterborough provided a gateway from trouble. Would not Braugh leave at the end of Lammastide, to ply her skills at other places? But when the market and fair folk left—as all such businesses do—where would a recovering Cwenburh and I stay or eat?

Hereford wasn't the precincts of a Monastery or Abbey, but so far had proven a harsh town with people of church or business keen of money. I hoped the sisterhood of Alfred's train might advise in these confusions, and I felt again the shame of judging them.

First I bought hefty lammasloaf—and immediately indulged in a hunk. I descended a path into the row-ditch where the butchers plied. A slab of a Saxon tradesman looked me up and down, his bloody leather vest pestered by flies which he batted away with an impatient hand. "A good bone is not cheap these days—to go along with that bread you are stuffing in your face."

He was indeed a vast hog of a fellow with bristles growing out of his nostrils, ugly in all manner, his character echoing his person. While I made business, his fellows were shouting great speculations about Cyrus's upcoming battle and how they might bet.

I still considered the gentle colossus's words about the 'strange doings' of his mention. Certainly a man fighting such a beast as a bear—other men in turn watching and betting on the outcome—was blasphemy of a sort.

I knew Our Savior preached gentleness and bloodless conduct for everyone, including the beasts of field and forest. Cyrus was a benevolent soul, and how could his plight ever be construed as God's Will?

I was again faced with thorny issues without ready answer. It was sad irony that just that spring I knew comfort and steadiness in life at Peterborough, with Cwenburh securely in that same life.

I had bungled that stability away and it would never return. God has by now, I pray, forgiven me.

While smelling the broth brewing from outside our makeshift chamber, I watched Cwenburh nibble away bits of bread like a ravenous mouse.

"Mistress Braugh did not seem upset or surprised when I did not have the money."

"Oh, I expect not," she replied, then paused, took a second thought, then offered, ". . . healing women are odd sorts, knowledgeable in the way of mysteries."

Later I slipped out of Cwenburh's convalescing chamber, for sleep was her greatest friend. I fell into talk with the carpenter; he was filled with the day's news.

At center of it of course was the newly reconsolidated train and its livery. It would have its first engagement for business beginning on St. Bartholomew's Day[25] at the sumptuous fair and market in Worcester.

"We have almost twenty days to prepare, Cuthwin. Ah, if you could only join us. But it is good the old bag Braugh needed to pass on her clever healing potions and powders to her daughters. She is not the sort who performs any service on speculation. Your knowledge, however, was a timely exchange, and indeed Cwenburh will have time and place to heal."

I allowed him to continue with thoughts of a rich future in Worcester. I knew nothing of Braugh's daughters—in fact, did not know she had daughters. Also, the venerable healing woman had not visited us in the courtyard for over two days—since I had regained my senses. When might she have conveyed such information to the carpenter?

Was there some preordained agreement that extended beyond myself and the business of the clasp?

I did not enjoy being part of a plan determined by others. That night

---

[25] Saint Bartholomew's Day. August 24th.

while lying beside Cwenburh, I dropped into slumber ruminating about this. When I woke, I was looking into the half-open eyes of Cwenburh, who reached over and took my hand.

"Oh, Cuthwin, I know by your feel you have caught wise to a plot surrounding you."

"When people unexpectedly know things I don't, it is always suspicious, Cwenburh; also, that Mistress Braugh did not show upset when I showed up without money to pay her."

"It is all my doing, may you and God forgive an annoying wife."

She explained Braugh had never speculated on the clasp, but through Matilda's early intervention, learned of my skills at letters. And starting then—and when Cwenburh was a little better, the arrangement was confirmed.

"I know—as does Matilda and her sisters—their way is considered an abomination before God. You're so filled with the ways of the Monastery because of your love for Abbot Elsin, I know you would never continue with the train." She moved a bit, and began stroking my arm with her other hand. "I would be too weak anyway, and so it all came into line. Our plot. Does a faithful wife sin if she does so for her husband's well being?"

I did not enjoy being forecasted by Cwenburh and so accurately. However, her revelation meant there would be no argument over why we might not join the train. She spoke the reason herself.

I was about to speak, when she squeezed my arm; that was not entirely the all of the matter.

"And Cuthwin, there is something else of more Christian urgency: Matilda asked me to take her infant when they leave for Worcester. To raise him as our own, God help and bless us. And I said I would ask you."

"What! Oh, my sweet Savior! We cannot feed or shelter ourselves!"

In the ever-present quiet of the closing night, we heard low-chiming bells summoning the faithful for Matins.

She looked towards St. Guthlac's and turned in that direction. "Could we attend prayers, Cuthwin?"

"Can you? Do you have the strength?"

She assured me she did, if I was at her side. The thought of us praying together in a church—something we had never done—overcame all else. My strength had returned entirely, especially with my belly full of bread and broth.

Slowly making our way out, she drew her breath in surprise when I just picked her up gently. "You are so much lighter now, Cwenburh. I could carry you back to Peterborough."

Being at service and saying the prayers together allowed time for thought and spiritual musings about the arrangement for us both. We realized that God set out great dictates for some, and this was ours. We had little or nothing but each other, and that came so close to ceasing I could not bear to think it.

Furthermore, we had lost our child, and through Matilda had been given another—this in trust by her, who had rendered us so much.

So there was no need to discuss the matter. It was almost the clearest instance of God's wise balance in the nature of things that either of us ever experienced.

We returned without words, and even being carried had tired her. We lay down together, and she held on to me and fell asleep at once. Having seen us return, good Matilda came in with a cup of broth; seeing Cwenburh asleep, she offered it to me. While I partook, she nursed her boy; but he fell asleep, and she covered the tiny person with meager swaddling and rocked gently side to side with it.

I knew already it had no name except 'Boy.' His father was unknown, and his future path would be following Matilda. One evening, she explained how her mother had been sold into this life when she was but in arms. It was not a life that accommodated old age, and her mother died of a terrible ague of the skin.

Still for a woman of Matilda's great heart, her sacrifice seemed too steep: "How could you bear to give up your own child, Matilda?"

"Because I am a harlot and damned before God, and I do not want the boy to share in that. I followed my mother, and look at the result."

"You are not damned before God. We are taught that forgiveness is always there for us."

She continued to rock the child and I knew religious argument was not appropriate—the life she led was so entirely foreign to me, it was hard to visualize its goings-on. I could have asked dozens of questions, but saw only one good path.

"Then stay with us in Hereford, as Cwenburh's sister, and the boy shall have an aunt. We will become a family, and you will be shut of this life."

She looked at me—astonished. She tried for words, missed them, and instead began to weep—shook her head, then surprised me more by looking up with a vast smile: "Cuthwin-of-Alnwick, you are a good man, and Cwenburh is a lucky woman. But years ago I was sold along with my mother to old Gertyn, and I am bonded to her. It would take several pounds for my freedom—for I am not yet fifteen, so am highly desired by customers. I bring in much during each festival."

Two pounds of silver coin was beyond my imaginings, and I stupidly had not anticipated such a bond chained Matilda to this life. Indeed it did, along with most of her sisterhood—to Gertyn, and before her Alfred and Gertyn.

As simple as our properties were, Cwenburh and I had our freedom.

I suffered silent crisis.

If I only had someone with wisdom and learning to advise. Father Abbott had played such a decisive part in the events of my life; if only he could do so now. Certainly it was not possible for Our Savior to hold no mercy or forgiveness for a soul like Matilda. Furthermore, damning her to the fires of eternity was something that every bit of my body and soul knew was not true—could never be true. The Archfiend Himself would recoil from the amount of good present in Matilda's heart.

She with the boy at her breast fell asleep leaning against the inside spokes of the wheel—one side of our compound. With them both comforted, I called for forgiveness if I were ever to not show compassion for a soul locked into such a path of toil.

I crept out from beneath the wagons and wandered from the inner court outside the row-ditch just when the sun was pushing up lazily from the east. I had much to consider.

Sabbath at Hereford was not observed nearly with the severity that it was in Peterborough, even though the holy seat of His Eminence. Dozens stirred before their pavilions and such—laboring the stiffness from limbs and attending the morning fire. They called to each other gossip of the hour—and on this Sabbath talk of the commonality strayed from the religious. Words of marvel described the great struggle the previous night in the pits outside the walls. Cyrus defeated the bear—indeed at one point, picking it up whole and pinning it to the ground, the poor creature bawling for mercy to the wonder of all the gamesmen.

Abundant coin was lost.

I purposely passed by Ahulf's pavilion. His great carved coin hung from its post—a morning westerly made it sway as if rocking an infant. I was thankful to find Cyrus sitting at the doorway in the early sun applying salve to a wound on his arm.

He greeted me and swept the ground beside him for me to sit.

"The bruin scratched me good—its claws came through the sheaths. It didn't mean to, poor dumb brute."

"Do you fight it often?"

"When the money is right."

And he went on to talk of his wanderings on fairs and markets, with Ahulf being his agent, as it were, though Cyrus always remained free. He especially looked forward to Bartholomew's Day at Gloucester which he boasted as being far more lucrative than Worcester.

"In Worcester, the city's holy men and local Hundred hold pit-fighting to be a great sin and condemn it, so collect a great fine upon each single event. They are especially greedy. All towns and cities normally impose a single fine for the entirety of our shows as they do in Gloucester. A good place, surely, one that also offers lively commerce for Ahulf."

I never before asked about the details and issues of harlotry—it wasn't discussed openly, nor did I contemplate details. So with Cyrus

I took opportunity to ask how such business was conducted and how it all worked.

Cyrus answered and it was not long in the telling. I became even sadder. I voiced upset that such evil doings were conducted for money on either end of such trade.

Cyrus wrapped the wound—gave his great arm a crank or two to see if it still worked. He drew back a bit, and offered me a long look, and a shake of his massive head.

"So, if Ahulf gives you three pence for a one shilling, four knife, is that more or less honest? Churches are never above dealing in coin and worth as well. Even for such sacraments as burials and marriages, coin is claimed."

I considered this. for the giant did not offer it in a contentious manner, but more brotherly. Seeing me in quandary, he rose to his great height and asked if I wanted to meet Ursus the Bear.

"He will be fed soon, and it is a happy time for the poor animal."

It would be the first time I had seen or visited a bestiary. The master was a skinny old Norman who plied the roads with his family members. He had—in addition to Ursus—trained birds of odd color, several badgers who fought all comers, and creatures similar to stoats; and his greatest property, a lioness named Sibyl.

There were also odds and ends of other God's creatures. Ursus was overjoyed to see Cyrus, and the Norman let him out of his cart, and Cyrus fed him by hand bits of joints and sweet roots and melons from a bucket.

It was a strange sight to see the two combatants so at peace. And no less the lioness dozing in her cart—lions I had seen were ferocious, pictured in a glaring array of colors upon the margins and headings of Scriptorium books.

Her owner was proud of Sibyl and his train.

"Not too many years ago, Master Cuthwin, I had a young dragon, and times were fat for us then, let me tell you. But, it flew off. It was these biting flies. Those damned creatures drive all my beasts mad—they are the devil's curse."

For indeed, despite his remote location from the row-ditch, there still swarmed a pestilence of flies and stinging creatures. His sons constructed a defense system of fires on four sides of his bestiary to utilize any one of the winds. In them they burned green resinous woods, obnoxious to bugs, though not much less so to people.

As we walked back towards the walls Cyrus speculated on Ursus's increasing age, and how the master of bestiary wasn't always forthcoming with proper feed. It concerned him, of course. He looked sadly back in the direction we had come and unburdened his news: "They will not come to Gloucester, but instead to Worcester. Ahulf could not make the journey sweet enough for the Norman skinflint."

So that Sabbath was a lesson in parallel matters for me—by not going directly at the problem, Cyrus had with sense accomplished more at the flank of things. Living things, human and beast alike, were bought and sold, both in whole by day and hour. It was the way of things, God's will or no.

I was filled with excitement after witnessing the bestiary. I regaled Cwenburh and her sisterhood about its exotic sights. She was of sufficient strength to listen as I spun great tales of wonders. After all, where might simple folk such as we see such curiosities as a lioness or bear? It was a wonder to behold and listen to.

Later Cwenburh and I lay beside each other.

She asked what sort of quarters we might find, for she would not have strength enough to travel by St. Bartholomew's Day.

"My services to put Braugh's potions into writing, in addition to paying our debt, will hold enough sway to rent shelter for three souls."

And we both fell asleep, held in the arms of Our Savior, blessed with the trust and optimism of youth, an endless commodity.

So it was in the second year of King Harold Harefoot's reign[26] that we settled for a recuperative time in Hereford. And it was here our nephew, who came to be christened Eadrig-of-Hereford, joined our family and subsequently brought us endless joy.

---

[26] 1037.

Within a few months fortunate events followed close—one against the other, as cattle following each other into paddock. Cwenburh recovered and was able to maintain, then increase, a flow of milk for Eadrig, who took nourishment as eagerly as a young colt.

My business became brisk. Braugh's two daughters arrived from Shrewsbury. The mother had ambitious plans in her old age: She desired to take up year-round shop in Hereford. She would then have her daughters split two traveling pavilions from her one, the elder going one way and the younger the other.

I found it remarkable that the daughters were far worse for wear than their mother, for both were quite decrepit though just touching their middle years. One had no teeth, the other's leg was shorter than its opposite; and the elder daughter also lacked her front teeth, and a part of one ear. Her younger sibling wore a colorful cloth of patchwork over one eye having had it gouged out in one sort of struggle or another.

But they seemed content with their lot—and, like it or not, I observed and heard much about both: My unstoppable source was the African girl, a terrible gossip who spoke a most awful Saxon. She said the daughters' infirmities resulted from ignoring their mother's warning: "Both as young girls, Master Cuthwin, put their quim and mouth to devil's horn beyond what was good for them. Now look at them."

Yet they learned the cleverness of healing craft from their mother then added to this their own experiences. Whatever fair or market they attended, their skills were in demand. Also important to their plans was each could read enough figures and letters to make out written directions for potions, salves, and the like. This made their mother's knowledge, in form of writing, portable.

My services then were of immediate value and I understood why Braugh was quick to make the trade with us for healing and attending Cwenburh.

While mother and daughters bartered and transacted diverse things to get their trains together, I wrote my fingers to nubbins. I sat long hours with a board upon my lap writing upon quartos of the poorest quality vellum, but I soon gave this up, instead working faster onto wet clay.

Braugh was not generous in buying good supplies, and soon after Lammastide the moveable shops dealing such materials ventured to other towns for various fairs and markets. Taking the thin clay trays home, I would transfer this deluge of ingredients for potions, elixirs, and salves onto bits and pieces of cheap vellum afforded me by the parsimonious old woman. Contrary to her statement there was nothing wrong at all with her memory or wit.

She relied on me to construct all into a book or folio. And, of course, two copies had to be made—one for each daughter.

It was with only endless coaxing that I was able to talk her out of the price for tapirs, and then only the cheapest sorts that spit and sputtered, and sent out rank-smelling smoke.

"I tell you, Cuthwin, I fear for our nephew's health with those awful things," Cwenburh warned me.

It was only after great argument with her mother that the elder daughter, Edith (of Sussex) convinced her to give us coin for a tiny alcove next to a butcher's house on the banks of the Wye.

Within less than a week, though still slight of flesh, Cwenburh fixed up what was essentially a mud-floor storage hut into decent quarters with fresh water only a stone's toss distant. This was a great boon.

The place became littered with clay tablets and their frames, and I sat amidst it all transcribing onto vellum. The butcher gave me advice on where to provide myself with better vellum. Soon—because of the eternal kindness of God—independent jobs began to come to me. I worked on these during off-hours work unknown to Braugh. I was then able to procure my own writing supplies.

It seemed that more than one or two odd guards here and there wanted letters written to their people miles distant. And the word of this spread so fast that soon both forms of work overwhelmed. Cwenburh gossiped and enjoyed company, and in truth I did, too—at least the hearing of it, God forgive.

Two journeymen butchers, both kin to the butcher himself, would often take repast with us at Vespers.

"Cuthwin, you should charge these cottars more than a ha'pence for writing them such priceless letters."

"Yes, it is God's great gift—a miracle. With your help, Cuthwin, these ragbags are able to convey plain word of home and people across leagues and time."

What I did for poor people was short and plain words, and took little time. But indeed, I was doing two or three such a day, and we were accumulating resources for our future—most of all, to buy livery tools to again ply my trade.

One Sabbath I found Braugh looming in my doorway, angry. It was her way to remain outwardly composed when angry, yet her words became even harsher. Her eyes were set like those of the hawk as she glared down.

"So, Cuthwin, you do me false, after I saved you from serfdom and your wife from eternal darkness."

This was ridiculous—I denied it at once, but she went on and—as I had guessed at once—my off-hours' labor had become known to her. She wanted a share, and we were right in the middle of this difficulty when Cwenburh returned from showing off Eadwig to the butcher's eldest daughter.

And the worst began—for immediately the two engaged like hungry sparrow hawks over fat crickets, and since Braugh loomed over the diminutive Cwenburh, the two were chin-to-chest argufying.

Within moments, Braugh discharged me from service. Further, Braugh promised to appeal to the wardens or even the Hundred for compensation for my faithless breach. There was a closing volley of hostile words with promises of foul deeds before the old harridan turned and departed. This display of shouted invective brought others around to join in the fray. All became a general confusion.

Such a fray was Cwenburh's home terrain.

There were great embers in her eyes as she stalked back and forth, bouncing Eadrig on her hip.

"She will be back, the greedy old squint. Where else could she get someone to do what you are doing, unless it be a cleric or some such who won't work so cheaply."

She set herself on the floor after placing Eadrig in the leather-lined cradle. I was not, as is my way, too upset about the goings-on; I was a free man, and had nothing written agreeing to any long-term labor with Braugh.

"See here, Cuthwin." From her bodice she removed a leather wallet with the clasp, then three shilling pieces and six pence. This caused me to draw breath.

"So much! God be praised, Cwenburh!"

She was a born saver of resources, and was the best reeve or factor anyone would want. Cwenburh pointed out that she had calculated my labors so far and I had paid back Braugh many times over, and it was she who owed me coin.

"At least two schillings worth, if not more. Working folk around here know the old bag is cheating you. And she just demonstrated to everyone that she is but a dried-up old cunt."

"Ah, Cwenburh, you have a tongue on you like a serpent, God help us."

But good or bad words aside, it is this day that became the starting point—the first milepost—for a long road that extended over thirty years. That same Sabbath I had definitely thought my career as liveryman was ending—or, had ended.

There was God's design here. Who else cares for common folk?

In those days poor people had no scribes about; only great men or landed sorts with money could hire a cleric or perhaps reeve to do such.

I enjoyed writing—listening to words, then putting them down to be passed along. And the more flourishes and other written craft requested by clients, the more I loved it.

Making the various inks was good, artful craft I took special pride in producing. Further, objects upon which one could write were more varied than thought by most—a clever contrivance could turn the most simple items into workable writing surfaces.

In the Scriptorium at Peterborough, Brother Cassartorius and Brother Ithamar had many ideas about all the implements of writing—

especially Brother Cassartorius, who brought with him the wily crafts of Italy and Lombard.

For seven years I paid great attention to all those tricks of craft that came to my notice.

So I saw God's great hand directing how my craft might offer poor and ordinary folk betterment. Cwenburh's skills were a priceless addition to our family endeavor. She saw how best I could apply this use and the when and where of it.

In a definite way, Father Abbot's sure, God-ordained will had led me along a crooked, difficult path to this useful point and I knew he would approve of it. I had found my rightful place before God. And true enough we began travels and encountered experiences and folk that enriched our lives as eggs might a rich cake.

Book 4

Cuthwin adopts the life of a traveling scribe. How a time of peace and prosperity came; also, through tragedy and the intercession of evil men, how he and Cwenburh become father and mother to Eadrig. He relates and describes his travels throughout Mercia and all England. Our truthsayer observes and learns the ways of the commonality and how ordinary folk prosper and how they are taken low by earthly circumstances, including famine and disease. Lastly that when great men turn against the preaching of Our Savior, they are seized in the foulness of pitiless sin and become lost souls, swept into the eternal fires of the Archfiend.

We spent the winter establishing my new trade of letters in Hereford.
It was a time of gathering and learning skills necessary in setting up a
traveling pavilion as scribe. At this time mine was an unknown public trade among the diverse community that moved from market to fair
from spring through autumn, a sort of traveling village.

It was not a type of life without its own practical issues, for moving
one's home and business nine months of the year from village to city
demanded skills of transport and business combined. There was a great
and I feel wise tendency for traveling pavilions of similar businesses to
stay in company and follow similar if not the same begang[27] on yearly
rounds.

This type of circuit was not the same each year because great men of
monastery, church, or manor had authority of each town or city; hence
they could change the fairgeld charged during fairs and markets. Those
who did business on the begang kept well abreast of their changing
circumstances. In one city, when a tax of a pound silver was demanded
one year, this made that city impractical. However, the following year it
might be half that.

My concern was the quality of my craft and our transport, and
Cwenburh's of business. The constant network of talk and gossip was
the life's blood amongst diverse businesses. The steadiest flow of information occurred mostly during winter when we stayed in one place.

And this wintering spot, which varied person to person, became comfortably accommodated for us in Winchester, the capital of Wessex,
a stoutly walled city promising the protection of diverse thanes with
housecarls of nearby great men.

Yet a grim hand reached out and visited terrible pain on us and many
more; Eadrig was not two years of age when a scourge of righteousness

---

[27] Begang. Old English, meaning circuit, course, passage, etc.

fell over the whole of the country. All those guilty of fornication—or party to it—were condemned by the Archbishops of Canterbury and York during high meeting of all churchmen in that holy city. Their severe resolve resulted in a Writ-of-Penance that rapidly went around all counties.

Saints' days and celebrations central to markets and fairs, they declared, had become scandalously desecrated by the mortal sin of fornication. Lords, their housecarls, then all thanes with their men were commanded in the name of God by this holy writ to eliminate this scourge, which soon thereafter was made a royal decree by King Harold.

In fact, it was maintained during this conclave that the King's creeping ague was punishment upon His Highness for allowing unrepented sins-of-the-flesh to descend upon the Lord's kingdom on earth.

These outrages of the body, it was held, were too often ignored—or even partaken—by powerful men, their housecarls, and thanes. Hence, contrition must be done by carrying out annihilation utterly of those who purveyed base immorality in the past or now.

It was during this time that Matilda was, we heard, burned at stake along with all her sisters. All across Mercia and Wessex, and into Anglia, their sisterhood was scourged from the land, mostly by fire. The horror of this news beat us low, for we had knowledge of this community, as it were, and knew that Our Lord always granted forgiveness and pity, especially to those who asked it. And Matilda, for one, was of a deep religious nature, and her worries about Eadrig's soul prompted her in fact to yield his care to us.

By her demise we became the only guardians of Eadrig. She would, when alive, take great risk to occasionally visit, especially during winter. Matilda needed permission of that gargoyle Gertyn, Alfred-of-Aylesbury's widow, to visit. A procurer by her nature, the greedy old bag was always in fear of her bonded 'daughters' running off.

I was forewarned about this shameful wrath through Cwenburh during the spring fair in Marlborough. For when great men make armed violence upon poorer people, they begin for a singular purpose—such as cleansing the land of harlotry. However, during their selfish actions, darker self-serving purposes expand. Finally it encompasses all people, innocent or not, how otherwise these men hold in scorn.

This invariably included those to whom they owed money, or who in previous dealing shorted them sufficient geld when asked.

Throughout the country, all healing women, always alert to such paroxysms of morality, scattered like sparrows, hiding their pavilions and properties and taking secure concealment until things passed. And healing women were not the only craft beset. Several freebooting thanes, deep in their cups, came into my pavilion on the prowl 'for fornicators,' they said. They kicked over several cases of unused vellum and growled, "They say you convey messages with demons here."

A long time before, I had fashioned a fine ash cudgel, and I grabbed that while Cwenburh took up a pot of boiling water, so discouraged they went off, most likely to seek out more drink.

It did no good to yield before such scum, for they would only become more emboldened. They understood that if they overstepped their warrant, the undersheriff, and certainly the Hundred, would not stand by them.

But, nonetheless, they harried everywhere that spring and summer, until the manufactured outrage passed. But it was too late for poor, dear Matilda and nearly all of her ilk; a few were excepted if they had protection from the patronage of clerics or land owners interested in their own personal needs.

We said many prayers for her soul at all the towns we plied that spring, summer, and fall. Matilda was a sweet girl who gave life to Eadwig. She knew the violent swings of her living, and as it turned out showed much sad wisdom in her actions. We swore never to allow Eadwig to forget his mother and how she sacrificed before God for his well being.

It was the murder of those who had helped us in Hereford so unyieldingly that began a lifelong instruction to me how God's words can be twisted for the warped motives of great men and women. Also, how the teaching of Our Savior can be utterly swept aside by the pestilence of money and land.

Then power itself becomes blacker than the eternal pit.

This led to our own sin, for we could not bring ourselves to forgive nor pity churchmen who did foulness to Innocents under the guise of holiness. Cwenburh never went to church again, but kept the Sabbath at home in prayer and peace; her only exception being Christenings and Marriages.

I never tried to persuade her otherwise. To the contrary, in the concealed corner of heart, I hoped unrelentingly for those false churchmen's damnation. May God forgive me.

Without anticipating it, financial security was extended to us by the Grace and Generosity of God. My skills, perhaps because of their newness and by finding a niche starved of service, increased until they were in high demand. It also expanded steadily until it included not just letters, but simple constructs of agreements, such as marriage and merchet contracts, minor charters, and writs such as that of manumission.

Soon I found there were not enough hours in the day, and I wrote myself sore-of-hand. It is an exciting and flattering thing to find one's skills in high demand, and it invites the sin of pride, a most seductive indulgence.

But the greatest event—and a direct result of having resource—was the taking of the Holy Sacrament of Marriage between us. It occurred in the handsome city of Bath at the great Abbey during Saint Bartholomew's Fair and Festival on the last year of King Harold Harefoot (1040).

To be wedded in the shadow of the holy St. Alphege was a great celebration of God's generosity. We afforded a humble mass with passing of the Sacrament of Marriage, and it remains the greatest experience of my life under the blessed auspices of Our Savior.

At our marriage celebration, Cyrus the Great lifted us aloft—each by one arm, while Eadrig stood on his shoulder thumping him on his vast brainpan. We had become friends with many who plied the seasonal circuit. Cyrus and his great, parsimonious employer and agent Ahulf became our oldest comrades on the begang.

Sadly it became evident that we must faithfully and patiently serve penance—perhaps for being young and foolish, and wanton in our ways. The generosity and kindness of God for saving Cwenburh's life came with this provision: Her child-bearing days ended during that siege of illness; she and I were not to have children together.

"This is why He has given us good Eadrig." Cwenburh was certain of this, so bore herself proudly serving this contrition. For myself, her time carrying child—especially at its birthing—was so horrible, I indulged in the sin of selfishness. If the price of having Cwenburh in good health was for her not to bear children, then God's exchange seemed great wisdom to me.

I never voiced this with anyone for it was anything but a saintly reflection.

Cwenburh made an aggressive, feared factor for our business. She developed a keen business eye. Though she increased wisdom and craft to deal respectfully with people, she lost none of her tartness if they should cross us.

"Cuthwin never commits to writing on speculation."

That was her absolute regulation; she collected coin up-front, and it had to be in the King's true-minted coin. She now wore her marriage clasp openly on her plain but well-woven Flemish kirtle. If one of the various women-folk asked—which most did—where she got such a fine item, she laughed and said I had bartered with a savage for it, a far northern Chieftain, to win her hand.

"I am not taken to wife by just anyone."

For she was almost exclusively of great joy and cheer, unless under the duress of an ague. Likewise if someone tried hoodwinking her in price or agreement, or worse yet, transgressed upon a friend or loved one, she became an indomitable fighter never backing away from combat and severe words.

Yet Cwenburh's kind heart and lively spirit came with a price for a husband. When good Eadrig was not quite four, while at the great St. Swithin's Day[28] Fair at Reading, I ended a day transcribing letters. My eyes were sore and my hand sorer. Cwenburh had warmed rocks for my arrival from work, and while wrapping my writing hand in the wonderfully soothing thick cloth with the rocks, I saw two infants in the corner.

---

[28] Saint Swithin's Day, July 15th.

They were just in their creeping stage, on a floor cover in the corner of our living pavilion amusing themselves with carved animal bones.

Eadrig, a calm and serious child, supervised them.

Cwenburh returned to work on a door hanging.

"They are twins, Husband, and aren't they beautiful girls?"

"Where is their mother?"

"She was burned at the stake by those bastards two Ides of April past. The kind butcher's daughter was wet at that time, but cannot sustain them. Her marriage contract to a well-heeled baker needs exclude them. Her mother refuses to keep them on. She is a great pitiless sow."

I was left to study the crown of her headrail as she worked. Her scheme unfurled before me as a carpet merchant might toss his ware before a customer—or a cloth merchant a bolt of linen or wool.

I recalled that desperate time, how her soul and spirit took in the great Norman hound we rescued. She decided overnight it should stay with us for the rest of its life, despite the fateful incongruity of it. Then there was Eadrig's placement with us, as it were, and how this forecasted Cwenburh's lifelong vocation to rescue and care for those violated by harsh fate.

Indeed, through the years, at an appropriate time in her many conversations, she would say, "God's will is not imparting misery on the innocent or the poor. And certainly not our Savior's way. I cannot speak for the Holy Ghost."

Those within hearing would gasp at this sacrilege, but she meant it and was not partaking in sarcasm.

So I rested—felt the swelling go down in my hand—and reflected how our situation before God had improved so drastically since those years before when times were bad. Though we were not rich like landed or privileged folk, compared to that first winter at Hereford, we were improved vastly, thanks to God's graces.

And we did indeed have Eadrig.

At this moment I knew it was no use arguing, for though we imparted much to any poor folk we encountered, we still had bounty accruing. In truth we spent little save on business and plain living. Our wedding and feast had been our grandest indulgence. But, as I recall the evening I was introduced to the girls, I did make the perfunctory husbandly motions of being involved.

"So, Cwenburh, how is our treasury?"

"Oh, very well, Husband. But I lament your soreness—your hand will not last much longer. So we must save."

"And rightly done it would be. Maybe we can sell these two imps to Danes when we reach the coast. As fair-skinned girls they would bring much."

This was approximately how I concluded the moment, as aged memory serves. It was my way, and Cwenburh's, to bring resolve to potential conflict with humor. What did it accomplish to sound a matter and raise ire when it was clearly ordained by God what should happen?

The twins were named Matilda and Elesa and had not been Christened because of fears surrounding their heritage. The scourge leading to their mother's demise had not completely dissipated. Despite this, when a calmer day arrived, Cwenburh decided it was time for them to take Holy Water, for cursed agues take little ones so rapidly.

It was a few months after taking them in, just prior to the festival and market of St. Luke's Day[29] at great Abington. She had begun negotiating for a personage to administer the Holy Water through the offices of a town priest. I should have intervened, but hoped it might go uneventfully.

He at once brought up their parentage.

"Since these are not yours, Daughter, whose are they? It is important to the Holy Father these Innocents' parentage was not product of sin or heresy."

In truth the more his holy and personal offices were compromised to christen such babes, the higher his benefice would be in performing the sacrament. These fees were non-cloistered holy men's entire means of making coin, which often supplied the ample demands of good living, frequently including wife and family.

Herself already had her fill of corrupt or righteous churchman, so negotiations degenerated into ill feelings and words to match. Events did not go smoothly.

---

[29] Saint Luke's Day, October 18th.

By the time the wardens came to me escorting Cwenburh and our twins—for I was at work erecting our pavilions, along with our fellows—these officers were in great cheer and joyful temper, and narrated the great argumentation that had erupted to me and others. Their words held out no surprise for me.

"Indeed, Master Cuthwin, it was a great day! This wife of yours told the greedy fuck that for all she knew His Graciousness the Bishop was their father. So there will be no christening there, by God!"

There was indeed a great hew and cry among the parish clergy and word spread with glee among folk preparing for fair and market.

Cwenburh was in our wagon, and I found her taking a cup of ale—dabbing a bit of bread in it, and treating both the twins and Eadrig, who as always begged for a morsel. Her nose was still filled with fire, and she did not care if there would now be a fine involved and possible punishment.

"Anyone come here bold enough to punish me, and I will hurl boiling water or pee over them. I did nothing less than unloose deserved scolding upon a thief."

It was with pride, God help me, that I saw fire in her. The right nature of her instincts could never be extinguished. So I partook of a brief repast with her while her raging spirit soothed.

The aftermath I could soundly handle.

The wardens would be eventually back, I knew, and would carry warrant from the Undersheriff, or perhaps directly from His Grace the Bishop. This great cleric held charter of many local soke and his own proud demesne, though charter for the market and fair was held by Father Abbot of great Abington Abbey.

I took immediate occasion to personally visit our treasury—for the end of it would be paying the required fine for the incident. What I saw there delivered a sound punch to my middle—testimony to Herself's understatement and frugality.

"Great God! Cwenburh. We are rich!"

"Husband, you know nothing of money. We are but modestly kept, by the Grace of God. Edsil the Butcher has three times that, God be Praised."

As it turned, our means were more than sufficient to overcome the twin's dilemma with Christening. I turned my attentions for remedy of the twin's problem to the cloistered world of the venerable Abbey, a world so like Peterborough I took to its ways as a hound to meat.

I knew those who lived by The Rule in Cloister often looked upon uncloistered parish clerics with scorn. Indeed, Cwenburh's recent conflict met with sympathy when I contacted one of the Brothers. This soul in turn sounded the matter with the Abbey Sacrist. Within days—during St. Luke's good festival—we withdrew to a small chapel ancillary to the walls of the Abbey of Abington. There, the Innocents Matilda and Elesa took the Holy Waters and made us joyful indeed, God's Will be done.

We were a family of like christened souls, and were all content. Prayer of thanks was made to Our Savior and to St. Luke, who was the patron saint of scribes. By this time, I was twenty-eight years of age, and indeed Cuthwin the Scribe.

During the years following the commencement of King Edward's rule (1042), there occurred a great famine and scourge of boils and ague countrywide. For the first time I saw want and misery bring low an entire country. Though strong walls and flooded row-ditches may stop an invasion of mortals, nothing stops famine and disease. What began during winter in the south, swept north as fast as a draft of fever through the warming seasons.

Animals died by the thousand-fold and prices for bread were driven so high it became impossible to buy. A great oven-like heat and drought locked the country, and the grain crops with others failed, and finally fairs and markets came to all but a halt.

A most miserable pile of vegetables and poorest quality spelt-bread was costly, and soon our family treasury was almost empty. The great flesh we had put on in the good times—nearly ten years of it—went away in autumn and winter.

As I recall, a sester of wheat cost somewhere around sixty pence. Hence, wheat and finer grains, and their products, were beyond reach of ordinary folk, and certainly the poorer among us.

A shilling bought little or less at market. What grew cultivated or raised upon croft was virtually no more. Beasts of field and forest, as well as God's bounty from tree and shrub were so hungrily taken, even they were driven high in price or trade.

Fate trapped us upon the Welsh marches in Ludlow, for there the disease took our draft animals, as it did most our begang fellows. What few fairs and markets remained south and east were shuttered. So as the Holy Book teaches, "Whether a tree falls to the South or North, the place where it falls, there will it lie."

So we remained the year and then some at fateful Ludlow. It was a time when we became instructed in the terror of unmet needs.

For a while such disaster bade well for Ahulf the Broker, and indirectly benefited Cyrus the Great, for that year they kept to the same circuit as we. Yet even after a while, Ahulf had nothing to buy or any means to pay in the event a customer offered him an advantageous item.

"That man would buy a Saint's toenail, and sell it as an arm bone," Cyrus would joke. Cyrus's wife and children were in the south, and he was desperate to stand with them during these times. The larger the town or city, the worse the times were, for many people were living close-packed; these times brought on even more demons and ill-tempers.

Because of this, Cyrus risked the long trip south a few days after Michelmas, which indeed was a dismal time by contrast to all the Michelmas days I'd known previous.

Ahulf, knowing that without Cyrus, outright disaster would come upon all his diverse businesses, therefore left with Cyrus, the great man towing everything in a pull-cart. Like so many sorry souls, when Ahulf and Cyrus set out south, the road swallowed them whole.

We never saw either again, and years later heard from Cyrus's wife that when he left for the north with our begang, prior to the famine, that was the last she saw of her 'giant.'

I often prayed for God to have mercy on their souls.

The winter in Ludlow was harsher than in the more southerly

Winchester, plus at risk of raids from nearby Wales. The Welshmen were always on keen lookout for advantage upon we Saxons whom they hated dearly. But that winter was cruel; snow and ice locked the town, and with famine atop it, people began to die, most from the cold.

In the midst of this misery was His Grace, the Bishop of Ludlow. This was the same red-headed cleric who took us prisoner, hanged Alfred-of-Aylesbury, then deceived his older brother, His Eminence the Archbishop of Hereford. We hardly held him in reverence or hope of kindness. If not for the cleverness of Sidroc-the-Old, we would have all been slaves for all His Grace intended.

His Grace's vast blackstone residence was an opulent eye in this storm, and at its rear door town-folk would go for used trenchers and any scraps tossed from it each Compline.

Remembering her time at wild crafting, Cwenburh, weather permitting, children in tow, would head out of town to glean from fields anything to grind down into flour; especially prized were acorns in the woods. This source lasted until she and other women encountered His Grace's men. They drove the women from the woods, occasionally breaking bone or inflicting contusion.

His Grace's pigs had priority to fatten on their usual autumn fare of prime acorn.

The womenfolk turned to gleaning in hedgerows for herbs, roots, nettles, and wild grasses. I was, God be praised, able to contribute through occasional small tasks of my craft; my customers came solely during these harsh times from His Grace's household, which galled me, may God forgive.

These I insist pay me in foodstuffs, no matter how meager. My payment would, I guessed, have to be stolen by them from within, but I prayed for forgiveness if this was so. Even a joint well-gnawed was good for soup when boiled long enough.

Roots, ordinarily scorned, were like gold during the sharp edges of winter. And that winter was the cruelest of any. Worse, fuel for any fire began to become historical. When any ague and boils struck, death was almost predetermined.

Our shelter was two of our pavilions made into one, braced against the outside walls of the town close to one of four gates. The River Teme, which quickly froze over, was before us, along with the stone bridge crossing. A pitiless wind blew down it from the harsh mountains of Wales.

Early on I was compelled to resort to cudgel to protect our cart from being broken apart for fuel by others, desperate—who already had burned everything burnable to keep warm. At that point, they still feared serious injury over cold.

They were fearful and perhaps ignorant of how the woods and hedgerows must be daily gleaned. Even those who labored thus found meager reward. All energy possible would be spent for the tiniest bit of fuel to be used sparingly in shelter, whatever it might be.

Finally, the burden of seeing children die of the cold and want of food turned the folk outside the town walls, as well as inside, to heinous, desperate wrath. As always, the Evil One fishes the most troubled waters.

Initially this rage was visited against us strangers who had become stranded at Ludlow. Seeing the turn of the blood's temperature, I had quickly relinquished our cart to the bedeviled crowds of men and women. A tiny wedge of our shelter, by giving them the cart, went unharmed. But how long might that last?

Since no one had food, and quickly anything burnable had been consumed, strangers were no longer the limit to this wrath.

Both his Grace's residences and two of Ludlow's church residences came under siege.

Terror resided everywhere. Desperate to control the mob, His Grace's thanes and their diverse men rode out from his residence visiting stark violence upon the rioters, for their Godless transgressions reaped pitiless revenge. But such was their extreme of hunger that even while death blows fell upon them, other thanes were dragged from their horses, their beasts killed and hacked up for meat in the midst of things.

Because of two separate such episodes of rioting, by the time spring came upon us, many widows and orphaned children had died, and little hope could be held out for our future. All life was now in ugly flux.

But with the sun, the River Teme thawed, and with the great river returning to life, its bounty began to stir. Where the river was navigable, the ability for a poor boatman to come and go was now possible.

Our lesson in the misery of want continued, however. Now His Grace decided it was not enough to rain violent control on people. The severest justice of the church must also be visited on those who rioted. Several of his housecarls and household folk were killed and maimed during the upheavals, and a half-dozen churchmen and their families assaulted— their homes completely ransacked for anything of value. One deacon had his brain pan caved and now lay fish-brained.

So on days leading up to the Festival of the venerable St. Patrick, the trials and hangings began.

Dozens of executions occurred each day on the direct order of His Grace. Even those in positions of authority viewed their continuance excessive. Finally, the Undersheriff came and dictated a letter to me, circumventing any Ludlow churchmen. It was to His Eminence's Secretary in Hereford, who was his cousin. By this it was hoped His Eminence, of supposedly a kinder nature than his younger brother, would order mercy shown.

Only then would order and peace return, for much repair had to be made.

When Cwenburh suggested a price, the Undersheriff responded gruffly that I would do it gratis or we might all end up being hanged.

Despite this ham-fisted treatment, he was known as a right, God-keeping officer of the town, and was desperate for order.

In fact, it was his oldest son—a lad known for great feats of speed afoot—who would run the entire twenty leagues to Hereford in one bound, as it were. I was told the letter would reach His Eminence's Secretary's hand within six hours times, such was the prowess of the young man.

His Eminence did respond, requesting his brother to show God's mercy. Sadly, however, not with the speed by which he was requested, so many more died during the days before and after Saint Patrick's Festival.

With the return of wild fowl and fish in the River Teme, His Grace's housecarls became ever-vigilant to poachers, hanging some caught. All fish, fowl, and eel belonged to His Grace or His Eminence's thanes.

But desperate people were many and the country—the Welsh

marches—were wild and rugged. The press of urgency makes men clever. I benefited, for being Cuthwin the Scribe, no one suspected my earlier craft on the fens and along the river Nene. Hence, at night when I sneaked out, I was able to tend snare and trap, yet was never suspected, and Cwenburh had the good sense never to appear better off than others. Even the humble muskrat makes good broth, and by and by the spring advanced, and the weather returned to center.

Business, at first meager, resumed. I remember transcribing various '2-Pence Letters' (as Cwenburh came to call them) for local churchmen, which are small letters taken straight to vellum—brief scripts.

In one, a subdeacon told a distant cousin that many wretched people dwelled in the demesne and wetlands and they were possessed by demons. These fiends compelled weaker souls to steal His Grace's and His Eminence's creatures to sustain their sinful, corrupt bodies and families.

When he left with his letter—grousing about me charging a poor churchman for such a simple act—Cwenburh and I were barely able to resist a prideful chuckle. At that day's meal we enjoyed cold grayling and broth, and would this evening.

"This day, Cuthwin, grace said before our meal will pray for the redemption of these fornicators and blasphemers who pass for Our Savior's servants."

When I admonished her for painting all churchman with a common brush—that she must show respect for the Holy Church, she persisted: "If that red-headed murderer is part of the Holy Church, then oxen recite gospels and roosters say the Holy Words."

It was another of her condemnations for His Grace, whom she loathed more than anyone else.

It was during the week of Whitsunday[29] that we and a few other followers of the begang managed to muster enough resources together to hire two former housecarls as protection. We would make our way from Ludlow while the weather was fair.

Ludlow was a low and miserable place after the retributions for the

---

[27] Whitsunday. Celebrated on the seventh Sunday following Easter.

riots. Though we, as a group, made friends there, we also made enemies within the residence of His Grace and other manors of his sworn men. We who followed the traveling life were suspect in their eyes.

"Our Savior fed hosts of the poor on a few fish and loaves of bread, and I give these folk more than that": This thought was commonly attributed to His Grace, as in what he told his thanes and housecarls.

There were only a half dozen of us remaining to form a train, and indeed we were greeted by an armed thane and his men on our way out the road that followed the River Teme. They squared off with our armed escort and we menfolk who carried only cudgel and haypitch.

"His Grace gave you thieves no leave to depart his precincts. You owe him rent and fines for his creatures which you stuffed in your fat paunches—poached from his Grace's demesne and waters. And he will have it before you leave, goddamn you all."

But one of our guards was armed with a Pict short-bow, a lethal and fast weapon close-in; furthermore, he was greatly prized for his accuracy and extraordinary speed. He had come at a dear price, but once paid, was loyal.

All eyes were on that lethal bow. The leather-crafter, our spokesman, was anxious for peace, as were all of us, so he said, "As true Christians, what you say is untrue. Have those in power not sent you into harm's way without care to your well-being nor your families? Do you not see this?"

The thane was mounted, along with two of his men—the others afoot, like us, save for two of the donkeys who pulled our two carts. But their mounts—all of the wretched animals—had bones and ribs showing, and it was a miracle they had not been consumed during hard times. They could barely manage any burden at all.

The entire thrust of this outrage was coin, and we all knew that if the thane returned without anything, he would in turn be fined or somehow docked items of value. Why else would he come on such a fool's mission?

So all of us in conference decided we could muster four shilling and a few pence together to resolve this peacefully. While we talked our bowman kept a 'kestrel's mean eye' on His Grace's men—and them on the bow. Our counter offer was taken at once, but the leather-crafter added wisely, gesturing to me, "And I would inform those necessary that if they pursue this falsehood about us, we will dispatch a letter to none other than Archbishop Eadsige-of-Canterbury. In it we will inform him of His Grace's outrages, and provide proof of them."

All in the land knew of this great prelate's loathing for the brothers His Grace and His Eminence. Also, that Archbishop Eadsige consecrated King Edward and had great sway with him.

My craft as scribe, in an ironic pass, became equal to that of a bowman with a Pict short bow, for His Holiness Eadsige had a hundred thanes and each of them a hundred villains. These would willingly ride west to reclaim in the name of the King all demesne and soke in holding to His Eminence and corrupt mitered brother, then skin each alive.

In this memorable way we left Ludlow, and to this day I have never returned there, initially for the bitterness of memory and also for lack of reason. Years later, the Norman invaders made short end of His Grace, Bishop of Ludlow.

The years immediately following the cursed famine, so-called by folk who lived through it, saw a slow recovery to life as it was before. We followed the begang, of course, for what other life did we have? But it was a lean circuit, beginning with Cwenburh and me carrying many of our necessaries upon our backs.

The twins and Eadrig followed, and if fortunate enough, they could ride in the tiny cart drawn by a single donkey—our entire company.

In my view the aftermath of the cursed famine was worse than the event itself. In addition to the lean times, necessaries such as an armed escort were not possible. Further, the road, towns, and even small crofts were choked with orphaned children and children and mothers with no support.

For these the famine continued.

Where would they live? What would they eat? Who would care for them? The healthier children were subject to all sorts of predations. Even those with a mother surviving who had not deserted were hard-pressed to survive.

Rogue bands of cotsets and diverse criminals wandered; sheriffs and undersheriffs were slow to eliminate them or did nothing at all. This human misery went unnoticed by landed thanes, their tenants and subtenants. Indeed, often they took part in the victimization of the poor and wretched as it offered them a plentiful supply of nearly unpaid labor.

Some of these miserable souls gathered around prominent monasteries, such as Peterborough or Shrewesbury, and the monks there dealt with them as they were able because of their sworn observance before God and the rule of St. Benedict. Yet even then some Abbeys and Monasteries, may God forgive me for recollecting this, did nothing but drive these wretched souls away. City and town clerics were less help, and great men of diverse elevations did little or nothing.

In the far reaches of the land, balls of fire and scourges of flames beset bad and good alike. These catastrophes were guided by the vengeance of God who was punishing the evil amongst the faithful.

But in recollecting these times from my own personal observations, I emphasize that no general statement about charity towards the poor can be fairly made about any specific persons or group. Every party and group had both merciful and cruel souls. None were exempt from the sin of selfishness and violation of our Savior's most central act, that of mercy and charity towards the poor.

For those traveling between fairs and markets, it was a dangerous time, and often it was necessary to stay in one place—or, at best, travel shorter routes to poorly chartered fairs or markets. So many adversely struck by the cursed famine businesses remained poor.

And these times were personally devastating to kind Cwenburh who witnessed especially the homeless children with profound sorrow and spiritual distress. Though always braced outwardly, I knew her toughness was powerfully tried. We constantly took homeless wanderers under our wing, sharing what we had when in fact we had little ourselves—our own children wanting for necessities.

"How might we recover if our resources are constantly drained by our charity? Look at us, Cwenburh!"

"We must do as best we can, Cuthwin, through God's help and the words of our Savior."

She weighed no more than six stone[30] and had not regained her former fine flesh. It would have been useless to argue with her and add to our already difficult times. Our own children took to giving charity as the water bug does to the pond, and especially Eadrig, a serious child. He was always somber of purpose and possessed Matilda's spirit by blood and Cwenburh's by example and love.

The twins Matilda and Elesa, however, would have tried the patience of Holy St. Nicholas Himself. Many times—not just now but throughout the troublesomeness of their childhood—Cwenburh was taken with great temper, hiking up her kirtle and chasing them about with great oaths and a switch. And God help me, I would intercede on their behalf, despite their guilt and mischievous natures, and all three of us would occupy troubled seas that day.

I remember, fondly of course, Eadrig lecturing the twins on better comportment for Christian young ladies—them listening intently, always intending reform. Waifs traveling with us would experience these scenes with awe, not remembering such times in their own lives.

Many a night following the cursed famine, our quarters—wherever they were—appeared more a camp of wanderers than of a scribe and his family.

It was close to the eighth year of King Edward's reign[31] when we made winter quarters near Wilton that Cwenburh came in contact with Wilton Abbey and Abbess Herelufu and her dedicated nuns. This Abbey was richly endowed of lands and means through chaste Edith, wife of the King.

This Abbey was great for its charities in number, magnitude, and nature, and this was because of the thought and strength of Mother Herelufu, herself a daughter of a great Earldamon. And it was through

---

[30] Stone. Fourteen pounds. Someone weighing six stones would be eighty-four pounds.

[31] King Edward the Confessor reigned from 1042-1066.

this powerful Abbess's ideas of charity, many of them new and held in dubious regard by the Abbot of Wilton, that Almoner Gunnhilda entered our life.

By this time, we had recovered most of our former economy and health. Eadrig was part of my activities, having learned to write a good hand from myself, almost as easily as teaching him the ways of mending a simple leather strap. In truth I was proud to instruct and to watch him learn so readily.

I, for one, would watch in wonder as he wrote with either hand almost equally well, for I had not seen that, even in the Scriptorium at Peterborough. Further, he had over time scrutinized my three priceless books I managed to buy piecemeal over the years: King Alfred's *Psalter* in our language, the venerable King's translation of *The Consolation of Philosophy* by the great Boethius, and diverse excerpts from the Bible in Anglo-Saxon, Norman, and the language of Rome.

Through good and bad times, I built these up, for a man whose business and love is language, it is unwise to languish in mind. So at just eleven years of age, our boy was an eager and important part of our means on the begang. All would have proceeded without event if not for this first winter at Wilton and Wilton Abbey, in reality two abbeys in one, both apart.

From this unlikely and most unexpected direction conflict came into my life, and I was not equal to it, may God forgive me and those whom I afflicted.

Gunnhilda at Almoner-of-Wilton Nunnery sought help from womenfolk who followed the begang and wintered there. She was an aggressive, resolute officer, and most effective when dealing outside cloister.

Often with a pair of monks struggling to follow in her wake—for nuns who didn't occupy office never went outside cloister—she would follow a route in the pursuit and assigned purpose of Mother Abbess's charities.

In these efforts, Gunnhilda required womenfolk to separate from the nuns in the Abbey. They were needed to help with the dozens of female waifs now growing up in a series of buildings abutting the Abbey.

"And not just well-born girls, but any under God's skies. Just think what otherwise might befall them if not for Mother Herelufu's ware[32]."

Cwenburh was Almoner Gunnhilda's foremost recruit. That first winter—when the ware was in its development—there was much to do. During it I lost the labors of Cwenburh in my growing list of winter projects.

For now I was reserving longer and more thoughtful commissions for the months when I was in one place. A most important craft was in psalters for more monied freedmen of station and soke, though usually only for town and city clerics who could read and required several personalized copies.

One day Gunnhilda brushed into the small shop I rented, almost knocked over Eadwig in her wake, and in her brusque way announced, "Mother Abbess needs a letter sent directly to the King Himself, and you shall have the great honor of doing it."

I told her at once I did not get involved in the doings of great men and women, and she must seek out loftier craftsmen than a mere begang scribe.

"Mother Abbess nor I nor our sisters write at all, or expertly enough. She orders it, and it is not your purview to deny it, Cuthwin-of-Alnwick. You and yours live and breathe on her demesne and at her holy offices."

"And, Reverend Mistress, it is because of the well-being of my wife and children I do not involve myself in the acts and business of great people. I am a freedman, I pay my taxes to Mother Abbess and Wilton Abbey, and I am an honest, God-fearing man in good standing. I must do what is best for my family."

Then after spitting fire and smoke, she was gone, vowing great retribution. Eadwig thought a moment in his calm way, for he was studying the Norman language in order to expand our services, and said, "She is a very overpowering Holy Woman, Father, is she not?"

At Vespers there were few words between Cwenburh and me, and later as she administered the warm stones to my writing hand, we avoided eye contact. Eadwig and the twins felt the discomfort in the air. I knew that after prayers at Compline when the children would be put to

---

[32] Ware. O.E. meaning protection or guard.

bed, a questioning wind would commence.

In sounding our differences, not unusual with us, we did not become disrespectful of each other's offices, for after that first year together, we never repeated those youthful follies.

But the truth was that by using me, Mother Abbess was attempting to get around Father Abbot, and thereby the Bishop of Salisbury, conducting some sort of intrigue. The three were at constant odds and loathed each other endlessly; that was the truth of it.

"But Cuthwin, you were rude to the Mistress Almoner, and she of such great charity and giving to the little ones."

"Dear Cwenburh, once you become a link in the chain of such powerful people, even if only by simple obedience, you risk destruction and ruin, and that is a fact. In the name of God and Our Savior you have seen that yourself."

"Do you resent so much of my time spent away from here? Is that part of this, for you are always so respectful and circumspect with Holy people?"

And, this was the first time this issue arose—this fulcrum which could bring friction between us. Cwenburh's sense of charity was powerful and giving, and may God forgive me for impeding it, no matter how lovingly.

By denying her question—and I did—I did little to convince her; also, wisps of guilt nibbled at the kernel of her question—if there be some truth in it.

Yet I was a student of events which are often like crumbs—leading in a certain direction where their eventual destination can be anticipated. The more keen the student, the shorter the trail of crumbs needed to be.

I did not want this situation to arise again.

At once I decided not to winter at Wilton again, even though—at the confluence of two rivers, and kindly accommodated by weather and resources—it was a good place. Returning instead next winter to Winchester would eliminate the matter. So I decided to bide the issue, easing through it with as much peace as possible, and—above all—to veer out of harm's way and keep our family free of thorny issues.

Within a week of the encounter with Reverend Almoner, I found myself looking at an elderly woman whom I knew to be a non-cloistered factotum for Mother Abbess. She was an elfin woman with wide blue eyes that locked on her subject with a mixture of wonder and craft.

"You do such wonderful work, Master Scribe. It is God's gift. Mother Abbott needs discuss this gift with you. Might you attend after Sext?"

It was less than a week after Reverend Almoner's visit, and I was not unprepared for its consequences—Mother Abbess rarely requested and was never denied when she did.

A scribe's wishes are nothing compared to the power of an Abbess or Abbot.

She received me in her residence: One portion given to her public necessities, the other inside cloister.

She sat on a stool working at her spindle; the room was unadorned, keeping with her avowed demeanor of humility and plain living. I knelt. She rose and made the sign over me. I kissed the crucifix that hung on a long, simple braided rope around her neck.

Abbess Herelufu was a comely woman, cousin to Queen Edith, and of great family, often discussed with pride by those at Wilton for Edith was raised there. These were influential and wealthy people with concerns not of ordinary folk, free or otherwise.

She signed a dismissive gesture to her factotum and we were alone. She bade me to rise. Abbess Herelufu sat back down, and did not resume her work, but looked me over as a wife would a plump chicken.

There was something—a tiny motion—it might have been a shrug and sigh; then she did pick up her work, but rested it in her lap

"Abbot Denewulf remembers you from Peterborough where he was Prior, years ago."

I felt as if kicked in the middle—Denewulf was a common name, and I had foolishly never expected the Prior of Peterborough—so far away from Wilton—to be the same as the feared Abbot here. I tried to keep my composure, but she must have seen her news struck home.

"Abbot Denewulf wants me to turn our poor waifs out. And Reverend Abbot makes abundantly clear to His Grace the Bishop that offering shelter and charity is one thing, but raising them from girls to womanhood out of cloister invites sin and diverse evil doings. In short, he opposes the ware—holding the idea of a ware being against the order of things, hence God's will."

She smiled a bit, then did shrug.

"Father Abbot has great influence, and despite the King's charter making specifically ours a double monastery, Father Abbot persists in his position. That is, as being superior to my office and all weaker women who stand before God and Holy Benedict's God-given Rule."

So this was the argument—it was always something like such amongst the influential at court. More germane to me, the severe Reverend Denewulf would, of course, have told her everything concerning myself directly or indirectly. This would certainly include Cwenburh's bondage, escape, and my dealings at the great Monastery, including owing money.

But I knew common Hundred law relented a debt after so many years, and indeed those years were double-passed. However, a bonded woman never was free of, in Cwenburh's sad case, the nature of her birth—as daughter of a slave and her owner.

She allowed me time to follow this trail of crumbs to its proper end—not needing to say what I must conclude: Cwenburh's long-ago status the two of us never discussed because of its thorny and intractable nature. Now it could be alleviated or just as readily revealed. Cwenburh and I were in her pincers.

"So, Cuthwin, to gently explain Reverend Almoner: The letter, before God and Our Savior, is not to the King but to his august consort, Gentle Edith. But true enough, it needs be of the highest quality and of the most somber nature. My gratitude for your craft will be in a Writ of Manumission for sweet and charitable Cwenburh, your wife. As elected Abbess, it is within my power to do that without prejudice."

"And, Mother Abbess, when must the letter to the Queen be completed?"

"I set out for Court within the week, God willing."

It was all done as the powerful get it done, by compulsory order or its close sibling. Such events are conducted above and beyond the feelings of ordinary folk who spend years learning their crafts—ultimately, they are on the beck and call of their betters when and how they require them.

Contrary to all my instincts I crafted a fine letter which evaded the purview of the Bishop His Grace and Father Abbot. I counted the blessed weeks when I would be away from Abbess Herelufu for good.

Some days later Cwenburh—who had been very pleased at me for relenting and crafting the letter—greeted me after my work. She, I assumed, remained ignorant of the reason I did so. Though a holiday, I had worked beginning at Prime, for I had a backload of work.

The children, including the serious Eadrig, had gone to a Saint's Day show with the baker's wife and her children; in fact, we were to attend later.

Feeling the balm of the warm stones creep around my wrist and hand, I looked over and saw her Writ of Manumission on a block—an edge of approaching spring light illuminating it.

"Mother Abbess has freed me, Cuthwin. I am a free woman."

"Yes, it is God's will, and a joy to me."

"It is in your hand, but witnessed by His Grace and Ealdorman[33] Fyndson."

"They applied their blessed hands after I had crafted the document. I do many writs, as you know. But that was a special joy to me. I wanted it to be a surprise."

"Oh, it was all of that."

She sat next to me, not busying herself with readying to go, and she seemed anything but joyful. I looked at this woman who had been with me constantly now for a decade plus five—since she had been an impish girl. Her intelligence was great. Yet those outside, I guessed, saw her as a capable, compassionate, busy wife and business partner, and she was.

But her intelligence was her own and subtle. I perhaps allowed myself at times to forget it as well. She was never slow observing causes and effects. At once I knew she either smelt the foul odor of the deed's truth, or actually knew it, then she passed along a fact most alarming: "I was visited by Reverend Prior yesterday. He says that Eadrig's prowess has gained the attention of Reverend Guthrith, and most of all Abbot

---

[33] Ealdorman. A high ranking royal official and prior magistrate of an Anglo-Saxon shire or group of shires.

Denewulf. He made special mention of your masterful decorative hand at letters. This means, Cuthwin, Eadrig is being eyed as a possible oblate at the Abbey."

My memory about this moment is crisp and will remain so. Brother Guthrith was Master of the Scriptorium at Wilton, and he viewed me with unblemished disapproval. I had gone against the order of things and God's Will by learning my craft, and worse—plying it in trade.

But certainly in the eyes of Father Abbot—enabling the Abbess to circumvent the normal order of things was another, fouler matter. Taking Eadrig to tonsure would add to his motive.

And Reverend Guthrith? He was a cruel and inept monk, and I would sooner Eadrig work in a watermill than under his eye. Anyone with any sense knew this as well. Abbot Denewulf's vengeance had begun. He would have Eadrig.

All thoughts of attending a Saint Day celebration drained from me in a moment, leaving a void.

"And what did you tell the Reverend Prior, Cwenburh?"

"First, you tell me if writing the letter to the Queen, which has started these troubles, was done against your will—somehow using my long-ago status as lever?"

Her eyes went to the writ—mine followed. She knew the answer; my policy of avoiding the doings of great people was absolute—then, and now. And at that moment, we were seeing the wisdom of it, God forgive me for such prideful reflection.

"It was."

She put her own hands around the warm stones—sharing with me their balm, in fact reaching further and taking mine in hers.

"Well, wise husband, Cuthwin, I told Reverend Prior to attend the stables and couple with the animals, thereby giving respite to young, powerless girl-waifs who are years from being women."

"Oh no, Cwenburh! Jesus save us! We are lost!"

The dark business of gossip about Reverend Prior and others had it so, and God forbid, many folks in neighborhood knew it to be true.

And within the moment, I looked at this wife of mine, and her eyes—and especially the animate corners of her mouth. These informed me at once, with a sort of relief, that her tale dealt a bit of revenge upon me for excluding her from the original truth of the dealing.

"Cuthwin! You think I would do that now? No. I said nothing of merit, one way or the other. Even Reverend Mother Almoner must pretend the unseeing about that pig so averts eyes heavenward."

So we sat there next to each other, our hands warming on the rocks, and sharing in the knowledge that we must go very soon—that the one advantage we had was freedom, plus the honest coin we had put by. And above all we had Good Eadwig and the girls to consider now.

I knew that it was God's hand which guided us now, and would—I knew—see us safely gone from selfish minds who sowed power for selfish reasons. These mighty ones enjoyed benefiting from the good but passed any bad to those who worked day to day, year to year. They saw this spinelessness as God's ordained right.

It was that way then and it is the same now.

God favored us by the King holding court far distant from Wilton at Sussex, and Edith his noble consort was with him. So though it was known that Mother Abbess carried a letter to Lady Edith, and who wrote it for her, nothing was known with precision about what it conveyed, save myself and Mother Abbess.

As I had learned on my first job of scribe—with Sidroc-the-Old—adherence to absolute confidence with all clients was necessary if I were to survive as a scribe, or at all. Even to this very day, seventy years after writing that letter, I adhere to that swearing, though it originates from myself.

But I knew the contents of the letter would not alleviate ill-will between powerful figures at Wilton, but increase it. So in view of the good fortune of this delay, I decided to launch upon the begang early that year. We needed to get clear of this snarl of acrimony.

Further, since we occupied the demesne of Mother Abbott specified to her by Royal Charter, my coming and going was technically beyond Father Abbott. He would surely keep me pegged to him until he knew precisely what was in the letter and had his revenge. The Abbey's Scriptorium benefiting from the gifted Eadrig was only, to him, a side benefit.

But I would rather face the perennial fires before allowing that blackguard to have my beloved adopted son.

We traveled far north that year on the great Ermine Street Road, heading for far York where we would commence our business on St. George's Day[34], which fell well after Easter. That year it was maintained we would do well to begin there and work south until the cold fairs and festivals of autumn.

It was an opportune time for attending business at northern fairs and such, for in the long-ago wake of the cursed famine, Northumberland had made the greatest rebound. Further, as I traveled back south, I could attend letters-to-family and business to see they were dropped off at appropriate places, which Cwenburh added to their fee, may God forgive us.

"It is not cheap, venturing throughout the country," she would tell our clients she judged to be somewhat more monied than most.

Our traveling family, as we craftspeople termed each other, was large, for many were eager to strike out for richer grounds. We made a great adventure of it for the children, and Eadrig was full of facts about it—he being our traveling wise man in such things.

"Uncle, they maintain that sullen, vengeful dragons fly up and down the great rivers in Northampton."

And he would raise great commotion amongst the twins by drawing such creatures on discarded pieces of vellum, thusly his superior hand provided much entertainment for the children of the train and also the adults. First and last, he was a boy of nearly thirteen now, and would have his sport with youngsters, as God allowed to those enjoying the carefree years of youth.

But viewing these drawings also provided great increase in scrutiny of Selvig and Essox, our guards—the former a grand old warrior, and the

---

[34] Saint George's Day. Generally on April 23rd, depending on that year's date of Easter Sunday.

latter a clever dwarf, as alert as the hedge stoat.

They spoke a strange tongue, were kinsmen, yet got angry if anyone asked if they were Danes. Whatever language they spoke, they were as fluid as robins, for their Saxon was poor indeed—Selvig's most rudimentary. He had fought in many armies and places, was grandly illustrated with scars and gouges, and swore by his axe and buckler.

At Huntingdon we paused over a long holiday in celebration of two saints. I returned to our pavilion to find great solemnity greeting me instead of the usual joy of kinship.

Eadrig sat in the corner showing his psalter to the twins once again, reading to them quietly one of the psalms. He had crafted the smallish volume over several years in memorial of his mother Matilda.

And it was none of your apprentice work, but a masterpiece for any age. To think a young craftsman, not quite out of apprenticeship, would produce such a fine volume. As mentor during its creation, I was enormously proud.

"Cuthwin, your nephew has a question for you, of which I would not discuss with him, and strongly disapprove of. You must intercede."

Cwenburh was not often angry with Eadrig, in fact rarely so. But she was now, and out of a corner of my eye I glimpsed a broken switch, and saw a welt upon the side of Eadrig's neck. This was a most extraordinary situation. Eadrig was calm, looked from his reading and wondered if the twins would fetch us sweet saint's bread the baker made that morning. This was indeed a task beloved to the imps.

He gave them a few coins, and they went off. He knew their absence was wise at the moment—always a precocious lad.

When alone I learned at once the time had come for we three. Truth never abandons those who follow the way of Our Savior, which certainly was Eadrig's way.

"Uncle, I have for many years heard that my mother was of uncertain morals; in fact, the word *harlot* is applied. Is this true?"

"Husband! I will not have sweet Matilda called such, in the name of our Savior who values above all forgiveness. She gave you life, for all your knowledge, Eadrig!"

Wrath was fully in her nose, and it would not do at this moment to have this out before faithful Cwenburh—it just was not in her nature to allow a beloved friend be maligned, even by one to whom she was devoted.

I asked her to excuse us with all patience, and Eadwig and I went for a walk. We strolled out from the town's precincts towards the country-side, in fact where an ancient watermill labored and eelmen trapped. The trees had leaved out fully—birds were returning and setting up their spaces with song. Beneath, cows bedded, chewing their cuds and slap-ping at the advent of insects with their tails.

It was a peaceful backdrop to what must be brought forth.

He was Matilda's son, and I knew she would want him to know everything as he entered manhood, and this is what I did, as kindly and directly as possible. We were both people who lived by words.

Dear Matilda had saved Cwenburh's life, and likely mine as well. And more than that, voluntarily relinquished the one she loved more than anything in the world, which was Eadwig, doing it for him and leaving him to God's will.

I explained how innocent children—infants, after all—like Matilda are sold into slavery like spindles or swaths of cloth, and are possessed by their owner for the remainder of their life. Furthermore, how they have no choice, none whatsoever, in their lot, and do what is compelled, and without foreknowledge or prejudice.

It is what they do each day, during—in this case—a very short life and manner of survival.

When I was through, he made the sign—and called on me, at that moment, to pray with him for Matilda, and we did. I asked if he held his mother in poorer judgment knowing that truth of matters.

He seemed taken aback, as I hoped he would be, for I had come to know and love him more than any man could a natural-born son, thank God.

"Oh, no, Uncle. Of course not. I will always value and love her memory; if anything, even more now."

At that most inappropriate moment, even a poorer memory than mine would recall the boisterous interruption: Two eelmen became involved in a shoving match over several sticks of eels. During a Saint's celebration they should not have been working, but despite this, were extracting God's bounty from the stream to sustain them in their cups which they had abundantly indulged.

Eadrig went over calling for peace between them, in the name of the Holy Saint, and calmed their donkey, who had joined in the fracas by braying its lament, refusing to accept the loutish eelmen's burden.

They were coarse with Eadrig, who returned to my side and shrugged it all off, and we proceeded back to town. He and Cwenburh, of course, would later embrace, for the great heat would have diminished in her blood.

And it was God's Word which provided me a future truth, first seen by Cwenburh. For several weeks, she lamented same during our most private moments. But it was on this pivotal day, while stopping by the river to study a kingfisher diving for small fish that I overcame my fears: "Eadrig, I think we will soon lose you."

"Oh, I would never abandon you, Uncle or Auntie."

"I know, but you must. Your God-given gifts are such that you cannot peddle letters from pillar to post the rest of your life working for pence. God calls you to greater things, and you know His truth. You have asked about great scriptoria often."

And we traveled back to our pavilion, my arm around him, knowing that we must now plan for this, and do it well.

Since this great adventure north would take us through Peterborough, it was incumbent on me to do more than simply ply old memories there. I knew that Eadrig's best course must be taken with the finest advice available, and such advice must be sought. Peterborough was the one place I knew it to be available.

I had kept close track of events at Peterborough Monastery and township, natural for me since I was more of Peterborough than Alnwick, my birthplace. And in the years of my business, which was the exchange of information over distances, it was easier for me than others.

I knew my teacher and master at livery, Gilbert, had died years previous, and that most others had too, save a few. And one of these, praise God, was Father Abbot Elsin Himself. Years before he had gratefully withdrawn to the life of an ordinary cenobite. Citing infirmities, he resigned as Abbot, retired to private quarters in advancing age, and resumed the contemplations dear to him.

But the fact he was a venerated and influential counselor throughout western Christendom pursued him everywhere.

It was fourteen years since Cwenburh and I set eyes on our native fens. By this time one would think, Eadrig, Matilda, and Elesa had grown weary of our stories there, but they claimed not, in fact urging us in the telling.

We had become quite the jongleurs. But now that everyone saw the real country of our youth, they seemed to be satisfied with our strengths as storytellers.

Our trip across the fens was only a few days past the Festival of The Annunciation[35]. And though spring arrived several weeks before, it was a wet time to travel. The road, never good, was troubled with streams overflowing, and bridges half-submerged by spring waters.

For all of us in train it was imperative to reach York for St. George's Week festival. We could not take long at Peterborough.

We were not more than half-a-day in Peterborough than Cwenburh, via the quick network of gossip, was an authority on events, which of late had turned intense between Old Father Abbot and the new Abbot

---

[35] The Annunciation, March 25th.

Leofric. The King had been consulting often with the Venerable Elsin about the current great troubles, and the aged man wanted little of this.

Hence, when spring arrived, Venerable Elsin took to his beloved fens to live simply upon a raised-reed house with one attendant. It was early for his move, for those wise to the fens knew high waters were still at hand and the ancient sage might float out to sea. Also there were few comforts—but he told all he was closest to God and his Son, Our Savior, only more in veneration to St. Guthlac, to whom he prayed thrice daily, and whose Festival Day was close at hand[36].

Some would assume, most tellingly the King, he cleverly designed distance from matters of the court.

When the King's messenger found Old Abbot Elsin retired to the fens, he ordered Abbot Leofric to command the Venerable Elsin to return 'where people who loved and cared for him could look to his needs.'

And here the conflict warmed, especially in the telling of it—for the old man was dear to the folk of Peterborough. Father Abbot would never order Venerable Elsin to do anything, his love for him was such. Lastly, and perhaps most significantly, the saintly man was leather-headed, and would not have obeyed anyway.

Hence, the week previous, two powerful Ealdormen and their party came from the King to consult Elsin and found the venerated man still upon the fens. When they went to consult, they were subject to hardship and even humiliation when one fell into muddy water and needed to be hauled out, contrary to the dignity due such great men.

Cwenburh reveled in the situation.

"Now, the fox is loosed in the yard! And Father Abbot is in great disfavor from the King."

In the end there was no way for us to see him save to venture out, stand hopefully on the boat landing—like all such landings in the fens— blow a great horn, and hope to be recognized. Worse, evidently his attendant was known to be grumpy and contrary, even to the Ealdorman's party.

---

[36] Saint Guthlac's Day, April 11.

"I think, seeing who sounded the horn, he shall pee on you," guessed the nephew of the leathermaster, our train's leader.

The next morning Eadwig carefully packed up his mother's psalter, and with it a gift, which by tradition on the fens must remain secret from fellow pilgrims. We packed a great quantity of good smoked eel and bread with a tank of fresh ale.

Ours was an expectant train which traveled single-file out the dike-path, which divided three ways at the landing. All around us swallows swirled—looking for early spring repast, for these hardy spirits preceded others of their kind hoping to gain advantage over slower travelers.

Gleaming white egrets fished—looking steady-eyed at the muddy water, moving stealthily through the reeds—then of a sudden striking out, and coming up with a struggling fish. Our youngsters looked on with fixed wonder.

I listened and gazed at this long-missed panorama. It was difficult for me to keep from talking on about the old memories.

"Soon, the frogs will begin talking, even during the morning. There are great times with those."

Several times Matilda and Elesa attempted to play in the turbid spring water which surrounded the trail with raised dikes and passages atop them. These industrious passages were crafted over generations of work by those who lived and died on the fens.

"Did gnomes or spirits build these, Mother?"

And Cwenburh fielded the dozen questions at a time the girls had, with Eadwig doing his best to help—their minds as quick and unquench-able as a tree full of rooks.

At the landing were a half-dozen shells and larger flat-boats, several more elaborate than normal—the only clue of trappings beyond the ordinary. And as with most landings, on a pole hung a great ox horn.

My excitement rose as I took the instrument, remembering the ways of its blowing.

All looked on as I took the horn, inflated myself like a bagpipe, and let fly, sounding a deep, long call—feeling pride at remembering. As the bellow of the horn faded, the stillness seemed even quieter.

We looked out on a sea of reeds, rushes, and tiny islands still not grown lush yet, but swaths of green signed early return growth. Below the rising sun, the complicated patterns of islands and channels wove their vast maze. These would puzzle any save those frequenting the byways of the fens—as movable as the tide itself over time.

It was a spring day. The clouds sailed in from the sea and a lusty brightness took hold of their edges by the rising sun—which later would dissolve them away to allow the land its full bounty.

Then we saw an object coming our way, still far from us.

And at first it was only tiny, and finally distinguishable was a boatman—one man poling along, his strokes even, unhurried—head up, alert to who waited.

All watched expectantly. He took up his pole, allowing the craft to drift towards us as he looked over this strange lot of pilgrims.

And at the moment, we both recognized each other.

"Jesus, Our Savior; is that you Frog? Do you remember me?"

"Young Cuthwin, I do indeed. Who is this horde you have brought with you?"

The girls hid behind Cwenburh; Eadwig stood straighter, yet at the moment looked to me, for I had spoken often of Frog, my greatest teacher at wildcrafting.

Frog tied off at the landing, stepped out, and we embraced; he had aged mightily, and in fact was missing two more fingers and part of an ear.

I made introductions with my family, and he took a long look at each, nodding as he absorbed each detail, his mind and eye like an osprey.

He took a breath that signaled a resigned penitent, but it seemed suspect. He gestured in all directions.

"Well, here I am. My uncle saved me from the gallows. The Undersheriff finally caught me at the traps, but Uncle Elsin used his great influence. And I had to swear on my mother's—his sister's—grave to serve him for five full years in good faith and obedience. No better woman than my mother lived anywhere. So see what I've come to. I carry on like a damned monk."

I had not known Father Abbot was his uncle, but it went directly to those times years ago when he often asked after Frog. Frog looked

Cwenburh up and down, making her blush.

"By God, Cuthwin, you have yourself a handsome wife. I stole many a fat fish from Wilfred-of-Loe's weirs, and was the better for it, the tight-fisted bastard."

It was the scandalous stuff. His position of contrition and penance had not ridded him of a frank tongue nor dulled his memory. Cwenburh gasped a bit, as did the girls, and then laughed under cover of her kirtle. Eadwig appraised him, and could not withhold a smile at his tart words.

Without further word, we set off; Frog poled the larger of the boats, while I did the smaller, following in his wake with Eadwig—the lad deeply and freshly astounded with every reed and backwater of the fens.

Ahead, the reeds and floating plants parted, then closed back around us; the girls and Cwenburh chatted at a high rate, and it was a wonderful time, praise God for his gift of the beautiful fens.

And soon, in more open water, we came upon the house and it was larger than most. The poles were taller, stout, and higher above the water. Plus, a yardarm extended to lift up burdens from the water, and the steps up were masterfully crafted; and sitting atop the peak of the house was a plain wooden cross.

Frog made fast at the base of the stairs.

"Himself will be overjoyed by this menagerie of plain folk you bring him. He is bored with grand people of great purpose and issue, the greedy bastards."

As we climbed the stairs, from inside emerged Old Father Abbot— older, more stooped, and helped along with a staff, smooth with use. But his eyes had not aged a jot, and they looked at each of us as we came out onto his level, but stopped on me, and he smiled grandly.

Frog made introduction to those he wouldn't know. We went down, all of us, on our knees so he could make the sign over us. Unlike sturdy-hearted Cwenburh, I have a too-ready way with tears and sometimes embarrass her. Yet, God forgive, the fact was, I was no gladder to see anyone else in my life outside of Cwenburh, even at those quietest times when she is starting the fire and greeting the new day with prayer, and singing gently a tune of her childhood.

It was a great morning, and soon Cwenburh was at ease, for talking with Father Abbot was like gossiping with any ordinary Saxon; indeed, that language was his favorite of the many he spoke—it flew fast and furious. And God forgive me for talking outside my place, but in truth, Father Abbot loved gossip, and would listen fondly to it—and partake briefly, until he would nod, asking forgiveness for his temporary lapse.

Then return to eager listening.

Finally, it was time for business, and he closely examined the psalter Eadwig had made—a tiny thing, lacking rich makings, but so elaborate in its doing. He was awed as others had been.

"Words of praise have preceded you, Eadwig, and they are accurate. Cuthwin, you are a great teacher, but surely this is the work of a prodigy—in miniature, may God praise."

"If you would only bless it, Father Abbot; it would be a glory to his mother, may Our Savior forgive and ease her soul."

"Forgive, Cuthwin? No, I think instead we should pray to forgive her murderers."

"By Jesus, even I will say holy words over that."

And all looked to Frog, whom we had forgotten for the moment. Eadwig handed over his psalter as Father Abbot was helped to his knees by Frog, and everyone joined in prayer as he blessed the psalter.

At Sext fatigue overcame him—by that time Himself had been awake since Lauds. He aired advice for Eadwig: "He should travel to the great Scriptorium at Monte Cassino in Italy; there is no greater place to see and learn great writings of all kinds. There writing and words are the highest praise men might commit in physical form—and accompanying art work—to the glory of God and our Savior."

We all looked to one another—for this advice struck us as if Father Abbot had suggested Eadwig venture to the sun or moon. No one could speak—how might I respond? Finally, despite its source, I raised the obvious with Father Abbot: "But Father Abbot, a young boy going that distance with little means, the ways of the world—and of the roads—are fraught with death and injury every league of the way, God Forgive me for saying. We love the boy too much for that."

He nodded, took the last bit of ale, and gestured to Frog, and with a bit of a shrug—in fact, at the moment I thought he might ask for more ale, "Frog will take him. He is expert in the way of the road, and I have a most urgent letter for His Holiness in Rome to be carried by the King's escort who will soon arrive here to take it. The two will accompany them. Then he looked sadly to Cwenburh adding, ". . . and Mother Cwenburh, he must part from you very soon, as necessity demands."

Frog took this in with no more note than he might an errand into Peterborough. "And I needs carry a weapon, Uncle. King's escorts are brainless sots."

Father Abbot closed his eyes for a moment, as if Frog's harsh practicalities might vanish. He looked at Eadwig, reached out and took him by the shoulders. "You Eadwig, do you intend to take tonsure at the end of all this?"

"Yes, Father Abbot, as God is my witness."

"Good, then your obedience will start now, at my word. You are to have possession of a letter of personal nature to Father Abbot in Monte Cassino—we were student-oblates together those years ago. Frog will return with the response, for I yearn to hear from him while both of us are mortal souls."

Struggling to rise, he made sign over us all, added that weariness was overcoming him rapidly, and that Frog would take us back. His wit, though, still moved with rapidity and clear direction.

"So, you and your begang will have one more day here? Eadwig will stay on at the Monastery with me until I leave two days after Saint Guthlac's great celebration. But only to France to see the legate. The King insists I start no later than then. I come in on the morrow; we shall meet then at Father Abbot's residence."

On our way back to the landing, Matilda and Elesa wept. They were not so young as not to understand how events stood. Eadwig, their brother—great companion and teacher—was leaving their life.

Frog seemed out of sorts, and tying the boats up, stood on the dike top, in fact taking me aside a bit: "The Old Man is sly. He goes to Rome. He knows that the so-called escort carries the King's command for him with it." He tossed a hostile gesture towards the distant King's Court, ". . . so the King will impose a sentence of death, the bastard—commanding an old venerable man like him to Rome over his own fucking problems."

He cast a look out on the fens, being delivered of so much life in the strengthening spring. He took heart and gave me a parting slap on the back and returned to his boat.

That evening late in our pavilion, I let Cwenburh know how it really stood with the old Abbot being ordered off the fens to traverse a ruthless road. Together in the dark, we prayed at length for Father Abbot, Eadwig, and the querulous Frog. We were proud of Eadwig and for such a wonderful mind and soul God allowing to enter our lives via his beloved Matilda.

Cwenburh only said what I thought—as well as Frog and others: "Such an ancient as Father Abbot will never survive such a trip. What sort of man is King Edward?"

"He is the greatest and most powerful man of all, and only God has command of him. Kings do what they please."

In the dark, holding each other, both of us recalled the night—how Matilda scooted under the wagon at the camp of Alfred-of-Aylesbury.

She had sidled up beside us, still yet a girl, uncovered her bosom where Eadwig sucked. "This is my newborn, Eadwig. I have spit on the hot stones, and they foretell that he will be a great man."

These were her first private words to us. Then she plied us for stories of our adventures—and how we had told her truthfully of our flight. We never thought such a soul could not be trusted. And her gift of trust and right carried to Eadwig.

That God's supposed ordained servants ordered her death flew in the face of right faith and belief. No—the act of murdering good Matilda and her sisterhood was by Satan Himself, his craving for souls always unquenchable. And any who did His bidding became damned before God.

The months following Eadrig's departure at Peterborough were sad for both us and the twins; also all members of the begang missed him as well. Despite his youth, he shined good spirits on us all.

Business at York, as we had been advised, was lively—moreso for me, as my valued and beloved assistant was gone. And finding business so venturesome, the begang, in a group decision, plied its way north, finding great profit as it went.

I became overwhelmed with work. I kept alert for any replacement, and eventually, that late summer encountered Ligulf-of-Darlington.

Ligulf was greyed, and earlier in life was a clerk somewhere, but he fell into disgrace and cast off to wander the country. He only alluded to it indirectly, and we never pried. It was enough that Ligulf was practiced in writing both Saxon and the language of Rome. Yet he was vulnerable to strong drink, poor meek soul that he was. He took direction well, though, and Cwenburh kept a weather eye on him after we gave him pay—just before each Sabbath.

We thereby always knew where to fetch him on the morning following each holy day. He certainly was no substitute—even by half—for Eadrig, but he took some of the pressure from me. He did simple missives well, though on some days had unsteady hand. So when recovering from his cups, he was of no use.

At the conclusion of St. Giles[37] Festival in Durham, our train set out south through prospering countryside with thoughts to avoid the Northumberland harsh winters. Praise be to God, it was a bountiful year, and fields and forests were festooned with God's riches. Indeed, throughout the land working folk busied with winter preparations, as well they must.

Our train's business of proceeding south was keen—anxious to make

---

[37] Saint Giles Day. September 1st.

as much daily progress as possible along the Northumberland Road, not a bad one for its kind. We added one extra guard to Selvig and Essox, a friend of theirs from previous battle-strewn days, skilled with lance and swing-ax. He mounted a massive but ageing horse he called Pisser, and both were favorites with the children. We carried all our coin now, and were especially aware of the notorious hazards of the road.

It was our fortune to encounter hunting parties of villagers, tenants, and sub-tenants bristling with pig-lances, thinning out the fatter wild pigs from those ranging the thick woods—property of rich thanes and tenants. On this year especially, the forest floor was rich with pannage, choice stuff for owners.

From these parties we purchased quarters of fat wild pig, and elected—especially if the weather was fair—to encircle and camp in the country.

Such times were our reward for enduring the begang—not having a home, save our pavilions and what we might fashion to augment them. The tiny villages and surrounding crofts were busy with the business of country and stream—especially with the now-fattened livestock which Saxons held dear to their life of independence.

It was close to the River Tees we made such a camp and rested. We looked forward to good traveling, for Edmund the Leather Crafts-man predicted good weather in the coming days. It was here three mounted men abruptly approached overland—their mounts capris-oned and themselves armed, clearly not out for leisure or sport. Having been caught unmounted, our guards moved between them and our train.

Expected were their demands for writs-of-passage, possibly posturing for bribes for their own reward in secret from the reeves or sheriffs.

One was clearly in charge, richly clothed and braced, his horse the same. When Edmund bravely walked past our guard, he bowed and, after identifying himself, invited them to our repast. Their mission was not a repast nor writs or coin.

"I am Aldwulf-of-York, I come to fetch one Cuthwin the Scribe for High Reeve, Sigald, thane and loyal servant of Earl Siward."

Cwenburh held me by my arm for an extra moment when I moved

forward. "Careful, Cuthwin. These men bring trouble."

I moved on and, identifying myself, asked after their mission's purpose.

"My mission, Cuthwin, is to bring you to the Great Manor of Earl Siward, for you are wanted at once by the High Reeve, Sigald-the-Dane."

"For what purpose?"

"For the purpose of obedience—I don't wonder after purpose, and you shouldn't either if you want to keep your head on straight."

It took even more courage for Edmund to step before me and hold up his hand for peace—and our guards prepared for the worst. He appealed to Aldwulf for more reasonable and less harsh grounds of talk. Aldwulf would have none of it.

"If you think the protection of these three mounds of shit give you strength to question my purpose and means, think again, old man. I come for Cuthwin the Scribe. When it comes to the wishes and commands of Earl Siward and his High Reeve, that is the beginning and end of it."

I had never been subject of such a request, and wondered at the nature of it. I brought up the central truth of things: "I am a free Saxon, and cannot be taken off like a bondsman or miscreant; I have family and belongings, and have done nothing wrong."

"You are annoying me. Are you coming or not? If not, I'll just dump you off before Sigald-the-Dane in whatever condition I can, telling him I've done my best."

Sedrig readied his weapon and planted himself firmly between all of us and Aldwulf.

"You will not take him by force, you tongue-heavy lout!"

Essox readied his bow, their friend managed to mount his horse Pisser, though without saddle or livery. He had hastily armed with lance.

There was violence in the immediate offing—all the harmony of a peaceful day unraveled in the space of a few moments talk. I would not allow myself to become the topic of harm to anyone.

"I will come, but you must tell me for how long? If consultation about writing or a brief task, I needs know, Sir."

"Know!? My place is not to know and neither is yours; our place is to do."

At this moment, the unexpected erupted—a surprise more for Aldwulf and his men than myself knowing her like I did. Cwenburh stalked angrily around our guards, stood staunch, feet apart and started in: "I will not have you spirit off my husband as freebooters might oxen or sheep. I am wedded to Cuthwin—bound to him under the word of God and sanction of our Savior."

At the same moment one Emily of Portsdown, Edmund's wife, cried in outrage from within their largest wagon. The great lady, nearly deaf, of great flesh and plagued by various aches of her bone ends, struggled against her two daughters to get down to earth and confront.

"What is this shit!? We have writs clear out to the heavens. Who bothers us, Husband?!"

This was the last development Husband Edmund could tolerate, and he withdrew some, commanding her to return—ordering daughters to push her back in, to not allow their mother free exit. Meanwhile Cwenburh did not relent.

"Only God pulls asunder wedded free Saxons, and how might we know where you fetch from—where is any writ? Any order? You could be from the Archfiend for all we know."

Emily, undaunted, cursed and pushed her way by attained footing. Dragging a daughter on each arm, she entered the fray shouting instructions to the skies: "Put an arrow in the bastard, Essox, you little turd. We pay you enough!"

Aldwulf whirled his horse, confronting Essox, then back—for Cwenburh had moved even closer, and I grabbed hold of her, pulling her back.

"Peace, Cwenburh. Do you want to get us all killed?"

Worse, had not only Edmund's commands gone unheeded by the wrathful Emily—both daughters began scolding the Earl's men for disturbing an old lady thus. Their pleas, however, flew in the face of actions: Once riled, wife Emily was feared more than dragons or beasts.

"By God, who are these ruffians that plague us so? Where is your spine, Husband!?"

Seeing the disarray the situation was descending to, one of the accompanying thanes of Aldwulf laughed—shook his head and looked to the heavens.

Aldwulf saw this and became even angrier.

"Silence, you harridans! I swear by God above, I'll kill every goddamned one of you." Then he too looked to heavens and declared, ". . . what have I done, God, to deserve such adverse duty before my Lord."

"Before your Lord? What sort of Lord demands kidnapping free Saxons from the road—who have every writ of passage so deemed, and paid high coin for them, too?"

Voices became so raised and swelled with temper that not one hundred paces distant, Essox's donkey heard and for its own reasons began braying so loudly as to deafen all.

Edmund stood bravely, but the scene had become so rattled by high noises and voice that he looked back then forward: Armed men were to the north, and his wife, daughters, and Cwenburh shouting, and the donkey braying to the south. Essox was ready with his bow, and could not attend his donkey—and the eyes of Aldwulf moved from Essox to his other antagonists. Now two other of the wives joined in the fray.

It was disorder itself that ironically decreased the ugly tension that had arisen through Aldwulf's harsh manner and threats. Now his two thanes, both young and of active eye, allowed themselves to exchange appraising glances with Edmund's daughters, young and fetching in their simple dress.

"Oh, fuck all! I want Silence. Silence! Silence! Quiet that fucking donkey, Goddamnit! Otherwise I will go back and return with forty men, as God is witness."

I gathered enough wit and presence of mind to believe the origin of this mission was indeed at Earl Siward's court, and his name attached to anything carried almost as much authority and weight as King Edward himself. Indeed, every Saxon—all residents who lived or wandered the land—knew well the deeds and powers of Earl Siward since childhood.

Though now of great age, all commonality knew too well his continued authority and unrivalled wealth throughout Northumberland, and even beyond those borders. His High Reeve would be fully bestowed of that authority and reach.

I appealed to reasonableness of this Aldwulf whose manner had not begun reasonably. Edmund and the other men did as Aldwulf ordered—I too asked for quiet, stepped almost to the stirrups of the man.

"I am a scribe, Aldwulf-of-York. So I need equipment even if for brief work or simple consultation, I must know what to bring and how long I will be absent. I am a craftsman with practical demands."

He tossed his head, took off his helmet, and glared down. "And I do not know Cuthwin the Scribe." He sighed, with feigned exhaustion, and glared at one of his men who approached the two young women, striking up conversation. The spirit of his business had suddenly become milder, despite his initial blackish tidings. "I do know that the High Reeve doesn't beckon people on order of Lord Siward for small, brief talk. So that is as much as I might guess. Come fully prepared. But, by God, come you will. The more willingly, the better nature you will find the High Reeve. This disorder," and he gestured towards our train, "will favor no one."

I asked for time to talk with my family, meaning Cwenburh, and was given it. Almost dragging her to the rear, I went to our two vehicles, one a wagon, the second a covered trap.

At once, I saw that—as I might have guessed—the timid Ligulf had fled. Cwenburh kept a weather eye on Aldwulf-of-York and the scene around him. He still squared with our guards.

"Cwenburh, for God's sake, these men come from the court of Earl Siward, the greatest of men. He does anything he wishes with anyone."

Matilda and Elesa ran up, laughing—now ten years old, they still saw more humor than evil in this world.

"Mother, Ligulf peed himself and is hiding by the spring."

Nearby the stonemason and his sons struggled to quiet the donkey, so there was still much ambient chaos; Cwenburh ordered the twins into the trap.

"Cuthwin, we are free. They are slavish brutes and have no business with us; no writs. Nothing! They are dung-covered fucks on horseback."

"Jesus and the Holy Ghost protect us, Cwenburh! They come from Earl Siward. No one would weave that as a tale. Look at his dress and mountings. Earl Siward is more powerful than all—friend of the King and Himself half ice bear. Put a stop to this unthinking wrath of yours. There are the others' welfare to consider—two-dozen people, our friends and all they own. He only wants me. We must think and do so fast."

Craft and caution dictated I go alone, then re-join the train as it went south, even if I was absent for a number of days. I would take the smaller of our horses and a kit of portables to craft basic work.

"Oh! On whose dragon's teeth?! Not mine, by God. You'll not go anywhere without us."

We argued—at odds, our voices getting louder—and within a few minutes discovered all looked at us, for peace had been attained overall save our division within audible to all. Aldwulf looked on with smugness—satisfied at seeing me struggling with his diminutive tormentor.

I reflect back the decades with regrets, as the aged will do. My responsibility as husband before God and teachings in the Great Book was clear, even if requiring means forceful.

Love of a woman, even one's wife, cannot forgive ignoring Scripture. However, Cwenburh and I had been together fifteen passages of the four seasons enduring all varieties of evil and joy. Though Saxon husbands rarely rough-handed their wives, they certainly commanded their family with firmness, and a good, holy wife obeys, as directed in the First Book of Peter.

On this day I was not equal to these holy directives, and failed to stand firm. Therefore Cwenburh and I, with all we owned, departed our friends and companions and trailed off to Sigald-the-Dane, High Reeve for the great Lord Siward.

Edmund assured he would not fail to inform this untoward development to the Abbot of Peterborough, who through Old Elsin, had significant regard for me.

What good might this do? I did know by not continuing south much business would be lost. We had a remunerative number of cold fairs expecting Cuthwin the Scribe in the south.

I have always suspected God was punishing me for not assuming the often uncomfortable role needed to keep a family in safe circumstances. We rode on toward the court of the High Reeve looking into the deceptive north wind, cunningly lacking its later cruelty.

I remained morose throughout the inauspicious ride to what we eventually learned was the grand estate of Oakheath Manor, one of Lord Siward's holdings north of the River Tees near Gainford. I was sullen over Cwenburh being so irresponsible a mother to expose Matilda and Elesa for no reason other than her stiff-necked humors.

Aldwulf rode without word, surely nursing bad feelings in wake of the chaotic delay and disrespectful scene that, of course, would be conveyed to the High Reeve. Great men only respected the rights of a freedman to the extent it suited their purposes.

All manors owed allegiance to a great earl like Siward; in fact, even the Palatine Bishop of Durham struggled to stand equal before him. Of Danish birth, Earl Siward had northern roots to account for scores of marvelous stories, including a claim that his grandfather was a great ice bear who ranged northern wastes eating animals whole.

The Old Earl ironically stood contrary to his fellow Dane in his adopted land, a powerful northern sentinel for King Edward. Earl Siward and his sons could serve up mere freedmen such as myself like pickled eels for repasts—these acts practically beyond the law of Saxon King Edward.

It was this order folk knew.

For Saxons and any in Danelaw, it was a part of the real fabric of life and fable in everyday life, teaching the common folks the order of position, and their own God-ordained place within it.

So tossing up one's free status in the face of one such as Aldwulf on a mission from Earl Siward's High Reeve was an act of insolence and futility.

My progress was steeped in a gloomy fog as I walked along beside our cart. Finally, I took some cheer—there was still time for a last-pitched siege of Cwenburh's prideful stance.

Progress was slow and Aldwulf left us to serve as vanguard and to sleep in comfort in the Manor for we instead needed to overnight along the river Tees. Himself left the two mounted drengs—for such is what they were—to overnight and escort us to our destination in the next day.

They shared our evening meal with us, but refused comment on anything remotely concerning our purpose, adding, "Aldwulf is our lord and a mean bastard, when he instructs us to say nothing, we say nothing. Too much has been said already."

Nearby was a good-sized manor, and several of its occupants came out and visited with the drengs whom they knew. Even the unquenchable cheerful twins had caught the sour mood between Cwenburh and me. By her quick words—hasty, and ill-thought—I had little room to negotiate with the High Reeve.

With her and the twins there, he had my family.

Feelings of regret did not come readily or sometimes at all to Cwenburh. At this point, I hoped she perceived the gravity of our situation. For a show of spirit and womanly opposition, we were now pole-axed. Several leagues behind us was the begang, traveling in the opposite direction along with all her acquaintances, friends—those whom she loved for years.

Old Emily would sleep comfortably this evening with those she had grown old with, and the only consequence of her was action was the absence of her friend Cwenburh with whom she joyfully gossiped interminably.

I swore to have it out with Cwenburh—we were not at the Lord's Manor yet. The dreng's orders did not explicitly include her or the twins. It was essential I try again to make her see sense and go back. For now, with others in ear-shot, I would bide my time.

Before the true dawn, I was up, and I saw our escort still slept. Parting the hanging over the end of our wagon, I got in, I tied it fast behind me—Cwenburh was up at once, staring at me, knowing I had serious purpose. I kept my voice very low—this meeting I wanted only between us.

"Cwenburh, by writing letters of import for anyone under allegiance to Earl Siward, I will become a walking threat if allowed to roam free once more. Likely as not, I will never leave the proximity of such men again while he lives. And you being my wife, these corrupt men will think you privy to at least some information sworn to the husband. For the love of God, you must get out now."

"I will not."

She drew her legs up to her bosom and allowed her hand to move the cover over the twins more; summer was failing, and the night coolness had begun. She refused to look at me.

"Cwenburh! For the love of our Savior, listen: There are great troubles now in the land between violent forces who struggle for power and money. Earl Siward is the hub of this. For years God has blessed us by keeping such avarice and pride away from us. Certainly you see this Cwenburh!"

"I see my vow before God as wife and mother, and that only."

"Then before God as it dictates in the Great Book, you must obey me, your husband."

"I will not. My vow before God and our Holy Savior comes before that in any book, Cuthwin-of-Alnwick. I've faced more deadly foes than those bastards—for and because of you—and I will continue to do so."

A vertigo took hold; I pressed both my hands to my head and leaned against the rib of the cart's covering. I drew away—forces were overwhelming me—with a severe and meaningful tone, which came out unexpectedly as a growl. I pushed on in unusual anger: "Goddamn you, Cwenburh-of-Loe, you will obey me. You will!"

"Goddamn you, Cuthwin-of-Alnwick, I will not."

It was hopeless. Dealing with Herself was akin to conversing with stone.

I slipped back out, my anger urging me towards crazy things— instead I stalked over to the nearby spring and sat, enduring the darkest thoughts in memory. I knew in heart and mind, those like Earl Siward were bringers of evil and misery for plain folk. Why in heaven or hell could not Cwenburh see that?! I loved dearly this recalcitrant wife who refused to benefit from her wedded husband's foreknowledge.

God forgive but I had ceased struggling to yield Christian forgiveness to those who were power-hungry and avaricious and who stooped to every conceivable sin before Our Savior, including murder. In the coming lent, again, I would pray and sacrifice for the holy strength to let my bitterness pass and take my Savior's kindness into heart and soul about these beasts who went adorned as human souls.

I sat in this shadowed wedge of peace. Looking about at the elms and oaks, their leaves just barely touched by advent of autumn, who might guess my fear and hopelessness before God? All now rested on our Creator's shoulders, and there was nothing I could do.

The Great Manor and rich sokes at Oakheath Manor occupied a deep oxbow in the River Tees diked off generations ago to turn to the richest of fields. We arrived before Sext, and passing by fields, we saw the great teams of ox and their tenders straining to look us over—these strange new arrivals.

Knowing people of village and croft, I was sure our appearance had not gone unanticipated. Words carrying news traveled at greater speeds than any ox or mule. Unlike most manors, Oakheath was not set amidst the fields. Instead it was built along the River Tees itself—the river to its back, the sokes and demesne of the Lord spread out before it, and the Manor and adjacent dozens of crofts and adjoining structures at its front. This way any approach by hostile forces was far more difficult—a defensive wall requiring much shorter length.

And unlike lands to the south, those in Northumberland and Durham were sites of warfare in recent years, so the walls around Oakheath were well kept—the gates double, and of weighty construct. Lookout platforms were to the side of each, standing a rod above all else.

Hostile invaders coming upriver could be seen in advance and the horn then blown. Surprises from the sea never promised anything but ill. But only one lookout was manned this hour and he glared down at us while we passed beneath.

Within Manor confines, structures of wattle and daub were kept well protected with white wash. These were extensive and at center no more or less complicated were constructs of simpler, smaller structures. This is unlike today's pretentious Norman styles to match the owner's wealth and position—stone and rock being the finest and most ostentatious.

At the time of Saxon King Edward, even a High Reeve such as the harsh, tragic Sigald-the-Dane maintained the practical directness of Saxon design. Function was always mainstay to those who kept a foot planted on everyday demands and needs.

Aldwulf-of-York awaited on a raised wooden landing—an area where goods and such were received and dealt with by various offices within; also, an aged and/or a richly fleshed rider could mount and dismount horse with dignity.

Aldwulf held arms folded over his chest and looked down at us—a superior smugness, one that foretold that a reckoning awaited within.

"Welcome to the Manor of Sigald-the-Dane, Cuthwin the Scribe. Sigald is within completing midday prayers. So wait and you will be called, for he is eager to see you."

The pair of drengs, their duty hopefully over, were anxious to return to their lands. While passing close to me, one took note he was not seen and warned in a low voice, "Be cautious now, Cuthwin the Scribe. From the look of the bastard, the arrow is fully notched. God keep you."

At that point housecarls came out from a side door—four of them—their corporal still gnawing a joint, then tossing it to a second who caught it and resumed—the former wiping his hands on his breeches. He squinted up at us and exchanged sarcasms with the drengs, who left at once. Then two serving women came out behind the housecarls.

"We are to take your woman and children within."

"I am a free tradesman. My family stays with me until I know the nature of my calling."

"Oh! A haughty one, are you? We have heard that. Well, you will soon learn there are no bishops or whore-mongering monks to interfere here."

But they stayed in place, neither advancing nor withdrawing. Cwenburh sat in place on the cart, and I stood to the side of the trap; the twins clung left and right side of her who was the last bastion between them and the Great Man's pleasure.

Cwenburh now realized circumstances confronted us as grim as any before.

Seeing developments, the serving women tried to withdraw, but the corporal seized the joint from his comrade's hands in mid-gnaw, hurled it off, and yelled, "Hold! you bags of guts, until told to leave."

We held our peace uncomfortably until within minutes a tiny gnarl of a man limped out, helped along with the use of a staff—a badge of office at his chest. His staff was intricately designed. At his side was Aldwulf. The official pointed at us with an emaciated hand, twisted as a cypress branch by the bone disease.

"You, Cuthwin, will follow me within. I am Bedalf, the High Reeve's clerk."

"I wish assurances from you my family will remain here unharmed while I am within."

"You might have considered their welfare when you allowed your wife to cast insult and outrage on the Undersheriff, which has thrust my Lord into a bad humor, Cuthwin the Scribe, no doubt about it."

It was shock added to misfortune—I had never seen an undersheriff go about without their medallion of office around their neck or at least upon their mount's livery. Even at this moment, Aldwulf was without this medallion, but there was nothing in law or practice that locked him to wearing it.

The clerk's eyes traveled to the cart then stopped on Cwenburh and the twins. He raised his free hand—as diseased as the one holding his staff—and gestured towards the Manor.

"Go in, and your family can wait. For the time."

The corporal waved his men and the women back inside, then walked closer to our trap and wagon. I followed the clerk and Aldwulf—Undersheriff Aldwulf as it developed—inside.

Two house serfs pushed aside a rich hanging, more elaborate and fine than most. They clamped it open at the command of a booming voice from inside, for the weather had become warm under the midday sun.

Inside, the very last wisps of a morning fire rose lazily, traveling a crooked pattern towards the hole in the arched roof overhead. This and two other doors admitted profuse light, and in it I saw sitting in a grand carved chair—a sign of power and rich providing for the High Reeve—Sigald-the-Dane.

He stared into the remnants of the great fire hearth, over which was suspended by stout gaffs enormous iron pots, each worth a fortune. Two women worked there under his gaze; each took a handle of a great pot and struggled out an opposite doorway.

They showed me to his front by pressure put on my shoulder; Aldwulf bade me to bow deeply, and when I rose I was eye to eye—the High Reeve being higher, situated in the grand chair.

"So you are Cuthwin the Scribe?"

His voice was deep, emanating from his vast, corpulent body; he was clean shaven, yet the Saxon words were roughened by their treatment with his Danish-speaking tongue, but nonetheless clear, foretelling many years in this land.

"I am, Your Excellency."

"According to Aldwulf, you were not so respectful of his office when he came to fetch you."

"I was not aware I insulted him, Your Excellency. It is not my way to insult anyone. I did not, though, realize his high office, nor did the others, a medallion of office not being in sight."

"Do these wandering tradespeople expect me to go about night and day with my medallion hanging out of my ass?!"

And then they all—clerk, Aldwulf, and the High Reeve—burst into laughter, the High Reeve's deep and resonant, like two stones being banged together underwater.

When they settled, Sigald took a great, patient breath and explained I had been honored by Earl Siward Himself to be his personal scribe.

"And now you have sullied this honor by being a churlish fellow. No one spits upon a great benefice from Earl Siward without penalty, Cuthwin the Scribe."

I made my apologies, pointing out I had shown no discourtesy to anyone, and that I was a tradesman following the begang, and it was my place. And that all of us should—must—keep to our places. I, not knowing the purpose of the extraordinary summons, was curious about it.

At that point the women returned—I assumed for the other pot—and the clerk Bedalf shook his staff at them: "Out! You slatterns! We are at business here!"

"And I am at business here, you twisted little turd. You surely are not going to heft this brute nor certainly clean it," retorted the elder of the women.

But this time, the clerk was not involved in the laughter, which was even lustier on the parts of Sigald and Aldwulf, Sigald even allowing himself a clap of his hand against his great thigh.

Such was the Manor way—for the business of each Saxon's workday went on like a troll's giant steps, unstoppable by such superfluity as protocol or manners.

The Clerk groused something I could not make out. And again, Sigald recovered himself and returned to his purpose, his voice reflecting a rapid decrease in interest of the situation concerning me or any other scribe.

"In any case, I will not sit here and bandy words with a tradesman: Suffice it to say, you are now the personal scribe to Earl Siward, The Great. You will be compensated with fairness, and I shall defer to my firebrand clerk here other details, save one: That wife of yours is fined five pounds silver. If you lack this she will be flogged for her outrageous impudence to an officer of Earl Siward. Consider yourself a lucky fellow before God and our Savior, Cuthwin the Scribe. Now, that is all for now."

I had wit enough to keep words to myself, and readily followed the clerk out the same portal; this time Aldwulf stayed behind. Returning to the platform, the clerk stopped above, gestured to the Corporal, and pointed to both myself and Cwenburh, who was understandably relieved at my reappearance.

"Now, Cuthwin, the five-pound silver, or the corporal will carry out the sentence-right now."

I looked at Cwenburh with all the meaning I could muster—parceling up a plea for common sense and bare survival in one vast breath presaging my request: "We owe the court a five-pound fine directly in lieu of a whipping. Fetch the box. The clerk's duty is to collect it at once."

Cwenburh was keeper of our treasury and factor to all things dealing with coin. She had sewn coin into Eadwig's spare blouse, plus a clever hidden compartment in his thick-soled turnshoes.

Her bartering terrorized me—each penny and shilling dragged out of her in bargaining was a great effort. I was constantly reminding her of courtesy to clients who were short of money—or who claimed to be short of money, for she was hard pressed to believe their stories of need.

She looked up in abject horror at the clerk on the platform, and just barely kept from tears, which to me, who knew her so well, was the give-away, for she never wept.

"We have not such a sum in all the world, Cuthwin."

The clerk's gnarled old hand moved a notch higher up his staff, and with the other he gestured to the corporal.

"Then, bitch, my corporal shall whip you forthwith."

I stepped back up to the platform, and seized the clerk's staff one hand above his misshapen talon: "If you or your thugs touch my wife or family, I will never write one letter for Earl Siward. I am now his scribe in service. You can take your chance with the Earl or his functionary for so eternally alienating my services, you little thief. Stay your hand if you have wit about you, and be patient."

We both knew where the five-pound of silver was headed—a bit for him, a little more for Aldwulf, and most for the High Reeve. Now, eye to eye, he certainly saw that I meant what I said, and I was summoned here to function in letters—beyond working at livery or mill.

I pushed his staff aside a notch, turning to Cwenburh, and now I had my own temper to deal with. Though rarely up, when it was I would be adamant. She knew this.

"Cwenburh, fetch the five pounds at once, and give it to this person, and by God and Our Savior, we will hear no more of damnable avarice."

Throughout the process of being shown to the tradesmen quarters and settling in, I remained in temper and sour mood. The previous three days had showered disaster upon us. Though she had gone contrary to my sense and wishes, I had to remember our plight was no fault of Cwenburh. She did what habit dictated by playing the knife too close to the bone. I, on the contrary, was born and raised at Manor, and knew only too well their raw-boned ways; my mother had died on one. I had spent my early years in its service. Indeed I had risked life and limb escaping—and the experiences of one's earliest days are etched deeply upon memory.

And Oakheath Manor was ominously grand beyond any I had known.

For the moment, the distaste of our fate was assuaged when we saw our quarters were substantial: A large house with surrounding modest croft for a garden and stock, itself abutting the end of the wall that extended into the river, then curled inward, a dozen feet high, and made of stout wattle and daub with many posts laid crosswise.

It looked to the open south, and would offer much warmth when winter's short days offered scarce sunlight in these northern lays. Bedalf the clerk had retreated inside with the five pounds, to divvy it up—to take partial credit for the fleecing given us.

Cwenburh was going through the pangs of losing such a sum, and finally when out of earshot of anyone, told me, "We lost one-half of everything we have ever earned to the bastards, Cuthwin."

"They will be after more, seeing how readily we managed five. Be careful in everything you do concerning these people. All the rules are theirs. There is no law but the Earl's law. And the Earl's law has no regard for flesh nor blood, freedom nor bond."

Several wives of tradesmen called striking up talk with Herself. I led the twins away—down to the river. The bank was steep, and I kept an eye on them, though still managed to ruminate on the future and how vastly different it was.

The two girls, now daughters to both our hearts, kept close to me, for the troubles and unkindnesses visited on us had broached their naturally joyful spirits. Smoke from nearby fires increased as Vespers approached, though now the keeping of hours according to The Rule of St. Benedict were far, far away, at least in spirit.

Cwenburh had been given small, newly picked apples, and she found us by the river, and taking her knife, cut them into fresh quarters for us. I began for no other reason than the immediacy of things, to recall my days on the Manor at Alnwick—my first memories of my mother working at the massive hearth.

And they all listened, ate the apples, and were together on the bank of the Tees. This flow of God-giving life was low and lazy in the late summer, a dimpling of a fish here, a scattering of skitter bugs under bended willow—the fish chasing these morsels down.

My account was interrupted by the sharp 'smack' of a kingfisher setting into the water on its downward swoop, and coming up with a struggling fish in its beak, landing within view. The twins marveled, and Cwenburh pointed at it, and explained the way of these tiny, beautiful birds—God's gifts for human eyes, perhaps his most generous.

She said how they, at one time, were fairies, but who had gotten at cross purposes with the spirits of the woods and waters for not marrying lascivious trolls and elves who always desired them. And all at a once, they were turned into simple, tiny birds, to feed upon fish their entire lives.

And so, for now, we ate apples and shared each other's presence, another of God's gifts so easily taken. Why such a gift was included in the odious power of Godless souls is only answerable by the Ancients.

As the months of autumn passed at the Great Manor at Oakheath, the enigma of our fate increased. A lunar month elapsed and I was not called to inscribe a single letter. Our house was left in rough condition by the previous occupants—a liveryman, actually—who had died the previous winter. The rather large garden that occupied our croft was unplanted and we had to purchase most food items at market.

Cwenburh, a woman who enjoyed market days, was however uncomfortable with the mood at Oakheath.

"There is something wrong here, Cuthwin. People's tongues are tied."

This discomfort, among others, gave her a turn towards an uncharacteristic irascibility of spirit—which began understandably enough after the thievery that greeted us.

"I suppose, Cuthwin, the great thieves have not discussed pay with you yet, nor have you asked. These market people are fleecing us, thinking we have ample coin to pass along."

I reminded her of my inactivity thus far, so my question would be ill-timed. But she remained critical of the state around us, including my efforts to bring our house in readiness for winter. But I avoided argument, especially with her.

In a further dark development, various manor peoples began to notice and remark how close the twins were to womanhood, and what sort of bride price such a handsome pair might fetch. Cwenburh, as any Saxon mother would, had ambitions for them both being settled on those of the begang, and she made this clear. For the first time she became unpopular with other women at Oakheath who considered this a show of pride. Cwenburh was resolute.

"One savagery they cannot do is abduct the twins, for then they would outrage God's Order of things."

Yet God's Order at Oakheath was out-of-balance, or 'cockeyed,' as Cwenburh put it. A priest and his deacon attended a small run-down church called St. Budoc's Chapel, a pathetic structure often with more poultry than souls inside, the former feeding on various bugs that lived in the descript roof and walls.

If Cwenburh ever resumed church attendance, it wouldn't be St. Budoc's, and even I was hesitant on Sabbath—and others too. For religious matters were long-in-the-tooth at Oakheath. Earl Siward infamously showed lifelong disgust with the church.

And this did not go unstated. The shriveled clerk Badalf claimed in open market that powerful Bishop Ethelric committed unspeakable acts with farm animals. Great hilarity greeted his words, but laughter at great men's expense has a manner of returning by the path it departed.

It was clear that Earl Siward—including his High Reeve, Sheriff, and all under-officers in Siward's many lush manors—were emboldened because of their famous Lord's close ties to the King. Hence, they were frequently at serious odds with Bishop Ethelric, infamous of temper and mood as Earl Siward.

I became amiable with Sceaf the Miller. Old and infirm, he had passed his duties to his sons and grandsons years before. He spent the autumn days at the river fishing. He would converse, but never of daily events of Manor, but only those beyond its border.

"I tell you, there is a storm brewing between Earl Siward and Bishop Ethelric. Ah, and it could drive a month of gales and tempests. From friend to foe—always the same with those two."

Finally I was called by the High Reeve's messenger boy to appear in order to draft my first letter. Taking up my tried and beloved equipment in its carrying case, my heart rose to renew my craft of a dozen-plus years. The High Reeve became forthcoming about my duties: "This is a letter to the King. So it must be handsome—fulsome in its meeting to the eyes at court. This was Earl Siward's idea when fetching you here. He had seen some of your art at York this summer."

As I learned, letters between powerful men are artful in what they do not say rather than what they do. They are often not interesting, even more mundane than those missives between wealthy merchants. In a contrary fashion, minor officers and ordinary people do not mince words, and say outright what they mean. Often they are so outright, I feel responsible as a scribe to suggest words of easier, less mean-spirited tone.

And in this first letter to the King—I had one day to prepare it prior to the courier going south—an ominous note was sounded when the High Reeve affixed the Earl's great seal to the wax and signed the Earl Siward's name. Then it was inserted into a courier's purse and sent at once on its way to court. This letter never saw the eyes of the great Earl Siward.

When I rushed to ask about my remuneration before he withdrew, the High Reeve looked down at me—his great eyebrows shot towards the middle of his brow: "I shall think on it, minus your rent, of course." And waddled out, his vast bulk heaving right to left like a ship at sea.

A wifely silence greeted me, these becoming more frequent. The long nights of winter were coming on. Cwenburh was dour about the lack of information concerning pay and rent and imagined many varieties of skullduggery on the part of them all. She seemed to imply—when she did speak of it—that my lack of assertiveness lent itself to such a slighting.

This less-than-unkind assertion was more frequent of late. I allowed myself to think on other issues. I was bothered about developments regards the signature of the letter, though who signed a letter was as confidential in my eyes as what was in it.

Through the years there were many instances when clients signed a letter with another's name. But a great Earl writing in the first person to the King Himself, was a serious concept to me. Was not a bad or inaccurate word here or there—imparted to none other than a King—of the highest concern to even a mighty personage like Earl Siward?

I had illustrated the margins of the letter—though rapidly—with handsome figures and additions for the Royal Eye equal to any cleric at court. Though Eadrig was more talented, easily, I had the more experienced eye and hand.

The normally grumpy High Reeve was impressed with my work.

"This is indeed well done with such a short time allowance, Cuthwin. Let the Bishop's catamites try and equal that!"

So having me as scribe removed any cleric from the direct route between Earl Siward and the King. Capable scribes and illuminators not part of a church or monastery were almost unheard of in the days before the coming of the Normans.

Those few who knocked about the country, like Ligulf, my short-serving scribe, had hands unequal to work demanded by great men and such. With me, Siward's court had notched a piece into place secure from any prying cleric's eyes. Yet to also exclude the great Earl Siward was itself grave business even for his High Reeve. I was a cog in intrigue, whatever it might be.

These developments were part of my unwelcome future at Oakheath as I prepared for winter. And it was when St. Catherine's Day[38] grew near, that the first word about our plight arrived from outside this auspicious Manor.

Soldag the salt pedlar arrived on St. Catherine's Day. He and his train of donkeys traveled with his usual assortment of sodden, unruly assistants to do heavy lifting, for Soldag was elderly and battered by a lifetime

---

[38] Saint Catherine's Day. November 25th.

of wandering and contrary living. Like many salt pedlars, he lived a free-ranging existence, never following a regular circuit or trade route. I found a cautious few of these ragged wanderers made excellent couriers for letters with necessity of delivery the year written.

"One salt pedlar or another will be by," Cwenburh would recite with knowledgeable breath.

I had fashioned my own tradesman's seal designed after a cross; therefore, this added emphasis when Cwenburh would remind them that the fires of hell would sweep them up if they violated the contents. The deciding factor for our use of a particular salt pedlar was how eager they were for the extra coin given—for they would want more in future. It was profit for them for no extra effort or outlay.

By All Soul's Day[39], salt supplies had fallen dangerously short and the bounty of salmon and other fish swarming the Tees badly wanted salt to keep through the winter.

Soldag feigned no knowledge of me, and it was his old wife who passed the letter from Peterborough to us, and Cwenburh guaranteed ample schillings for carrying a return missive I would write that night.

The letter was from the Prior of Peterborough Abbey on direction from the present Father Abbot and was entirely disappointing. They learned of our plight through Edmund the Leather-crafter. Father Abbot advised me patience and the acceptance of God's mysterious ways, and above all to pray for Earl Siward. This great personage needed God's strength all through these 'times of troubles' during which no mere monk could offer any help. When I read the message to Cwenburh, she scoffed and tossed her head in frustration.

"Other than they have no belly to do right by God, what does that mean, Cuthwin?"

"There is great trouble upon the King, but I know nothing of it, save that it is growing, and he requires Earl Siward's allegiance. And in God's name, we must let it stand there, Cwenburh."

We sat there captive to the stupidity and waste of great men's devious and violent ways, so contrary to the Grace and Word of Our Savior.

---

[39] All Soul's Day. November 2nd.

Everyone was cowed by them, for in the end, it were those with sword and other weapons who ruled. Even Father Abbot could not challenge the will of the King.

The plain folk who worked and prepared victuals for each winter were without power over fate, save what the Lord might provide.

Cwenburh sat beside me, uncurled her apron, and revealed shelled walnuts, their meats shiny in oily halves. Taking my hand in hers, she put two of them in it and snacked on the first herself.

There were so many things to ask or to impart between us, but the silence in the house was rare, for the twins were always rambunctious—with a half-dozen ideas each half-day for one thing or another.

Grayness had settled over Cwenburh and me, for rumor between manors along the Tees had it that marriage negotiations were in the offing. It would begin with the ceremonial delivery of a marriage braid, and we knew the rumors to carry truth—for Matilda and Elesa were fetching and healthy, and both held much promise to a freeborn husband and his family with land and means.

These negotiations called for keen mind and planning for any Saxon parent even with a single daughter, but for two at one time, it promised exhaustive discourse and bargaining. And I knew that Cwenburh—who considered our presence an outrage, and unlawful—was sorely placed for her role in this. Worse, the twins heard the same rumors—even prior to Cwenburh—and were anxious at their calling, marriage being so mysterious and unknown to them.

So we ate walnuts in silence, and finally finishing this repast, Cwenburh said, "Answer Father Abbot as you wish, Cuthwin, but please ask after my dearest Eadwig. I pray every night for him, and give thanks for his having departed so close to this calamity. He is, thank God, free."

Before she could rise, I took her by the arm, and gently sat her back down. "Cwenburh, know this for sure: I would pay any amount of money, yield any property, before seeing harm come to you, and I say this before God. It is my husbandly duty I cherish most."

She rose, looked back at me—holding her eyes directly on mine, as was her way when intending emphasis-of-meaning: "Cuthwin, I knew and loved you for the man you were the moment I laid eyes on you at the table of that swine, Wilfred-of-Loe." She allowed something of a half smile, and added, ". . . my error is sometimes forgetting that, God forgive me."

This has remained the highest praise ever given me during this lifetime, and I am grateful before God. I prized her words from she who was my wife. Her words visit me to this day, over fifty years later. Though the country has changed from under me—now old and cripple, marooned in a strange, even crueler world—her words remain my joy, Praise be God.

Book 5

How great tragedy strikes Cuthwin at Oakheath; his life is hurled onto the edge of the Eternal Abyss by Demons of Greed and Violence, thereby falling into disarray. How he struggled with terrible adversity and wanders Northumberland questing for any sign of his family. Seeking peace at his childhood home of Peterborough, he instead is subject to calumny and must seek sanctuary. This concluded, he ventures back north resigning himself to the foul vicissitudes of fate and the workings of evil-doers. Despite this, God has mercy on him, and he begins to experience reversal of bad fortune.

On the second day I was able to feign meeting Soldag the salt pedlar by chance. I had known the rogue for close to a dozen years, and he was always the same, crafty of eye and cautious—and always on lookout for extra coin. The repugnant clerk Bedalf had just concluded a negotiation for geld with Soldag. Before leaving to scamper back to Sigald, he saw me; a glint of smugness was distinct in his tiny pig-like eyes. Lifting his staff, he poked it in the direction of the manor.

"Himself intends to travel tomorrow morning—striking out for the Manor of the Great Earl Siward—and he will take you along. Make sure you are ready at Compline, for with the bell we are off."

I had no inkling of this trip, but why would I? These sorts traveled frequently and I was but a conscripted servant. With my family at Oakheath, I would come back with the faithfulness of a rising sun and the greedy swine knew it.

Soldag and I held conference under the privacy of an awning stretched between his two carts.

"Cuthwin, you seem to have changed life styles."

He hid my reply letter to the Prior of Peterborough, then fish-eyed the ten schillings I placed atop the cart brace. He swiped his old paw across his frazzled mouth and its drooping mustache. He wanted more.

"Ah, Cuthwin, these are bad times. I could have my balls cut off if they caught me with such an article—or worse. I tremble for the danger of it."

"When did events get so bad, Soldag?"

"Oh, there are great tensions between the King and those here in the north. Everyone speaks of it."

I began to take back the coin and gestured for return of my letter; I sighed with great disappointment, for I had heard of no such troubles. "Still," I added, "I could understand before God and Our Savior how you could not carry it."

Of course the old stoat was anxious for the coin, and immediately added that for a few extra shillings and on the strength of our ongoing friendship, he would undertake this awful risk.

I left him with the letter and his shrewdly wrought fee, resolving, when asked, to mislead Cwenburh in the amount extracted from me, for the sake of peace-of-mind. For in truth, I knew there were troubles upon the lofty levels of the Earldom and country itself.

I gathered this not from the content of the letters sent from the Manor, but from the royal couriers arriving—on some days two or three. Of course, since the High Reeve and his clerk were fluent in both languages, they had no need of me, and it was noteworthy—to me—that so few letters went out in response to the royal missives.

And no texts of the letters I crafted revealed anything of unusual merit regards troubles or threats; instead they were of placid and steady tone.

By the next morning, I had prepared a sort of traveling craft-case and in truth it was stuffed with more necessities Cwenburh claimed were required for my trip.

"For all I know, dear Cwenburh, I might be crafting letters in the midst of a copse or field—I need room for the necessities of my craft, for the love of Jesus."

She had misgivings at my departure, as did the twins—for during the eleven-plus years they rarely saw me leave for more than a day. I promised great benefices upon my return—and Cwenburh asked to keep a weather eye out for news of the times.

She too felt unsteadiness within Oakheath Manor. Now both watch towers were maintained day and night On nights, distant watch fires were lit: Twenty furlongs or more before the walls, they cast light over the fields. Those coming up to the fires would be illuminated from the towers, but themselves be blinded of objects beyond it, such as the walls and those who might man it.

Now this could mean little, for often freebooting raiders, notorious brutes, were rumored to be in the country, and fires would be lit and towers manned by keen eyes.

So residents thought little of these signs. Those womenfolk who would talk with Cwenburh told her we were new and would soon get used to the ways of a great manor.

At the time for departure, we said prayers together, and Cwenburh kissed me farewell, and said, "Remember, Cuthwin, Our Holy Savior on the cross and the sign of his passion, and what it conveys to us."

At the time, since she was always a most devout but plain-speaking woman, I simply took note of the unusual artfulness of her farewell. As we rode off, my family looked on until I saw them no more.

I was surprised at the fast pace we set—me mounted on my trap's mule, a tame beast the children named Puddles. The capaciously fleshed Reeve traveled atop a gigantic satin-black steed—massive as an ox. In fact, this magnificent beast was one of a pair—the second following unmounted to serve relief when its mate became sore-at-back from the weight of the High Reeve.

These two were profusely caparisoned, the jewels of our procession, which in the manner of such a train involved nearly two-dozen thanes or housecarls, all mounted and armed. Alongside him was his toady Bedalf on a tiny white pony.

Young factotums ran alongside the procession to fetch and carry, and in all we were an imposing force.

No brigands and freebooters would think of harming us.

Puddles was not used to a high pace, and would not—or could not— keep up, and I often had complaint from the Undersheriff—for once again, Aldwulf-of-York was present, and commanded the protecting train. He finally threatened to slay Puddles if he did not pick up, claiming we would eat him that night.

I did what I could, beating on the poor creature's flank with a switch, for Aldwulf's sense of humor was too often blended with the serious. After a surprisingly brief repast at Sext—with the High Reeve shouting out that daylight was wasting—we set out again after helping him switch great mounts.

We continued into a valley that was narrowing, with thick groves of thorn and beech extending to the bottomland which soon separated the two with not more than five furlongs between the forested hillsides. Here Puddles just stopped; the animal was spoiled and fat, always pulling our trap at snail's pace in the begang, and I knew the end had come for it.

While I struggled with it, Aldwulf came back fast. He was angry, and one of his men accompanied—for now the train was several furlongs advanced of me.

"There it is," he looked at me and shook his fist at the creature. "You see, Scribe, they are good for nothing but grief." And he then motioned to his man, and, while whirling his horse about, barked, "Give it several moments to recover itself, for sake of God's kindness, then slay it."

And galloped off. The dreng left behind took off his helmet, for though late autumn it was a warm, clear day, and at once I saw he was one of the two who had originally spirited me from the begang those months ago. This was to prove God's good fortune.

I used an old trick with Puddles. I had kept the paw of a cat in a pouch. I had remembered this over those many years from my years at the stable.

"What's that dried thing?"

"Cat's paw. Puddles hates cats, and will search them out to kill them."

It stirred the recalcitrant creature, and looking around for the enemy, its ears went back—and it stomped its front hooves.

Now, more than eager to move, the young man reached down and touched me on the shoulder—casting a nervous gaze towards the Reeve's procession, now at the point when, following the narrow valley, it was going out of sight.

"Wait, Scribe."

He put his helmet back on, and there seemed a force in his voice that reminded he was fully armed. Seeing they were out of sight, he looked down at me. His eyes narrowed and he gestured towards the hillside.

"Get quickly into the woods, and flee. There is much retribution ahead, and it will be grim indeed. Now I must slay this animal to display blood."

My mouth dropped open—struggling to find words, I appealed to spare the beloved but bothersome creature.

"Do what I say! I am told to slay both of you. Spare yourself—in the name of Jesus. I am a croftsman and cannot kill an innocent, unarmed man, but I will if I must."

He then drew that massive broadsword, and I leaped away as it came down on Puddles, killing it as neatly as if he wielded a bolt of lightning.

Then, wheeling his horse he kicked into a full gallop away. Knowing something hideous was at its start, I pulled—fought to get my traveling case from under Puddles, saying a quick prayer for the beloved family animal and myself.

With the case so heavy, I struggled off through the chest-high grasses, entering the shady midday shelter of the woods. I continued uphill, my heart throbbing, gasping for breath, for it had been years since I had roughed it overland.

Reaching the arched backbone of the hills, I cast looks north and south. Which way should I go? Certainly Aldwulf would discover his dreng's disobedience and seek me out—probably sending several to do so.

I decided on the opposite direction they would expect, and proceeded north—parallel upon the hill's spine in the direction of the Reeve's train—away from Oakhurst Manor. The case's broad leather strap ached—I had strung it across both shoulders and upper arms, leaning into my burden.

This was entirely undoable for any distance, and I had not gone a league when I came across a massive pile of boulders protruding from the dark earth and litter, piled up through the ages. This, and those like them, were common upon hilltops, and made excellent promontories.

Here I collapsed—ruing how fat and lazy I had become over the years of being a scribe. I thought desperately of Cwenburh and the twins; I wondered what sort of evil had come upon this day.

Having at least the good fortune of high ground, I unburdened and, staying on my belly, crawled atop the highest rock, and two-hundred feet below and five furlong distant from me, three mounted men waited patiently on the high ground.

And it was then I witnessed a most extraordinary and grisly deed. For indeed, it was the Archfiend or his minions who ruled that day, and I know that to be true to this hour.

The Reeve's procession swerved towards a defile, now apparent to the west. None of my former party could see the three awaiting men. And when they did emerge into sight of these three, the Reeve and his toady halted at a half-pace, but his men closed in and it was Aldwulf who reached over and took the reins of the massive steed that carried its master.

The High Reeve's own men were betraying him—or had.

The factotums afoot fled like hares towards the woods, but were intercepted by two of the drengs who had taken up rear guard—and from horseback struck the Innocents dead with battle axes.

I guessed the calumny underway had been fully planned by Aldwulf; his men were its legs and hands.

Seeing how it stood, Bedalf threw himself off his horse, but as he went to kneel before Aldwulf, another behind him unsheathed his sword and beheaded him—so swiftly, that it seemed hardly possible. For I had never seen warfare—where armed drengs plied their duty to their masters. Trained men became fiendishly adept with arms, and here I saw it in fact.

Only at this moment, the three men awaiting led their horses at an easy walk forward. It took no great perception to discern that the middle horseman was a young noble of great authority, for his steed was elaborately caparisoned in silver and gold; his body armor gleamed, cleaned and polished daily, no doubt.

They rode up to Sigald-the-Dane. The man, certainly an Earldamon said a few words, almost as if in greeting, then he drew and brought the death knell down the middle of the vast man, almost cutting him in two down to the saddle.

Blood rolled over the unfortunate horse, but the Reeve—both halves leaning in opposite directions, stayed mounted.

Perhaps it was the result of his blow, and this mawkish sight, that caused laughter from everyone—audible even from where I hid. While some began to outrage all the bodies, Aldwulf—joined by the two alongside the Great Earldamon, Himself—remaining mounted, commenced to carefully search the Reeve's baggage.

It does nothing to continue in detail about that hour and narrate the foulness that unfurled below me. Suffice it to note it is the Holy

Teachings that tell us that men imbued with greed and power who do such violence must answer before God for their misdeeds.

I knew that when finished with this outrage, they would backtrack and my escape would be noted, and I was the dead man's scribe—privy to whatever betrayal or crimes he was conducting, or at least as they would think.

Taking precious little time, I opened the case and lightened it: Keeping food and spare clothing, which was very little, I dumped all else on the ground, for letter writing was glaringly off-purpose. For my scribe work, I did have two small knives and a few tools of more general use, and of course I carried my old knife in belt. I picked it up, sad it was still heavier than wanted, for the case was leather and mounted upon crafted frame.

I thought at the moment of taking out the clothes, using them as a hackensack, and casting away the case, but for the time, opted against this.

I proceeded as rapidly as possible north—once again, staying contrary to the direction of home. It was my second best advantage; the first was that all the men were mounted heavily armored and would have no chance whatsoever of chasing a fleeing person in heavy woods—especially one who kept his head.

After that, expecting a scribe to lack any skills in the woods or at croft, they would insist on staying mounted until Aldwulf saw the fruitlessness of their pursuit. Then, only if ordered, would those most subservient, leave their mounts, lighten their personal armor, and pursue on foot, carrying light weaponry.

Time was with me.

Daylight would be lost before Vespers, for it was late autumn, and the north sky would swallow the sun earlier each day. The night before me would be a three-quarters moon.

Traveling rapidly by night, I would at wisest opportunity, reverse direction and head back towards Oakheath Manor. Having traveled this land all the previous fall and summer, I knew its lay in general. Though I would not equal a native-born person, I did have general knowledge of the rising range of hills and mounts. I would be familiar enough with proximate larger towns and villages and which lay in what direction.

And more than all, the River Tees and its tributaries would be my master guide, for the courses of rivers and streams were my mentors.

With the moon fully risen, I kept it well to my right, skittered from one hilly range to another. I would climb to the first arched back of a 'Giant's Shoulder,' which is what countrymen called the piles of bounders, common at hilltop. I encountered one of these soon enough.

Because these are popular night camps for such miscreants as poachers and thieves, I used caution upon approach.

Turning south, what I saw caused me to nearly cry out. A great light pulsed far distant on a precise point of the horizon: A fire consuming great quantities of stick, wood, and straw could be none other than a village burning—and in that direction, there were was no such large settlement other than Oakheath Manor.

Fires by accident were common in villages, and indeed all human settlements, but on this particular day and night, assuming accidental fire was far-fetched.

Aldwulf and his party, perhaps with the Earldoman leading, returned and put Oakheath Manor to the torch. Whatever transgression the High Reeve committed was reaping thorough retribution.

Wild with the darkest thoughts, my caution discarded, I proceeded to the bottomland and, by the setting moon, walked quickly south. Knowing the ways of greedy, violent men, I assumed them to be more eager for booty than to disarm and follow a runaway scribe—and no officer would risk ordering such a profitless enterprise when there was a rich manor to loot.

When the moon first touched the western horizon, it was not yet Lauds. By this time, Polaris had risen over my left shoulder, and I carried forth— by now my pace driven by desperation. I stopped only for water.

At this time when I was losing all moonlight, I saw the first column of wolves[40] paralleling my course south. At their rate of travel, they made many leagues each hour. Despite my desperation to go on, I was terrified of these ranging beasts, and swerved away from level ground, and took

_____

[40] Wolves. Common in 11th century Britain.

to the edges between forest and lowlands. I had to be prepared at a moment to become tree-bound, the only defense one armed or unarmed man had.

Frog was full of wolf stories, as were all men plying the out-of-doors at night. The beasts were a menace to herdsmen, and cunning beyond what one might expect of a Godless creature on four legs. Indeed, many swore them to be inhabited by demons who sought to carry your soul to a nether world populated by fiends and goblins, your flesh being their reward.

You rarely saw them but heard them frequently all through nights adjacent to their hunting grounds. Nights, especially those with any favorable moon, were their stalking time, particularly in winter.

All beasts of croft and stable would be completely ill at ease through the nights, and needed extra oversight and soothing.

By sunup I had seen close to a hundred of the beasts, some in packs over twenty, all threading their way towards Oakheath. Keen in sensing flesh, this explained why they had no interest in a single person such as myself.

At this moment I steeled myself, for surely a calamity had overtaken Cwenburh at Oakheath. I prayed to Our Savior that his mercy was with her and the twins.

Despite all efforts, I did not come within view of Oakheath Manor until past Sext that day—by this time I had been steady paced for nearly the full turn of the moon and sun. Despite my frenzy, I approached the expanse of croft between me and the River Tees with stealth—staying low and looking out where the Manor and diverse structures had stood. I would do no one good dead or in chains.

My spirit sagged when I saw Oakheath Manor was not there any longer, at least in substantial form.

The walls were mounds of smoldering ash exhaling sad, twisted cords of smoke that drifted eastward with the late harvest wind.

One of the watch poles had been pushed back up, supported hastily, and I went lower still when I spotted a single watch atop it. He shouted at some of his fellows on the ground and began to climb down, but was threatened back up with a staff-bearing elder who sidled forth like a land crab—and there was something familiar in him.

It was Soldag, the avaricious salt pedlar.

I followed the edge of the croft towards the portion of the burnt wall that met the Tees. Soldag or no Soldag, I maintained caution. I emerged from the massive poplars and oaks at the portion only a furlong or less from where my abode had stood. It was burned utterly; nothing living remained.

I came closer to Soldag and the watch tower—then saw the first pile of smoldering casualties, victims of the slaughter. Caution was cast aside; I came out into the open, looking over and up at the pile, the stench of it having remained with me since. At the moment, I lost stomach and fell to one knee, retching and weeping in the same moment.

"So it is you, Cuthwin? You are not slain?"

Pressing my palms against the ground, his voice seemed fractured. Before me, Soldag's turnshoes were a blur—he bellowed once again at the watch: "You worthless turd! Climb back up there. They will be back. Either they will pull your nuts off or by God I will do it first."

Helping me to my feet, he turned me away from the ugly pile and looked me over. My eyes cleared and I looked out on the manor house, its former greatness now in slabs and pieces, smoldering.

Taking the back of my head, Soldag put a vial to my nose, and at once an overwhelming smell of mint cleared me.

"Oh, yes! That does it for such situations, Cuthwin. Come over here and sit. You are due many shocks, I am sad to report. Seems Sigald-the-Dane was pissing in his own bed, and that says it all."

I saw Soldag's men looting the remnants of the Manor. They had backed a cart up to a portion that was mostly unburned and were loading booty rapidly, shouting at one another.

Soldag swore to himself, then pitched into another loud howl, quite a feat for such an elderly, knotted man. "Goddamn you all! Fight later, get booty now! I will decide what goes to who, you witless oafs. Now hurry!"

In ordinary voice, much like describing the price and quality of salt that year, he took his staff, gesturing this way and that.

"Important skill to learn, Cuthwin, is to search where drengs and their halfwit scum have not when fleecing a rich manor. It is surprising how much they miss. Back through my seventy years, I have much experience, God forgive."

"Have you seen Cwenburh or my twins?"

"Those attacking afoot stripped the bodies of anything of worth. Children would all be taken live as loot, of course. They stacked the adults as you see, then befouled their mortal remains by fire."

"And Aldwulf, was he behind this foulness?"

"I cannot say. I was some hours distant when I saw the fires, and learned details from the three that survived." He pointed behind what had been a woven rick for grain. "They are over there dying. One or two might still be alive. I do not know if they were the attackers or the attacked."

Again he leapt up and, waving his staff, spewed outrage at his men. I forced myself on. I was desperate for an eye-witness account of what happened to my family and at once searched out the survivors.

The three were not of the Manor or Village, and had deep, fatal wounds; they were hirelings who followed their sponsors, armed only with cudgels or staffs, their pay being loot. These three somehow fell into bad ways with those armed with steel.

Two had died, and a third still lived. His remaining eye looked up at me, sapped of its color with approaching death. His mouth worked at words. I knelt and asked, "Can you tell me what happened to the women and children?"

"Mother," he muttered.

And then he died.

Though returning thanes and company were not spotted, Soldag called his party off, eager to escape. He offered me advice: "They are looking for you, Cuthwin the scribe, surely as birds have feather."

"Do they know I live?"

"What difference! In fact, you do, so get out; in a few hours, the wolves will return, at the least. I would offer you shelter, but if any of these high-born pricks found me giving comfort to a treasonous High Reeve's scribe, we would be goners, no matter how far distant from Oakhurst. I am sorry for your loss, Cuthwin. But the dead are no longer with us. Take it from an old dun—save yourself. Look to your left—there lies one of the scum's cudgels, and it is a good one . . . and you will need it."

And he was gone.

In later times I have reflected on Soldag, and all such men who take opportunity in grisly circumstances, but I had no such contemplations on that day. I thought only of facts—the fate of my beloved Cwenburh and twins. Taking up the cudgel, I braced myself stronger than ever before and began looking through the pile of dead souls. Words used to describe such a ghastly task would be unequal to the task, God help us all.

At nightfall I had, as Soldag suspected, found no children, just adults. Even determining this was difficult in the wake of the outrage of a funeral pyre.

When the sun sank in the southwestern horizon, at its lowest point dusky shadows extended shrouds over the remains. I saw movement in the croft, great furred backs and tails, occasional heads looking out. The wolves came in several directions without a sound.

Retreating to a massive oak, I ascended it, hauled up my case, then my cudgel, and secured there upon an immense arm of the ancient tree. I turned my back towards the remains of the settlement and Manor and faced the Tees, its waters threading towards the sea.

Through the night the sounds of the beasts struggling over the bodies were appalling. There had been no livestock left, such being walking booty. Different groups of the ravenous animals fought over possession of this or that, and I prayed most the night that none of the spoils would be Cwenburh.

Somewhere towards Lauds, I felt the Lord's scorn upon me for my selfishness. Shamed, I prayed for the survival of others and for the departed souls being so desecrated.

I allowed dawn to declare a strong presence before descending, cudgel at ready. I staggered at seeing what remained of the grisly pile, and had to brace against the rising stench of it. I withdrew towards the edge of the croft where thickets greeted the field, but heard cries and whimpers. Investigating, I discovered one of the consuming beasts, maimed in the fiendish struggles with its kind, two of his legs nearly bitten and torn through.

It tried to run from me but could only manage snapping and snarling in its ghastly fury. Its green eyes had every bit of savage life it was born with. For the first time, may God forgive, I felt anger and fury mount—more than at any time in the three days since my donkey had been decapitated—the beginning of this carnage. This beast's bloodied fur, its bared teeth—untamed eyes glaring—challenged every precept that differentiated beast from God-given souls.

Such bestial fury through the curse of Satan was a contagion—moving from beasts like him into a human soul who lost God and Our Savior's good words. This base animal was as evil as the immoral Sigald-the-Dane—and within an instant my cudgel was brought down with all my strength upon the wolf's head with the ugliest result.

Perhaps I could think I simply put an end to its plight, but this was untrue. For the time it took my cudgel to sweep downward, I fell prey to Satan's most seductive words for retribution: It was certainly not any form of mercy towards this beast's misery.

Now that I dictate these doings and reflect back at that moment of violence, I offer it as proof for the folly of people calling me Saint or Holy Man. I am no more saint or holy man than any ordinary person who has threaded his way through this life.

When, on rare occasion I thought of myself shriven of all and able to join God with a decently cleansed soul, I think of that wretched animal snapping and snarling at me and I feel my cudgel as it traversed down. Ultimately all God's creatures have the right to his Eternal Mercy, and mankind too, no matter how badly it conducts itself. We all live under the heavens' immutable chance for forgiveness.

I believed that then, yet as God is my redeemer and eternal Pardoner, I suffered so numerous blows, I grew unsteady at heart regards men and women now, a half-century later.

Men returned to Oakheath Manor late in the second day. I heard them shouting—and the sounds of their horses crashing through underbrush. Climbing a high oak at the second evening, I looked back and could see the towers back up, and dozens of men—and women—moving about beneath.

Indeed, those responsible for the High Reeve's end were re-establishing the demesne and all extended crofts quickly. Boats plied up and downriver as search parties afoot looked on both banks. Thank God, they did not have hounds.

Most were no more or less adept at forest and field than any cottars or those used to walking. Avoiding search parties like these was easily done, if one kept one's mind and wits carefully honed. I did not—could not—assume they were looking for me, or were not. Caution and stealth were now the constant of each passing hour.

I accelerated my withdrawal downriver and struggled for an assessment about the standing of the matter in wake of this catastrophe. I had to keep rational. I had no indication whatever that Cwenburh was dead; most notably, despite a difficult search, I had not found her bridal clasp from Hereford in the embers. The murderers and their scum looted everything, but in their haste—or simply repugnance of the process searching the burning bodies for loot missed some. Most notable were metal clasps. I found nearly a dozen of them; they remained recognizable though damaged.

As the cynical Soldag had predicted, I found no children or youths, for these poor souls—which would include Matilda and Elesa—brought premium prices on the slave trade.

And God help us all. What came of Cwenburh if not murdered on the spot? Always wary as a wood rat—she could have escaped, and if a miracle would be granted by God, she had done so with the twins.

If so Cwenburh would flee as far away from Oakheath as physically possible, and seeking them out was my highest and holiest duty. And if I must search, and I must, then it was necessary to discover if I were indeed a wanted man. But if I were thought dead, I was blessed by such misinformation. Also this meant the good soul who spared me would escape terrible punishment for his disloyalty.

Any place frequented by travelers along the well-traveled road to Durham Town would be filled with rumors of who was wanted, for what, and where. Retreating towards trouble and not from it was always my most unexpected hence trustworthy ploy. This would indicate Durham Town as my wisest destination. The origins of all the wickedness at Oakheath was there.

In the ensuing weeks, it was as if the butchery at Oakheath had never occurred. No one claimed to have heard of it, nor had seen anyone looking like Cwenburh or the twins. They would certainly stand out—for no other reason than Cwenburh's nature, plus the flaw upon her face, and the twins because of their appealing looks.

Were such outrages as Oakheath so common, they were not worthy of travelers' curiosity and gossip. The winter would cease for nothing, but moved over Northumberland turning things grey and naked—skeletons against the sky. Visiting birds were gone, animals went into burrows or laid low, and people traveled less.

My outer garments fell into tatters, and those spare I carried with me in the case experienced the same. Not only had I lost several stones, I allowed an unruly beard to grow, and within several weeks of moving slowly north and northeast—always wary—I was quite a different-looking person than I at Oakheath.

Save my scribe's case.

Before going into a peopled setting, I would hide it, for its fine and specialized construct would certainly draw attention plus undermine my story of being an itinerant liveryman looking for work.

It was now past St. Nicholas's Day. Winds rose from the sea, and frost swept into my body as I struggled daily for warmth. I made hot camp during day to warm rocks, and bedded them under soil and litter at sundown, sleeping atop them, a skill I learned as a herdsman in the north. But mornings came cruelly late, now well after Terce.

Finally, after many weeks of plying within and without of Durham Town's precincts for any information, I decided I was forgotten, as indeed was the entire incident. Concluding that caution was no longer necessary, I began to risk traveling openly. I had a few shillings and could buy a winter outer garment of the roughest sort and a few other needful items. I gave thanks that stealth was no longer needed, for cold camps at night were for younger, happier men.

I had stayed twice at combination livery-and-grain houses; at the time of King Edward, their proprietors made good coin providing them as makeshift stopping places for the commonality.

Still, by habit, I had hidden my box not too far distant, and carried only roll—a makeshift purse. And on one evening two riders rested their animals overnight, and bedded within with myself and others. They were not thanes or drengs, but rough and tarnished by travel and the making of many cold camps. Having means for ale, they fell halfway into their cups, and regaled other travelers with their adventures and travels.

They were coinmen.

"Why, once we apprehended a cotset who yielded us a pound of silver. He had buggered a great Lord's daughter! Now there was the luck."

There was laughter at this as everyone saluted the fall of sodomists and how justice stalked all evildoers. A cartman asked who they sought now, and what their worth might be.

They recited a list of various criminals, describing each one. Then one pointed to the rafters of the stable and, with mock dignity, intoned, "But the number one enemy of the Earl and King we pursue is Cuthwin-of-Alnwick—great purveyor of treason to both our Earl Siward and the King, may God help him, for we surely will not."

A traveler—a musician—entered the talk. "Surely, this infamous scribe must be half eel to have escaped young Earl Siward."

Both coinmen went somber—and confronted the poor soul, their ale-induced fellowship gone.

"And how did you know him a scribe, Fellow, and it was the young Earl and not the Elder interested?"

"Well, I have heard."

"From who? Tell us. This fucking scribe wasn't even known to be alive until not two weeks back, and then only to a few. So, from who?"

One was on his feet and beside the musician in an instant, grabbing and pulling him up as if filled with rags: "So, from who, you little turd?"

Several travelers withdrew out the heavy door hanging into the cold, and others went low into the hay and feed; I drew back behind a paddock barrier, but watched and listened, my innards chilled into a knot.

"For the love of God, friends. I am just a musician, have mercy."

Both coinmen were beside him now, and a knife appeared in one's hand as if materialized by a demon. He placed it under the musician's ear. "So, from who did you hear this profitable news? Otherwise, I will start with your ear and work down, you piece of shit."

"Please, I heard it a week back from a salt pedlar named Soldag. He had made good coin for selling the information, and he told me he sold it to the Young Earl, I swear to God."

They released him, and with a violent kick sent him off, throwing his belongings after him.

"Get out of here you little worm—get out into the cold and freeze!"

Others who had not already preceded the musician did so at once. Both coinmen, now in poor spirits, returned to their bedding and sat; their silence could be heard everywhere.

Finally, one kicked his cup sending it bouncing against the beam behind me. He spit into the straw and looked momentarily towards heaven, "Well, Brother, soon half of Northumber will be looking for this damned scribe. We should have . . . ."

"You are the sot who flapped his mouth about it. We had the inside word, and the advantage. First to the trough is the key to our trade, goddamn you."

Then his comrade spotted me—or a bit of me, protruding behind the barrier.

"So, who is there? Have we amused you, Neighbor?"

I moved into view and held out my hands. "I am a liveryman looking for work and know nothing of anyone's business but my own, and keep it that way, friends."

"A liveryman?"

"Yes."

They looked me over a second time, then returned to their morose thoughts, one standing suddenly—looking knowingly to his fellow. "I do not favor it here any longer. There is another sack of fleas downroad a league. We will go there."

And they did, despite the hour. At that moment I would not have given a ha'penny for the hide of that musician, for he spread news that could eliminate their advantage—the poor man was in their way.

As they led their animals out, one hesitated and looked at me. "Make sure you keep to your own business, Liveryman."

And they were gone.

Quickly, I left by another way and made for where I had hidden my case and made cold camp. Should I curse the day I met Soldag the salt pedlar? I suppose I might have, but such was the character of that ghoul and scavenger that selling information about a living person seemed mundane in such a cursed soul.

I had befallen knowledge through God's Will that unknown might have cost me far more than nights in cold camps. Somehow Soldag had not found advantage of place to sell the information for several weeks, and perhaps did not even know I was assumed slain.

That night, I wondered after the young man who had spared me, and what might happen to him when it was found by Aldwulf-of-York his man disobeyed his order and his weak-heartedness had come to the knowledge of a man greater than he.

In my prayers that night, in addition to my family, I added the young man, whose name I did not even know, and through the years pray Our Savior will look kindly after him. I owe him time and it can never be repaid.

My scribe's case, unique and elaborate in craft and design, was my lingering problem, yet my heart sank when I thought of abandoning it. I knew no matter how I looked in attire, it would identify me as no ordinary wandering cottar or freedman, and that could bring on disaster.

It had been a great holiday gift from not just Cwenburh, but others in the begang, including and especially Edmund the Leather Craftsman and Analf the Joiner. There was no other portable case like it. They designed it for my work after years keeping their clever craftsmen's eyes on my needs.

And of course Cwenburh was at center of the idea and afforded the materials, rich in wood and leather of the finest kind.

To me it was beyond worth, yet whenever I hid it, its retrieval would draw me back. But these were life-threatening times, often necessitating flying for my own safety and certainly not returning anywhere. I felt the fool for not disposing of it earlier.

Lamenting the need through the night, at dawn I knew I must take anything of necessity from within, and as one might burn the remains of a beloved animal, bid it farewell. Scraping away ice and snow, I started up a larger fire than usual.

I began my sorting.

Since it contained what few basic tools of my trade remained, it became—atop that personal significance—a most agonizing task. Its weight had raised calluses on both hands. Carrying, even dragging it over, up, and down daily, I wore rubbings across both shoulders, despite the padded harnessing I fashioned.

At least this burden would not be missed. So placing the most necessary items within a makeshift wallet, I hefted it a few times and confirmed its ease of carry.

Prodding the fire high, I dragged the case towards it and took sorrow-laden breath. Had not our Savior wandered with nothing but his staff by which he drove the money-changers out of the temple? Did this teach me not to cling to material items?

I went to close the lid of the case, when an item caught my eye. I opened the lid again; on the rich cloth lining within—itself fashioned with loops and hooks for many items—I looked closer. The lining was entirely visible: There, on the upper and lower right inner edges of the lid, burned skillfully into the cloth were the figures of two tiny crucifixes.

These were fresh additions.

With a gentler, more appraising touch, I hefted the lid and realized it was far heavier than I ever remembered it, especially empty. Cwenburh's strange words of good-bye following her farewell kiss returned to me of the sudden.

Taking my small knife, I cut away the cloth covering of the lid, and between it and another cloth were six wide ribbons, themselves sewn into the cloth; running my fingers down the first, I felt they were double-layered, and between them were sewn coins.

This was the same work, or similar to it, Cwenburh provided Eadwig for his journey south to Rome and beyond. Continuing with caution, I cut out the ribbons. Concealed within were fully two pounds of silver pence, and the tiniest, most artful piece of jewelry: a peacock with tiny green eyes. It was gold.

So within was a fortune, by our standards.

Through that morning, watching the case burn to fine ash-grey embers, I thought back to the moment of our farewell, and wondered—marveled—at Cwenburh's gift, for she was born with instincts laced with the fey.

She carried in her mind great whirling bestiaries from which she spun tales. Also, she saw fate and other great visions in many natural markings, and always trusted to her instinct for the future, and we would argue about this in the friendly way we did. We were great at such discourse, and the children—and especially Eadwig—would listen with wonder and amusement as we traveled.

"Auntie," the serious young scholar would ask, ". . . have you seen these griffons actually pick up people and fly away with them?"

"Only after eating moldy bread!"

She would toss her head back—swipe the air at me, and warn, "Make sport of me, Cuthwin. By Our Savior, I shall pray keenly for you after one swoops down and spirits you away—poor doubting soul you are, scornful of God's natural creatures."

So this fire that now consumed my beloved case radiated memories imbued within its fabric: voices and times of the past, near and far. Cwenburh, in her craft and knowledge of me, would not tell me of our fortune contained herein, for I would have shunned the entire case rather than leave them without all we had worked and traveled for.

I was out of tears and laments. I now thought of Herself: A marvelous blessing God gave me—young and foolish—on that day at Loe a full sixteen turns of the seasons ago. Had she been taken from me by that same God? I bent towards the fire, now sinking low like all earthly fires, and prayed for God's mercy. A greater spirited soul had never ascended before her, nor would it after.

I sat praying, not wanting to turn my back on the burning core of the fire; I swung a bit, left and right, hesitating. A voice within warned, *Cuthwin, you must carry on.*

I wandered until winter without learning anything of my family nor of what happened at Oakheath Manor. At Middlesbrough were haul-outs and yard-arms where ships came and went with diverse cargo. Also, this area's misfortune was that invaders from overseas beginning long ago would often land and up-to-present strike havoc wherever they raided.

After some time here I met a leather merchant, a good soul who for a few pennies allowed me shelter in his stable after I had bought repair material for my wallet and other portables. After several days, seeing that I was on something of a quest, he asked after it.

I did not lie, but told him generally I had lost my family in these troubles, along with the tools of my craft, I being a liveryman. And it was here I found the first true information, and it proved dismal indeed. The merchant lived in the area for many years. He was anything but strange to the slave trade.

"These sordid men who deal in slaves come with ships of many oars, the bastards. Oh, they make a life of it, they do. I see them all, for they use leather restraints coming and going, for the pigs cannot afford chain."

"Then, in the last months have you seen twin redheaded girls just short of age?"

"God help me and you, I have. Sold oversea—were hotly contested by several of the Danes."

He could see I was struck dumb—it told him the truth of it and he lamented such business, a kindly man.

"Oh, I pray for your loss and God's mercy. I beg for forgiveness by Our Savior's virtue for being the bearer of this information. By now they could be thousands of leagues distant in any direction of the heavens. I know this is meager enough balm, but God spared them—your daughters live and are worth more healthy than otherwise. This awful assurance and prayers is all a poor leather-monger can offer."

I prayed that night that God would be kind to Elesa and Matilda, for only he knew where they were. Even the King himself lacked enough resources to dispatch ships over the seas and into countless harbors in search of our poor wretched girls.

The chances of Cwenburh surviving continued only as the merest thread of the possible. But, I—despite the devastating outcome for Elesa and Matilda—would carry on hoping for the intervention of Our Savior. One thread was Cwenburh: By the act of hiding our funds with me, obviously she anticipated something dire.

She was not one to be caught unawares. I deeply felt she lived.

Having purchased warm but coarsely woven clothing to maintain an impoverished appearance yet survive the raw winds, I went to Durham amidst Twelfth Night celebrations. Having done business there in late summer, I was more confident with the surroundings.

Though not prime time for pilgrims to pray before the shrine of St. Cuthbert's, this greatest of God's servants incorruptible remains still drew faithful from all Christendom. Because of this I had ready my excuse for wandering there; and more shelters for travelers, nowadays called 'inns,' rather than religious premises, made daily living more comfortable.

Still, I slept light and looked and spent like one with only the lowest of means rather than a freedman with a fortune of silver and gold bound around his upper thighs. A knife, cudgel, and sober man offered little or no reward to predators who preyed on weaker and more promising targets.

But by the spring of that year, I lost heart at finding word about those who survived the devastation at Oakheath. However, I did learn it resulted from the treachery of High Reeve Sigald, the details seeming to revolve around money stolen. The mounted caparisoned warrior who cleaved him was young, certainly not the aged Earl Siward.

But it was Sigald's foulness and greed that resulted in the ruination and mayhem at Oakheath; that all save Sigald and possibly his clerk were innocent of wrongdoing meant nothing to great men steeped in anger. I was able to gather no more information despite a grueling winter wanderings, town to village—back to town.

I greeted spring at Great York—a town larger than all others, well south of the troubles in Durham. Without any word at all, I fell into a despair and was weary of plying the roads and paths—with risk hidden at all corners and junctions.

Knowing I must continue—Cwenburh would be sure of that—I decided to return to the begang by way of Peterborough, and resume my former identity. While venturing south, I would write a letter explaining our family's misfortunes to Eadrig—and possibly to learn something of him, especially if Frog had returned from his great ambulation.

A raw, unyielding winter held on to land, sea, and mountains, driving back the coming spring—snow falling late, ice locking everything unseasonably. This drove thanes and cottars to delve further and further into winter and spring supplies until there were no more to be had.

Making my way across my old homeland on the fens, my spirit, instead of being enhanced, fell. I saw the cruelty, again, of winter's hand; yet this year the grip of winter relented, and I did thank God and Our Savior. I knew too well what it was like when folk died in famine. With the improvement in weather, the worst of this would be avoided.

Yet the cruelty of bad men was impervious to even the powers of weather, being driven instead by the darkest of shepherds. Our land fell prey to them, absconding our fates from under the eyes of God and Our Savior whose absence challenged faith in their eternal goodness.

I prayed to shrink away from these thoughts, but doubts began to grow within, as wayward seeds sprout after being scattered by the most ill winds. My faith weakened.

When I slogged through the spring mud and the familiar gates of Peterborough town, I sought out Edmund the Leather Craftsman's son, who had given us so much help the previous summer.

His wife was shocked when I came to the door and identified myself—for I still had full beard. She cast a wild look back, and lowered her voice—it being stern and sharp: "What have you come here for? Do you want us ruined, like you and your family? What took you to fall in with such evil men, and to involve poor Cwenburh and the children. Get out before I tell the guard, God save your soul."

And the door hanging swung close, and I saw it being tied firmly down.

This was an extraordinary greeting. How might they be so misinformed after the letter I sent about our abduction to Father Abbot through Prior Wulfgar? I explained precisely the nature of our abduction—and reading his response I knew he understood. I stood, staring—had this woman taken leave of her senses?

Surely her husband had not.

Yet they were as one in such matters of local knowledge and fact, or at least seemed as much in my memory.

I sought out a wine and oil merchant who kept a pilgrim's shelter used by those not partial to the rules of Monastery hospitality. He had never known me.

There—after thought—I shaved, went to a merchant and bought

clothes, clean and moderate to the eye, and for the first time in a hundred-plus days felt a little of my former self.

When I returned to pick up my belongings, thank God I spotted the Guard and the Undersheriff before they did me. Backing into hiding, I heard them heaping foul language on the merchant for giving me shelter, and what I heard shattered my already tattered hopes: "Give shelter to a traitor, you prick? We should hang you here! Now where is he, or it's the worse for you?"

It was my own acquaintances who now turned me over. Only a half-year before they gave us profuse hospitality and information.

Traitor?

I at once hid deeper in the darkness between houses and sheds. To leave Peterborough—wending my way along narrow raised dyke roads and expecting to avoid mounted men—was impossible. They would ride me down like a dog.

I whirled, and knowing the way only too well, made for the Monastery gate. Reaching the Monastery ground proper would be my only chance for fair hearing. Also, the proof should be kept in the Scriptorium folders—my letter to Prior, and the return copy to me, as weak as it was.

"Stop right there, Cuthwin-of-Alnwick!"

In the long row leading to the Monastery gate, the mounted watchmen emerged on the far end. Cut off from it, I knew that any entry gate must now do.

And it was Our Savior who watched over me: A nearby side gate was wide open, for at the moment a shepherd was pushing six fat ewes into its premises, and though my desperate retreat startled animals and shepherd, like the once agile youth I had been, I vaulted over the sheep and landed inside Monastery grounds.

Here, the law was Father Abbot and the Lord.

Carrying cudgel and with a knife at my waist, I made my way to the front of Father Abbot's quarters, and by that time, there was such a commotion, including the ringing of the Monastery bell, that several monks at office gathered, and, putting down my weapons, I turned to the closest:

"I am Cuthwin-of-Alnwick. I seek Holy Sanctuary from these men, who falsely accuse me and mean me harm."

It was a whirl of events: The Undersheriff rode up, his great horse gasping steam from nostrils, wide with excitement. He pointed at me—actually thrust his arm at me in sword-like motions. "This man is a traitor. He has inflicted treason on the King by consorting knowingly with traitors. No hearing is needed, before God."

The guards ran up, not far behind; bent over, their slothful ways in town not equal to sudden exertion, they struggled for breath.

At once I recognized one of the monks as an oblate, and another far older without any sign of office at his waist—yet he quickly ordered in the language of Rome for the oblate to run for higher authority.

But he held up a single hand, standing between them and me.

"Reverend Prior will be here. Stand fast, please be to God. There is request of sanctuary here."

Prior Dundage walked sedately into the court, and though far greyer now than when—years ago, he had been Gardener—still possessed the sheer height of command—being taller than any then and now.

The Whipmen followed, and two other Brothers—both held office, one Subcellarer, the other Sacrist—and in fact still Brother Aethyl, now bent and carrying a great staff. He looked me up, then down—shook his head: "Oh, Cuthwin, still up to your rascality?"

"Rascality!!! This turd has committed treason against the King."

Reverend Prior raised his hand, pointing at the Undersheriff. I'd forgotten that his voice was as commanding as his presence.

"Where are you, Master Undersheriff? Must I remind?"

Reverend Prior motioned towards my weapons, flicking a tiny gesture to the oblate at his side, and he at once swept them up.

Prior Dundage took his time, looking me up and down—back up at the Sheriff, who, remembering his place, calmed down. Undoubtedly, half of his family would owe rents and other fees to the Monastery, and a Prior was the leading edge in the pursuit of such matters.

He took a breath, deciding something, and asked where the King's Warrant was for such an arrest of a free Saxon craftsman.

"I don't have it at hand, Reverend Prior, but follow direction from the

Lord High Sheriff, now two days' distant."

"Cuthwin, what do you say? God help you if you lie."

"That I am innocent of such crimes, and am a faithful servant of God and follower of the loving words of Our Savior, Jesus Christ. I would swear my innocence as bond against seizure by the Archfiend."

He looked up at the Undersheriff and pronounced temporary sanctuary for me until Father Abbot returned from France. "He escorts the mortal remains of the Venerable Elsin, more honored than any other man by all within and without cloister at Peterborough."

The Undersheriff became sullen, for clearly there was abundant reward for me, to be shared with the dogs behind him, and he withheld swearing, but his neck and jowls swelled like a rooster.

"Lord High Sheriff, Reverend Prior, will hear of this by courier, and he will not be pleased, and I think Canterbury will not either."

"God's grace and love go with you; and Father Abbot's love and reverence for Canterbury and all there is widely known. But this matter must wait; Cuthwin, on my orders, will remain within and be held account for any true warrant."

After the Undersheriff turned tail, conversation amongst Brothers began; but Reverend Prior held up a hand, directing Brother Aethyl to escort me within. I was taken to one of the havens for wanderers and pilgrims. Since I had nothing but myself and what I wore, Brother Aethyl glanced about to check we were alone and had enough sense to see I was altogether sad to hear of old Father Abbot's death.

It sapped any relief enjoyed from receiving sanctuary.

"I shall bring you blanket, spoon, and bowl. We are keeping a day and night vigil for the Venerable Elsin who we all loved, me no less than all, and certainly you as well, Cuthwin. He was fond of you because of your love for Waddles, that cursed donkey of his, may God forgive me."

I sought out a tiny chapel used by travelers, skipping the repast at Sext. I had lost so much, and now Father Abbot Elsin who spared me from terrible consequences of my youthful adventures. I thanked God in prayer that he lived to give sign over Cwenburh, Eadwig, and the twins Matilda and Elesa. And, once again, me.

In the name of the Father, Son, and Holy Ghost, Abbot Elsin lives in heaven, assured of God's eternal grace. I believe this to the present hour despite my numerous weaknesses of faith which would have alarmed this most sacred of men.

Christendom with England had lost much with the departure of Abbot Elsin. In the wake of all my loss, I cared little about my mortal person; hence, I lived under temporary sanctuary soundly enough. I was plagued by no worries; if hanged, I would meet my end shriven and join those I loved who dwelled above in the comfort of Our Savior.

I asked for chores at the Livery from Elfgar, now Liveryman of Peterborough. He was a terse, massively built Saxon, a great nephew of Gilbert—who began his apprenticeship under my former teacher and loyal ally.

I occupied myself with repair of tackle; while working I prayed for the souls in my past, including Frog and Eadwig. I hoped he would have word when Father Abbot arrived with the remains of the venerable Elsin, for Frog would never abandon him until home on the fens.

Despite the advent of spring, bad times still carried on from the long winter. I would save my bread, and breaking it into pieces, feed it to the pigeons who lived in the stable. I hoped for forgiveness remembering I bagged these birds, who also had sanctuary. My planned escape those many years ago remained vivid—and how Abbot Elsin gently applied for mercy for them after convincing me to stay.

By this time, my belongings had been the route of trade via the wine merchant. But they received reprieve by order of Reverend Prior; hence were returned to me worse for wear. He ruled all with a stern, steady hand in Father Abbot's absence.

The funerary train of the Venerable Elsin arrived with great sorrow and ceremony at Peterborough on the same week the first swallows returned to the fens. Abbot Leofric accompanied the vanguard, walking barefoot and wearing only sack-cloth and a simple wooden cross strung along a coarse fiber line.

Behind came the remainder—great men and scholars of Monastic Houses in France—friends and associates of Elsin. Some walked, and a few who were elderly rode. We all lined both sides of the gates of Peterborough Monastery, the bell striking regularly, singing out mournfully these somber hours.

Outside the gates, all were on their knees while Father Abbot elevated the cross about his neck, announcing in the language of Rome there would be fourteen days of mourning. During this time the Abbey and Town would observe solemn vigil—celebrating Holy Elsin's transport to the eternal joys of heaven.

No business beyond that necessary to attend daily sustenance was done for those inside the walls and in cloister, excepting for tending to the needs of honored guests, who arrived daily.

The Venerable Elsin's remains were opened to viewing and prayers by ordinary folk outside and inside the Monastery confines, then afterward only for churchmen or officers of the land.

I attended these through the entirety of the first day and well into the third, then returned to my quarters unable to sleep because of demons of past times. Giving up, I went to the livery resuming work on a complicated length of trace. It was not quite Matins, the oblate on fire watch was already asleep like so many before him, and I worked on, contented with the moment.

Only the beasts moved in paddock and stall as I worked.

From the corner of my eye, I saw movement through the top slats between myself and the entrance. At the moment I heard the bells announcing the cessation of viewing for ordinary folk. Whoever it was held a moment, cautiously.

Then, satisfied it was safe, into view came an elderly woman, but one who walked erect and strong. She hesitated, swept away a head-covering revealing bright blue eyes darting left and right, making sure no one was near save the sleeping oblate. I at once recognized Esa, Wife of Ordgar, the fisherman and eelman.

When passing through the previous year with the begang, I heard

Ordgar had died, and the fishing enterprise was no longer expertly conducted, but time prevented me from visiting this kindly soul, God forgive me.

"Cuthwin-of-Alnwick, events have gone badly for you of late, God help us all."

She kept her voice low, but I recognized it at once. She was invariably kind to me, for one who knew almost nothing of my mother, Esa held special sway.

"It is true, Esa. You look well, and my spirits arise to see you, God knows."

Then we embraced, retreated to a nook in the livery, and from beneath an outer mantle, badly tattered, she took a small sack with bread and dried fish.

"This is for you, made the best way."

Lowering my voice more I asked after Frog, and why he had not returned with his Uncle's procession, for I knew he had knowledge of Eadwig.

"Oh, Cuthwin, would you not guess!? Without protection of his beloved Uncle, his enemies raise old issues and want to hang him. He disappeared before Abbot Leofric took ship in France with Great Elsin's mortal remains, God be Praised. He is a cunning one." She paused, checked to see the oblate still slept then added, ". . . he is on the fens, the rogue, what there is left of him. Know this: Your Eadwig is arrived and safe at his destination, God be Praised."

She, of course, had seen Frog. He emerged from hiding and confided recent events only to Esa, for whom he had powerful affection. I gleaned this by watching and listening those years ago, mainly in wake of one incident: Frog embarked on a great rout when he got word—incorrectly as it happened—that Ordgar had beat Esa. He meant awful retribution.

When he returned—having first visited his cups grandly—he acknowledged his was a false start, and that Ordgar was a good sort.

Now, for sure, I wanted to see Frog badly, and she took my hand, squeezing it with her powerful Saxon-wife hands.

"He cannot come here, and for the foreseeable future you cannot go there, and God forgive, I will skull either of you who try. Somewhere in you, Cuthwin-of-Alnwick, is a streak of Frog."

She kissed me, covered up against the night cold and left me with the provisions and utter joy that Eadwig has reached his destination. My adopted son was with Holy Men and going about his great purpose given to him by God.

Upon cessation of the holy vigil and the funeral mass—full of singing and great words of praise, closed to the commonality—Venerable Elsin was interred at the Monastery.

Within a half day, I looked up from where I read in my quarters, coming eye to eye with the Whipmen—whose duties had shifted for the better to messengers for Father Abbot.

"Cuthwin-of-Alnwick, you are wanted at once before Father Abbot."

I followed them over that familiar path, last taken when only a youth. Now instead I saw a different Father Abbot behind the same simple table, Reverend Prior standing to one side. My gut tightened when none other than the Undersheriff and the High Sheriff—though unarmed—stood to right and left of him, their eyes fixing on me like a kite spotting a fat grasshopper.

I knelt, received the sign, and stayed there.

The High Sheriff stated the King's case, which was simple: The King had ordered warrant on the basis of sworn testimony from Earl Siward, his numerous thanes and loyal tenants and subtenants in his Earldom. Earl Siward assured the King that anyone who had cooperated and done tasks for the wayward, greedy traitor—the late High Reeve of Gloucester—was a traitor and must face judgment.

At that he moved his hand to the warrant, already unrolled before Father Abbot, who made no move, no response; his right hand held a large cockle shell, which he would examine absently, then put down— tap several times—as these arguments played out.

Reverend Prior Dundage motioned to my letter to Father Abbot through him, and a copy of his response, adding simply, "Father Abbot, these are true letters written prior to events."

Father Abbot looked directly at Prior and nodded. "I have read all these."

Again, he raised and lowered the cockleshell while ruminating, tapping it once or twice, turning it around, yet did not speak. With no exception, if Father Abbot doesn't speak, no one speaks without permission. But a High Sheriff is a powerful person, used to his privileges of office. He gestured to the writ and said, "The King expects each of his subjects to do his duty."

It was a bold and careless offering; he was not on his own ground. The cockleshell was set down firmly, and Father Abbot lifted up his head, looking at the High Sheriff with a strange, unreadable countenance.

"And we have great love and affection for the King and Queen, but the issue here is of sanctuary for Cuthwin-of-Alnwick, which I grant indefinitely. I see here a loyal, good soul wrongly accused, who has lost his family after odious abduction by those vacant of our Savior's sacred words. He and his family carried the blessings of the Venerable Elsin, and produced a prodigal son who serves the Church before God and Our Savior."

Then straightaway he stood, made the sign over us all, and exited by the private entrance, though first turning the cockleshell sculpted side down, and straightening it a notch.

The High Sheriff and his underling swelled in their wrath, and after a nod from Reverend Prior, the Whipmen made to escort them out. The High Sheriff raised an arm, pointing at the departed Abbot.

"The King will hear of this within the day, or two at most, Reverend Prior."

"No doubt." Then Reverend Prior looked at me, and gestured to me to stay where I was; then watched as the angry officials followed the Whipmen out.

Prior Dundage was equally unreadable as Father Abbot—he gestured for me to rise, and thought a moment. "You are knowledgeable about the ways of a Monastery, Cuthwin, and know what Sanctuary is, and how those with it conduct themselves. There is no need for you to work or such. Prayer is your best refuge."

"I will pray, Reverend Prior. But I also wish to work, as I always had. I would like to do copy work; my hands require the practice."

"There is a different Master and Assistant Master of our Scriptorium and I must ask them. I caution you against hope for their consent. They both know you plied the skills learned here for profit throughout the realm. This raises issues, Cuthwin. So be patient."

There was noticeable ease of Monastery folk towards me, and for the first time Liveryman Elfgar had more than a simple word with me, and complimented my craftsmanship. I told him I would serve anyway I was of use. I did not hear back from Prior Dundage, so assumed no word meant my desire to practice my craft met with scorn. No surprise there.

Time was of no consequence to me, nor what the King might or might not do. God had taken everything from me I loved, save Eadwig, who lived far distant and safe, God be Praised for this gift, if for none others.

I would hear of word about Frog from time to time through Esa, who I found with little surprise had gone to care for him upon the fens.

"He is infirm now from the wanton ways he followed, and needs a wife. His wits are still about him, though, without doubt, and he can yet rob a trap or two, though he says all we eat or trade is honestly gotten, God forgive him."

I spent hours in contemplation and ruminations about the fate thrust upon all of us who work and survive from season to season by our wits and hands. If God had mercy on us, why did he rain misery mostly upon us, and so comparatively little on the cruel, greedy souls who held vast offices of authority and lands?

Then too were churchmen of town, village, and manor who often strayed from Our Savior's words. They would sell all sorts of benefices supposedly given to plain folk through the goodness of the Lord.

Worse, those ordained before the great office of the Bishop of Rome or his delegate to celebrate the mysteries and give absolution lived lives often contrary to how I understood them to be proscribed.

I had spent thirty-plus sets of seasons watching these things. While enjoying sanctuary at Peterborough, I spent four more years without word of anything, though snippets from the south informed that Eadwig knew my state but was rightly warned away from writing to me. I was, by Royal decree, a traitor, and any letter might be intercepted and used mightily against the sender, even a son.

And then Earl Siward, Earl of Northumberland died, God help him.

I knew this would change, or might change, my situation. The greatest and most wrathful of great men cannot defy death. For outrages from the likes of Earl Siward sent me spinning into an abyss of self-pity and even heretical views. I believed mindless Fate ruled beyond any realm held by God, and that Fate was more in league with Satan than it was God.

I told no one, not even my confessor, a simple priest/monk named Issin who worked sometimes as Gardener when the appointed Monastery officer was ailing. He tried to assuage my soul of my prideful enmity over past events: "Cuthwin, my son, such calumny befalls most poor folk in this cruel world and you cannot separate yourself from the whole—for all are able to be forgiven by God."

I would say my penance, work at harness and tackle, and watch one day turn into a week, and it into a year. How deep is mortal folly to view such as I, Cuthwin-of-Alnwick, saint or saintly. In truth, I struggle through prayer and sacrifice for redemption of my own soul and to save myself from the fires of the Archfiend, greedy reaper of wretched souls.

When I learned King Edward issued me clemency, I felt very little by way of joy. He signed a writ freeing me of false accusations by those who duped the late Earl Siward with false statements; however, I never came to feel any gratitude to his Royal Person.

I felt grateful only to Peterborough Monastery which gave me sanctuary for those years. I do recall thinking what I might do. First thought was I might become an elder oblate, and stay there—perhaps this way gaining admittance to the Scriptorium. I had not practiced my craft in five years, and did not know what skills I might yet possess.

The liveryman—who had grown great friends with me—voiced warnings about the entirety of the good news.

"First off, be cautious of what Kings say—good or bad. I would not believe them. Those noble turds cannot tell truth from their own spittle. I would watch your backside outside these walls."

He and I sat before a hot brew of wild serviceberry leaves, his specialty.

When I confessed thoughts of becoming oblate, he slapped his knee and looked to the rafters overhead. "Oh, may God and Our Savior bring you to your good senses; you know better than that. Save for a few of these monks, most could not raise a pimple on Abbot Elsin's ass, God forgive me. His holiness and my kinsmen Gilbert's mastery of craft is why I came to be liveryman here, none else. They are with God now."

He continued, raining diverse opprobrium on all Monastic offices. In the four years there—though I slept in privilege in sanctuary quarters—I heard much. There was substantial truth to his words.

He twirled his empty cup, looking reflectively into the small fire in his workshop and night-quarters.

"I had a good wife who gave me many children and died giving me a ninth, God keep her. Now my eldest daughter mothers the lot, a good soul. I have yet another marriage suit for her. It is as good a bride price as a father might wish, and I cannot deny her this."

It was the way of so many folk: The eldest daughter would mother the remaining siblings until the father re-married, or she might leave to be married, the marriage contract forbidding her continued care of her siblings.

I had made hundreds of contracts in my time, and some were bitter indeed for a remaining parent, especially a lone father with many children.

It was now mid-summer. The kindly weather lent itself for travel, and if I were not to become oblate, I should leave. But first I would seek out Frog, for I had wondered if I might take pilgrimage oversea, taking Eadrig half the fortune Cwenburh had left us—which I kept safe always. It belonged to all of us, and there was no trusted way to get it to him other than on my person.

I did not know, however, where Frog hid; great and minor officials wanted him for past warrants, and now new outrages.

God and Our Savior, I was sure, extended forgiveness to Frog: For as a kite cannot keep from eating fat insects, so it was Frog resumed his thieving and diverse outrages, even though mostly crippled and no longer able-bodied.

And in less than a week after news of my writ was public, Esa came to market to sell some split-reed baskets, always premium items. During those times we met openly.

She heard of my renewed freedom at market the previous Sabbath and, like Elfgar, advised caution.

"Good Cuthwin, use wise sense. Rich, powerful men can't be trusted—you must give clouded water time to settle, God help us. Give up your name for time being; Frog's main weapon is that people do not know him by sight. He changes names like he might turnshoes, the poor heedless sinner."

For me to see Frog strained even Esa's resourcefulness. Several rewards were offered for him, a few by the Undersheriff, others by rich thanes who owned vast holdings. These great men held in demesne, croft, river, and wetland those God-given resources which Frog utilized as skillfully as Esa wove her baskets. Unfortunately for her, it was common knowledge that Esa knew the whereabouts of Frog, but she never offered proof enough for her own warrant.

In Esa, Frog met his match for caution and resourcefulness.

"Oh, yes. I am always followed when I leave market. They think I don't see, but I do. God help me if I were ever to try and trade fish or fowl, they would warrant me at once."

Finally, after a week I returned and she asked if I remembered where many years ago—almost two decades—several eelmen butchered a stolen calf, and were summarily hanged. I did. In fact, it was called locally Hangman's Crossing, for two prominent raised pathways parted the fens there.

Close by was a dilapidated boat-landing. There at Lauds at the setting of the half-moon during the next few days, Frog and I could meet, having yet a few hours of dark.

"If on the third night, he does not show, I would continue on, for God was wise in putting off the meeting of you two."

How she regularly got to and from where they stayed, she did not mention.

At that same market, I bought several sets of turnshoes and a new heavy-made traveling wallet. Much walking was ahead; furthermore, I was given my knife and cudgel back.

The last step prior to departure was to seek permission from Father Abbot, who was about to attend court to the south. Prior Dundage escorted me in and reminded to thank Father Abbot Leofric for representing my interests over the preceding years.

Abbot Leofric stood looking out a window with glass. It was the first I had seen, and when I knelt, I struggled to keep my head down and not stare.

He asked me to stand, smiled, and beckoned me forward. "Tap on it with your fingertip. Most glass I've seen was exceedingly dark, or colored—used in artistic celebration from scenes of Our Savior's Passion."

And he made sign over me, and in fact he and Reverend Prior then said short prayer for me.

I rose, thanked him and respectfully slid ten shillings upon his table,

"You have sheltered me all these years, and my wife Cwenburh and our family would want Peterborough Monastery to have benefit of our past blessings through Our Savior, God be endlessly praised. All I ask are masses be said for Cwenburh and our two girls, wherever they might be, God help them."

I was humbled when Father Abbot, then Reverend Prior, embraced me in turn. They assured I would always be welcomed there. With that great spiritual and kind conclusion, I left Peterborough Monastery and town for the first time in four-plus years.

Of course, great stories were told many times about the hanging at the crossing of dyke/pathways during the time of King Cnut. This infamous locale was distant from where most might suppose Frog might come and go.

I arrived there the first night under a luxurious half-moon, which fes-tooned the fens with its vaporous light. Under it, nightjars hunted, and secretive bats darted down into the reeds, then up—fluttering in place a moment as they ate their prey, then flew down for another.

The powerful memories of the fens overwhelmed, and the remains of the old boat landing brought back better times. In the relics of two fen-boats, actually piles of pieces and splinters, I made my camp and admired all above me. The moon set perfectly in the northwest, and now complete darkness cloaked all. Yet, after eyes adjusted, the stars and objects strewn above illuminated faintly as they arrayed towards the mouth of the Great Ouse.

"If you intend to travel on the continent, you'd better be more aware than this, Cuthwin-of-Alnwick."

Frog emerged from the reeds, quiet as a stoat, and offering the short-est of embrace, checked about, then sat on the old wharf, keeping as wary as the fox.

The five-plus years were hard on him; the hand with missing fingers was stiff with bone ague and he favored entirely the other. He had a great cleft over his right eye, and in the darkness I could make out no more.

Perhaps, I did not want to; time and harsh living were his lot, God forgive his ways.

He told me how the journey to Monte Cassino Monastery went with him and Eadwig. He scoffed, recalling how their progress was painfully slow with the Venerable Elsin and the King's Escort.

"The whole snarl of them, save my uncle, of course, were fornicators and swine—crooked bastards. They skimmed money everywhere with shelter keepers, and I trusted them no more than I might snakes. The holy men were not much better, just stupider."

Seeing the way of things, the Venerable Elsin, now growing weaker each day, ordered Frog to separate, and make his own way—making four times the daily distance. Though Frog did not say as much, his character would conflict with the escort and the clerics.

Frog removed his hat and motioned towards the distance—perhaps, in his mind, the Rome of years before.

"So indeed, with Himself commanding me, I left—Eadwig in tow.

You know, Cuthwin, that boy is a marvel of patience and intelligence. We became great friends, and he is equal a student of wildcrafting as you were. Though unlike yourself when young and adventurous—he kept strict the Commandments."

In just three months' time, a wonder of progress, they reached the venerated ancient Monastery at Monte Cassino where Saint Benedict founded all that became The Rule.

Wondering after my destination, Frog took me by the shoulder and gave it a shake.

"If you go to France, you will not last a month. Their ways are a plague with the foulest sort of robbers and murderers up every tree, behind every rock and stump. Holy Pilgrims, if they traveled alone or as a few, have their things relieved from them. Even I had uncommon close calls, and me with your dear Eadwig entrusted to me."

His plan back then was simple as it was potentially slow, but it used the imagination of survivorship: He lived off the land and waters as best he could, kept close to the coast warily contacting no one, and making camp in a secret place, often cold if he thought caution for the best. It was essentially the same going south.

"When we did enter village or town for market, as we left we were always followed by human jackals, who soon lamented their mistake— they crashed through thickets like pigs. I should have slit a few throats, but because of Eadwig's pleadings, broke a few arms or legs with cudgel. They would flee yiking like dogs, the foreign-speaking brown-eyed fuckers."

At that, there was an awful shriek—at once, both of us knew it was a careless muskrat snagged by the great fen owl, dark and deeply spotted—its life ended at the cutting ends of the soundless hunter's massive talons. Despite his decades, Frog's head turned at once in that direction, and he shook his head at the work of nature, so dumbly cruel.

Any further thought of traveling south on the paths through Normandy and beyond chilled within, and I knew at once, my greatest strength still lay in writing.

"Frog, I think I must first write letters to good Eadwig. I know of ways to send them south. I could not send or receive letters while in sanctuary without involving whoever I sent with treason in event they were intercepted."

"Oh, a great pig's snout for all that treason, sanctuary, writs, freedom, and prayer means—all that shit. Stay on the fens with Esa and me, Cuthwin—we will steal the fuckers blind, and eat hearty during all seasons. You have a great gift for it."

Despite the clandestine nature of our meeting, he laughed at this thought—slapping his thigh with his good hand then of a sudden taken with a cough. He knew I would not do that, but I felt richly complimented he thought me capable.

Quieting, and spitting out great phlegm, he nodded, looking over at me. It was now the false dawn, and he and I looked out upon that and knew soon he must withdraw. We both gazed at the expanse of fens as the light eased across it, and we shared this peace of our God-given souls, though I know Frog would never admit as much.

"Cuthwin-of-Alnwick, we have shared many sunrises, but I'm afraid this is the last we will witness together."

"May God help you, Frog. You cannot go on as you are; they will eventually catch you."

"So? I have the one great gift anyone could have, and they won't harm her. I tell you Cuthwin, Esa is too smart for any of them."

It was difficult, this parting—made moreso by how much this soul had imparted to me, making so much possible. Not the least of these gifts was making me wise in wild-crafting, enabling Cwenburh and me to survive, first as youths, then, when older—and under God, keeper of our children.

We embraced, and he faded into the rushes like he had appeared. I only barely heard the sound of a pole against a boat, then nothing.

And he was right: I never saw Frog again, but I have always prayed that Our Savior's eternal forgiveness embrace him, and that God preserve his soul. For Esa, she had no need of my prayers. Save for Cwenburh, no finer soul lived under God's grace.

I thought this day on the rich providing fens that perhaps hundreds of more days were before me. Little did I know that as only God may command, my time ahead turned into twenty-times that.

Day spread out its candle of golden hue throughout as I walked away from Peterborough, unsure of what to do, and even more—where to go.

Mine was a hollow freedom, may God forgive my lack of gratitude.

Knowing I must have time to pray and consider all, I took shelter at the Spalding Monastery. And, may God forgive, I decided to yield to the expediency of untruth in God's own house, telling them I was Egbert-of-Alnwick. I thank Our Savior that the humble monks extended hospitality to me, and asked nothing more of my name.

I decided to take Esa's wise words to heart: "You must give clouded water time to settle, Cuthwin." I must live on in untruth if I were to do any of my former family any good—and to reaffirm Cwenburh's good sense in providing me with the family's fortune, most still bound around both my limbs.

At chapel I performed many stations of our Savior's Passion, and while doing so I decided to return again to Northumberland where the outrage occurred. To do otherwise was to forever leave behind even the most delicate of hopes.

Acquiring surface, quill, and pen, I wrote three letters more or less identical to Eadwig, telling him I would settle in York, and the name I adopted.

I wanted to take no chances it would not reach Eadwig: During the ensuing weeks, I selected three different carriers: one of church, the second a merchant, and the third a three-times Pilgrim resolutely set again upon Jerusalem.

I dawdled north to Great York, and in the leisurely interim grew a close-trimmed beard and became accustomed to identifying myself as Egbert-of-Alnwick. I decided not to return to any begang, but instead remain in York. While wandering I learned nothing—accomplished nothing—so staying put I could do no worse.

The York of that year—the decade before William the Bastard laid murderous waste to it—was a mighty center of Saxon and Dans law life. It was the largest town I visited on the begang. During our prosperous dealing there six years before, I became familiar with the layout of York. Some say its buildings went back to times when giants ranged the earth, wrestling with loathsome dragons and other such beasts for possession of the rich lands.

I recall now a half-century later, I returned to York in the late summer when they were still digging out from a terrible late spring flood that occurred the same year. Though God blessed the Vale of York with that opulence, this fertile land and waters could become hostile and flood.

York was a port city. Shallow-bellied ships transported goods upriver from deep-watered Hull, their holds stuffed with materials from all over the God-endowed world.

On the week of my arrival, the tides were bad and nearly a hundred of these smaller river boats crowded the course. Their crews were mostly in their cups, and factors and other merchants had even more time to negotiate and wheedle. The boats' holds were filled with larger, more profitable merchandise, mostly wool or hides of ox and other beasts, and of course the vast barrels of cured eels, prized in all Christendom.

So all was in chaos, made moreso by priests and other religious sentinels in keen expectation of their benefices. These sorts walked here and there, ringing bells and blowing horns—shouting warning and invocation against all, for it was the sixth day, and approaching Sabbath. Righteous gelds would be levied in the name of the Archbishop, who along with these officers, would take a share. Ultimately the Archbishop held all power in York and could never be disregarded in business matters.

But despite these officers and their authority, a considerable show of roguish behavior greeted me the day of my arrival.

Several dozen boatmen lay hold of one of these greedy church officers (May God forgive my saying such) and took away his bell. After rousting him overhead, they tossed him in the river. They then gamboled along, ringing the bell in his stead, and in their crude Danish tongue invoking everyone to commit all sorts of sin and disgrace. Laughter followed them everywhere until the Archbishop's mounted thanes appeared.

Cunning, despite being steeped in heavy ale, the boatmen scattered like fleas. Frustrated, the mounted thanes took to beating anyone they saw laughing at the expense of God's ordained men.

Such was York in the days when Saxons ruled, before the greedy Norman had beaten Saxons with their demonic horses and sullied our land with rock and stone castles filled with criminals and excommunicates.

I set about my plan in earnest, for in all this chaos, one Saxon with ideas for a business would not even be noticed.

In the twenty-plus years since I commenced life as a scribe, the craft caught on somewhat and it had sprouted into a recognized occupation outside of monastery and church. There were not a few around who wrote and read Saxon and the language of Rome—some, even the Norman language.

On my way to York, I always stopped either at fair or town to see a scribe's work, which varied from poor to acceptable. None, in my view—and may God forgive me for the sin of Pride—did expert work. They wrote letters, and had done with it. Yet their prices reflected an opinion of themselves beyond the actual. I made mental note of all these.

My first efforts in five years while writing the letters to Good Eadwig were painful, but demonstrated that almost twenty years of craft, learned at one of the finest scriptoriums in Christendom, imbued skill into my sinews.

In York I decided to combine my two crafts: One was dealing in writing materials, including the many inks and fine quills and growing use of copper point—priceless implements. Also, I would in an adjoining half-shop, as it were, return to the business of a scribe, first exercising muscles and knowledge long dormant before opening that portion for the commonality. I expected only top form in myself.

At last I made use of the coin gained through one business to open another. Yet true to the way of things, a snarl of city, church, and other laws, regulations, and diverse officers needed payment; otherwise nothing could be done. So I played things keen with coin and word.

An approach had occurred to me some days earlier, in the form of a wreck of a shop along the river bank. It was owned by an old dissembling devil by the name of Idwal-of-York who claimed he was Saxon, but spoke with the mark of the Welshman. He would become angry when anyone, even innocently, asked after his Welsh blood.

"You snouted pig. An illiterate like you would not be able to tell the difference between someone from Wales or Geatland." And he would eject them from his shop. Back when on the begang, and in search of vellum or parchment for finer writs, I would enter to find him in an ale-stupefied sleep, wrapped in a floor covering.

He took a liking to me, and considered us fellows-in-knowledge, he claiming literacy in 'several languages of great sophistication,' which he was not. Once, curious about his origins, I employed craft, may God forgive. I had come by a letter littered with so many Welsh word forms I found it almost incomprehensible. Taking it from me, despite being bleary-eyed to the extreme, he read it with ease, and said it was some sort of brutish stupidity, and for me to have nothing to do with it.

"All Welshmen copulate with beasts and wild creatures that dwell in lair and forest," he said.

Now five years later I found the shop in even greater disarray—half filled with mud, and even a few dead birds, who never again would see distant marsh or lands. The shop reeked with stench. Idwal teetered on an upper platform, and what little merchandise he had was strewn here and there, some of it spoilt.

He looked at me over the rim of his cup, while in mid-argument with an unseen woman at the rears. He cursed her profusely in Danish, then turned to me: "What do you want?"

"Vellum."

"I do not have any, may God help me."

"What surfaces do you have to write upon?"

"Ask after his bare ass. That would make great surface," and a stout Danish woman swept aside the door hanging and stormed in, managing this comment in mangled Saxon. She snatched the cup from him and gestured towards me with it.

"What did you want? I own this eyesore now."

"Actually, Mother, I want to buy this shop, complete with license, writ and charter, and of course merchandise and furniture."

"How much?"

"Five shilling."

"Pig's ass! Twenty."

"It is not worth half that. Ten."

"Fifteen."

"Twelve."

She stopped and thought. Despite his mental state, Idwal's mental processes caught up with events. His brow furrowed, and he reached out to the woman; his knobby hand belied his voice—signing more a plea than a remonstrance: "Who said I wanted to sell, you unparalleled harridan, you backdoor whore?"

And in a first for my forty years, I saw a wife draw her thick arm back and soundly backhand who I supposed was her husband, sending him head-first into the foul muck, some of it a half-leg deep.

"I own it, and will do with it as I please, like you did, you little Welsh fucker," then wiped her hands upon her apron, nodding with finality. "Done. In silver pence, eighty of them—each with King Edward's figure upon it."

And it was this way, using the Venerable Bede's reckoning, in the year 1056 past the time of Our Savior's birth, I came to own what I deigned to call Eadwig's Letter Shop, in York, upon the bank of the River Ouse.

My shop took all my resources to bring to fruition—to represent an outlet where anyone or any group could access reliable writing equipment and surfaces. But from the very first—after I'd hired a boy to scoop mud from the floor—I crafted a wall sign reading, "I am missing my wife Cwenburh-of-Loe. For anyone who knows her whereabouts and can describe her, I will give 5 grams of fine gold."

And though my business increased steadily through fall and winter—some customers read, some not—yet the words on the sign spread. Finally, a subdeacon, greedy and heavy with ale and meat accrued through geld of his office, came in and pointed to the sign with his staff.

"Only the Archbishop or Earl Themselves may post such a reward. I fine you five shilling for such impertinence, but you may keep it posted. And where, in the name of God and the Archbishop would a nubbin like you come by five grams of gold?"

From my time in Hereford in wake of our poor child who died in birth, I had no use for malfeasant church officers. But unlike Cwenburh, I held my temper and instead used wiles, God's gift to me.

"It is not my sign, Your Holiness, but done by me in interests of my brother-in-law, who is illiterate. He murdered a priest and his poor wife fled in fear of his temper. Oh, he paid extraordinary weregild to Father Abbot, may God forgive him.

He stepped back wiping the ale-induced sweat from his roundish face. "God protect us from such men!"

I took out a bucket of stout ale, richly done, and paid my fine. He stuffed it in his wallet and we struck up conversation about another matter entirely.

After imbibing his share of ale, he left, and I knew would hear no more from him, save for an occasional petty renewal of his fine. By this time, I had been established in York more than a year and had taken on a young apprentice named Oslaf-of-Hull. He looked up from his bench when the wretch staggered out.

"Master, do you think he might be that stupid to believe your wild story?"

I drew myself up in great feigned indignation, and thoroughly reprimanded him for assigning such mischief to his Master. And going out to replenish my bucket, I opted I might assign extra work to him, and he shook his head, for God help me, my sense of irony is easily gleaned.

In years following, I had people who knew a Cwenburh approach me for the reward, but they always had the description wrong—anyone who truly saw my Cwenburh would remark after the formation of her mouth, and of course her nature.

I received two long missives from good Eadwig. My heart would soar each time I did. In them he would sorrow to the diverse tragedies subsequent to leaving us, yet now he primarily worried after me, his 'father'—which is how he addressed me, making me proud. He prayed for Cwenburh, who he likewise called 'mother,' and also the twins, his sisters. God, he maintained, had made them his family in addition to the blessing of having good Matilda as his first mother. Eadwig assured God would show mercy upon them, and forgive those who enslaved them.

During the second letter he informed about the recent completion of Holy Pilgrimage with Father Abbot to St. Joseph of Campasino. There he had received a holy sign that Mother Cwenburh lived. And also, in sure sign of his obedience to The Rule and God, he pled with me to revert to my true name, for it was a great name indeed.

"Father, you cannot involve yourself on continuing deception, in God's Name."

And on this second letter, I learned he had raised his goals and was on the way to ordination.

And such was our great reward, only if both his mothers could know.

The first sign advertising the reward for Cwenburh yellowed and was eaten from its place by vermin, so I put up another. So much time passed, I lost count of the number of signs I had gone through.

I made my regular devotions at the many churches and chapels in York, but my spirits flagged as did my body. Though I took caution to be in best form during my times at work, on off-times I began to imbibe in heavy ale. By Compline most days, save the Sabbath, I was solidly in my cups. The ale purchased the benefit of allowing me to sleep, yet it did nothing for a heavy heart.

I maintained a modicum of control on this for I saw too many souls lost through the cups. And the craftsmanship of my work, God be praised, once again returned to center. Hence, my business increased even more until Oslaf and I could barely deal with it. Oslaf was a wonderful apprentice and, three years shy of his journeyman time, he was doing premium work. His ill fortune was ambitious parents, his father a prominent fuller. Also at odd intervals, I kept two youngsters as couriers and for odd jobs.

God and Our Savior be praised, all but me seemed content enough with the daily business.

I could dictate or write another long tome about the working life and skills of a journeyman scribe, but I will allow this brevity to suffice: Much of the skills needed for working as a scribe have less to do with writing and writing equipment and more to do with patience and perseverance.

Many clients have their stories crooked—fixed in their heads in ways difficult to write on surface, if not impossible. They are a jumble, and Saint Paul Himself could not make sense of it.

A scribe is obliged to take a client through their missive step by step, and put it in a sort of order. And one day in the midsummer prior to King Edward's death, a particularly scatter-minded clerk sat before my desk. He struggled with the topic of the letter he needed written. Venom and parsimony clouded menial thoughts.

"I tell you, Master Cuthwin, by withholding price this scum of a Reeve is trying to shit all over my Master with this barren business, and it is false. May God strike me if she isn't as fertile as a young mouse. He owes my master coin and much of it."

It was late into the morning—his business was about the sale of a slave woman who was promised by the seller, his Master, to be fecund, yet turned out to be barren through an old injury occurring prior to the sale. The seller, his Master, vehemently denied this.

"And I must say that the other my Master owned—a God-given mirror image of the one he sold—had many children, and died having a fourth, may God bless her departed soul."

"You mean they are twins by birth?"

"That is it. Exactly."

I knew from the initial outflow of his information, this slave had originally been sold to his master ten years previous. My attentions drew keener.

"Hair color?"

"Red! Should we mention this in the letter?"

"Perhaps, also their names."

"Names! Slaves!? My master is High Reeve to Osmod-of-Melter and such a landowner owns fifty slaves and does not know the names of all his fucking slaves, Scribe. This asshole of a Reeve will know who I mean."

Completing the letter, I feigned how lucky this foul swine was: That very day I was traveling to the township of this miscreant Reeve who was complaining in petition how grossly he had been hoodwinked. "... And I will deliver it in person, with no extra fee involved, for you and your master do much business here."

It took me only a few hours to prepare my traveling belongings and to make sure that Oslaf not undertake any projects that taxed him too greatly. After assuring he had stock, I told him I would be gone for possibly a week. He was surprised by the suddenness of my trip, and had to constrain himself not to ask why. I think something was lurking in my heart—making it sink: I strongly suspected I had located either Elesa or Matilda.

I was torn from the death of one to the continuing life of the other, even though enduring the misery of a slave. I cursed myself for being misled so easily to think they had been sold overseas—not questioning it. Having been sold, or somehow being sold back into our country, it opened rights due to free-born Saxons.

It was late spring and good weather. I set out for Doncaster at top speed, ignoring the spreading magnificence of the land and waters. But that was the first day. It occurred to me, despite this anxiety—even excitement—that I had become cooped up in the large town of York. I was born and raised in croft and open land, and being confined amongst buildings and the chaos of living close to hundreds of other souls did me little benefit.

In Doncaster I sought directions where the manor was and reached it just before Terce on the third day. The Reeve at issue was a stout Saxon whose name I am proud not to remember, functionary to a wealthy tenant with two hundred hides from King Edward.

When he heard the letter, I initiated the ruse I had decided upon: "Actually, I am more than just the bearer of a letter. I am to be one of the witnesses before the Hundred on this matter. So I must see the woman to fulfill my duty. Even perhaps talk to one close to her, so I might bear witness of what you say to the Hundred."

"Good enough, Fellow; there is not much to see nor witness, but what there is will suffice for proof against that pig you represent."

He instructed a sub-Reeve to accompany me to nearby stable and barn with cottages to one side.

What I saw caused me to curse God for the first time in my life. It was poor Matilda, whose namesake was so important in my life, in all our lives.

She was crippled severely, walked with difficulty, was blind in one eye, her features were askew and, worse than all, her mind was gone. At the base of her brainpan was evidence of a horrible injury—a deep indentation, which was so profound it was difficult to understand how she survived.

Seeing my horror, the sub-Reeve laughed, and gestured towards her—a sweeping motion, as if casting seed upon soil.

"There she is, Scribe. She eats and shits. She is not fertile and has not enough sense to bed a man properly. We were sold an old herring as a fresh young salmon."

Overwhelmed, I was taken with vertigo and sat before I fell. He left chuckling, leaving me to a maelstrom of thoughts. A kind woman offered me ale, then went to Matilda and put her arms around her. She sat her close to me and explained, "They say it was a demon so plagued her, but if it was, he had a Saxon or Danish hand on that cudgel that knocked her senseless."

"Has she been that way long?"

"Always—in the five years I have worked here. On good days, she can attend simple things; on others, she sits there and drools or weeps."

Since it was growing late in the day, she offered me shelter for the night. On the following morning I decided to complete business and set out by Terce. I was in the most severe mood in all my memory.

I returned to the Reeve who, mindful of his great position, kept me waiting before coming out to do business.

"Here is my offer: Take her back, for half her purchase price and I will add nothing for her keep."

There was no reason to dissemble any further. I felt beyond propriety or consequences. I would harness the truth and trust it would confront an animal like the Reeve, scaring him sufficiently to keep his lord and himself out of trouble.

"Who you have here is my freeborn daughter, Matilda, a healthy and normal Saxon girl stolen by unlawful scum and sold into slavery. So you have traded in a freeborn subject of King Edward. I will take her and if you hinder, you will be impeding one who does much business with the Archbishop of York. It will be bad enough now, but at least you can maintain ignorance. But no more. I have told you plain."

"This is an outrage!"

"Enough of that, Reeve. What depraved cotset hurt my daughter so? Does anyone know?"

"How? Who? It happened at your client's sokes—with little view to property. So take her then. And by the way, how will you get her back to York? Carry her on your back?"

"You have guessed right, Your Honor. She appears to weigh little more than a lamb."

"Lamb!"

Word quickly spread how Matilda would leave the demesne of the Lord not as a slave but as a freeborn woman violated by beasts. Out of direct view of the manor, a half-dozen women and even more children gathered, shedding tears and making their goodbyes, though for the moment Matilda remained oblivious. The children petted her arms and then she did look to each of them with a trace of a smile.

My host for the evening, eyes narrowed, reminded me: "See the evil-doers hang by their balls, Master Cuthwin. They have ruined a wonderful soul." And she gave me bread and cheese for the return trip.

"Matilda, you need ride on this seat." I tried to smile, but little came of it, ". . . and I will walk one way and you will look over the top of my head counting swallows like you once did."

I set out on a slow pace, my wallet slung at a side, Matilda on my back. It was not a dozen furlongs before she rested her head upon my hat. I tried not to be angry and not to yield tears. By God I would see justice done.

I did not pray.

Even God can deal out a death-blow to the human heart so powerful it presses you to the ground forcefully separating despair and faith.

My soul was cold to the touch for ensuing months. I made Matilda comfortable, hired an elderly Danish lady to come in, and had a carpenter construct an alcove for her in my small quarters.

Oslaf learned to keep silent regards any questions about her, for he at once perceived my less-than-benevolent state, and in fact witnessed worse. Now he—and all—knew my true name and the story behind things.

He was present in the shop when that human foulness—the clerk in employ of the perpetrator's Lord—Osmod-of-Melter—came, having heard of my return. He was eager for a response to his query.

He carried his wand of office, and a youngish boy attended him; the stupid fellow stood before me, puffed up like a fens toad.

"What is this, Scribe? You did not notify me of your return on my Master's business."

Without word I showed him to where the Danish lady was working yarn; that day Matilda was able to hold up her arms as device.

"My God! In the name of heavens, you brought her back! So you may keep here, then, you fool."

"Who did that to her? And where are her nephews or nieces—her sister's children?"

He noticed the strain in the air; even Oslaf withdrew from his bench, watching. The clerk lost spine—his eyes narrowed, and his lips began to quiver. His tiny attendant scrambled off.

"What is that to you? That is not your place, Scribe."

"Because they are both my adopted daughters, raised from infants, and I have fair witness to that. They were free souls, stolen from my home, and at least one maimed in a blow delivered by a criminal. Further, any sale of them after that is contrary to Saxon Law, and writs and receipts are not only no good, but can be used as testimony in my claims." Here I plucked his wand away, ". . . and if my nature did not make me averse to it, I would brain you or any other thieves or murderers who followed. Now get out from here, you vile bastard, and tell that to your cursed master, this Osmod-of-Melter. And tell him I will see justice is paid, and then, *goddamn every soul of you at Melter!*"

And I broke his wand across my bench.

That day I wrote to Eadwig, telling him how Matilda still lived and her condition following the tragedy of her kidnapping. Also, how guilty I felt not pursuing his sisters in England, instead believing a single man, who indeed could have been a demon.

And worse followed bad: The next day I found the Danish woman amusing herself by mistreating Matilda during the time she must make water, and I kicked her bodily from the shop. I had never before struck a woman.

Oslaf, who was only months from completing his apprenticeship, implied he would be leaving then to work at a cousin's some distance from York. I guessed my mean-spirited state had turned him contrary to buying into my shop.

This was unfortunate. My shop was, despite all this misery, a success, and any enterprise proximate to York dealing with writing and its accoutrements came to me for supplies and services.

I sat in my quarters and Matilda lay sideways on her palette. I knew I could not care for her alone, and though I had more than sufficient means to hire someone, might not the same thing happen again?

It is against the nature of things to purchase love or care with silver. I could not resolve what to do, yet I loved Matilda. While she lived, I would do anything for her, just as any of her family might.

"Cuthwin?"

I was knocked sideways by the sound of my true name, and at once was eye-to-eye with Matilda—a single clear, beautiful blue eye.

"Cuthwin?" she repeated.

"Yes, Matilda?"

"I am Matilda. Yes."

She nodded, rolled over and looked at the ceiling; then after a tiny dash of a smile, nodded off. There are not sufficient words or lamentations in the soul to convey this moment's import. Half in a daze, I pushed slowly through the hanging that separated both shops from my quarters, looked at Oslaf and said, "She spoke my name and hers. May God forgive me."

The day the Archbishop's Canon appeared with his assistant for the second time, Matilda was now speaking sentences—simple yet distinct, always referring to items around her. If I asked her if she was happy, she would nod and assure me she was.

If she was hungry, I would hear, "Matilda is hungry, Cuthwin."

These words brought me more joy than any time subsequent to my departure from Oakheath Manor a decade before. And this cheer was not even sullied by the serpentine world of words and diverse legal matters resident in such personages as one of the Archbishop's legal canons. This scholar cost me dearly, but in the crime perpetrated on the twins, justice must be had. Even though a civil matter, this scholar's knowledge would work sense from the convoluted ways of law.

He was a loquacious fellow—with a sad fondness for complexity. The more of it he saw, the happier he became.

"Cuthwin, this business confounds. You used a false name, swore to it, and now bring writ against an honest Saxon thane and/or his officer for bonded souls not yours, but the offspring of yours. You are under *Writ of Bonus Activas* to stay away from Osmod-of-Melter's sokes. God forbid you do that again. That business promulgated harsh times."

It was true: One day I set out to confront Osmod-of-Melter, and when I reached there I was immediately driven away. Thank God, I carried staff and had knife; otherwise, I think his threadbare housecarls, emaciated and lack-luster as they were, would have assaulted me.

As to using another name, I knew there was nothing under canon or civil law against using a false name as long as you didn't swear to holy or royal contract using it. I was not a scribe for so long without learning a little law.

This Canon would drink ale, slap his hand to his forehead, and marvel at this matter's labyrinth of issues. This was his third session, and each time cost me dearly for his tribulations. After each concluding moment, he drew himself up into robes, and with his student and page walking before him to clear away lesser mortals, would stride off muttering how unique my petition was.

Oslaf was not of high opinion of the Canon: "I tell you, Master Cuthwin, he is upon your back like leeches."

Oslaf mentioned no more about leaving, and when the day passed and he became journeyman, we celebrated mightily with all tradesmen around, for this is a great time. The next day he came to me, excited with news that would change much.

"Cuthwin, a girl named Gunnhilda-the-Mute has taken to hanging around our residence. My mother, charitable soul that she is, feeds her. She sleeps in the stable with the family donkey. Though struck dumb by God, she understands well enough, and might work well to look after your poor Matilda."

So that winter Matilda and Gunnhilda-the-Mute developed affection for each other—one afflicted soul reaching out to another, God's mercy be praised.

The holy days were spent in prayer and, amongst the more boisterous, celebrating. Though I could not bring myself to pray—and certainly not to attend church with regularity—I did my part enough to bring no attention to my uncertain spiritual state.

As is becoming clearer, Time confirms that the stuff of sainthood resides far from me, for it is known widely that saints do not lose faith—never let go of their faith in Our Savior and his Father. Not even death through holy martyrdom separates them from the beauty of faith and constancy.

I believed in the Father, Son, and Holy Ghost, but I had no faith in their benevolence and involvement with the commonality, in ordinary folk who by then—I had watched close to fifty years—were subject to affliction of sorrow and violence just as ants or swarms of bees might be. Often evil times not only passed over great men, but some were its perpetrators.

And when might there be a reckoning? This awfulness finally over-filled my cup when I saw dear Matilda so senselessly maimed. I promised everything humanly possible and not to rely on God. These human foulnesses of right and wrong who brought such horror on my daughters would feel man-made justice.

"Master Cuthwin, two young frauds are out in front claiming their fortune in gold. I have driven them off twice, but they come back, I am sorry to report."

Oslaf and I became used to such claims. At minimum those knowing a Cwenburh were a weekly occurrence, and I interviewed each, regardless of how flimsy their stance. But this time, I found, was as Oslaf described: One claimant was a young man just experiencing the rising of pith, the other a girl younger by several years. He spoke for her: "This sprig knows a Cwenburh, as God is her witness. She and I were sold to a fuller, and are on way to his establishment here in York."

Behind them, the fuller's man lurked—a massive cottar carrying a staff, his eyes grey and pig-like. The young man—rather than he—seemed to be in charge.

I looked them over and saw at once the girl had either no vision at all, or very little. She squeezed her eyes tight looking for me until I spoke: "If so, what does she look like and where is she?"

"I cannot see, not well. Her face was always a blur, Master."

Oslaf sighed and looked askance at this three-person show.

"Then how can you describe this Cwenburh?"

"She is old and kind, and not called Cwenburh, but Mother. I only know her name because I overhead her tell one of the girls. She takes care of girls in the name of God and Our Savior at Saint Mary's. Until Mother Margaret sold me to a fuller, I lived there as well."

The tiny Saint Mary's Monastery was only a league from the wall of York, and if this Cwenburh had been my wife, surely by now—with the sign being up—I would have heard of her prior to these two—if indeed they were speaking the truth.

"Master Cuthwin, this little one has been put up to this. I say call the guard and have their livers boiled," Oslaf advised.

And in a rustle and scramble of turnabout, they fled as sheep escaping the shearers—the massive fellow following, staff thrust lively into ground with each step.

I stood there only mildly surprised at what lies people perpetrate for silver or gold.

"Oslaf, who read the sign to them? My sign? Did you?"

"No. Somebody told them about it, the little swine."

Despite their apparent falseness, her words gnawed at me. For Cwenburh did at one time take care of girls, and was ambitious to do so again. And she would, of course, seem old to a young girl. But if they had both been sold to a fuller from this place, why had not the boy been able to describe her?

It bothered I had not asked after this.

It was late spring coming into summer, and I had in mid-winter previous purchased a tiny pull-wagon at good bargain, using it later to give Matilda and Gunnhilda rides. These outings they loved. The next day was beauty itself, so we went afield, ascending the river path which passed close to the Monastery of Saint Mary. So while passing, I thought to check out the meager thread of information.

Leaving Matilda and Gunnhilda on the edge of the croft adjacent to the Monastery walls, I gave Gunnhilda a stout bell in event she needed to summon help.

Supposing that such a holy place for women would never grant me admittance, I sought out the public gate where alms were given or asked. But when I rounded the corner where the river met the wall of the Monastery, I instead encountered an outer building—connected by covered walk to the main establishment.

I heard the screams, squeals, and such from young girls at play easy to follow. The building surrounded a square, but before it were four massive oaks—one with a swing. And under this, enjoying the fair sunlight, were several dozen girls.

Watching them, sitting on the edge of a horse trough was Cwenburh-of-Loe holding a switch across her ample lap.

"Oh, the noise! May God and Mother Abbess forgive us all. If you must murder each other, be quieter about it!" she cried to the girls.

My legs might have grown roots that reached deep into the earth, so transfixed was I. Though she had aged, it was Cwenburh-of-Loe as surely as I was Cuthwin-of-Alnwick. At that point, she swept vacantly in the air—perhaps at a bot fly—with her switch, then, looking left, she saw me.

I stood only twenty paces off.

Like me, she appeared to have taken immediate root into earth through the wooden trough. It took no vast perception to tell she recognized me at once.

We had both frozen so perfectly in place that if viewed by others, we might have appeared to have turned to stone via the divination of Cwenburh's elves or fairies.

I cannot guess how long we might have continued dumbfounded, transfixed by this miracle of place and time. But the children ran up, clamoring, laughing: "Oh, Mother. Have you seen a ghost?"

She looked at them, and handing the switch to the largest child said, "Edith! You have the switch and you are now in charge. I have a visitor to attend."

The youngsters looked to me knowing this change was on my account so were very curious.

Cwenburh rose from the trough and, as if sleep-walking, approached, a step at a time. She put a hand to her mouth, stifling a gasp, and kept it there.

She stopped a half-dozen paces before me. When I tried to form words, I found a bound tongue. I tried again and managed, "Jesus, Our Savior, is that really you, Cwenburh-of-Loe?"

"Yes, as God has desired. Are you my husband, Cuthwin-of-Alnwick? As God is my witness, they told me you were slain those years ago."

"I was spared by a good soul and have sought you out ever since, not knowing if you were dead or not, may God be praised, though I am not worthy of it."

She resumed, closing the distance, and when before me raised a hand and put it on my chest, pushing slightly. "It *is* you. You are not a phantom."

I clasped her hand to my chest and began an emotional dissolve. Though all the little ones were looking with eager eyes on their mother and this visitor, I ignored propriety and lifted her hand to my cheek, her touch so long absent.

"Cuthwin, you are not going to weep, are you? Husband, you are made of such gentle cloth."

"Oh, no more, Cwenburh. I am roughened much."

This strangeness was too much for the young girls; despite their colleague with the switch trying to hold them back, they simply rushed around her and surrounded this woman—their mother—all asking questions at once in several languages.

Cwenburh gently withdrew her hand, fell back into her motherly tone, and pointed at the switch: "What is this mischievousness?! What might you do if Mother Margaret saw you!? Now Edith, take these ducklings back to their pond or I shall use the switch, and do it surely. Now, and no questions."

The little ones' wonderment brought us back to the reality of this day—the ten years receding for the time.

She looked after them, and while doing so leaned against me. I knew without her saying that these tiny creatures were loved unquestionably by her; further, that I must fit back into her life gently and with patience. I was but a letter writer; she was, however, the lifeline of these little spirits, just experiencing the onset of a life that needed as much preparation by love and care as possible. And how infrequently children received these when abandoned.

My mind moved to a single issue, for there was a terrible shock in store for Cwenburh not one hundred paces away, and I had little time to brace her for it: "Cwenburh, I have news of the twins and it is not good. Prepare yourself."

Now she took firmer hold of me—this time to keep upright.

"God spare me. Last I saw, the bastards knocked me out looking for where I hid them. When I woke," she looked up at me, "they were gone and there was fire all around me."

"They were sold into slavery. Elesa has died, but I have Matilda now, though she was injured by brutes, and is not right in her senses. She is behind me—beyond that wall with a deafmute, her friend and caretaker, by name of Gunnhilda."

I led her by the hand, rounded the edge of the wall. Gunnhilda had Matilda out of the cart and was fashioning a bird nest from grass and straw, or rather Gunnhilda was while Matilda looked on following each of her friend's moves.

They did not see us at once, but since Matilda was in full view, Cwenburh brought her hands to the side of her head, drawing a great breath.

"O, who has done this to her, Cuthwin?"

"I am not sure, but it was on the soke of a creature named Osmod-of-Melter not ten leagues from York."

Cwenburh moved towards her slowly so not to startle her. When Gunnhilda looked up, she did start, dropping her work. Cwenburh reached and touched her arm, "Gunnhilda, don't fear me. I never did you harm, child."

She knew her! But how could a deafmute understand?

"She is deaf, Cwenburh."

"Gunnhilda is very clever and can read the words in one's lips. So at one time she could hear. The poor thing ran away from here."

Then she turned to Matilda who picked up the nest and sorted through it. She looked up at Cwenburh, reached out and took a strand of Cwenburh's hair between thumb and forefinger; holding it for a moment, she let it go and asked, "Mother, where is Elesa?"

Having Cwenburh back in my life and me in hers was a wonderful gift from God, but it came with a not-insignificant problem in the form of Mother Margaret, Abbess of St Mary's Monastery. She was an aged cousin to the deceased Earl Siward—a family still powerful. Yet the charter for St. Mary's was small and had never benefited from an Abbot with ambition, and though a 'double' monastery, the male component still tended to have precedence.

This Abbott was a weak sort, and years ago had yielded any authority to Mother Margaret, also his cousin. No sort of preparation by Cwenburh would have fully braced me for a woman like Mother Margaret.

"Indeed! A husband reappears after ten years; how extraordinary. And Cuthwin-of-Alnwick, where were you keeping yourself these years?"

She was hard of hearing and pig-headed, and neither of us knew if she wasn't hearing because it did not please her or if she seriously had not heard. Her question, once again, ran over the top of both of our previous explanations, and by the time we completed our first 'examination' by Mother Margaret, I was ready for holy orders.

"She is a loving soul and cares for the little ones beyond measure, and is God's sole protector of them."

Under a two-day furlough, we were permitted to return to my shop in York. Cwenburh was under command of Mother Margaret to serve at least another six months in service to St. Mary's, and—she had told Cwenburh in private—". . . do not yield to the demands that all husbands feel is their right."

"But Mother Margaret," she responded, "he is my husband before God, sworn in the Holy Sacrament."

"Very good. I'm glad you agree, my daughter."

We stopped at an ale shop, bought something for the Sext meal, and sat on a bench at a nearby church, a woolen wrap around us both. It was an utterly clear day, and the wind had desisted, leaving it crisp and beautiful along the outer perimeter of York. Sparrows, laboring throughout winter, sought out crumbs at once.

But bright day or dull, it galled me to have this old woman intrude herself in this miracle—how we had found each other.

"Did she hear you?"

"I cannot say. It is difficult. She is seventy-plus years before God on this earth."

Cwenburh saw I was saying much with eyes only. We partook silently in the hearty cheese and heavy wheat bread—an indulgence of good times. I forced myself of an earlier resolve, to not insert myself in her life too gracelessly; and I certainly did not need counseling from a difficult old woman, Abbess or no.

She broke off crumbs for the sparrows and looked sideways at me. "Cuthwin, we have been apart for ten years. Now we get Sabbath together, and sneak at other times—as we did at the old mill house when not much more than children"—she smiled and brushed off her hands of crumbs—". . . that is something of our vigorous youth that God has given us in return."

"And I say before God, Wife, it is winter and we are no longer children."

"Cuthwin, it will be for not much more than five months, and I get to have Matilda several times a week at my room."

"Thank God our daughter is female."

"Gunnhilda is female, and she stays with you." She began to put things away so we could get back to the shop before Terce on this Sabbath, and I caught the oddness of her last statement. Looking steadily at her, I was about to ask about it, when she continued: "Gunnhilda is a fetching young lady, though mute. Did you take her to bed before I came back into your life?"

"What! God forbid! She is a child, Cwenburh."

"She is sixteen. Her appearance tempted several priests, but Mother Margaret was quicker than a cat seeing it. During the uproar caused by this, the poor thing ran off. One of the lustful clerics is older than you, may he be damned to hell. The barnyard prick could have gotten her with child. Like you, she is a gentle spirit. You could father a child with her and you would abide both."

I could not hide my confusion at a number of issues her words tossed into the fray.

"I believe we were both present when exchanging holy vows and repeating them to God and Our Savior, were we not? I did not know if you were alive or dead, and you were alive, God be praised."

"I bedded a man for nearly three months; I would have died otherwise, that second winter after I escaped—I just could not survive out. I made my confession, have prayed for forgiveness. I am weak. I should have told you before. . . . "

The bread and cheese turned to stone in my gut. I looked over at this good, God-given woman, my wife, and saw in her eyes lingering abject misery and hardship.

"Cwenburh, you would have been a fool to not have, you must know that? Why ask forgiveness? It is they who should ask forgiveness of you. God has allowed this foulness just as much as Satan, and brought us both low—allowed our innocent child to never draw breath—then killed one of our twins and mutilated the other. Forgiveness be damned!"

"Oh, Jesus forgive you, Cuthwin; you are not lost, are you?"

"Are any of us the same after Oakheath, and all the wretchedness that followed?"

There could well have been many things said at this moment, but we used the good benefit from the wisdom we gained after twenty-four years of cruel experience by staying silent.

To survive, we both had yielded to ugly realities—doing things we never wanted: I by losing so much of my faith, and falling into bitterness with Our Savior's teaching, and Cwenburh by losing nearly all those things a mother most values.

She stood, extended her hand and turned towards York. "Cuthwin. Husband! Spring will be here in a few months, then I will move from St. Mary's into your shop—our shop. I must let the little ones down easily—plus teach that young novitiate how to mother, poor thing. And resist Mother Margaret's constant ploys. Now come along."

When extending her hand to me, she smiled, and for that smile I could have gone on pilgrimage to the ends of the world; hence, we joined hands and returned along the path into York.

We were just six days into the year[41] when every bell in Great York struck out, peeling the lament. King Edward had died in the south, attended with all the greatness of his court and entire Witan[42], and immediately it was decided that Earl Godwinson would be King. He was crowned and anointed at once.

It was much news to arrive at one time and all York was in tumult.

He had reigned for twenty-eight years, in fact since I had been twenty-three years of age. I could barely recall another King on our silver pence.

"Master Cuthwin, in all your years, had you seen King Edward?"

"No, Oslaf, I have not."

Oslaf furrowed up his brow, looking out the shop upriver towards the Cathedral. I kept my own opinions, busying myself with an ornate psalter for a wealthy churchman. My work, God forgive my pride, was now up to its best, and such a commission was not only a flattery for my craft, but enabled me, even at a half century, to improve.

I would soon begin another, but this one for Cwenburh, though the stubborn lady still could not and would not read. But she could hold it at prayers and that was enough for the effort and love I would put into it.

Events of great people in the south had little currency with me.

This is the situation with those who work: We must do it to survive, and often, as the Bible teaches, take joy in our work if lucky enough to be free. There are inevitably other daily problems and situations connected with work and family. Ultimately though, after giving ample thanks at church and prayer, we are left to meet our responsibilities.

The lofty and powerful had their own pursuits and grand enterprises,

---

[41] January, 1066.

[42] Witan. Counsel of nobles in Saxon England. They elect the new king, though William of Normandy (later "The Conqueror"), disagreed with this.

and that was God's order of things, and each of us under the sun looked after our place.

On Sabbath that week, Cwenburh admonished me while at dinner of plump guinea fowl; Oslaf often joined us in our tiny household—Gunnhilda having something to do with this. "Husband! I have seen a vision—we will see the new King. They say he has but one leg, and the other is wooden up to his hind quarters."

Matilda—who was beginning to track more and more conversation—laughed, and Gunnhilda joined.

"Oh, for the love of Our Savior, Wife, where did you hear that?"

And so it went, never relenting. I carved the last of the bird and aimed down its unfortunate limb at them all. "Soon, this King will be dragging his tail behind him, spitting fire, and shedding scales onto the faithful."

But I was mocked, and these were Sabbaths of good fellowship—such a relief from the week of hard work, and the excitement of rumor bursting every conversation.

Within weeks my personal aversions to business of the south came to an involuntary end. All freedman or freedwomen of means and property in and proximate to York were requested under Holy Declaration by Archbishop Aldred to attend the great Minster of York. There King Harold would make declaration two days hence—the coming Sabbath.

"See there, Master Cuthwin, good Cwenburh was of right vision."

I assured Oslaf she was right almost half the time, but he did not see the humor in that.

In York my fellow shopkeepers often gathered during cold winter times at the stout barn and group of sheds the collier kept for coal and peat. There was a rich, amply fed fire, itself the social point where gossip and all sorts of talk dominated. I was careful to attend often enough not to be held as haughty or seen as holding myself above my place as an ordinary craftsman, always a problem for a scribe.

But on this day, when this uncommon summons loomed, all were anxious, or worse. They knew too well their money interests depended directly on the affairs of archbishops, earls, and wealthy thanes.

But the King? And one newly crowned? We of York learned of the King's death in one breath and in the second the crowning of another.

This rush was an issue.

Many were suspicious of a king wholly decided in the south without approval in the north. They were specifically most unhappy with His Eminence, Archbishop Aldred-of-York.

"He was there. They say he even consecrated Harold Godwodsen. He might have represented his flock better."

Tempers rose and settled in the flock like a great beast breathing. I knew that to say anything, even a whisper, against the King was treason, and I had had my fill of that. And to voice disparagement about the Archbishop was no less foolish.

When asked, I was careful to say few words. Those I did use did not indicate a commitment, save to say I had never heard of any great man taking trouble to speak of serious matters to the commonality.

Reaching home, I felt my head swirl with the arguments and alleged facts and claims. Matilda and Gunnhilda were busy at their wool-crafting. Serving me dinner, they watched me carefully at my bread and stew. I guessed with dismay the volley of speculation about our new King was not over.

Gunnhilda gestured to me, then made sign to Matilda—who motioned emphatically towards me again. They had developed between them a complicated system of signs and interpreted word through lip movement, gesture, and even odd grunts and laughs. Matilda dawdled her spoon in her stew—she didn't eat much—and looked up. She spoke slowly so Gunnhilda could read me: "King is a dwarf with one ear, tiny, little."

I shook my head—adding emphasis to my weary denial: "The King is *not* a dwarf. And he has *three* ears."

To get these two laughing was my only escape to the peace of reading the Bible or another good book—then they would leave me alone.

Mother Margaret had, Cwenburh said, declared Harold Godwinson a rogue and no king of hers. Despite the Abbott's command, she took to bed with an ". . . ague peculiar to those of great age."

At the great gathering I would have complete company: It was Sab-

bath and Cwenburh would not miss such an event. We decided to load
Matilda in the wagon; of course Gunnhilda wanted to accompany, and
with her came Oslaf, my journeyman, a freedman and very interested
in my business.

On the great day we set out along the River Ouse on an extraordinarily
cold January morning bundled in the warmest attire possible. Thank
God and Our Savior I could afford same.

In the days before, Normans scattered the land with their elaborate
stone constructions, and prior to its destruction a few years later, York
Minster below was stone, but above was of wood, and loomed a hundred
feet above the city, it being the highest structure in all of the north.

The gathering was to be at Nones[43]. This itself was strange for on
Sabbaths the Minster was busy, it housing many altars and places of
devotions and sacrament, not the least being baptism founts and
alcoves with hangings. In these, sinners were shriven prior to taking the
Holy Sacrament. Hence, Archbishop Aldred, a most devoted Eminence,
would have to clear the capacious structure of the faithful.

But that is what His Eminence did, this extraordinary act tipping the
scale for this occasion's exceptional nature even more significantly.

The Minster's two grand stained windows were striking visual elements of its imposing façade. These reflected the low, weak afternoon
light in an eerie halftone, creating two large membranous eyes that gazed
out on the people of York who wended their way towards it.

The sun itself, setting so extreme in the southwest, seemed to indicate—to remind all—where the profound events had unfolded in the
previous two weeks.

I don't know how many thousands dwelled in York then, but since
it was before William and his Normans destroyed it during the invasion
and battle, there were far more people than years later, God save their
departed souls.

At least several hundred were already there just before Nones. For a
keener view of events, I knew utilizing another entrance would put us

---

[43] Nones. Ninth hour of the spiritual day.

at advantage. Veering around the steps that led to the yawning double doors, we trekked the snow-strewn path towards the east side entrance admitting us to the transept. Doing so, we made entry into the middle of things.

Events there were in great excitement.

It was a scene of wardens and guards being ordered about right and left by a tall, elderly priest—he creating more havoc than order. I recognized him as Father Deacon of the Minster.

"By Our Savior's Grace, all of you see no one comes into the house of God armed."

Of the moment, from the direction of the choir, a bishop unknown to me entered, wearing plain habit, but with the special fringe unique to that office; plus, unlike an ordinary poor cleric, the cross and chain were of gold—jeweled and fine.

"Please, Father Deacon, remember Our Savior is the Prince of Peace; all will be settled and go well. His Eminence would see it no other way. So let us have peace, God be praised."

He smiled genially—gesturing expansively for us to rise, for all had gone to their knees. Switching to the language of Rome, Father Deacon—who stood a head higher than most with a nose like goshawk—followed the bishop, imploring one thing or another until they went out of sight towards the front.

From behind we were being pushed forward, for others also schemed this a better place to enter and view events.

The remaining authorities were subdeacons, their meager, threadbare robes hastily patched or tied together. They moved in to exert the tiny authority they did have. They were a pathetic lot, lucky to have tiny benefices by which to eeke out a living from the faithful.

A liveryman and his wife, known to preside over the largest and best-endowed livery in York, pushed by them and proceeded haughtily into the shorter section of the nave. His stout old Saxon wife looked admonishingly at these deacons who made to catch the husband's elbow.

"What is this?! We will stand where we please in the nave. This is our church."

And there was subdued laughter, and these puny men became

indignant. "This is God's House, and we its minders! Must we call the beatle!?"

But this only resulted in chuckles, for these mawkish enforcers were notorious drunks and fornicators, and on any Sabbath would be lost in their cups by Nones.

Between the nave and the choir was posted a line of wardens and guards. They were not deacons or subdeacons, and their presence was unusual: No ordinary sort, even if in their cups, would go beyond them.

Behind us the entire Minster filled, everyone pushing chest to back, and the talk rising to a drone. It was past time and yet no great personages appeared beyond the barrier of guards. Children were chased by the subdeacons; they, however, evaded the awkward clerics by dodging around them and scooting between adults. There was laughter here and there. Children were not expected nor supposed to attend, yet a few mothers could not resist violating this unspoken protocol, knowing a memory of a lifetime would be unfolding.

The result was an increase of noise until the drone became a steady, low roar. Finally, the elderly Deacon Priest stepped onto the first steps of the choir, banged his staff down, making a great racket.

He leaned forward, his imposing frame a pillar and shouted, "Silence in the Minster! You all know about prayer, do you not? If you cannot have patience, then pray for our beloved departed King and his grieving widow."

Despite the enormity of the cathedral, the priest's voice rivaled that of a hunting horn. Everyone hushed in fear he might level that voice at them.

Bishops and their entourages commenced entry from right and left of the ambulatory, the former bearing their mitres, attired in the elaborately embroidered vestments of their office. We all knelt—a sea of people, causing a rumbling bespeaking the presence of several thousand.

When Cwenburh whispered if one were the Archbishop, I shook my head and with a gesture bid her wait. He was not in evidence.

A few of the very aged clergy upon the choir were provided finely carved benches—for they could not stand long, nor get to their knees—nor rise, even if they did.

327

It was the same amongst the commoners. Those who needed them either brought stools themselves or by a family member. All others stood.

Without announcement, fanfare, or indeed any sign at all, save for the sounding of a small bell, Archbishop Aldred entered. Everyone— even all clergymen, despite their offices—knelt. Following him were even more churchmen, and I supposed, members of the King's court, for they were not dressed in vestments.

All knelt on the platform or steps leading to the expansive and grand altar, probably in order of grandness.

But His Eminence—of great age then, thus a small boy following him in event he needed help—ascended all the way, turned and looked out. Unlike everyone else, he wore only black vestments, plain, save for a great chain and crucifix around his neck, still swinging slowly at his waist.

He carried the imposing golden mitre of the Archbishop's office, and wore the pallium from the Holy Father—its whiteness glaring in contrast to all the other blacks, but even this lofty accoutrement was adorned with a black ribbon across it.

He spoke loudly in the language of Rome, and gestured for all to rise, and when the commonality—confused—did not know if he meant them as well, he raised his voice, and his Saxon rang out in great voice, "All rise until told to kneel."

It was dim in the Minster, and massive chandlers were carried in alight. With all of us so packed, the grievous history of fires in the Minster came to mind. It gave me not a little balm to see that each of the stands of candles was monitored by a young acolyte with a wetted blanket.

In increased light, I saw the men of court wore scabbards without swords. No one entered a church armed, yet empty scabbards meant their weapons were not far behind. This explained the earlier upset.

Then Harold, King of England, entered from a separate entrance in the ambulatory. He was alone.

When the Priest-Deacon with the massive voice stepped forward to announce, Harold held out his hand, stopping him, his gesture preceding the Archbishop's, who did the same.

Harold had none of the dozen malformations and strangenesses of body reported during the preceding days. Contrary to all that, he was well-formed, and a head taller than everyone on the altar save for the Deacon-Priest. His hair was striking—completely white and long, resting across both shoulders as might a ruff, his squared features clean-shaven.

He was no longer a young man, but he moved without a sign of age. Even more curious than His Eminence's plain black habit, the King wore unadorned clothing, far more modest than those of his court who stood to the right and left of him.

These great men too were confused for not having been bid by the Archbishop to kneel again before the King; but there was no doubt of it, the King had declined this, and his word carried.

Then I and all others became riveted by an extraordinary event no one had anticipated save the King and Archbishop.

The Archbishop extended his arm, and bade the King to ascend the steps and stand next to him. A priest emerged from behind and moved forward carrying a small crown on a silver cushion. His Eminence handed his mitre to the boy as the priest presented the crown to the Archbishop.

The Archbishop elevated the cushion and crown intoning, as best as I might recall, "I Aldred, Archbishop of York, servant of Our Savior, consecrated this man, Harold Godwinson, King of all England, after he was designated same by our lawful Witan. I did this through the will of the Almighty and authority of that same Witan plus our Holy Father Pope Alexander, Bishop of Rome and all Christendom, may God be praised on the highest level, Amen."

But instead of putting the crown upon Harold, he lowered the cushion, holding it before his chest.

Then Harold stepped forward and, though his voice was strong, it did not carry as well as the Deacon Priest or His Eminence. But most were close enough to hear easily: "I will not wear this crown until my loyal subjects of York have honest say in this, and this is why I have come here. To stand before you. What have you to say? As God is my witness, none shall bear malice from me for any question."

But every freedman present knew full well that if the Witan elected Harold, Harold it was. Though Northumberland had much of Saxon England's power then, which now seems so long ago, it is different today. But, wisely, the new King wanted our approval.

The wealthy liveryman, who to this day I view as the bravest freedman in the Kingdom, shouted, "Your Highness, will there come trouble from overseas for this?"

Harold smiled, looked to all sides of him, and despite the tightness drawing across the faces of those from court, extended his hand to the east. "Yes, it will. But I know in my heart," and he extended both arms towards all, then allowed them to fall to his sides, ". . . that every loyal God-fearing Saxon and soul of Daneslaw, especially those of Great York, are more than equal to any and all troubles from without."

Then, as in a single germ of impulse, all started in one shout, spreading to the entire congregation—thousands of Saxons, "Let Harold be crowned King Harold."

With that, the Archbishop handed off the cushion after removing the crown, and Harold turned and was crowned King of England.

Looking back over the subsequent years, and all the infamy and disaster that followed that afternoon, I still cannot help but respect King Harold's candor, for he was right about the troubles, but tragically wrong about prevailing.

He was to live only ten months more, and would die a Saxon's death in defense of his people and home. Any Saxon lamented that day, or would, but any of his subjects present that day at York Cathedral—at that hour—were convinced of King Harold's God-given grace and love. We believed he would drive away any who would make slaves of us and render the Saxon life and kindred into ashes and ignominy.

And so it was at that moment, my desire for renewed faith in God began to return, though it would take more time subsequent to the ghastly sight when I first saw the terribly maimed Matilda.

Finally the day arrived when I had a decision before the Hundred. The relationship between the Canon and Cwenburh was contentious, making the scholar work harder for his fee. Worse, she forced him to be more direct in explaining things and work with renewed alacrity.

"I think this wife of yours, Cuthwin-of-Alnwick, must be the very severest sort of woman to live with, as God is my witness. You have my sympathy and admiration."

The decision was sweeping: The technicalities were more crisscrossed and complicated than a spider web bridging a wooded path. Cwenburh would have none of the long explanations other than understand who was paying his fees.

"Yes, Mistress Cwenburh, an outstanding decision. But now the serving of the order and collection of the weregild is another matter, of course."

"Of course! But not like your fee, Master Canon."

I managed to extricate the Canon from the shop before he was further admonished by Cwenburh—her blood quite up.

"For God's sakes, Wife. It is Sabbath."

Matilda sang along with one tune or another in her head while Oslaf read to Gunnhilda from the Bible in the far corner—she watching his mouth intently, smiling with the process of hearing the right Word—and admiring the reader. They had fallen under a sweet spell.

Cwenburh fixed Matilda's hair while pointing hither and yon with the brush and planning retribution upon the very elements. I faced her anger squarely—it was an old situation that came easily to me.

"Cwenburh, we cannot afford thane, even drengs—or whatever— to go out and serve the writ, let alone enforce it. Osmod-of-Melter has toadies and his own drengs, and they will protect him for the life of them."

Later, in my alcove, which was now our bed and only truly private quarters, I convinced her of the futility—even danger of life and limb—of going out to Osmod-of-Melter's without force of arms.

We became quiet, enjoying this time that was denied us for so many years. Then, Herself drifted to other matters; she felt very much as a protective aunt to Gunnhilda.

"You know, Cuthwin, Oslaf's parents will absolutely disapprove of Gunnhilda as wife. That cannot be. You know there is trouble coming there?"

"Yes."

The poor girl's deafness would be viewed as a demon's curse by his parents and family—a very stiff-necked religious family, to the person.

In my heart, I was sure there was far greater trouble coming our way, carried by its own share of demons. As Cwenburh slept against me, I reflected on the King's assurance that there would be trouble, and when it began it would—like in times past—commence in the north.

Wealthy York being prime reward for the victor.

Before first light, we walked back to St. Mary's—once again risking admonishment for spending time together somewhat past Sabbath. These times of stealth were tiny payment for our miraculous coming together, though I would air a few husbandly complaints. As Herself went out of view behind the wall, a last gesture of departure, it occurred to me she was now proximate to the half-century mark.

The terrible times left her with something of a limp, and she had scars over one eye—their cause never given. Her long, fine hair when freed from its bounds was nearly all grey, with only a few central streaks of black. But in body she was still as solid as a block and more generously fleshed.

"Are you still smitten with me, Cuthwin?"

And it was true, we did exchange such stupidities still, as old as we were. I could not wait for this spring to arrive, to be free of Mother Margaret's avaricious hold on Cwenburh's place and time. It would pain Herself, I knew, to part from the homeless waifs, and there would be many visits.

That was just part of how things worked with Cwenburh-of-Loe.

Through the week it was a lonely time for me. How quickly the human spirit is spoiled—going from being used to absence, to a rapid desire for constancy of people and things heretofore absent.

At our livery, gossip session rumors from the south would be bandied about, and most concerned with William of Normandy.

"He won't sit idle, that one won't." The woolen merchant was the most traveled of the shop owners in York, and he stood before the fire, warming his backside and espousing the politics of the matter: "Normans are a greedy lot to the man of them. And Duke William no less. After all, he is a bastard born and swollen with the heritage of Norse raider, the turd."

And back and forth the pros and cons of the matter would go. My concern was that it was only a few days from Shrove Tuesday[44]; it was not season yet for warfare with the sea to traverse with many boats carrying an army and horses.

I was beginning a plan—that when Cwenburh got free from Herself at St. Mary's, to sell the shop to Oslaf, whose family were increasingly anxious for him to have it. With the funds we then had, we could move far south and acquire a small croft in a remote area. There we could enjoy liberation from daily labors while still young enough to be relatively free from aches and agues that gain increase with age.

What is living if not dreams?

The weekday loneliness and the press of these plans—atop my desire to renew my faith in the words of Our Savior—brought me to the small church of St. Mary Bishophill, as had become my habit. It was quiet here where my struggles to pray to reassert faith could be carried on more personally.

Certainly, I needed spiritual guidance on how to proceed. All was accelerating at an uncomfortable pace as we approached Easter. If only Father Abbot Elsin still lived.

I had donated a bench within, and it sat in the shadows before a massive candle that marked the hours, itself casting a most peaceful,

---

[44] Shrove Tuesday. The day in February or March immediately preceding Ash Wednesday, the first day of Lent).

ethereal light.

"Why are you not on your knees to pray, my son? Do you sit before God?"

This deep, masculine voice yanked me around, as if I had a cable attached; looking at me was a tall priest, a cowl pulled over him, just the hint of his face. His habit however was not that of a poor local priest. This churchman I did not know.

"I am sorry, Father, but I thought I was alone, and I had forgotten myself in thought."

"I forgive you, my son."

And he slowly moved back his cowl, and there older, grown into a fine man—a priest—was a person who no ageing or costume would conceal to me, his father.

It was Eadwig.

I now maintain to all that the greatest relief God may endow upon the cruel separation from loved ones is revealing them, for me there is no greater joy.

Eadwig and I took hold each of our shoulders, turning a half circle and examining one another; finally, we simply embraced, making open declaration of gratitude before God. Then we sat upon the bench and talked, and the words came as if a spring-swollen stream burst through a barrier of branches and weeds.

He had but a few days in York. Eadwig had gotten permission to travel with all speed north from Canterbury where a legate from the Holy Father was holding hearings of sweeping import regards the current and mounting troubles.

Indeed, Eadwig served the Legate as secretary and interpreter, for by this time, his imposing brain was stuffed with diverse languages and works of vast knowledge. Of course by letter he knew of his mother and Matilda, but I assumed he had seen neither. No words could brace him for Matilda, yet, I struggled to do so. He put his hand to my shoulder: "Father, it was at your shop I found out where you prayed. I saw her. May God forgive those responsible for what happened in act and intent. I find it difficult to say that, may God forgive me, dear Father. But it is true. I loved my sisters truly."

Such harshness even of Eadwig was testimony to her injuries, for my spirit turned darkness when I first saw her.

"Their fate—Matilda's current misery—made me say hasty things that have thrown my soul into question before God. Cwenburh, who has always possessed the stronger of faiths, worries about me. She is strong enough, but I struggle with the matter, Eadwig."

From within his habit, he took out a writ from a wallet, and held it up, opening it for me to read. He had anticipated the entire matter of serving the writ.

It was short and direct: Four days ago, Eadwig was given powers of inquiry by Cardinal-Bishop Columbus, Legate from His Holiness. Eadwig had translated with rapidity a long legal tome from the Greek, a language strange to his Eminence.

"He asked me a return favor but I asked none. He insisted, and I told him of the evil fallen to my twin sisters, and I wanted to get to the bottom of it, as did my mother and father. And we shall do this, Father Cuthwin, though I know it might be viewed as prideful. For God gave me the power of languages."

We walked to the shop in a troubled silence, for it was too late to venture forth to St. Mary's for all were abed there. Before walking into the shop, I turned to Eadwig, "You know, there will be severe moments out on that turd's sokes if writ is served. Osmod-of-Melter is a violent, hateful swine with many toadies."

"We must pray for God's will to be done, Father. What he did met the disapproval of civil law, and now he must face God's."

There was steel in his voice and words, and I knew this plan would go ahead, and do so with alacrity.

When we entered the shop, Oslaf and his father waited there to discuss our upcoming sale. They became flustered by sight of a cleric in high garb. Gunnhilda went to her knees, whereas Matilda just reached out with a big "Hello Eadwig," for they had talked and became at once siblings again—all in several minutes. Eadwig laughed. "Up! For the Love of Our Savior, I'm a monk and priest, not a Bishop!!"

It was only at that moment—when there was a chance to sit—when I noted that Eadwig seemed beset by an affliction of his bone-ends.

"I rode here on a dispatch horse with two of Earl Leofwine's thanes and their drengs—assigned to assure my well being. God help me. I usually walk everywhere I go, thank God. For love of my family I made this exception. Now see how I am rewarded."

He so confessed with a great laugh and slap to his backside.

Eadwig returned to being every bit a Saxon in a Saxon household where bone ends were of prime concern: He was at once administered strong medicine by Gunnhilda, who was learning the ways of wildcrafting from Herself, who had begun almost at once to instruct her in the ways of being a wife. She half-pushed, half-helped him down, drew up his robes—which brought on great laughter—took off his turnshoes and began to apply the salve and rub it in.

And God help us all, he was so trapped we all took advantage: He was plied ceaselessly for stories of faraway places, and he was as much a storyteller as both his mothers. It went this way into the evening when all curiosities were justly served by us.

It was as little past Matins when finally we rested.

It was approaching mid-morning when we arrived afoot at St. Mary's Abbey. I know it might be better for me not to go along—for Mother Margaret would have nothing of a husband during the week—with Eadwig along, I thought she either might make an exception, or perhaps through simple respect give us leeway.

I sat to one side when Eadwig saw his mother chasing after children in the yard with tiny mantles in each hand, for it was a raw, windy day, and a few of them were not properly protected. A young novitiate attended—Cwenburh's student replacement.

The young woman saw Eadwig first and next Cwenburh. She motioned for the novitiate to continue the chase of the girls, then walked towards Eadwig, who had moved back his cowl—protection in the cold morning wind.

When she saw me sitting discreetly to one side, the cat was at once in the barn, and she ran forward and embraced him, and he her. They talked—she in fact whooped—and casting a look at me over her shoulder, and with Eadwig gesturing to me, they entered the Abbey proper. I knew they were going in to get permission for a family gathering from Herself.

Eadwig was always a strict observer of protocol and respect to elders and those of position—he knew the order of things.

I knew them, but didn't like them.

The young novitiate herded the children in—or at least out of my sight. And the wind increased, and I moved further into the lee, and settled—and was experiencing the trepidation—anxiety—of venturing out to Osmod-of-Melter, trying to factor how it might be done painlessly—with no violence.

But another danger intruded: Mother Margaret swept into view, caught sight of me and walked towards me, another novitiate in tow. She—as was her unnerving practice—looked me up and down, as if I had been a demon sprung from the earth,

"Father Eadwig will join you back in town, Master Cuthwin. He has deigned to bless us with midday prayers, and with his mother take joyful repast herein."

I felt my knees meet the cold earth; she made sign over me and left before I had cleared the end of the fence.

Joy, fellowship, and the humble status of plain Saxon folk and how they enjoyed good times meant little to Herself. I sought wisdom and restraint to think nothing more of it, and while returning—my back to the wind—found solace in the more immediate concern of this dismal business pertaining to Osmod-of-Melter.

Early the next morning Eadwig led me to where the squires were equipping each thane's courser with proper drapings. They would not have burdened their fine beasts with such equipage on the express ride from Canterbury, so had borrowed some from local notables who played host to them.

Eadwig frowned.

"Please, may God forbid, good men, I want no harm to come to anyone this morning. Remember the words of Our Savior."

It is not often that truth and reckoning are meted out at the same table and often it is not sightly. The elder of the two thanes looked sadly at Eadwig. His face sported a scar over his eye and, not yet fully clothed, he displayed on his forearm a scar from a burn.

He bowed to Eadwig; his voice kindly, contrasting with his bleak, pitiless countenance, spoke: "Father, bless you. Yet I served under arms these twenty years. And I have sworn to Earl Leofric to advise as well as serve. I tell you, give your father Cuthwin the writ. It needs be in his hand. Attend today elsewhere, Father, and let us to this Osmod creature and do what needs be done as God wills. These things often get ugly, and are no place for a man of Peace, let alone a Holy Person of your fine makings and high standing, God help us. May Our Savior curse me if I say wrong."

The other thane nodded, and gestured north—as if pointing to the distant Osmod. "My cousin speaks true, Father. I have spent years squeezing out pence and shilling from these little toads, and they piss in every direction before yielding, pardon my crudeness, Father."

Eadwig had the authority to go—but I knew thanes, and the violence they could mete out.

"Eadwig, they say right. Gunnhilda will attend your bone ends, and those in my shop will be honored. Remember you need rest for the trip south, God help us."

He and I looked at each other, embraced, and he said he intended to visit the Minster then allow his bone ends to be assuaged—he had that edge of a smile that was uniquely his before the age of five.

The elder of the two thanes mounted and looked at me—nodding, and gesturing before him: "Master Cuthwin. I am John-of-Canterbury, currently thane to his Eminence Archbishop Stigand. When we arrive we must show solidarity and be stouthearted, beg your pardon. This brief errand is a break in the monotony from court and church matters. But my cousin and I have done our share, God help us. And our two drengs who follow are not without experience. So this said: Do you want to serve this writ and see it through?"

It was plain. Those sent with Eadwig were beyond your ordinary guard. I had four hardened warriors with me—and I had witnessed what such men could do. But I took harsh grip on the situation: Osmod-of-Melter was a base murderer and violator of free women born and their children.

"Yes, I am, as God is my witness."

The two thanes nodded to each other and we set off.

Not having mount, I rode double behind one of the drengs, a massive fellow with a long bow alongside the flank of his horse, its wood a high gloss from years of use. The day became clear and notably warmer. We all rode along silently, and John-of-Canterbury must have ascertained our destination earlier, for he went directly.

He was a somber fellow, along with his cousin, and though the drengs began to talk one to the other, I was frankly anxious about the upcoming and listened to nothing but an inner voice warning me of impending brutality.

People meeting us along the road would see the mounted armored riders and caparisoned horses; their eyes would widen in fear and anticipation.

We arrived at the southern bounds of Osmod-of-Melter's sokes before Sext. At this, the two drengs—one giving me hand down to the ground—after gesture from John rode off in opposite direction going out of sight.

"Master Cuthwin, walk ahead of us with the writ, but stay close to my horse, and get behind it if there is trouble."

At the high-wall John's cousin took the horn from its sling and hurled it into the shrubbery, laughing.

"Wouldn't touch my asshole to that."

So with no warning we passed through into the manor proper. There was a scurry of surprised serfs, free workers, and housecarls coming to alert and going for their respective places.

Emerging from the closest structure was a man I deduced was the elder Osmod's son. I heard from the liveryman he dealt with daily affairs, the father being infirm.

The wretched clerk I dealt with in my shop—how I first came to know of things—came out with a pair of housecarls, who immediately withdrew, being quicker on the uptake of things. I assumed they went to arm. There was no sign of the Reeve.

The son and his toady approached another dozen steps, then stopped alongside each other, their eyes locked on the lavish mounts carrying their riders with heavy arms. The clerk moved his gaze to me, disdain written across his thin rat-like face. He motioned towards me with his staff.

"This is Cuthwin, the gnat who made all this trouble."

I wasted no time.

"I am serving proper writ from the Hundred. I must have it read to Osmod-of-Melter, or have him read this fair copy Himself."

"He has the ague, and cannot come here. I can hear it for my father. I am Osmod-the-Younger. Then having done with your business, Cuthwin-of-Alnwick, I want you off our demesne and sokes."

The clerk looked nervously towards closest shelter; clearly the son responded with more strength than this little fellow thought healthy.

Just then, with something between a snort and shout, the Reeve loomed into view; deep in his cups, he staggered towards us, raising his arm: "By God, young Osmod, I be your father's Reeve." Half dressed, he finished tying his breeches up and the same moment pointing away from the manor. "Get the hell out of here, all of you. Cuthwin-of-Alnwick, you miserable swine. Your writ isn't worth the paper to wipe my ass with."

John-of-Canterbury's comrade and cousin urged his horse forward a few steps and once proximate to the Reeve hammered down atop his head with his chain-mailed fist, knocking him unconscious. This was done offhand as if working a gate latch. He laughed and shook his head.

"Drunken fuck."

Outraged, the son raised his hand a sudden, giving signal to others, shouting, "Have it that way then, you bastards."

But when nothing happened at his sign, he looked around helplessly; the clerk gazed transfixed; the Reeve stared dumbstruck, a ragged head wound bleeding profusely.

John-of-Canterbury's two drengs rode in. Each carried one of Osmod's housecarls across the saddle, dumping them off before the son.

One dreng hurled a broken bow towards a paddock. Both housecarls lay beside the Reeve, they too senseless. One's legs twitched in ugly spasms, then stopped.

I don't know if I blinked or looked away, but whatever I did, when my attentions returned to the son, John-of-Canterbury's broadsword was to his neck. Lifting slightly, young Osmod stood on his toes to avoid having his throat slit.

"No more of your stupidity! We will talk with Osmod the Elder. Now fetch him," he looked to one of the drengs. "Go with this piece of shit, and see he does it."

"No one needs fetch me, you bastard." An ancient hobbled along before a house slave who carried a stool. It was Osmod the Elder, and with a glance, all of us saw that he was a personage very different from all before us. He was gnarled—scarred about head and face; the arms and hands projecting from his tunic were as sorely used as the rest of him.

The stool placed, he sat—moved his staff before him, took a left and right grip on it, and looked over his visitors—nodding. Only one of his eyes functioned, the other squinted and long absent.

"I am Osmod the Elder. By way of God, the King, and Earl Siward, I am the owner and master of this demesne and surrounding sokes these forty years. Though I am seventy and eight, if I were armed properly and of fair bone and muscle, I would take broadsword to you all and dance in your guts. Now read me this writ, though I can guess its content. Go ahead, don't shit your breeches. Read, you lettered prick!"

I was flabbergasted to witness a swing of spirit and energy so extreme and sudden. John-of-Canterbury smiled widely, and exchanged respectful looks with his cousin, then quickly returned a weather eye to its ancient speaker. I stood there, and John looked to me and nodded. "I would read, Master Cuthwin, before someone gives this old boar a weapon of some sort."

So, I did. Finished, I looked up in time to see the elder swing his staff and strike the young slave across his chest.

"Bring me ale, Godammit! And serve these two thanes some as well—they look of tougher thread than the piles of fish guts I preside over!" And while the lad fetched, the elder looked to his son with disgust.

"By God, your mother was made of bone and cleverness, but in forty years you learned nothing."

After slaking his immediate thirst with a gulp of ale, he handed off the cup to the boy. Our two thanes drained theirs and tossed cups back to him.

"First off, I bought both the twins as slaves along with others. And where does it say a landed thane who has served Lord Siward faithfully for fifty-plus years cannot buy and sell slaves? Heh! You will get nothing from me on strength of false writings."

When I started to respond, John held out his hand, stopping me.

"We are not here to argue. Get the coin, now!"

His son looked up, and interjected, "We do not have such a sum, for the Love of God."

John eased his horse forward, and while passing the son, back-stroked him with the flat of his sword, knocking him flat to the earth. He glared down at the father,

"Listen, Osmod-of-Melter. You did duty to Earl Siward so know I will get the silver one way or the other. I have served Great Lords for twenty years, and you know their ways as I know those of the late Earl Siward. You are an ancient thane, so in respect I give you this one chance. So far, little has happened to anyone of merit."

The old man thought—looked to each of us, and shook his head as he saw his son struggle to regain his feet. He nodded—as one would recognizing the coming of foul, unstoppable weather. He gestured to the son: "Get it."

"What?!"

"Get it, I said. You don't know your bung from a rat-hole."

When he returned with ample leather sack, there was little talk: The elder explained gruffly that the twins' children had died during a great ague, "...along with many of my other bondsmen," so he included their weregild. There was no mention of their fathers or how Matilda became so maimed. So the matter was over.

When we turned back on that wretched soul's sokes on our return, my wallet was heavy with silver, but my cart heavier.

John drew a hearty breath, and nodded, observing, "That was far easier than I had anticipated."

Then began chatting of great matters to the south, and I rode behind clinging to the dreng, my stomach ill at ease. I was not sure who was hurt or how badly, and indeed had not seen the stricken bowman move after being dropped to earth and his spasm cease.

When I cast a parting glance back, no one attended him or his comrade. Melter and its master was a heartless place and sadly their brutal way of doings things had been reciprocated in a way contrary to Our Savior's teaching.

Our daughters Matilda and Elesa met disaster there, and silver was not justice. I had grown up with Saxon common justice, but now that it supposedly was completed, it seemed lacking before God. But once again I was confronted with this reality: What more could a common person do? It had been a Godsend, if it could be termed that, that powerful men at arms had come to our service, if just for hours; otherwise, no form of justice would have been done.

I returned to my shop and learned Eadwig was at St Mary's Abbey with his mother. It was Friday, and poor Cwenburh—in my view—was still confined by the Abbess. I was in a dark mood, but it helped when they both entered the shop at Compline, a bright surprise to end the day. Eadwig was proud of his diplomatic skills.

"Abbess Margaret bade Mother early reprieve due to my departure tomorrow."

Cwenburh hugged me with unusual intensity, for she had imagined great harm coming to me at Osmod-of-Melter's, despite the men-at-arms accompanying.

I briefly told both what happened, and that I was of a dark frame of mind. Cwenburh braced against the unfairness of it. It was enough we both realized that.

Eadwig was silent, then the inevitable question arose: "Was there violence?"

"I'm afraid there was, good Eadwig."

"Did harm come to anyone?"

"It did, but pray God, not death. But that was never far off if there had been further argument about any matter."

"Upon returning to Canterbury, I must make penance, if that is possible. I just could not see any other way, God help me."

Cwenburh sat, and I was surprised that her temper had not risen quickly; in fact she held, and was instead sad but collected about the hopelessness of pursuing it any further, at least in this life.

"God help us, Eadwig. And the twins, and their children and all other souls held in bondage by that gnarled old wolf."

We sat there. Guilty? Horror stricken? I cannot say then as now. Matilda and Gunnhilda had made many stacks of the silver coin, and were counting them—then arranging and re-arranging them. We looked at it—as though it were dead cat meat. Cwenburh stared up at Eadwig, then to me.

"Would such a pig tell the truth about the children of both?"

"I think to save weregild, Mother, he would have."

Eadwig in one breath said what I feared, then dissipated it in one statement: "If I had time, I would go out there. But I received dispatch from His Eminence the papal legate today. I must go."

There was a strained note in this news—he looked to each of us.

"I have kept a truth from you, and I hope you forgive me. It appears my election as Abbot of Eynsham Abbey is a foregone conclusion. After the end of proceedings at Canterbury, I go there to assume my responsibilities and meet the Reverend Brothers. I will pray fervently for the forgiveness of those who so violated our family throughout. May God and his Son, Our Savior, help and guide me."

"An Abbot! May God be praised. Wonder in heaven! Matilda must revel to see her boy so honored. And me, your second mother, God be pleased."

And Eadwig looked at me.

"And the only father I knew. How does he feel?"

I could only steady myself at the impact of the news—our Eadwig, an Abbot.

"Oh, Son, I cannot describe the joy."

He went on to explain how it might not be a joy, for he was a compromise candidate. A corrupt Abbot had utterly denuded the Abbey of all funds. In recent years it had shrunk in number and local attention of holy influence that all monasteries must have.

"Yet those brothers, including their Prior, are suspicious of this strange Saxon candidate pulled from the edges of Christendom, as they probably see it. A plant by the Archbishop of Canterbury, who," he ducked a look towards the floor, and shrugged, ". . . now, being without any funds, our first duty will be to beg for everything. But, that is part of the rule."

He ceased, laid his head atop Matilda's and since she had now fully recalled her brother, on one level or another, she had found renewed devotion, God be Praised. Cwenburh rose, looked at me—it was strange, even fey, but the same notion swept over us as if we were one. Cwenburh gestured to the silver, "Not with that would you need beg. God cannot put the twins' pathetic remains of justice before man to any better, more lasting use than with you, their brother for such Godly enterprise."

"Oh, Brother, that is right. It is so shiny. It will make good work for you in faraway Bethlehem."

We cannot know how Matilda became fixed on the idea of Eadwig living and working in Bethlehem. Had it been Gunnhilda? But she knew Eadwig did not live or work there. We all looked at Matilda, and at the moment I remembered both Matildas—one's soul inside the other.

There was a scramble of emotions, and when Oslaf entered, he found this strange, silent family scene—sitting around a King's ransom of silver, or so it looked, as if we had just summoned it from the earth.

When he looked every way at once like a confused owl, I could not help smiling, then outright laughing, "It is fine, Oslaf. Come in and help us with Father Abbot's funds."

And I am afraid that did nothing to put the poor lad to rights regarding that strange circle. For a circle is what God or fate had cast around us all. It was not a full circle, but we all savored that moment in hopes of times to steadily improve. But justice, there it was—the missing arc for those who worked with lands and skills, at the mercies of more powerful men and women.

Book 6

A baleful hairy star[45] appears over the land, burnishing God's punishment over night skies. Too late, people reassert their faith in God and Our Savior; hence, doom and sorrow are at hand. False prophets inspired by demons seize the hours, causing havoc, including visiting grievous injury upon Saint Cuthwin.

After great battles between diverse Kings and Earls throughout that same year, Saxon England falls to Duke William of Normandy at Hastings who slays beloved King Harold, his brothers, hundreds of housecarls, and thousands from the fyrd. William is at once crowned King of England by minions of his half-brother. Immediately subsequent to his rule vast, unmerciful chaos descends as William and the Normans bring death and ruin to Saxon England.

God's unstoppable hand sweeps the land clean—sinners and the devoted alike—and Saint Cuthwin loses everything he values, and seeks shelter and balm in the eyes of Our Lord and Savior upon the stark coast of Kernowec[46].

---

[45] "Long-haired star," Anglo-Saxon chronicles. Halleys comet, April 1066.

[46] Kernowec. Modern day Cornwall.

1

A few days past Easter I was at the shop assisting Oslaf, now Master Oslaf. An extraordinary number of letters were being written due to the rumors everywhere of the high possibilities of war in the south. Merchants especially made plans, sending missives in all directions vital to their trade; my former shop was overrun with business. Hence, I voluntarily stepped in to help.

And concerning war? We know there was considerable truth in the rumors; in fact, had not King Harold himself supposed as much before us all?

Eadwig, not prone to pass along unsure rumor, told me prior to his departure that while traversing France and Normandy with His Eminence, he had heard nothing else but talk of William waging war. All knew that Duke William harbored bitter grievance against King Harold for taking the crown in violation of an alleged earlier oath to William.

Upon learning of Harold's rise to Kingship, he grew sullen and withdrew to pray and ask of guidance. None of William's minions were admitted to his person at this time. Those in his inner circle, however, knew William would without doubt invade, even though most of his wealthy liegemen and thralls opposed it.

Even Eadwig pointed out that "William is a wrathful man with considerable riches and steadfast against King Harold, God help us all."

But by Holy Week, those in the north, and especially York, had taken advantage of twelve weeks leading up to Our Savior's Passion, and there were many Easter feasts.

The winter had been no harder than usual, and thanes and crofters—plus the young Earls of Northumberland—enjoyed larders and ricks still ample.

All sorts wandered into York during these times. Markets and such during the weeks preceding Easter were littered with all stripes of the commonality.

Everywhere a new addition would ply the land, mainly wandering monks. Those who followed The Rule of Saint Benedict had great contempt for them. They had no brotherhood or semblance of office or benefice, and indeed if they had or had not taken tonsure was unknown, save by their own testimony.

At York that Easter, several wandering monks were around, but one—from Ireland because he spoke with strongly accented speech—was popular in his preaching, drawing great crowds with impassioned sermons about Our Savior's passion.

The name he brazenly borrowed was Patrick, and most called him Patrick the Visionary. He would pass the bowl after his sermons, and made a modest amount of coin this way, also keeping two so-termed acolytes with him.

With the burden of business preventing us from hearing the rumors spreading wildly through York via croftsmen fleeing the countryside, it was not until—quite out of its usual time—the great bell at the York Minster sounded—without stop. Thinking there was a great emergency, we ran to the square.

There was a growing crowd—clearly most had left whatever they were doing and came a'running, as we had. Upon the rising platform of steps before York Minster, Patrick the Visionary preached, and already the crowd was approaching a frenzy.

He warned that God's Wrath was upon us, written across the skies, and this claim seemed to catch a note of fear with everyone.

By questioning this person and that, I learned with horror that beyond the confines of York, where the previous night skies had been clear, a massive ball of fire was descending towards the land.

"Where did it strike?"

"It hasn't. It is coming directly at us; it is the size of the moon. It is God's wrath. We are lost! And this holy man is telling us why and how all souls might be absolved."

Indeed, this wanderer had changed the tone and good nature of his Easter Week preaching. He now advocated the destruction of false prophets who he claimed filled churches and monasteries. He pointed up, and then behind him at the Minster: "God has spoken to me. Upwards is the punishment yet also redemption! Rid yourselves of these parasites of Our Savior's preaching. They even use a serpent's venomous mouth to deceive you about the time of Easter itself. Blasphemy!"

Several thousand now milled about with their number swelling rapidly. At once I anticipated that the Earl of Northumberland's housecarls—resident a few leagues out of York—would be called upon. Whoever was in charge at the Minster—the Archbishop being in the south for the marriage of King Harold—would have gotten message to the Earl about this heretic's incitement of the crowds.

At that moment the elderly Deacon-Priest, a brave man indeed, came out with two of his sub-deacons. With his great voice, he told Patrick the Visionary to get gone and stop his preaching apostasy and violence, or he would call the Guard; if not them, then request the Earl's actions.

Speaking around Patrick, and over him, he called on everyone to pray to the Almighty, "For in prayer God comforts all."

But Patrick the Visionary thrust his arm at them laughing, then turning to the crowd his face assumed an ugly visage: "Have you not seen their greed and immorality! Who has not been bled dry by them? They charge money to put the holy water upon your babes in arms! Charlatans and dupes are damned before God. This great hairy star is God's Wrath upon them and whoever follows them! Now is the time, while God's Wrath has not struck: Show him repentance—put every one of them to the torch!"

I vividly remembered the mob rule before the walls of Ludlow during the famine, and a sickening feeling took hold. I urged Oslaf at once to get out.

"There will be mayhem, Brother."

The Deacon and his men, seeing how things went, fled into the Minster with the crazed people in pursuit. At our back, we could hear hateful words and shouts swelling.

Simple fate made matters worse.

That night it was clear skies above York. The malignant body above spiraled closer. The sight of it caused my bowels to loosen with terror. No one in and around York had seen anything vaguely like it during their lifetime. Certainly it could only presage the most heinous calamity. Its brimstone and fire tumbled earthward; some fled while others hid anywhere from the sight of it gyrating above, every hour drawing closer.

Those wise in the reading of stars and planets maintained contrasting views: Some supposed the ethereal spirits dripping from the surrounding fuzziness carried serpent venom. If any struck a human, they would be consumed in a ball of demonic flames. Worse, if not shriven, would be dashed to the eternal fires. This added to the tumult.

Not a few seers gave readings and interpreted signs from the innards of animals; still others sold talisman and by clever device passed along the secret of ancient mystics to avoid the awful might of the star's heavenly strength. A few espoused wisdom gleaned from wood nymphs and gnomic beings privy to all such things.

The star illuminated things more than it had the nights before. Oslaf's oldest brother lived close to the Minster; at sunup he carried a most awful warning to his brother: "Oslaf, all of you, Master Cuthwin! Patrick the Visionary has the heart of the crowd; the churchmen have fled, save the Deacon who was torn to pieces and tossed into the Ouse, God help him."

"And where are the Earl's thanes and housecarls?"

"Not in York, God help us!" He eyed back to the streets, for a great commotion swelled in the near distance. "The hordes are busy finishing their looting of the Minster, and are spreading out to smaller churches and such. I advise you, while they are so involved, flee! I am. Soon all property and money will draw them in."

Indeed by now most shopkeepers had shut tight and erected stout barriers over anything, but I feared for all holy institutions.

I knew that once sated with small churches and chapels within York, those proximate outside its walls could be next.

One of the closest and most prominent was the Monastery at St. Mary's. The Abbot and Abbess within the walls had nothing to repel such a mob. Most vulnerable outside the cloister's walls were Cwenburh and her wards plus any who helped her with everyday needs. And of course, Matilda, for these two days she had been with her mother.

I set off at once, despite pleas from Oslaf.

"For God's sake, Master Cuthwin, what if the crowd comes across you?"

I advised that he and Gunnhilda and the two shop boys stay within—behind the boarded-up doors—and if anyone broke in, crawl in the space between the walls joining the shop to my quarters. I always knew it to be good cover in emergencies.

Then I was gone, feeling confident Oslaf was of good sense and would act wisely.

On the way out from York, I saw smoke rising and curling upwards into a clear spring sky. People ran towards the smoke, others away—away was the direction of a woman carrying a child; she shouted a warning to me. I recognized her from my visits to the fishmonger's pier.

"Get out! They are burning all the holy places. Lawlessness is everywhere."

I moved faster paralleling the river. Upon the Ouse, a number of punts were frantically being poled upstream by fleeing occupants. On the opposing bank, people ran alongside, pleading for them to take them on board.

On my side of the river under trees now heavy with burgeoning of buds, I moved along in cover then emerged into the open. Looking up, I saw to my amazement and horror that the ghastly falling star was visible during daytime. A most unnatural outline of dull light against the blue of the sky—its brightness otherworldly.

My ominous musings drew my attentions from the immediate, departing from my constant practice of keeping eyes ahead and to the side. So when I emerged from under some willows, I ran into two cotsets.

"And what fine-clad fellow have we here, brother mine?"

Both were brutish fellows armed with cudgels. My wits scrambled, regretting my vanity in wearing a better grade of garb though I was not traveling the open road.

"I am a plain fellow going to St. Mary's to seek absolution."

"You wear fine clothes and are nicely shod, Master Plain Fellow."

And the only warning I had, and then not much, was the beast who spoke—his eyes looked beyond me, and I was about to turn, and a great stroke of pain and blackness struck me at the same moment as a massive force threw me forward.

There had been three of the bastards.

I occupied a dream world with people I did not know and cannot recall in detail; whether it was a vision of purgatory or the gates to it I do not know. When I woke, I was looking up at the trees feeling a great cold in my bone ends. My vision consisted of black-and-white smudges, but I knew this was real and not a phantom place. And I could hear.

"I tell you, they left little for us."

"This old cottar is slain, God help him. He lived long enough."

Then I was picked up by the legs and dragged a ways, at once tumbling back to the phantom world—but this time I found Frog waiting. He said nothing, but sat on the raised house in the fens fishing with a plain pole.

He turned towards me, looked, then immediately went back to his line with one hand while eating a trencher with another. It went on: People, things and places drifting past like those on a river bank might while polling along in a dense fog. I was surely upon the fens.

"How long, pray God, have you left him lie here, you bastards?!"

That voice was Cwenburh sure enough, and she was in a temper. I remained awake, tried to speak but could not—to move my legs and feet, but could not.

Someone took my hand, and I knew at once it was Cwenburh.

"Cuthwin, can you hear me? Do not die here like a miserable wild creature. Can you hear me? Give a squeeze to my hand."

And I did—praise God, my hands worked.

"Ah! He hears. By Jesus, Our Savior, he will live! Come on, you louts!"

So it was this way for a long time—I would hear things, could use my hands, and one thing sure, became warmer. Most voices were

Cwenburh's, then Oslaf ordering Gunnhilda to do one thing or another, Matilda confused, asking questions.

And then laughter of young girls. But I could not make sense of this, for my mind was addled, and familiar words came together in uncertain order. Only if someone spoke very simply and briefly did I follow all.

Cwenburh perceived this, but I could tell a Healing Woman attended. Her presence I detected by my nose, both that and my taste worked well, for she smelled like rancid lard and her potions and balms tasted and smelled worse.

And like of old, Cwenburh would argue with her about price.

During quiet times, Cwenburh, a little at a time told me what had happened, and events subsequent.

"Cuthwin, they hit you most across the back, less in your brain pan, God be praised."

I joined Gunnhilda in the mute world, but feeling was returning to my lower regions—I could now feel the need to make water and complete the act itself.

Time passed without notice.

"I tell you, Mistress Cwenburh, he shall recover fully and you owe me a pound silver, holy woman or no."

"We shall see."

"See? See?! Our agreement was I work by time not deed.

"What is time if no deed is done?!"

It was the first time I awoke and made absolute sense out of what was said, and without knowing I was falling back on my God-given gifts, I said, "For the love of Our Savior, Cwenburh, give her the coin."

There was a whoop from both, and the Healing Woman proclaimed, "And see! He even speaks wisdom."

I also could take a bit of solid food, though first being given a good dipping in heavy broth. I had spent April and into May in the shadows, and Cwenburh attended me full time. Her time under oath to Mother Margaret evidently was over and had been concluded early. I came to the hasty conclusion that the gravity of my injuries had mitigated even this harsh woman's dark view of husbands. Cwenburh revealed a different story.

"The crowds reached St. Mary's and burned the outer buildings, the swine. I barely made it down to the river with the girls. It was mayhem. They nearly murdered Matilda, because of her disfigurement—and would have if I had not stepped in with a stave. They were all cowards."

And like quarreling rats, they looted relic, plate—anything of value—breeching easily the wall of the Monastery grounds. And, God praise her always and bring her sainthood, but Mother Margaret held to her grounds, and the poor woman died a martyr. It was then the Earl's men belatedly arrived and commenced their Godless reprisals.

Cwenburh had seen hangings before and after the famine at Ludlow, but never in this rapid and rapacious a manner.

"Father Abbot pled with the Earl's men against this, but it did little good."

They hanged dozens—distributing them like butchered geese here and there between the Monastery and Minster of York—from any point high enough—disallowing anyone to take them down. Within a few days of the sight and smell of this carnage, the Earl's men judged fair enough warning. Hairy star or no, this was the fate of thieves and murderers who brooked the peace in Northumber and sanctity of holy places.

Foremost amongst the Earl's men was a familiar name, Aldwulf-of-York now High Sheriff of the entirety of the Earldom. And it was the inevitable irony of fate that Patrick the Visionary, the originator of the riot, was never apprehended.

Daily healing and rest were my lot. Cwenburh rented a large building adjacent to the River Tees with a residence at the rear previously owned by a recently deceased coopersmith, dedicated to decadent living and devotion to his cups. Resident with us was Gunnhilda who for practical purposes became one of our family. With this came concerns for the young girls from St. Mary's, yet so far Herself had not broached this topic.

Cwenburh informed me of the rising matter of Gunnhilda and Oslaf, the two now completely in love with each other. Obedient Oslaf was vigorously—even virulently—opposed by his parents taking a mute as a wife. Gunnhilda living with him at his shop was disallowed. His stiff-necked mother and father assumed children fathered upon a deaf mute would be born cursed by demons.

Oslaf's rebellion—slow in coming—was in the offing.

When not in company with one another, they were in abject misery, and would sneak off frequently.

"Well, Cuthwin, there will be a little one coming soon whether the two old squints desire it or no. They are the demons."

In the spacious residence, where a half-dozen children had been raised by the cooper's several successive unfortunate wives, reassembly of my brain pan was the main concern. The Healing Woman, Brigit the Pict, and Cwenburh quarreled about what I looked like prior to the cudgel's fall.

"I tell you, he is my husband, and I know what his brain pan looked like, and that is nothing like it. He looks like a rabbit."

"Ah, nonsense. He looks fine. I know my business."

"Well, you might know your business, but I know Cuthwin, and he doesn't look like a rabbit."

And they would argue on: Then, Cwenburh, holding off her fee, would have her unwrap my sore, miserable head, and re-shape it with one of her wicked instruments, causing me unparalleled agony.

Howls of pain rattled the old roof planks and made the waddle flake off the walls.

Finally, I conveyed to them that even if I looked like a stoat or a hedgehog, for the love of God's mercy, leave me be until the bones fused.

And thank God, they showed mercy.

During the earliest days of my healings I was so occupied by swallowing potions, elixirs and having my head reshaped, I asked few questions. One that lingered was with Mother Margaret murdered, her highly placed influence would be no more.

True to my suspicions Father Abbot was opposed to having a shelter for homeless girls, likely knowing himself incapable of controlling his notoriously errant monks from such proximate temptation. He began to complain of its great expense, always the enterprise's weakest link. It was impossible to sustain the effort without the skills of Mother Margaret.

With the girls' outbuildings and such destroyed, my associative faculties returned to me enough to suspect where the girls were being kept. I was being spared burdensome details. So I used my time abed to associate the details with the clearest facts. The girlish outcries continued, always from the same direction, and if anything became more audible and numerous.

I was familiar with the old cooperage and knew well the building fronting the river was big for the needs of such work. Also, frugal Cwenburh would never pay for space not needed.

In May I was much better. One afternoon I was enjoying Cwenburh bathing me with a warm cloth. The smell of wool was strong on her, and since I was naked before God and my wife, this was one of the few times no one was allowed in.

Of course the shearing of wool and the newly taken fleece would be everywhere in York now. Home spinning was a good way for womenfolk to earn coin, and even with a sadly compromised brain, I deduced Matilda was busy in the main building spinning.

And she was not doing so alone.

"So, you teach the orphan girls to spin, Cwenburh? How many remain after the mayhem and chaos at St. Mary's? I assume we are continuing the responsibilities of St. Mary's now?"

She stopped her work, placed both her hands upon the rag that rested on my chest.

"I knew you had gathered all events together Cuthwin," she sighed, looking back towards the building. ". . . Eighteen."

"How will we feed, clothe, and shelter *eighteen* children, Cwenburh?"

"Actually, twenty. I misspoke. Two more came in yesterday—hidden away across the river. Got across, somehow, thank God."

"How will we feed, clothe, and shelter *twenty* children, then? And me being next to dead, unable to work, perhaps ever."

She resumed washing me, then became somber: "The weregilds. Eadwig has my touch with the future, and left us half. He did not want to argufy about it with you. He knows you consider it cursed." She paused, knotted the cloth in her tiny fists. "Then our considerable savings put with that. Cuthwin, cannot you accept the weregild was God's far-seeing gift for these waifs, no home, and too poor for even a speck of bread?"

"And if the winter is cruel? Even feeding three or four mouths takes art and experience. Silver cannot be eaten."

"We must pray then it not be cruel."

"Pray?! Did prayer do us or others any good at Ludlow when the Bishop sat inside provisioned and those outside ate thorns and pig droppings."

"Cuthwin! Again? You still talk such blasphemy. What would Abbot Elsin say to you? What?!"

She soaked the cloth and now rubbed it across my forehead, seeing I had gotten irate. What she said struck hard. I knew Father Abbot as a man of profound faith and compassion before all else, and his faith held out before money and policy of church or King.

Cwenburh bent, and looked in my eyes.

"Will you not pray with me now, Cuthwin, for God to forgive the blasphemy you have just allowed?"

"Prayer?! We must get out of Northumber, Cwenburh. There were troubles before and there will be even more troubles to come."

"Husband you cannot go north, south, east, or west for some time. Those bastards struck you, stripped you of every thread upon your body, and left you in a swale for the rawness to slowly kill you. It was God's doings that Oslaf and Gunnhilda even found you. It is only prayer now."

I lacked strength to argue, even if in my heart praying was of uncertain spirit. I could not sully Cwenburh's unshakable faith which I envied. Nor could I question her nature to help unwanted children, and in truth I did not want to, for I loved her for it.

We had been separated by evil forces for so many years, I vowed we would be parted again in one way only.

I wanted out of Northumber, and if healing was the only way to do it, I would do so. The experience of years told me that with the amount of resources we had, we could afford a virtual begang of wagon and escort. Then we could thread several hundred leagues south, get a bit of hideage before we ran out of silver, and face being left to our own resources with a brood of mouths. But the season must be kind, might God help us? But that took faith.

So at least one of us had that.

To an Innocent like Cwenburh who believed in the eventual goodness of God, pounds of King's silver seemed to offer an eternity of God-ordained promise. My own beliefs? Might I become a vagabond blasphemer like Frog? So she and I prayed together: I prayed not to become wild like Frog while Cwenburh asked God that the season be good to us. This made prayers possible for us that day in sad, doomed York.

My recuperation was slow. The ready repair of youth departed. The recovery seemed faster above my waist than below; indeed, my feet and legs did not function well at all. The irony of being wheeled around in the same vehicle I had built and designed for Matilda amused me.

Rumors of great matters became a fireside activity at the livery, pieced together after the riots. Mostly they concerned the doings of King Harold, his Earls and Nobles. King Harold became the center of a conversation of a social circle of loyal businessmen who helped shepherd me through my grievous injury with good fellowship.

Often we would repair to the cooperage; I in fact became something like the sponsor of them. Cwenburh would settle in the girls after their evening prayers and join us.

It was acknowledged Duke William would invade the south in late spring or summer, but summer was nearly gone, so this fact flew in the face of our fears.

"I tell you, I have been dealing with hardened boatmen for years, and they all say that summer will be the only time a great army could cross."

Not a few reminded that Duke William was a hateful, vengeful Norman. Further, he would claim his rightful place even if he had to part the seas between France and England!

Yet talk always returned to the business of York, foremost, and above all else was the raising of church and town levies. In fact, all were raised. This of a sudden dragged Herself into the fray. Cwenburh's shelter for girls drew a levy equal to that of an animal dealer or wholesaler in flesh for market.

So the troubles began—Cwenburh maintained a state of readiness for any official brave enough to confront her.

"We do not raise girls, as you would sheep, the greedy bastards. When they eventually are placed with fullers or some such, the money still goes to Father Abbot, he being no less greedy than the King."

And daily concerns maintained their usual flow of days as we approached September that always begins with the grandness of St. Giles Festival. Hence, the entire town and countryside were still recovering when the skies opened and great sorrows descended. Perhaps as some said, this was in retribution for the bawdy revelry of the Festival. Panicked boatmen grounded their craft hard in the mud and ran through York shouting, "Harald Hardrada has landed beyond Hull with Earl Tostig—they both have joined. Their host of boats and men will be coming upriver soon for blood and loot. God forgive us all."

This was the most unexpected news possible. Nothing from the north had mixed with the countless forms of gossip about Duke William's grievances from the south.

Harald the Giant (as he was known) and Earl Tostig were indeed ugly surprises. These two embittered nobles struck all with equal horror to that of the hairy star, but unlike the interpretation of a heavenly invasion, their motives and reasons needed no speculation. Though little specific was known about the personality of Duke William, the natures of Harald the Giant and Earl Tostig were known throughout the earldom and everywhere beyond.

No seer or reader-of-sign was required to know Earl Tostig, brother to King Harold, who had his earldom seized by the old King Edward two-plus years before. Crazed by hate, he meant to regain his domain and do it by violence, then once in control, mete out bloody retribution.

The murderous Tostig's ejection by King Edward was a great balm for all in Northumbria, and especially York where he was a bane to business and folk alike.

Now he was back with Hardrada who had long-established odious legends alluding to his crafty hoodwinkings, followed close by murder and destruction of those he deceived.

Rumors preceded him: "He stands two heads higher than all men, and eats his meat raw and kills men by enclosing his hand about the head of enemies and squeezing their brains out. And worse, he enjoys such."

Cwenburh and most others voiced these fantastic attributes. Fantastic or not, the terrible men's approach was monitored daily. It took no little common sense to gather as much together and evacuate York while there were still leagues between them and York.

Even without Harald the Giant, Tostig would be deranged with a desire of revenge—especially on those in York who participated in his downfall.

Two days passed, then witnesses arrived in York with tales confirming earlier accounts of the giant king's ruthlessness: Harald Hardrada's forces burned a small village to ashes without seeming to have purpose or aim in it. Then worse news followed: Harald Hardrada and Earl Tostig and their combined forces of boat and foot were en route up the Ouse in force—hundreds of ships containing all the needs of warfare.

Earl Morkere, now lord of all Northumbria, also had boats and forces on the river. But all knew the young inexperienced Earl and his brother could never successfully deal with so many Norsemen, even if not led by Godless monstrosities like Harald Hardrada and Tostig.

There was no time to ponder who would engage who, or how it might turn out. Whatever happened, the young Earl would be no match, and if he and his men engaged, they would all be slain.

The bounty for looting in York would be a rich reward for any army.

I looked on as quick preparations were made by Cwenburh and my household. I warned from experience, "You must not only go, but get well hidden in the thickest of woods, burying anything of value. They will follow and search. The children are fodder for slave dealers."

It was not long before I was confronted by an agitated Cwenburh who had become uncharacteristically hasty in her thinking.

"Husband, you need go with us. We have a cart, and strong boys to push it."

"What in the devil would the great men and their scum want with me, Cwenburh? Am I slave material? Would I have great wealth? I am not so rich in prospects that I am afraid to meet God. But you have the girls, Matilda, and household—everyone—and the resources to survive. You have what bloodthirsty swine value. Go! I shall be left alone by my desire. Remember the last time you went contrary to my instincts."

"In faith I do, Cuthwin. You did not need to voice it."

"Cwenburh, I fear your stubbornness—I respect it, but fear it. So, I'm sorry."

"And if they set the place afire?!"

"And if the hairy star comes back? Or Patrick the Visionary and his ogres? No, just go to the forests, hide, use all the craft that these others do not have. You are half vixen, Cwenburh. We learned together. Lay in wait until you see which way events turn. Survive! They say King Harold will without a doubt come north. And he is not the young Earl with a piddling of men and such. And you have left me with much bread and meat. I shall share a daily feast here with the birds."

We embraced, and I held her close for the sheer magic of it. She knew what I said to be hard truth. The wheels on the cart used to transport me caught every rut and hole, and even the smallest of the girls could walk four-times that speed. To Danes or Tostig's thanes, any one of those girls was a fortune as slaves. This was the cruel reality about those who invaded.

What followed was a mysterious but blessed day of quiet which gave all time to prepare. I hobbled about using two stout sticks; I went to the door, sat, and watched others exit York. Some would stop, bid me well, knowing I had no chance to retreat.

Not to raise such sympathy I went back inside. Besides, I had a better vantage at the back where the cooperage had a dock on the River Foss. It was dilapidated now, and at the lowest, tides were dry, an expanse of river mud extending between it and the river.

Between tides, groups of fat, lazy gulls stood, flat webbed feet planted in the mud. Their ebony backs caught the late summer sun. Around the flats, and darting beneath the old docks along the Foss, a few remaining swallows hunted—catching quantities of bugs needed for a long migration—one that would bring them south to enchanted lands.

Hobbling out upon this old dock I sat—here was privacy, and I could see downriver to where the Foss joined the Ouse. As the great tide pushed in from the never-tiring sea, it drove the river waters back; they would rise, and the invading boats would arrive. It would make another dreadful sight I would endure. The sun passed further overhead, and as it warmed the lazy gulls, it did me, too. Despite the sadness of this day, I enjoyed the first quiet moment I had known in a long time.

I awoke to a warm night and bugs stinging me—taking my blood. The tide was fully up, but everywhere along the river front it was quiet. Boats had been left there days before, their owners fleeing inland. The river had risen and most of these craft drifted about on their tethers.

Above there was no moon, and only a few tiny torch-lights could be seen carried, those coming down the opposite bank. Following their path, I saw them grab the lines, draw the boats in, and get aboard.

They were thieves of course, always the last to leave, and first to harvest the bounty from other peoples' misfortune and fear. But there was not a sound, aside from the frogs upon the marshes singing their constant unfathomable jabber.

Looking below me, I could see it was an extraordinary high tide, most advantageous for larger boats ascending—they would have planned their arrival for that, of course.

I withdrew, returning to my pallet. I gathered together a pile of round stones, perfect for throwing. These would give pain to thieves and other petty sorts who ranged up and down streets, stealing what they could from households who had fled.

I woke just at the commencement of false dawn. I tested the air for sound and scent, for I was warned that Norsemen in such a mass stink of fish.

Outside it was a hush; only the first bird songs were heard as the dawn woke them. Between the cracks in the cooperage's battings, light grew bolder; but all was quiet.

This ceased with a thump on my door. The visitor then tried it at once and found it barred. I took up stones, and got set.

"Master Cuthwin, I know you are within."

It was, God help him, Oslaf. With rich inventory and coin-in-house, what imaginings could have made him stay. I bade him come in the rear way, and soon he was beside me—looking forlorn, offering to start a fire.

While he did so, I was sorely tempted to give vent to worry and frustration: Why had he stayed? Glancing to me, while getting the fire going, he explained. His voice was heavy with despair: "Oh, Master Cuthwin, Gunnhilda has hidden in the wall and she will not come out. Further, the poor thing wants me to join her. I cannot get her to see reason; she is wild as a she-badger. Maybe this is what mutes do when threatened. Anyway, my people took all of value. My mother and father are very angry."

"They did not take everything of value. You are the person of value. What if Tostig's thanes or the brutal Norsemen cut off your hands? For the love of God, get out. Reach in there, drag her out and, if needs be, tie her up and sling her. She is as tiny as a wren."

He sat down at the hearth, crossed his legs, and glared into the fire.

"She is wedged in there like a dormouse. I cannot use force. I have not the heart, and she is heavy with my child."

So on this most fateful day of Saxon history, with violent men plying their way upriver to loot and kill, I sat in my bed and listened to Oslaf's quandary. While doing so, the good soul made us hot spelt porridge and worried after the future.

"My mother and father know of her state by me. They are invested heavy in the shop. It is God's command to obey your father and mother. And they are right."

And that was the way of working Saxons. What could we do about events around us? So I reclined, proud to enjoy his friendship and confidence. I admired that he cast aside all threats of great men and their thirst for power and wealth; also, he finally was fighting his hidebound parents.

Instead he worried about the tiny woman who was not more than a girl, now big with his child. This was very well done—in this I was identical to Cwenburh, God forgive.

Even amidst this catastrophe, my faith in God increased—for surely it was He who gave strength to poor Oslaf. Ordinary folk like Oslaf, who were faithful and God-fearing and practiced the teachings of Our Savior were the stuff of genuine grandness. Had not I faltered in my time?

For nothing short of God sending an avenging angel from heaven hurling balls of fire before her might the Almighty rescue us from fiends like Tostig and Harald the Giant. If only I could pray for such in good heart and spirit.

It is terrifying when the axe, as it were, has risen but not yet fallen. And the axe of Harald and Tostig continued its pause. Upon the river and in the nearly deserted town, no marauders or host appeared, despite the city being without defenders.

Thousands of townspeople were salted throughout nearby woods and crofts, with all their valuables and much of their household items stashed away with them.

Some of these sent family members into town intermittently to confirm there was still no sign of enemies. Yet all was not safe, for ongoing eyewitness reports confirmed Harald the Giant and the demented Tostig were harrying not far off. They were stealing all fodder and food from every croft and manor, and when done, burning and killing many.

Cwenburh and I exchanged messages and I found frustrating her ignorance of writing now more than ever before. She knew better than anyone to stay put.

"Why have the bastards not come all the way up the Ouse, God help us?"

The liveryman and his eldest daughter trekked in and called on me. Word had circulated to those hiding about those of us who had stayed in York, mostly the elderly and infirm like myself. By this time, I had coached Oslaf in the art of persuasion, and Gunnhilda came out of her hole to wait things out with us at the cooperage. They were welcome company, for over the years solitude had become strange to me.

Oslaf made occasional forays throughout town, curious about the strange calm. It was then he met those fleeing from the countryside southeast of us. This seemed a portent, but I could not parse the continuing delay in York.

It was now the fourth day since the town's evacuation, and those in hiding were bug-bitten, uncomfortable from their sleeping pallets and lack of home comforts. Further, the children were troublesome. Switchings, with parents screaming for order, made all the camps even more maddening.

The liveryman shook his head and complained, "I tell you, Cuthwin, out there, I am almost of the opinion we should send word to the murderers to get it over with. We can make a new town, but we cannot repair our brains with all this madness."

On the fourth night following, I again took my seat upon the old dock, and at sunset saw an immense conflagration beyond the junction of the Ouse with the Foss—towards the south. Since the wind was from that direction, the smell of burning wood overwhelmed and smarted the eyes.

Oslaf sat next to me taking a repast. I knew time was short.

"Oslaf, it is time for you to be gone. See that. It is from Fulford. It is a harbinger of disaster. Get out and into the woods to your family."

"I am angry with them for saying cruel things about Gunnhilda. The poor girl read our lips—my mother's lips—and now she prefers the hole in the wall to the presence of Mother."

"Indeed, did not the stubborn lady know she reads lips well?"

"No. Furthermore, Gunnhilda can speak or cry out, though it is a strange sound!"

"How so? How did you find out?"

He struggled around words, until I was sorry for the question.

"I just did."

I saw it was hopeless and put my hand on his shoulder and gave it a reassuring pat. "Time to be a man, Oslaf. She is here—unawares—take her suddenly, toss her over your shoulders and spirit her off to the woods."

He looked at me and, after an initial anxious face, understood. Such an action with Gunnhilda would be like grabbing a stoat by the back legs. He smiled and turned his attention towards Fulford, for the inferno grew; massive, black, greasy smoke rose many furlongs into the sky and now began to be felt in our lungs.

Since the work area of the former cooperage was so large, I suggested he and Gunnhilda could ascend into the beams and rafters above and hide.

"Greedy men seeing nothing but an old crippled man—and in a hurry—do not look up, Oslaf."

Abruptly, the peace was disturbed by a voice from the far side of the river: "Hallo! Hallo! Anybody!"

It was a boatman and, seeing the light from our fire inside, he approached closer. Its two polemen repeated, "Hallo in there! God's peace to you. Poor injured souls here need help, Our Savior pity them."

Having armed at once, Oslaf stood by me with a cudgel. When the boat ran up into the mud, I sounded things, "And God's peace to you. Who are you? What do you want?"

"We transport those who flee from what remains of the Young Earl's army at Fulford. They were defeated, most butchered by Harald and Tostig's men, God help them all. The few surviving, like these, run for their lives."

"Those who need shelter and help are welcomed here, but they must come up unarmed."

"Oh, there is no fight left in these poor devils."

We helped six into the cooperage and not only was there no fight in three of them, the other three had wounds deep to their innards and their hours were few.

The punt-men did not take risks for nothing—but for silver or anything valuable in trade. They collected same from survivors who had anything and were desperate for quick transport. In addition to these six souls, they had scavenged valuable armor and weapons to be cached and sold later. They hurried off, back towards Fulford, before saying another word. Their passengers were not happy with them.

"Those boatmen are carrion crows, the turds. There were dozens of the fuckers lingering on the river for such miserable opportunities."

The speaker was a massive Dane who carried what he told us was his son, and this is the moment we met Thorkald the Dane. He was a housecarl of the Young Earl Morkar's brother and fought with them.

"The young dimwits didn't stand a chance before the sly Harald and that maniac Tostig."

Thorkald had fought for a half-score of warlords for thirty-odd years, and had rarely seen a battle go so wrong and led so poorly.

His son was wounded the worst of all of them. Within the cooperage, we saw our share of the tragedy at Fulford at once, for the mortally injured died with merciful speed including, sadly enough, Thorkald's only son.

"He was but seventeen, God be with him. He would not stay home and his aunt grew weary of him."

Thorkald wept miserably. Gunnhilda attended him. Above his neck-piece he endured an ugly gash, and though it must have pained him awfully, he sat without flinching while it was washed clean.

"His mother died after bringing him into the world, and God seems to have forsaken the both of them," he told us.

Two of the three who survived started out to the northwest the following day towards their homes, both being fyrdmen—doing their annual duty to the Earl. They wanted no more of York, Fulford, or anywhere else there was struggle.

When Thorkald tried to leave, we insisted he stay—his wounds would just suppurate and he would die, unless he got rest and perhaps even access to a Healing Woman. His wound was deeper than it first appeared and he had bled badly.

The necessity to carry his son to safety drove him to trade his buckler and armor to the boatmen. Now all the injury caught up with him. Soon, he fell away into unconsciousness as his body absorbed the shock of the injuries.

I was sure the victors would be upon York to collect their reward. With the young Earl out of the way, there was nothing before them.

I brought Oslaf and Gunnhilda to me, and taking their hands, pulled them close. "Now look! There is no doubt about them coming. Oslaf, Gunnhilda—go to where Cwenburh and her girls hide and stay with her. She is half fox, and no one will ever catch her. Do this now. She will be beyond the others, so be patient and search."

Since Gunnhilda now loved Cwenburh above all other women-folk,

I had no reason to repeat my advice. Picking up what food I could and stuffing it in a large wallet, I drove them out as if they were poultry. There was no time. Fulford was only a league from where we were and anyone could travel that in an hour.

That left me with the unconscious Thorkald, which of itself was ungood. When they found one of the Young Earl's housecarls here, they would murder him and possibly me as well.

Despite being maimed, I dragged the massive Thorkald a little at a time, doing what little I could to conceal him.

I put out the fire, barred the front and back entrances, and throughout the day heard survivors passing on the river, and others in the street, trying doors, only to move on. From outside, the place would look like others—threadbare and abandoned.

The streets remained quiet, the river quieter, and soon the smell of the conflagration around Fulford went away. The tide rose, but when I peeked through the rear door onto the River Foss, I saw nothing.

I did what I might from what I learned with horses and cattle years before, cleaning out Thorkald's wound. In doing so, I removed all his clothes—discovering that his wounds were more extensive than we thought. Just the old wounds foretold a body that was a composite of scars and badly healed bone ends. I covered him with blankets—for there was nothing more I could do. I prayed his battered soul was far better off than his body; I feared he soon would be in need of the former and not the latter.

God in his unknown ways of mercy and wisdom saw fit to save York for the time. Harald and Tostig's forces, like vultures swollen with their pickings, heard that King Harold and his army of nobles, housecarls, and fyrdmen were hurrying north. Tostig and Harald Hardrada, confident after crushing the young earl at Fulford, rushed to meet the King, knowing their two armies would crush his one.

With King Harold out of the way, the practical Harald the Giant knew he would be King. Any pretender would need to deal with him and Tostig.

Five short days later they met intrepid King Harold and his Saxon army at Stamford Bridge. With justice of heaven behind them they were victorious—killing his brother Tostig and rival Harald. The remaining invasive force fell into rout and ruin and scattered like dogs.

We of the north were jubilant beyond description.

Without exception all came out of hiding.

The timing of our King could not have been better, and throughout the north it was accepted that Duke William had used his great wealth to secure the use of the combined forces of Tostig and Harald of Denmark. In making this dark bargain, William took extra time and extra resources to prepare for invasion, explaining why he had delayed.

Now it was thought that invasion from Duke William would be put off for at least another year, giving King Harold time to secure himself.

In those wonderfully few days following the King's grand victory at Stamford Bridge, York opened like a flower. Shops and businesses were at once rejuvenated from the evacuation; churches and monasteries renewed their rebuilding after the Patrick the Visionary riots. The mood was equal to any festival.

More thoughtful minds were ignored.

The indestructible Thorkald lived, though reduced to bones and sinew. His past military service was extensive having fought on both sides of the sea since a boy of seventeen. As William's defeated surrogate force grew to fact from rumor, Thorkald's experiences with powerful men enabled him to see matters with a more lucid mind.

He was not optimistic.

"I cannot speak to the timing from the north, but Duke William would never throw in with Tostig or Harald, let alone both. I fought for William once and against him another time. I learned, we all did, that his heart is set on Britain and King Harold's head. He is an intrepid, wily fighter. Listen sharp for news from the south; my guess is events are fast occurring there."

And the worst happened.

Within the week, dispatch riders from the King rode through—beseeching everyone able to join the King in the south for the sake of Britain. Duke William had landed unopposed, and was readying to take on King Harold inland.

While Cwenburh tended Thorkald's wounds, along with Gunnhilda, this was a great teaching opportunity for the young woman—I sat by with that news. Cwenburh's question showed good sense and matched my own.

"Thorkald, why would not the King easily defeat one army when he just defeated two, God be praised?"

"They're Normans, Mother Cwenburh, and fight from atop horses whose size is not much less in bulk than an ox, and caparisoned in leather to protect them against weapons from the ground."

Thorkald continued to be our expert advisor: His past experiences were so thorough that as rumors flew from the south, he saw through most of them. Cwenburh and I guessed that as a professional soldier, his natural modesty would not admit that long ago he had moved beyond a soldier, but commanded and trained many foot soldiers for numerous lords and earls.

"Do not think Duke William has not come with his Normans. He is grisly in his ways when encountering resistance to his will. I fear for King Harold, especially as we have heard nothing. Few survive after losing a battle to William."

We would have given anything for him to be wrong, but he was not.

About a week before Saint Crispin Day[47], news came from the south that King Harold was defeated and slain at Hastings by Duke William. Saxons in the South did not accept him as King; hence William's forces burned and looted their way towards London, defeating all in their way.

With that catastrophic development York fell into a lower state of mind than ever. Boat traffic up the Ouse all but ceased. People began to horde food at once. Grain prices shot up even more—threefold; meat became even costlier and all else followed. In fact, all food grew dearer within the city due to these speculations. Archbishop Aldred had been

---

[47] Saint Crispin Day. October 5th.

absent for some time. This itself caused unrest, for if he had been attending Harold and his brothers, had he even survived?

Unlike in croft and fields or tiny villages, towns of size had great dependence on markets and the goods flowing to them each week.

York was even more a market city. There were twenty-five or thirty-thousand people with daily needs for sustenance there. Disruptions due to the troubles fending off Harald the Giant and Tostig knocked many farms and such sideways. Their looting and destruction disrupted harvesting, storage, and transport of all crops. This was the primary reason prices soared in York, rather than genuine want due to a poor harvest.

By the time of the festival of Saint Andrew[48], I had grown much stronger, as had Thorkald. He used a great staff to get around—and because of his military background it made him feel armed of a sort. I could now walk without support, though slowly.

We became quite the companions in our infirmities, and it gave joy to Cwenburh to have an extra man to oversee.

Thorkald was having masses said daily for his departed son, so we were on way to the church at Micklesgate for services. Not quite there, we heard with apprehension the great bell in York Minster ring—not anywhere close to an appropriate time for such peals. It was so close our heads rattled.

We diverted there and arrived at the spacious square before most. What we saw brought Thorkald to a frozen halt only a rod below at the foot of the long wide flagstone stairs: "Jesus save us. Normans!"

It had been years since soldiering in Normandy and France with free-booters. Yet Thorkald's knowledge of Normans was fixed with a profes-sional respect for those who lived from battle to battle.

There were a dozen of them.

They had brazenly ridden their proud-fleshed palfreys up the stairs—each animal worth a fortune anywhere—and there remained mounted high above us. They were armed and arrayed before the twin archway doors of the Minster, the animals' braided tails switching back and forth.

---

[48] Saint Andrew (The Apostle). November 30th.

Theirs was brazen conduct that was to reap an extraordinary result.

The bells' tolling deafened, so we could not hear the talk in the gathering assemblage behind us. When the metal giants of a sudden ceased, the voices from the crowd seemed at once quite a din. A glance to the rear revealed the crowd exceeded any I had seen there before.

One of the Normans raised himself high as possible in his stirrups and yelled in broken, barely understandable Saxon: "Quiet before your new Lord!"

A pall fell over everyone at his word. Both doors opened and Archbishop Aldred emerged with his bishops, and other churchmen all in fine vestments. He carried his mitre, and compared to the hearty Eminence who appeared with King Harold earlier that year, he had aged markedly.

His vestments hung on him, and he was not much more than bones.

We all knelt, and even the Normans dismounted and went to one knee, though keeping a weather-eye on the crowd. They were a grim lot of Normans indeed.

Invoking the words of God and Our Savior, His Eminence made the sign over us, then handed off his mitre to an assistant, and with both hands motioned for us all to rise. At once, the Normans remounted. Several of their mounts defecated and urinated—the product running down the stairs. Several of them laughed and made light of it in Norman.

"These bastards overplay it," Thorkald muttered, for it was poor enough to ride up onto the entryway platform, but quite another to find humor in its unsavory result, to so befoul a holy place.

The silence ended, and talk sprinkled through the crowd—like pebbles cast over the surface of water, each word producing a dozen others.

I craned a backward look; indeed there were thousands crowded into the square and approaches, meaning all exits and entrances were clogged with York residents. Not one of them had any love for mounted armed Normans who conducted themselves like pagan tribesmen.

Archbishop Aldred commenced speaking, and without device of word or gesture—in no way couching his message conveyed the disaster: King Harold was dead; likewise, his brothers were dead, and his sons in hiding. His Saxon army was defeated and mostly annihilated by

William and his Normans. Duke William had this week been crowned and anointed King of England by His Eminence himself at Westminster. This anointing was done with full agreement by the Holy Father, Alexander, Bishop of Rome.

William's first act was to confiscate all lands and rights in the name of the King, both in croft and town—though giving us rights as tenants if we maintained our taxes. We would live on for the time being under our old Saxon laws. Lastly, our new Earl of Northumbria, a Norman, was vested with King William's powers, full confidence, and trust.

Absolute obedience and loyalty were expected and William demanded an Oath of Fealty from each of us.

Finished, His Eminence looked up sadly, took back his mitre and, with clear sadness, gave way the center to the Norman who had called for silence. Using the same inept Saxon, he ordered in a loud voice, "You heard His Eminence: All kneel and clasp your hands together and repeat the oath after me."

No one moved. We all stared. For to the person of us, no Saxon or person raised under Saxon or Daneslaw ever conceived or dreamed that a Norman would become our absolute ruler, much less take away all our land and property in a single clap of greed and power.

For both these messages to fall upon our shoulder at once was like convincing all to believe crickets recited psalms and birds chirped the gospels.

"I said, all kneel, clasp your hands together and repeat the oath you shall hear."

At once, His Eminence stepped forward and struck up a conciliatory tone with them in French, but within a few words the exchange became heated, with one of the Normans—in charge, but unable to speak Saxon, or not wanting to—pointed at us, made an emphatic gesture, which cut the Archbishop short.

All within the same moment, the crowd's energy increased in heat and volume, and the Archbishop, his anger also roused, stepped forward and pointed at all the Normans, raising his mitre.

I was close and could understand enough Norman to appreciate that His Eminence threatened them, for their horses fell back somewhat, and the men looked at one another.

Looking hotly at His Eminence, they turned—glared out over the crowd, the same spokesmen shouting, "We shall come back, and you will do as ordered right enough, you whipped halfbreeds."

While he shouted this on the crowd, His Eminence and the churchmen re-entered the Minster; then the Normans began to withdraw, easing their horses down the stairs. No one moved out of the way.

Most men present at least had a staff, a few others knives or some such portable weapon—and many were young enough to be in strong flesh. They were thoroughly angered at this devastation delivered by the enemy. Plainly put, the haughty Normans realized at a glance that despite their arms and horses, they were but a dozen, and surrounded by at least three or four thousand angry York residents.

The final epithet had done it, and several from the crowd called, "We will not allow you Norman dogs out of here alive."

And in a surge which pushed aside me and those too aged or infirm, the crowd moved forward on all sides as if a single beast.

Thorkald yelled, "Grab my belt—follow, Cuthwin. We must get out."

The Norman horses were unsure of themselves on stairs, and if on flat ground might have bounded forward and their great weight may have saved the rider, but not on the stairs which were numerous before the Minster.

So with mortal outcry, the Normans bellowed, their horses whinnied in alarm and tumbled downward, rolling over on rider and attacker alike and beginning a frenzy of thrashing to regain footing. But it was useless; in seconds, all were down and pounced on by the masses.

Thorkald pulled me away, and a parting grisly vision was of the mob tearing riders apart, weapons raised and lowered as high and fast as possible, and all of them red with flowing blood.

Horses tried to rise, but several of their riders had lances, and these had been seized by some of the crowd and thrust into the animals, bringing them down for good.

All was a ghastly jumble before this irrational livid tide of humanity, and the Normans were dead and torn asunder before Thorkald and I were shut of the area. Behind us were screams and the pathetic outcries of the slaughtered horses. It had been a calamitous error for all involved—the murderers and murdered. Now, blood ran profusely down the steps.

"The horses are now so much meat, and their riders will join their brothers in hell, the stupid shits."

Thorkald moved me along through the streets, and despite his infirmity and emaciated form, I was impressed with his strength.

When he reached home, we barred the door behind us, and while I told Cwenburh and others the horror of things, Thorkald likewise barred the rear doors to river and dock. He then busied himself by moving aside a strip of batting and pulling out his sword, possibly secreted away on the night he arrived—despite his wounds and lamentation of his dead dying son. He faced a horrified Cwenburh.

"Oh, may God help us, Thorkald. What possessed them so!?"

"Hate for Normans, Mother Cwenburh. We must prepare to be gone. Any Norman Lord brooks no such calumny from commoners, much less Duke William, now so-called King. He will kill all of us sure as there is Satan in hell."

I too knew—so well—that Thorkald recited the absolute truth and time was precious. Cwenburh herded the girls together, and all fell to their knees in prayer.

By killing a dozen, the mob had assured the near total destruction of York.

Thereafter, God seemingly abandoned all Saxons, as it had King Harold at the calamity with Duke William. In fact, we learned that Holy Father Alexander-of-Rome gave his blessings to brutish William in his invasion of England. The carnage that followed William's conquest—his elimination of Saxons by class—showed he lacked the remotest foundations of Our Savior's gospels. Also, I believe to this moment that it was God who had temporarily abandoned the Holy Father, afflicting him with the sins of ambition and avarice.

So it was the Saxon folk who in varying numbers survived William's scourge and lived on under the toil of the Normans. True, the Saxon nobles and clerics who acquiesced fully to William lived on as well.

But, it was the commonality who raised the foods, crafted the needs, and mended the broken that continued life under the teachings of Our Savior, necessitating watching their Saxon ways vanish in the years that followed. It is my belief, perhaps foolishly, that God resides with the innocent, not the guilty.

Book 7

Saint Cuthwin in company with others travels to the south from the tragedy and violence at York. Despite Cuthwin's struggles, all he loves is swept away by the demonic actions of savage Normans and Saxon turncoats. He then deals with the anguish of this loss and its earthly necessities. Resuming travel to the south he joins with devout Eadwig and survivors of his holy station. After seeing his most blessed son off to Rome, St. Cuthwin travels west to the wilds of Kernowec. He maroons himself on a rocky islet off the coast with modest belongings. There he meditates in prayer with God, His Savior, and the diverse Saints. He works for the purity of his body and soul, and thusly becomes Cuthwin the Fence Builder. He is consulted by various faithful as he grows to great age and wisdom; therefore, by his ninth decade of life, becomes known throughout Pydar as Saint Cuthwin, the Fence Builder. During this time, he begins and completes the telling of his august life to the Brothers of St. Kea Monastery.

Here through hard work and contemplation of all his travels, he lives on to advanced age and wisdom.

In the months following the bloody scene before the Minster, the question was not *if* one should flee but *to where*. Thorkald's assurance of the grimmest retribution by the Normans never diminished, despite the ongoing series of Saxon resistance in the north.

Still, what concerned myself—and Cwenburh—was always where to flee?

A hodgepodge of news, rumors, and actual fact mixed a demon's brew. As a scribe myself, and former master to York's best known scribe and shop, I was privy to events north and south. The business of copying and letter writing became so hectic that once again I was called in several times a week to help with the overload. Oslaf was wearing his hand out.

In addition to these sweeping concerns, there was disruption in his shop and house. When Gunnhilda gave birth to a daughter, Oslaf's overbearing parents rejected a child birthed by a mute. They convinced extended families on both sides to shun the child and mother.

Oslaf's home became an isolated place.

Cwenburh got involved. She was blessedly having luck in finding freeborn positions for her girls, three being apprenticed to local, responsible fullers. But she and I differed on the situation in Oslaf's household.

"Is not there enough strife in our everyday life not to take on more, Cwenburh?"

She was irrepressible when it came to right and wrong and showing compassion according to Our Savior's teachings.

Somewhat diminishing his positive stature before the womenfolk, Thorkald had taken a homeless widow to bed on occasion. The poor thing, somewhat on the homely side, mistook the occasion for permanence.

Hence between armies being raised to the south, west, east, and north, I had to deal with domestic issues, plus those of proper craft at the shop. It seemed, as Oslaf said, "everyone wanted to write every soul in England and Northumbria."

After Compline, Oslaf would come to the cooperage and, in private—from one scribe to another—we would share contents of missives, and it was not good.

Normans and their thralls would come north, only to encounter well-armed and expertly commanded armies of Saxon or those hostile to Norman rule who prevailed each time.

Thorkald got word of these battles, and gave them little hope in the long run. "Duke William is not here; when he is, and has time, he will come north with great force, as sure as the Lord created all before us."

Eventually, by the spring of the year, we decided on the opposite direction of the troubles—north, to Cumbria.

As if our plans were privy to demons, word arrived from Cumbria in the form of refugees: Several vicious dragons, they asserted, loosed themselves upon various villages and towns there, employing special venom and brimstone fires upon the kin and those loyal to King Malcom of Scotland, the feared Lord of Cumbria.

Clearly these worms were messengers of retribution for the many heathen violations perpetrated in the far north.

That put us back at the beginning, for nobody sane would venture into a nest of dragons awakened from long slumbers due to one outrage or another. Cumbria was eliminated, which disappointed me badly, for seeking safety in the opposite direction of the troubles and violence struck me as best.

Now it was summer, this one hot and dry. Most of this time, the whereabouts of King William was not known with any sureness: Some said Normandy, some said Mercia. Then, typical of base evil-doers—the greediest and most opportune of them—appeared to fish in sullied water.

Once more, ships and men came from Denmark under princes there; in fact, the first of them had arrived. So with Danes coming from the east with hundreds of ships and William and his army eventually coming from the south, there was no more hope. It was time to leave.

In the midst of these troubles, despite all, Oslaf, paying a greedy priest coin, was united to Gunnhilda in Holy Matrimony. At the cooperage, we had a fine wedding feast for them, making a wedding briar in an alcove for them.

As a morning gift, before all of us, Oslaf gave Gunnhilda an arm ring of pure silver, set with a single, marvelous pearl in the middle. About that time, his father, very much in his cups, burst in and made a scene. Thorkald—also in his cups—tossed the father onto the street, and Cwenburh did what she could to comfort the bride and groom from this outrage.

Matilda mistook it all for a mime, and laughed and pounded on the boards. I knew this was the death knell of peace and domesticity for Oslaf, and it was a grand exit at that.

Surely it was at this time that God's Grace fell upon us: We received a letter from Eadwig, now Abbot at Eynsham Abbey. He urged us to venture there, where Abbey lands could be rented to all or any of us, joking that he had good rumor the landlord was just and fair.

He assured us that the troubles between King William and Saxon Monasteries had been well resolved by His Eminence, the new Archbishop of Canterbury. In fact, Abbot Eadwig's letter was hand-delivered by Prior Walter of Hempstead, who with two other brothers from Eynsham Abbey, represented Abbot Eadwig at the funeral mass for Archbishop Aldred.

To us, with our family being together again, this was an overwhelming temptation, though Thorkald took a cautious view of it.

In fact, Thorkald and myself had repaired our health as well as old men can. One true and God-given gift was that we had become as a family: Ours consisted of myself, Cwenburh, Matilda, Thorkald, and the now-fifteen girls; also a young boy named Alf who had pretended to be a girl and was found out.

Alf, at eight years of age, was an imp and tested Cwenburh and Gunnhilda's patience and Christian forgiveness.

Thorkald demonstrated that turning Alf over and spanking his bottom did far more with him than any other appeals. Soon Alf wanted to be a soldier like Thorkald and stuck to him constantly, asking about his adventures in diverse armies. Additionally, the hapless Sara—devoted to Thorkald—was now swelling.

Cwenburh and I, having good silver coin, knew this was the key benefit that made this trek of fifty leagues possible. We had learned much about traveling being on the begang for over a dozen years.

In the end, Eynsham and Eadwig it was.

We purchased wagons and animals—with an extra rouncey[49] for scouting ahead and replacement in the case of loss. Taking main roads would be dangerous, so calling on our experience and Thorkald's knowledge, we would ply the lesser ways with terrain inhospitable to a large army, mounted or otherwise. Though this would add distance, safety was the highest consideration.

It was several days after Lammas when we set out. Oslaf and Gunnhilda—now with an infant daughter—I knew would be hardest for us to bid goodbye on that morning. We were surprised—to say the least—when they both arrived with a foot-drawn wagon, Oslaf announcing, "We would like to go with you? I could set up shop close to the Abbey— the closest town? Would Father Eadwig mind, do you think?"

We of course—in fact, joyfully—welcomed them, but I felt responsible to ask after his shop—his investment, his parents.

"I told them they could have it. I would no longer tolerate their cruelty to Gunnhilda and my daughter. Anyway, I was the shop; without it, it is but a place to buy writing materials. I take my craft with me, and I thank you, God, and Our Savior for that, and for my wife and child. They are my world now, God be praised."

This was a bold step. We all gathered in a circle that day and knelt in common prayer for God's protection en route. I will always prize the friendship of good Oslaf as one of my crowning achievements over the ninety-odd years, and if my influence was such that he came with us that morning, I pray to God for forgiveness.

When we left York I looked back—stopping in my track and gazing at what had been my home for seven years. I would never see it again—nor within a year would anyone else—not like it was. That moment became etched vividly in my mind. I turned and caught up with the others, a sadness in each step.

---

[49] Rouncey. A horse that may both pull and be ridden.

We directed west, away from all old established roads.

The heat is what I remember most. It was difficult for the animals; the children rode during the heat of day; also, they rode in the early mornings before sunup, children's blood being thick early.

The girls were over seven or eight years of age by now, but not yet women, and they walked well enough when content. However, growing weary, they would often fight among themselves, and in temper they would sit—obstinately vowing never to walk again in company of the other—in fact, they would swear to die before moving.

Not a few times, Cwenburh—or now even meek Sara—just grabbed a recalcitrant ward by the leg, and dragged her along, saying, "Then, in God's faith, we will drag you, rather than leave you for the wolves or gargoyles."

Being three-hands taller and thicker than most men, Thorkald was a powerful hiker, even with the imp Alf atop his shoulders serving as 'look-out,' as he put it. He would always precede us by many furlongs, coming back to alert us to one thing or another.

Thorkald had a diffident relationship with Sara. He and Cwenburh, who had become like sister and brother, were always on the margins of arguing about Sara, for Cwenburh took her part absolutely. I avoided talking directly—even indirectly—about the entire situation; I thank God for such practical wisdom.

The strain of a long trek always tired the children and Matilda first, and then Sara and Gunnhilda, though despite her years, Cwenburh retained the strength in being able to walk forever. Because of this all, we often set camp before sunset. We had so much daylight remaining, Thorkald, myself, or both would get astride Mouse. This was the name that for some unfathomable reason the children gave 'their' rouncey. We would ride a long way to serve as van for the next day.

From the first day, there was an uneasy silence upon the land. There was no clear reason that we could see: It was summer, and save for the heat of the day, a favorable time for travelers. The roads, though smaller and ill-kept, were nothing an experienced traveler could not deal with. Yet we would encounter no one, not one traveler. Neither I nor Thorkald liked this, and he was uneasy but would voice it only with me.

"Since my sixteenth spring, I spent the following thirty in hostile land, Master Cuthwin, and quiet is never good, God help us."

Each evening camp Thorkald remained on the highest scrutiny, and it took little convincing from Thorkald for myself and Oslaf to stand night watch from Matins through Prime.

Throughout the first week—entirely uneventful—we had almost perfect traveling conditions.

Thorkald informed all adults about the answer to the mystery of seeing few people when the children slept and would not hear: "It is as I suspected, we pass by people who have hidden from us, probably hearing us furlongs before the seeing. There is fear everywhere we travel south. I think I might nose some of these out coming from the south and ask them what is ahead."

The next day, well before Sext, Thorkald walked in pushing three frightened cottars before him, two women and a man. Seeing that we had children and women with us, they became at once easier about being marched in by strength of arms. They were indeed fleeing north.

To the southeast, the man spoke of great trouble with sacking and mayhem everywhere. Mounted thanes, housecarls and lower forms swept down taking everything edible, then burned all remaining while the occupants watched from hiding.

"They laughed and made sport of it, God curse them."

"Normans?"

"We could not tell. I have never seen one."

They had known nothing of the royal troubles; in fact they thought Edward was still King. What was significant to them—as all who live by their hand—everything was being looted and burned by men of power.

The man had enough of it all. "My wife has kin north."

We gave them bread and some flour, and they proceeded north.

Thorkald was uneasy about them—or indeed anyone we might meet.

"With all those girls in view, we carry a small fortune, even if we had not a pence with us. No one on the road keeps a cautious tongue. To inform someone of our human bounty would warrant a few coins, surely. We are too open, and must employ more craft. We might consider making hidden camp and keep a surer watch."

Cwenburh began to be saddled with guilt. She feared the girls might be swept up in any one of many troublesome situations. In the night she and I talked of all the events and fears of the day past and coming.

"I might have settled the girls early with fullers or millers; anything. Especially the boy."

"Oh? And everything that was happening by the week? No, Cwenburh, we barely had time ourselves; it seems that every Godless army under heaven invaded us within sixty days' time."

I had, by her example, become somewhat reconciled with the compassionate teaching of Our Savior, and at the end of each evening, we would pray together—and always included many prayers for safe passage. We did everything we could; now we were in God's hands.

To Thorkald's dismay we did not travel on Sabbath during the month of August, unless forced by lay of the land. On the day before, the old soldier would face off with Cwenburh who maintained that to break God's law would be to invite more trouble. They would quarrel, standing close like mismatched jackdaws.

Sara would try to mollify events, but too often she just drew mean comment from Thorkald, and it all went around and around.

Oslaf and I kept our silence. In my view, our party needed the rest of body equal to the rest of spirit and soul, and Sabbath contributed to the mix.

Like most of Christendom we rested on Sabbaths.

It was not yet Sext the day before Sabbath, and by Thorkald and my reckoning, we had come about twenty-five leagues from York. This is the first time we encountered a settlement of more than a few cottages. It was a frightful sight; with God's grace and fortune we had come across the disaster before all others.

Thorkald and I had scent of it before sight, for the wind carried the carnage to us.

It was days since the event, and the stench overpowered. Hundreds of rooks gathered; wolves scattered the bodies, consuming most. It was smaller but equally gruesome to the butchery I saw in Oakheath Manor.

"Let us get back at once."

Thorkald's voice was crisp with urgency. We turned back striding quickly—so fast, Thorkald would have left me had he not intermittently waited for me to catch up.

At camp, he said nothing. Unhitching Mouse, he removed the rest of his arms from the wagon. By chance, since Alf had been making times miserable for girls, the boy was confined to the wagon—yet in fact escaping. He was then tethered by a line around his ankle to a barrel with the girls minding the imp didn't undo it and run off. If not for this business, surely he would have seen the carnage from atop Thorkald's shoulders.

Mounted upon Mouse, Thorkald warned us all to make camp early—a cold camp well hidden. Then stay put until he returned. He went back in the direction of the carnage at a trot—armed with sword and lance and stout Danish helmet. He was private with his plans or intentions.

It was difficult to answer all questions at the same moment, but with Cwenburh, the full weight of what we saw was conveyed when I likened it to Oakheath. She at once followed Thorkald's instructions.

Even though our camp was a league distant, occasionally the wind would carry whiffs of death with it. A few of the children became ill; overhead, more rooks flocked in that direction—black demons intent on bounty.

Cwenburh directed the making of the hidden camp. Though only a hundred paces off the narrow roadway, it was virtually invisible.

Oslaf and I were shifty, worried—why should we not go forward; we had stout cudgels by this time? What happens if Thorkald is overpowered by whatever worried him?

By now Thorkald and I were fast friends, yet he never talked about his soul to me; but piecing together what he said variously, I understood that he felt fatherly guilt over his deceased son.

"He was too young, Master Cuthwin, and I should have opposed it."

Never a word about his soul, or God's punishment for his profession as soldier, but few souls prayed more fervently.

Every hour he was gone, our anxiety rose. Cwenburh and I sat next to each other, for the burden of losing our friend and his wise counsel was forbidding.

Then, late in the day, he returned; Mouse was spattered with gore, as was Thorkald. So weary was he, we thought him wounded. He slid from the rouncey, removed his helmet, looked around, and offered apologetically, "I washed my weapons, but I was too tired for the rest, God forgive me."

Then he collapsed by the hearth, no fire yet burning.

"We can have a fire; they are all dead now."

I sensed another dreadful fatigue, this of mind and heart.

"God forbid, how many were there?

"Dozens, Master Cuthwin."

We stood around him in a circle; he allowed Sara to help him off with his sullied outers. When the fire began, he sat heavily next to it, looked into the flames with eyes heavy and sadder than any I ever saw. He managed to gain his feet, then crawled under the closest cart and fell into a deep trance-like sleep.

Sara joined him there with a cape; she put it over him, Thorkald rolling over towards her. Then both slept.

We prayed together until the Sabbath arrived, and then—me taking the first watch—our group rested as best we might.

It was a warm, humid night, and the creatures were quiet, unlike those creatures on a late summer night. I looked hard, listened harder, but heard nothing. I never knew the life of a soldier and wondered if all the killing and violence is forgiven by God—or if such killing can be forgiven by God?

Cwenburh crept up behind. She sat next to me. Being always fey, she read well my musings. "Cuthwin, I think God's forgiveness is boundless. I feel sad for poor Thorkald who thinks himself doomed."

"He has said this to you?"

"He has."

We leaned against each other. I was having problems with my own faith, so had special empathy for others who too had misgivings about the heart of God. Cwenburh became even heavier against me and I saw she had fallen asleep.

I offered up a prayer, thanking God for bringing my wife back; she had done considerable to repair my torn spirit.

Silence spread from under the canopy of elms and oaks—their branches reaching almost to the ground giving sanctuary to everything underneath. I listened and watched, gently wrapped my arm around Cwenburh, and felt the night pass us by in the form of a frail breeze from the north. But though cooling, it did not carry feelings of optimism. In this foreboding moment, the strangeness of memories intruded. My mind wandered back a half century: There was the round face of my mother, Sarah-of-Alnwick. She tells one of her great stories, though I cannot tell which. She smiles grandly upon me, her son, always to be Cuthwin-of-Alnwick, indubitably her son. In these memories I slept.

No one spoke much upon rising; we made a very small fire with the driest of wood, and the smoke barely rose above the branches, and then in the tiniest of threads, disappeared.

As usual, the girls were cranky when we resumed. Thorkald walked ahead a few furlongs, and seeing he still was in a somber mood I over-took him walking alongside. Even at a stroll his strides quickly consumed the rods.

He knew my concerns about the events. He explained that house-carls, thanes, and such on the business of harrying and looting had human jackals called 'drudges' following in the wake of the horsemen and squires.

"These drudges fight from an unspoken agreement: After the town or fort is lost, they are given leave to scavenge for anything remaining, Drudges know their business, are ruthless, and follow their ways for years.

It was them I saw. They saw us, too, and were following, of course."

He offered no more. I knew he would pick up the pace now, and get farther ahead, but about that time Alf caught up—having awakened fully. He was too young to perceive Thorkald's mood, and the poor little waif asked to follow him on watch.

"Boy, how might I refuse a fellow soldier?"

He slung him like a wallet up on his shoulder, and off they went— Thorkald's strides twice mine.

I let the carts catch up, and by mid-morning the girls were over their crankiness and bounding about like hares. Sara and Cwenburh chased them around making something of a game of it. Matilda tried to intercept one of them, but though she had become far more mobile, would have more luck catching squirrels.

Coming up last were Gunnhilda and Oslaf, him carrying the infant, while he was being hand-fed last bits of bread by Gunnhilda. I had momentary regret about Cwenburh and I never having had that experience—to carry our child, passing it one to the other, and looking down upon it, surely one of God's greatest gifts.

But this was envy, and I struggled to sweep it away. Beneath the canopy of aged, towering oak branches, we traveled the road which paralleled a small stream, but a trickle in summer.

I walked along, for all of us had fallen into our usual formation and pace.

My first warning was feeling the fall of heavy horse in the ground, then the sound of them from my rear. I looked back to see with unbridled fear a dozen horsemen trotting up slowly from behind us; the litter-strewn path muffled the palfreys' hoof-falls.

Olsaf had fallen back to act as rear observer; and this duty hastened his tragic end. I turned towards the arrivals—for at the moment, none of the others had seen them yet.

Seeing fear in my eyes, Cwenburh turned and saw them, and then all the others. The lead horseman dumped a dead Oslaf on the ground. The half-dozen other horsemen came on slowly, threading their way between and around the wagons keenly appraising them.

Gunnhilda ran, and fell upon Oslaf, and Sara only had a moment to take the infant, her face a mask of dread.

I made them to be Norman and Saxon, a grisly assortment. I stopped, bending down to attend Oslaf to see if he lived. Cwenburh managed to warn: "Here come more, Cuthwin."

Indeed another dozen approached from the south—they joined their fellows, they too appraising their windfall. Two of their horses had dead men draped across them. The second in line tossed Alf on the ground, his leg twisted and broken, and bleeding badly.

Two of them—Normans—were arrayed with better tackle and armor than the others, and their palfreys were fully fleshed with the sheen resulting from expert grooming. The one removed his helmet, and looked back momentarily at the bodies slung across their horses. I understood the Norman only with difficulty, but I understood and saw enough. "That lout of yours fought like the very devil, and killed two of my housecarls, the old bastard." Then he took a breath and asked, "So what have we here?"

"His name was Thorkald. Is he dead?"

"Dead? Of course he is dead. That boy there will soon follow him. He was handled a bit roughly by one of my dumb Saxon shits. He fled but tumbled into a gorge. We wasted time retrieving him. He is worthless now."

He switched to a plain, matter-of-fact Saxon, the type used for the routine business of arranging for a sale of cattle or sheep.

"Now listen carefully, Saxon: The adults will live if they give me no trouble, like that damned giant on your van. We will take all else worth more than a pence, especially those price-worthy as slaves. I am Baron Hervey de Bourges, liegeman to Hugo of Bourges—your new Lord in this demesne and soks. Address me as Master."

At this one of his men tore off the covers from the wagons, and all the girls who had hid there were found, and our true human composition was revealed. There was immediate jubilation; the fellow next to the leader shouted, "By St. Martin, we have made a fortune. Where did you get all the young quim, you old kipper? Are you some sort of whoremonger—husbander of whores? Praise the Lord, but we are well set here."

Cwenburh got at once between him and the closest of the girls—a group of three huddled against a wagon wheel. Her Norman was more fluent than mine: "Mind you, these are free-born girls, all of them on their way to Eynsham Abbey, wards of the Abbot and Abbess of St. Mary's in York."

Oh, the horror of that moment: She had forgotten how worthless our lives were to brutes like these—greedy beyond description.

I stepped forward to pull Cwenburh back to me, but had a lance put smack in my gut, almost cutting. Master Hugo looked down at Cwenburh while drawing, "I told you not to make trouble. Are you all deaf?"

And he murdered dear Cwenburh with a single back swing of his sword. An instant base act by this foul sort of creature erased all that was so rich and meaningful to every soul she touched.

I knocked the lance aside, and fell next to her bleeding body.

"My God! What have you done?!"

Matilda dashed in next to me, also slipping beneath the lance and falling on her mother. In her anguish, as at any time she became over-wrought—her speech departed, and instead her tongue formed only a mishmash. Our poor girl had aged prematurely of late: her hair was grey, and most had fallen out, making her wound and the shape of her head even more apparent. Worse, Gunnhilda joined her at Cwenburh's fallen body, and true to Oslaf's word, she did make voice—a strange wobbling screech. At once, another horseman to my rear warned, "My God, demon women, look at the one and listen to the other babble."

And reached down, wrenched first Matilda upwards; drawing her close he unsheathed a knife and slit her throat. He then tossed her aside quickly, seized Gunnhilda and began to cut. I yelled—rather bellowed, "Mercy, for God's sakes. She is a deaf mute."

He completed the act and tossed her atop Matilda; their blood joined.

"Avoid their blood, brothers; it is the stuff of demons. It has venom in it."

I went senseless with shock and dumbness—a sort of grief perhaps experienced by helpless cattle at slaughter.

Some of the murderers dismounted and began to look through our belongings. They already argued over the division of coin to be gleaned for this grand find of many young girls, whom they all referred to as virgins. Pulling Gunnhilda's daughter from Sara's arms, they quarreled over whether an infant would draw any money at all, some saying it would, others not.

Master Hugo shouted at them to shut up. "Let the slave dealer decide, you greedy, ignorant turds!"

All the while Sara remonstrated for the girls' and infant's well-being as best she could, until finally she was struck hard in mid-protestations, sending her to the ground. Their master's voice was weary, dealing with his victims' repeated stupidities.

"Careful there. She is swelling with child, cannot you even see a pregnant Saxon, you dumb shit? She will draw extra price, plus we will need help with this many young virgins, God be Praised. And mind you they stay virgins, you worthless lot of pig fornicators."

Master Hugo's fellow pulled me off Cwenburh, and pushed me before his master, who had dismounted and sat on the tongue of a cart taking a hasty repast of meat and bread; a squire brought him a cup of fresh water: "You know old fellow, your lout killed a cousin of Baron Hervey de Bourges. I was supposed to be looking after him. Now I have much to explain."

"Tell his Lordship he will burn in hell as will you all."

Another sat close by, also taking refreshment. He laughed around a mouthful of food. Master Hugo squinted at me, squelched a smile, then shrugged the matter away. "He is in France and will be absent some time or I would tell him. Otherwise I might keep you around. Skinning Saxon pissants alive and tossing tanning salt on them amuses His Lordship and all of us." He thought a moment, handed off his cup to the squire, and rose, "...but I said any who would not give me trouble would live. From the looks of it, you're worse off alive anyway."

He ordered all to mount up—some led riderless horses whose owners had duties driving the wagons. They rode off with everything, leaving behind only those whom they murdered. All had encountered a calamitous end. For the living, there was only a procession of young girls—a swelling Sara carrying Oslaf and Gunnhilda's daughter—a slave train headed for a pit of serfdom perhaps even in a foreign land.

All this loss—the taking of my dearest at heart—within the brief span of a few minutes by the hand of a wretch who would probably forget his deed a week later.

For the moment, I thought I was the only one who lived, until I heard a moan from Alf. Going to him, I saw his legs twisted and broken, the bones protruding, and he had lost so much blood his face was white as a mushroom.

I was smitten: The dying boy and the slain bodies—and wherever they left poor Thorkald—would be dragged off by wolves. I had to do something and quickly. It was ghastly—all of it. The boy groaned; I looked about gaping—helpless as a fish.

The boy Alf breathed very slowly and I recovered enough where-withall to make the poor boy comfortable as possible. He never knew a home or any comfort beyond that short time with us.

I knew it was not yet Sext, and decided I must first deal with the living and attend the dead when I might. So much devastation was visited on all so matter of factly, I was stupefied. There was no horror in my heart nor instinct to lament—or urge to cry out to heaven. For the hours following this disaster I lifted limb like a puppet, and I thought simply. I could—in my mind—realize the infamy that had befallen, yet I cannot ponder that God saw fit to spare me.

I made a fire—or somehow there was a fire; it could have been just as readily made by the murdering scum. I did put pine boughs on it over dry wood. There was little wind and the smoke lay thick over the bodies, keeping the flies and vermin off. I prayed over Alf, but well before sunset he passed into the arms of Our Savior, Jesus Christ, protector of all innocents.

Suddenly I heard the jingle of metal against metal, and loud talking, then the stomp of hooves.

I darted into the stream, crossed it, and ducked under overgrowth of water celery and such that lolled over the bank.

From cover I saw three men afoot leading a mule piled almost to overflow with diverse booty, a virtual shopkeeper's animal being led to a fair.

As they came, the trio argued, but spotting the smoke and bodies, one called out the alert and went over to each lifeless being, coughing because of the thickening layer of smoke.

"Norman assholes left little. Oh, God curse this wretched smoke! They took the whole lot of it—probably pried the very wheel tracks out of the mud, the bastards. Not much here. Clothes."

"Clothes. Balls! We have all sorts of clothes. Look sharp: purses, wallets?"

"What?! These are gone, or they never had them. Kick that fucking fire out. Jesus save us!"

They did so while looking greedily around.

They were the lowest sorts. I saw slung over the mule, Thorkald's turnshoes, his tunic, and even his linen underclothing. I reached down into the stream and removed four fine smooth throwing rocks just somewhat larger than a hen's egg. Only one of the three men had a cudgel, the others staffs, and all had knives in waistbands.

I would not stand here and watch them take the clothes from my murdered wife's body, so I made some room for a good throw, dug my feet in and waited.

Better, I knew, was for them to move on, but they were the sorts who—like after the carnage at Oakheath—utilized the dead for their advantage. As Thorkald called them, drudges.

They decided Oslaf's clothes were best—absolutely clear of blood. The man with a cudgel—closest to the mule—left the others to attend Oslaf and instead turned Cwenburh over, appraising her shoes; then he started to remove them.

His head was uncovered, and smaller than a large melon—within two wagons lengths of me. I took aim, was almost ready to throw when a great exclamation aired from the two drudges who worried poor Oslaf's body: "Ayyyye! We are in luck. They missed it. Jesus bless us!"

His companion dropped Cwenburh's leg, and moved next to his two sordid colleagues. Kicking one aside, he reached down and snatched away what I recognized was Gunnhilda's morning gift. Like all newly wedded Saxon husbands, it was given by the proud Oslaf on the first morning after the holy words graced their union.

It was a beautiful silver arm ring—designed and wrought by the finest silversmith in York. That morning Gunnhilda had sat flat on the floor, stuck out her leg and tried to slide it over her foot. She was an odd girl; she struggled to reach her foot—her belly being so large with their daughter—she bit her lip, fighting to slide an arm ring over her foot.

At that moment, this unlikely scene strained even my sense of protocol versus the almost unstoppable urge to laugh.

Oslaf stopped her and put it on her arm; she sprang up—showed it to everyone, then took it off and put it on Oslaf's arm. He had said, "No, no! It is for the bride—for you!" And he put it back on her arm, and she laughed—and it went back and forth.

Odd girl, such an odd girl.

Afterwards you never knew whose arm it might be on, for it became a jest between them—but perhaps more than that: Cwenburh was sure Gunnhilda understood it as their symbol of linkage.

And that morning it had been on Oslaf's arm, and his long woolen tunic had hidden it from the Normans.

But not from these three.

They whooped and capered—the one holding it aloft. It was worth more than three mules piled with sundry equipment from croft and stable and they knew it. Abruptly, they became members of the worried rich.

"What if they come back, the bastards?"

They stood stock still, looking up trail at once, like stoats trying to catch scent.

"Let's get the hell out of here now and go back south."

But like most mules burdened too heavily, their beast would not resume at their demand. Not only was it loaded with twice the weight it should, I saw at once it was strange to them.

"Oh, damn the beast. Piss on it. Easy come easy go."

They cut lines, shoved everything off it, and quickly sorted through for what they judged the finest articles. Stuffing each of their traveling wallets full, they slung them over their shoulders.

They started back south at almost a trot.

Then I was alone.

I re-crossed the stream, fell upon my knees beside Cwenburh, and thanked God I had not become a murderer, like so many else that day.

With a fine stone—at such close range I still retained great accuracy. I had aimed for his long, ropy neck and it would have killed him at once. Then, leaping over and grabbing his cudgel, everything after that was a guess.

But, praise be to God it did not happen.

I dragged the bodies together, pushed aside the pile of junk the mule carried, and found a badly chipped adz, its handle broken. It was not portable enough for the cowardly bastards.

I remembered Thorkald up trail. I judged there to be enough light remaining to find and fetch him, return my dear friend here for burial with his family. I rebuilt the fire, put even more dry wood and green branches upon it, and left a vast developing fog of smoke behind me.

I proceeded south in search but could see no rooks gathering—a sure sign of a body. Finally, I knew I had gone too far. How far ahead had Thorkald gotten? So involved was I in searching, when I turned—a rod or so behind me—I saw the recalcitrant mule following dutifully, dragging its line behind, deciding on its own accord to join me.

Going up to it, I led it to a nearby oak stump, and stepped up on it. A massive-sized jackass, it looked back at me, and allowed me to slowly climb on. With its line the only sway I had, I surmised it was used to riders, or at least some.

Into the night I dug graves. My mind—its memory remained stilled. I moved uphill a ways to dig the six graves where the stream would not flood. I allowed a good high fire, working by its light though that night. Perhaps I needed its energy rather than light, for the fullest of late summer moons rose casting light across all—summoning the ghost world that live in all forests. I attempted unsuccessfully to hobble the mule, yet it grazed contentedly enough until it caught scent of wolves; it then became upset and began voluble braying. Its infernal complaint rattled the tree trunks, but served purpose of telling the wolves that with fire, man, and mule, this was no place for an easy meal.

I lamented my failure in finding Thorkald's body, for the carrion beasts would certainly not. Only tiny wedges of the disaster began to peek through my mental shroud of misery.

I labored the best part of three days, and did a respectful job of interring my poor Cwenburh, daughter Matilda and friends, making stone markers with their names upon them, and holy sign atop each. During these hours a profound sadness and despair crept into me, and I would sit long periods in reveries, sometimes weeping.

Twice travelers passed, said prayers at the graves, gave me condolences, even bread, then moved on. An elderly couple returning to the village of their birth told me that north or south, it made no difference.

"There is nothing but mayhem now," the 'Frenchmen'—as the man termed the Normans—inflicting destruction on Saxons. "It is this new King William, Pilgrim. He is without mercy."

I spent the fourth or fifth morning pacing before the graves praying— not wanting to leave. My family, save Eadrig, were here in this peaceful grove, their eternal resting place.

Matilda had such a poor life after her violent abduction from Oakheath—and the boy Alf, hardly no life at all.

The cruel and utterly thoughtless horror of Cwenburh's murder had a dark, menacing hold on my soul. I resolved to forgive them in the name of our Savior, as she would have done, no matter how long it took. But in those initial days, I plumbed baser desires, even praying that immolation be meted out to her murderers in the eternal fires of the Archfiend.

I knew then, as I do now, that regardless how long I lived and where I might be bound after death, memories of wonderful and loving Cwenburh would go with me. Holy words written and spoken maintain there is a paradise in heaven. If so it will have a long, languid river flowing through. And Cwenburh would certainly be alongside it, young and stouthearted in faith and youth. She would be sitting on the low branch of an oak, legs swinging, waiting for me—praying for me.

For as it says in the Old Book, mortal souls before God have life spans that are a mere handbreadth to God, and wherever or whenever my end would arrive, it would only seem a breath and loving sigh to Cwenburh, who waited.

I had not gone two leagues when the mule and I—it had decided not to bear my weight yet followed me closely—scared off wild dogs from a gravesite a good half-furlong above the road which still followed the course of the stream.

They had dirt on their muzzles, and ran in terror from the mule who had come alive and given chase for a hundred paces or more, bucking, kicking, and braying. Like all its kind, it harbored lethal intent for wolves or wild dogs.

I came to the edge of the gravesite, and save where the dogs had been digging, it was so fresh that the dirt tamped down over it was smooth, wet with the dew. At its edge, the dirt was crumbly, so all work was recent.

Whoever did it drove a wooden cross at its head, and I could not help but conclude it was Thorkald, which would explain the absence of birds and such when I came looking for his remains.

Informal graves were dug the length of the deceased, and this grave was long indeed—giving me more assurance it was indeed my friend.

Surely that old couple had not done this; otherwise they would have mentioned such a considerable piece of work. I was never to find out what kindly soul or souls performed such a holy and considerate burial for Thorkald the Dane.

I felt sure enough it was my friend to remove and put aside the wooden cross, replacing it with a carefully stacked pyramid of stone as high as Thorkald had stood. Then I covered the grave itself with heavy stones, making repeated trips to and from the stream.

After carving his name into the wooden cross, I replaced it atop the pyramid.

I made prayer over poor Thorkald, who had given his life for us. I did not have the holy man's insight into the ways of considering his rough, violent life. Yet if Thorkald could not be forgiven by Our Savior, what would it all mean?

I no longer cared who I did or did not encounter; I had nothing left to rob and lived a mortal life I wanted no more part of. The immediate required me to find Eadrig, and tell him of the disaster, and I could not take thought or intent beyond that.

In fact, I headed directly east, taking up a main road. At once I encountered more people. They said they were Saxon, the same as the couple. There was havoc all over, they reported, and the land was being rooted up by virtual pigs—Normans as well as greedy evil-doers of my own kind.

Atop this mayhem, hunger stood worse—those driven from their land had little to eat, and twice the mule was foolishly taken from me by Saxon scavengers. It would return later—somehow fighting itself free, and having adopted some sort of ownership on my person.

One time, he had blood on its hind leg, and checking, I saw it wasn't its own. Was it inhabited by some sort of demon? I wanted no traveling companion, my thoughts exceedingly heavy. I especially did not require this mule, a veritable four-legged feast for every hungry rogue or thief who saw it—and me with it.

Finally, the week preceding St. Crispin's Day, I arrived at ancient Oxford. Many of the buildings and residences were burned. Seeing me approaching with a mule, survivors would duck out of view. Their fears need be extreme to fear an old man followed by a mule.

I called at a small church, struggling to prevent the mule from committing outrage by following me inside. I finally took its lead and tied it to a tree, resigning myself to endure its braying after entering the church.

The church was looted, the altar stripped of holy ware; all candle holders were gone, shards of candles lay on the floor. A back door was open, and pigeons had come inside—up on roofbeams they sat, cooing, looking down.

"I see you are Saxon."

A young churchman—a subdeacon—came out from what remained

of a side alcove; he carried a stave and came forward cautiously, looking me up and down.

"I am indeed. I am looking for the way to Eynsham, Friend."

He poked at the corner of his mouth, still looking me up and down: "Old man, might you have anything to eat?"

"Nothing."

He lowered his stave and shook his head, allowing a half-smile.

"You will find no alms at Eynsham Abbey, Friend. King William's brutes have ransacked it and likely killed everyone, leaving nothing behind for anyone else. The Abbey was Saxon through and through and, worse, loyal to Harold, for his father chartered it. . . . Is that your mule making that infernal noise?"

I decided he was an untrue fellow and felt no compunction regarding the use of craft. I needed to find Eadwig, especially if what this person said were true.

"You give me direction to Eynsham, and you can have the mule."

"Did you steal it?" he asked. Then he rubbed his hind end with his stave and shrugged, " . . . no matter."

And then told me directions—reaffirming what I might have guessed.

He followed me out of what remained of the woe-begotten church. I untied the animal and gave it to the greedy fool.

At once several of his fellows emerged from under whatever fissures or burrows they occupied, all carrying cudgels. I walked towards Eynsham. I soon heard great violence to my rear. The mule was proving to be too wily; hence, seeing the cudgels, its fierce senses knew the roasting spit awaited. I was not clear of the walls and gate when it came trotting up behind me—the line dragging behind with one of the poor devils clinging to it, all skinned and raw. Despite his desperation, the maimed fellow let go, moaning, and rolled over on his back.

If it had not been for the distraction of the mule, they would have set on me for my clothes and shoes at the church. I was re-learning basic lessons.

It was but two leagues to Eynsham, and the lands I traveled by were half reaped, some not at all. Then just prior to Eynsham I encountered more burned structures and fields. As the ill-intended churchman said, the Abbey at Eynsham was no more. Its gate and walls had been made entirely of wood and all were burned—weeks before, evidently.

A few of the inner foundation walls and such had been of stone and lay there covered with ashes, sad sentinels to what was a small but chartered monastery.

Yet I still refused to believe that even Normans and renegade Saxons would kill monks, and especially their Abbot. Danish raiders, perhaps, but never the former, at least in my memory.

I had not gone far when I encountered fresh graves—several dozen. My body chilled, for proximate to the burned remains of the Abbey, it boded poorly. Elms and beech formed an archway above, and a tiny creek wove its way along the far side of the area. All the graves were recently made, with fresh-milled slats forming crosses on each. Whoever did this, though not identifying the remains, selected carefully the place where all these unfortunates' eternal remains might rest.

Duties of my own, only too recently completed, enabled me to know caring work when I saw it.

The sun was growing low in the west, and the shadows from the copse gently embraced the newly dug graveyard across the creek. I went to the creek and saw the entire bed had been torn up—from dozens of horsemen using it for clear riding. The water now ran clear again.

No birds sang.

Turning, I saw with some relief that the mule had wandered away, as it might when it found graze or gave way to some whim. I threaded my way down the creek, then saw a path leading up into a thick oak woods.

I heard horsemen.

Without thought of age or decorum, up I went into an oak, my old bones yielding temporarily to necessity. Though thirty years before, I would have reached the topmost, at least I ascended far enough to be out of view.

What I heard was clear Saxon: "I tell you, we can look until our eyes grow hair. He and that mouthy Prior have gone."

"They would find it difficult, Brother, one without a skin and the other without fingers."

"Only on one hand."

I eased around the tree so could see both: The speakers were two Saxon thanes, each with a dreng. Their mounts were thick with tatters of brush and such. They were picking it off and throwing it down while the one continued his complaint. They passed around a sack of ale.

"It is close to vespers and Himself cannot deny we did our best for that sodomite Gilbert de Ghent."

There was laughter.

"A Norman sodomite is the taker; the giver is simply taking repast. So Himself bends over for de Ghent, and, friend Wulf, we bend over for Himself." He looked to the two drengs. "As you two bend over for us."

"Piss on you, Ceol."

They all had another laugh, but the thane called Ceol drew a great breath, took a last draught of ale and shrugged.

"But, in the end, we have looked every goddamned place for that fucking Abbot and his Prior. Let's get the hell gone, brothers. Tomorrow, we will bring hounds."

So their great palfreys were reined sharply to the south and they were gone.

It relieved me enormously to hear Eadwig was yet alive, but gave me urgency to find out if he was injured and in need of attendance.

Returning to the ground, I gathered my senses, and realized that in survival Eadwig had the same teacher as I did—Frog. When Frog plied an area, he was always certain to first ascertain the best hiding places; and if there were not any, to simply make one.

His favorite was on the highest ground possible, and close to the troubled area, which in this case would be the burials. And invariably close to water.

Returning to the graves, I looked west and there was something of a rise—gentle and sure, more a dome. Darkness was approaching and in the northeast side of it, the shadows ran deep and concealing.

I ascended, and within a short time emerged into a clearing and was gazing down where the thanes and drengs had been. It was quiet; I had poor chances of finding them, but if near they would find me.

I made a fire and warmed a trencher, then another. I drained half my ale. Slowly, the smoke rose uphill, gliding between the ashes and beeches. I struggled against the temptation to call out, for anyone might come to a call.

Heavy with bread, I stared into the fire and nodded off with the ease of old men, the God-given gift to the advancing years.

I awoke to a gentle hand placed upon me.

"Be easy, Father."

Eadwig held his hand to my mouth, then bent down and kissed me full on the head, for indeed I woke to a great discovery.

We embraced in the dark, and I knew the endless joy of holding my grown son, for whom I was so proud. It did not require an intellect like Eadwig's to reckon why I was alone. He knew.

"Father, I have seen so much sudden death—murder. Know I am equal to it. Just tell me and then we both can lament."

I did.

The senselessness of Cwenburh—of all their murders—came atop me like an ague. I once more showed selfishness, and shook myself back from my own lamentations to the teachings of Our Savior.

"Eadwig? You? Your Prior? You are injured."

"They cut Brother Prior's fingers off on one hand, and me, they scourged with whip; but I am—with the help of God—generating another skin. Do you have food, Father?"

I had dried eel and bread, and putting out the fire completely, I followed him through the bramble, entering their lair beneath a great fallen log. Behind it, he had dug an alcove.

Bother Prior—Eanbald-of-Norfolk—was in a painful condition. His wounds had festered initially, and Eadwig struggled to act as healer. Much violence locally was due to the calumny of the Saxon turncoat Lord Edwin, cousin of the slain King Harold. To Eadwig, such mortal treachery required no musings.

"Saxons are making their decisions, Father, and many make them in their best interest, and these days that is with King William. And King William is scourging many monasteries and rescinding holy charters. I have been ordered to Rome by our Holy Father, Pope Alexander. I leave tomorrow; it is a miracle we joined. You will of course go with me."

"I am sorry to presume to add more, Father," interceded Brother Prior, "but we are also under banishment by King William and his turncoat Saxon Lord, who both hold sway from the Holy Father Alexander."

"Brother Prior! God help us. They almost cut out your tongue."

"Forgive me Father, but is it not true?"

"We cannot deign to second guess the Holy Father, Brother."

We retreated into silence on what was a painful topic between us. Eadwig looked at me with intensity.

"Now Father, you must go with me. They will kill you once they learn of our relationship. A faithful pilgrim has a boat waiting, and from there I will leave. I have many friends in Rome who are a joy in my life."

"No, Eadwig. I will never leave England. I am old now, and will seek out solitude, for I must make amends with the Lord and our Savior. I have not the faith of Cwenburh, and certainly you. Rome is no place for me. It perhaps never has been."

Brother Prior nodded—he heard what I meant with his mind and not his heart. Eadwig began to say something, but I held up my hand.

Eadwig took his lip between his teeth and struggled not to weep.

"When upon this earth will I see you again, God help us?"

Prior took loving opportunity to duck out of the alcove and go outside.

"Perhaps, Father Abbot, it will not be on this earth, God permitting."

"I cannot abide this when such a place as Rome awaits. You would live an honored life rich under the Lord, as you should."

I lifted my arms and placed them on each of his shoulders. "I am already honored: by Cwenburh, by yourself, and by the twins. I held you when an infant, and like Matilda, I always knew you were special. You cannot fail us all now, Eadwig."

When the timely Brother Prior returned, he joined Eadwig and me who were already in prayer, and it was special for me to do such in this august companionship.

In the morning—like stoats emerging from burrow—we checked all directions, listening, looking down upon the landscape.

"Frog used good sense in selecting places, did he not, Eadwig?"

His smile shared that fact with me, and I saw from Brother Prior's eyes that he had heard the story of Frog.

Below, in the most proximate opening, the mule grazed, waiting. I had told them about it, preventing one so astute as Eadwig to take it with them.

"Praise God, Father. That is a giant beast."

We moved downhill, and within a short time joined the troublesome creature in that same opening; from here we must in opposite directions. This was a point I knew would be the most painful of all, though I was immensely grateful Eadwig would be safe, for he was all my family now.

"Father, other than to go west until you meet the sea, do you have other plans?"

"Well Eadwig, I will favor more northwest than west, but you have the best part of my plan, God be praised."

"So, now we shall all pray."

And we did. All of us were keeping up our mutual courage. Trading embraces, Eadwig gave me his final blessing, then picking up my arm, put a small bundle in my hand.

"This is for you, God be praised. I have kept it for you. Do not open it until I am quite gone."

And we made our farewells.

I turned heading northwest. Hearing the mule's heavy steps behind me, I smiled, recalling Brother Prior's warning: "Beware of that beast, Master Cuthwin; he could be King William's demon."

After a respectful distance, I opened the tiny bundle.

In it was Cwenburh's clasp.

It was my fatuous intention to have nothing further to do with my fellow man, and by heading west where it was alleged British land ended, I would find no people. I was wrong; all the way west, here and there God ordained people to maintain themselves on his given lands and waters.

I avoided the small crofts and villages, only occasionally partaking of a market on the day prior to Sabbath. Yet as Frog advised Eadwig when they traveled in strange country, when I left I reversed my path to see if I was followed.

Several times I was followed, for what reason I cannot know—whether it be for curiosity or ill motive. My continuing comrade was the mule. It was ever vigilant for any and all, and its massive ears would firstly twitch around, then if what it heard displeased it, deafening braying would follow. It began to make itself more useful: It would carry a pack, and this improved my progress over rough ground. I began to begrudgingly realize that it was a blessing of sorts, for at night I slept with the soundness of an infant for it never was unawares. Taking the Lord's ways as a command, I finally named it Samson for its size and strength. God help me, it was my beast through God's unknowable intervention.

The people I came across were a rough sort, the more west I ventured. They were given to a language vaguely recognizable as a sort of Welsh, of which I was not particularly at ease. But what I knew was enough.

I reached the vast, wild ocean coast on what I reckoned to be near the Day of the Dead, though by now I was not sure. I was to become increasingly removed from time of day and year, instead owing more to the sun and moon and how they moved through the heavens. On moonless nights there were the stars, mainly Polaris, that gift to any traveler on such times.

Paralleling the intricacies of the coast southwest, I made camps where providence allowed. I would gaze with sacred wonder upon the vastness of the wild ocean whose mysterious horizons were known only by the stoutest-shipped Norseman. The sun was setting more southwesterly and it was getting colder, but not with the meanness I was used to farther north.

A great bounty of animal life began, such as I never saw before, especially fat hares whose haunches wiggled with fat and fine flesh as they fled far too slowly.

About an hour after sunset, wolves would approach—large packs of them, and I by old habit kept a fire through the night. Each night, though, I was given great amusement: Samson would wheel about on first whiff, and if they were foolish enough to come within sight of him, he would give pursuit, making voice one could hear back to Oxford.

Each day, I would stop at small streams and load up with round, wonderfully smooth and ideally sized throwing rocks; Cwenburh, somewhat prideful of her throwing ability, was in constant consternation over my ability, better than hers, may God forgive my pride.

So may Jesus's eternal Goodness forgive, I hunted the plentiful small game by the simple ways learned in my youth. In my heart I took pity on the creatures for I had seen too much innocent bloodshed. Something spoke to me that these small, vulnerable bodies were not without God's protection.

I decided to cease eating the flesh of warm-blooded creatures, the sort saved by Noah in his ark; were they not the creatures that approached and loved our Savior and offered him great succor? From that time, I sustained this rule increasingly well each year.

The first winter I made permanent camp within the coastline of a deeply carved bay in a swale where a stream ran oceanward. It was a God-given place of shelter and plenty, and my prayers were lovingly answered. Had the evils of the Dark One finally left me in peace?

In the vicinity were arrayed wild grasses, mostly green through the winter. I even found wild spelt and other edible plants. And of course I fished and plied the rocky pools and sand spits. This way I began to learn about the edible things along the coast—in the pools formed by tides and higher in the rocks. In short, I survived easily, as did the Samson. We saw nobody, for which I thanked God.

I read one of my Bibles when light enough.

In fact, I became sure enough to make large night fires, for God provided fuel in massive abundance, both washed up along a wide sweep of beach below me, and up and down the draw followed downward by the stream.

So even by the fire I could read some if I wished, God's will be praised.

More than anything, I wondered: After all the years that had preceded me, what sense I could make of them, and how did all the words and teachings of Our Savior and God fit in?

But other than reading the words, and thinking of general experiences, reflecting on the events of them, going deeper than that deranged my thinking. Eadwig had said that the act of knowing God's ways was beyond us. It seemed so to me.

I never argued this with him. For I was a scribe, not a scholar, but Eadwig was both. So even if we had plumbed the depths of the matters, his breadth of knowledge would be much beyond mine. Yet my beloved Cwenburh was never far from my heart and soul.

My lack of knowledge and background for matters of serious thought were sorely demonstrated to me in the book he insisted I take. That night he offered me a half dozen from his cache in the alcove saying he could attain easy replacement in Rome. Frankly, it was the last I desired—the *Consolation of Philosophy* by the venerable Boethius. Eadwig, years before, had mentioned it in his letters, urging me to read it. I would try, but become bored by the difficulty of parsing the language of Rome, then the intricate, confusing matrix of its content.

Finally, in a return missive, I admitted, writing from my heart, "Well, son Eadwig, the work is little consolation to me, I am ashamed to admit."

In truth its scholarship bounced off my hide like pebbles from the flank of an ox. But on that night before our parting, I had not heart to say I preferred another title, and took it, thinking I would try again.

But I found it still held the same problems for me.

My mind labored enough with other earthly paradoxes: Firstly was Our Savior's teachings, and the Christian world I saw and lived. After all, that is all I ever knew. Also, that is all Cwenburh and the children, save Eadwig, knew. There were the good times and the bad, and as the

Bible taught, God made both. But the loving teaching of Our Savior was at terrible odds with so much of what I had seen. Not the least of these paradoxes were the murders of those I loved, and even those who were strangers.

Then my contemplations became stymied. I reverted to looking out on the vastness of the wild seas, for this coast was as untamed before God as any I had ever seen. After the violent storms, the land would explode with the massive waves striking the dark, foreboding brows of the cliffs and rocky islets. They would, one after the other, assault the land with fury I never thought endurable.

God forgive me, I learned more by watching these, and thinking after them, than from anything else that first winter.

I did, however, find purpose in work. Sometime after the rising sun blessed the land with an increase in light, I commenced daily work on a small chapel and altar. I desired a place of peace to pray and contemplate. I did so with rock, placing them together with mortar, poor indeed because I had no knowledge or experience dealing with rock. Many times, it fell apart, and now nearly sixty, learning came slowly to me.

I could haul one large rock slung on my back, and the mule, if in the mood, could take two slung across its back. By and by, with patience, my tiny edifice came together. With my small adz and axe, I fashioned a cross of the old sort, and did work on this until I reckoned it to be close to my first Easter on this coast. The tiny alcove was my gift to Our Savior's great passion.

During this time, I contemplated an offshore island which fascinated me beyond all else. I gazed out at it for hours. It was a half-league offshore, thus caught the brunt of the roughest seas, parting them as a soldier might a shield against the onslaught.

Its solitude spoke to me in wordless magic. I became increasingly fixed to go out there and live—to withdraw completely.

◇8◇

On the clearest days as spring approached, I saw that it had a flat south-eastern end with grasses. In fact, the entire islet was treeless. As each day passed, the grasses became greener. They swayed in the almost continuous prevailing winds, these creating waves in the heavy growth, rippling with the flow of air.

Then legions of birds arrived to nest and make more of their kind. They swirled above it, riding vortexes of swelling winds—soaring then following them downwind, turning, rising, and holding, then going back and repeating this.

And all the time, each kind made more and more claims on nesting places. These claimants becoming so thick that most locales atop and on the sides of the islet were filled with each sort.

It was then a group of boatmen approached offshore—the first people I had seen. I withdrew into the vale and looked out. There were over a dozen of them in three small boats; all rowed, but two had sails not set. Each was filled to the rails with belongings. They turned into my deep bay, keeping to the lee of the point where they made a skilled, peaceful landing.

In fact, they made land near the stream mouth where I lived that emptied into the sea creating a network of small streamlets cutting through the sands, the sweet water returning to the salt.

There were both men and women, and they did not expect anyone to be in that bay, and I wondered how to announce my presence without alarming them. It was obvious they were fishermen come to make spring camp, for one of the boats was heavy with plugs of salt and loose staves from which to assemble barrels.

Samson destroyed all possibility of a gentle introduction. Catching scent and sound of this community, he brayed deafeningly. That immediately decided things: Three of the men immediately picked up cudgels looking up the stream in the direction of Samson's racket.

I walked down the path I had worn over the winter, came within sight of them, raised my arm to greet them, and stood.

Samson came up behind me, and that decoded in my favor for the men: Certainly someone intending evil would not have such a ridiculous beast with him. Lowering their cudgels, they approached, two stopping and one handing off his cudgel to his comrades, and drawing close.

After several garbled tries in what I assumed was a kind of Welsh— both of us making great effort, I understood him to say, "God save you, Brother. What brings you here?"

I explained as best I could in Welsh that I was a wanderer, an old man come to live out my life in peace.

"A Saxon?"

"Yes."

That seemed dark news to them. They nodded somberly to each other, but explained they were doing precisely what I had supposed, and would spend many days in this bay catching and salting fat codfish.

When I told them I was once an eelman, they seemed to recover good grace to my person, and invited me and Samson down to the beach.

And it was this way that I met Gyrth the Elder of Pider and his family, who were to become my first friends in the west. These people along the danger-strewn coast of northwest Kernowec proved through the severe test of time and their own endowed goodness to be my God-given blessing.

The chapel I made, despite its being my first primitive effort in rock, was a fortuitous decision, certainly driven by God. It was welcomed by the Kernow fishermen who plied the sea for the fat-bellied cod who inhabited a bank offshore. They depended on these fish for their survival each winter.

Being away from their village, they felt comforted to have a special place of devotion available enabling them to thank and pray to God for their sustenance as each week moved along. They could not remember but being anything other than Christian.

I enquired about the island directly offshore, its owner, if any, and who went there, and my intentions to go there. They to a man shook their head with long faces.

They strenuously advised me not to venture out to Ynys Penfras, as the island was known. It was inhabited by a pitiless Gwiddonod, which was a sort of witch, devouring people and animals who dared trespass.

In fact, according to those in Kernow, during the times of King Mark, a crofter, hungry for hideage free of geld fees, occupied the island with sheep. His son while tending them was eaten and all the sheep with them. When he transported more sheep and another son there, being of a greedy, careless nature with many sons to spare, the same misfortune struck.

Then even he gave up, despite being of Danish or Irish blood, notoriously ruthless. The villagers were filled with great stories peopled by all sorts of beings and creatures. Cwenburh would have been overjoyed by them and they her.

Since they fished around Ynys Penfras—which meant plainly Isle of Cod in Saxon—I asked if they had seen the Gwiddonod, and what figures she took, such dark spirits having a changeable nature. Indeed, did they know if there were more than just one living there?

They had not seen her, God forbid, for events they narrated occurred years before. However, they averted looking, for to set eyes on such a demonic being would risk losing your soul.

But I was to learn Kernow people were skillful and wove their old pagan beliefs into their present thinking. In fact, they preferred I stay on the mainland—seeing I wished to end my earthly wanderings here. The mainland they assured was far better than an offshore chunk of earth; furthermore, I could build many more things, like chapels. Equally, I would be available for diverse society and stories about far-off strange places which, during evenings, I told. These they thoroughly enjoyed.

And God help me, I enjoyed same, but it was contrary to my decision to seek solitude, and I knew I must not weaken—be drawn from my path. For they were wonderful simple souls who were surely at peace with Our Savior and his Father. Their society was the simple and honest sort I was used to. True, I found they still practiced reckoning Saint's festivals and Easter by the old ways. Despite this they were God-respecting folk devoted to Our Savior's teachings. Most admiringly, in my view, they were without desire to know or care about the ways of great men and their violent institutions by which I saw and witnessed so much odium.

They had not known King Edward of Mercia was deceased, and they did not consider him sovereign over Kernow anyhow, nor any violence-prone Saxon. Me, as Saxon, they viewed as a great exception to most.

Gyrth the Elder spoke it thusly: "In truth, Cuthwin, a hard-scrabble Kernowman's greatest desire is that all great Saxons and Normans cut each others' greedy throats. We mean no disrespect to you, Cuthwin, of course."

Many Kernowmen were great seafarers and knew much about Normans and Norsemen, enough to harbor a healthy aversion to both their societies.

Yet I begged these new God-given friends not to tempt me with their joyful society, for I explained to them my vow of solitude—so I might understand God's words and actions I had witnessed over nearly sixty years. During those first months of fishing, I told them of my family and events following. Most all, of good Cwenburh who I missed more than anything or anybody, and whose murder I refused to accept in the face of God.

Soon they accepted and understood my desires for solitude, understanding that I loved them very much, but my vows to God dominated all else.

Yet they remained adamant about the evil presence upon the Isle of Cod. When I insisted on going there anyway, they decided to ferry myself and even Samson out to the island.

"Samson," I advised, "could swim or stay, at his own whim."

But for some devilish unknown whim, Samson had inveigled himself into the hearts of the Kernowman's children, allowing them to ride anywhere their mothers would allow. I warned everyone thoroughly after the beast's disorderly ways, but the process went on anyway.

As they told me so often in Peterborough—God's ways are mysterious.

Heeding the advice of Gyrth the Elder and especially his wife, Alma, I went out to Cod Island equipped with a stout wooden cross—to be held before me whenever the gorgons approached. "They dare not consume both you and it, so you will be safe," I was assured.

Another identical cross was set into the bow of their boat; hence, we would be all protected. "Gwiddonods fear any sign of Our Savior, Cuthwin. It makes their eyes boil out."

In the last day before going out, the children wept over Samson's banishment. Worse, he would surely end his days as a meal to a Gwiddonod, for "poor Samson has no hands and could not carry a cross."

God help me. Who cannot grow fond of children and become averse to sadness in Innocents? Will they not know that soon enough, God Forbid? Much to my later regret, I asked if they would transport the animal to their village. It could be useful there, and I assured the children I would not risk Samson's gentle soul being sullied through consumption by a Gwiddonod.

But the mule was too large for transport by boat. "God forbid, Cuthwin. We are not Normans." But two of the striplings and one young adult he allowed astride, and they would ride him back to the village, actually preceding the boat home—judging by Samson's pace.

In the early autumn they transported me to the Isle of Cod. Two of the men—Old Gwyth and his son—piloted me out. They waited until the calmest day possible, for the coastline of the island was impossible in all places but two, and even those two required an ocean surge to be gentle for a difficult landing.

During the brief transport I recalled not being in a boat for many years and how I missed it. The majestic turquoise waves coming in from the vastness slowly lifted our boat. This strangeness I never experienced on the river or upon the fens. The swarms of birds had all but gone, but there were still many ink-black snake birds diving for their meal. As I drew close to the islet, it loomed larger, ever more imposing. We parted through the thick mats of olive-green vegetation that grew like a barrier around the island. All this swelled and subsided, as if the great ocean were a breathing being, sleeping in deep peaceful repose.

"We will have little time, Master Cuthwin. Be prepared."

I had things for protracted living with me, more than I wanted, but those insisted upon by Old Gwyth and his people. They reminded me I was not a tonsured churchman; indeed I was a contrite and modest soul before God, like anyone.

"By Our Savior's word, Cuthwin, there is nothing then to force you to withdraw and live like a savage, God forbid. So by God and ourselves, you will be provided for."

When we approached what was deemed the best spot, I saw at once it was the smallest of beaches. The tide was low—our time chosen for that phase—and we had an accessible shoreline two rods long and three rods deep, there meeting steep inclines towards the island's crown.

My belongings were quickly run up to the highest spot, and while holding my cross, I embraced my friends who were tearful and begged me to relent: "I tell you, in our village, and those close by, there are many fine widows who would welcome such as you, Cuthwin, God help you."

I heard often from Alma detailing each widow's strong points. Yet I bade them gratitude and farewell. They vowed to look forward with great joy when they arrived at fish camp the following spring and saw I was uneaten by the monster.

And saying the Lord's Prayer together, they got back in their sturdy craft and went off.

I had a heavy heart that moment, God forgive my lack of strength.

In dictating this portion of my life, it occurs that much can be made—and said—in the details of how an ordinary soul learns to become a proper hermit. But it is more correct to say that each man or woman must search within their own heart and soul what that best way might be.

One thing is true: In locales where it appears that survival itself is seemingly impossible, a person learns a soul and body with God's protection needs little.

However the mind, at least mine, needs far more, and if the order of the mind is left unchecked, disaster awaits. I do not know what might have happened to the first hermit who occupied this forlorn Isle.

But the fact was there had been others before me.

Judging by the signs of age, the earliest arriving soul simply died in a tiny alcove he built. Some of his remains were intact, others scattered. All were heavy with signs they had been pecked and cleaned thoroughly by the birds. They were ancient—the lightest of touch and they crumbled to dust.

His alcove, assuming it was a man, was built exposed to the elements, facing the prevailing winds. I assumed he would curl up there at night and sleep. It is difficult to think he could have lived long with such exposure to the elements.

The other shelter, however, I found distant from the first. This person had built a large stone house, now fallen inside itself, and his remains were in what must have been a pallet. His bones were not as ancient as his brethren, not nearly as much. The remains were bound together fully, some of the ligature surviving. They too had been picked clean. Against the wall were a stone cross and a round stone that had held some sort of votive light. Before that were four flagstones—kneeling stones—worn to a polish by hundreds—thousands—of long sessions.

There were the thinnest remains of clothes, mere skins, and these the creatures had left alone. These were now a fine white and grey powder.

My eyes returned to the bones, and it occurred to me they were tiny, and it had to have been a boy, or at most a stripling, but that seemed wrong at once. My eyes returned to the bones again. Slowly I counted the ribs—each in an even row.

It had been a woman.

I did not know if the elements killed this second pilgrim, but she surely lived on in contemplation for quite some time. I did not know if either had made any contact with a Gwiddonod, or any other demonic creature, though that might explain the sorrowful demise of the first hermit.

But there was no question about the anchoress who constructed the substantial hut. I now drew close for a detailed inspection: In the remains of her frail hand, she clutched Our Savior's cross, and no such creation of Satan such as a Gwiddonod would come near or harm her, God be praised.

It would have been sacrilege for me to occupy this hallowed ground, and I worked the following years, fashioning a chapel over and around it in stone and wood, celebrating the sacrifice this Holy Sister made. During that first circuit the moon took above me, I built my own modest stone hut a furlong or so distant from where she had prayed and died.

The Isle of Cod was not uninhabited. To my dismay, there were sheep surviving. They were scrawny woe-begotten creatures. The ewes had been tupped to skin and bones by the rams. They were a forlorn lot of rams, yet randy in their ways, and they would leave the ewes no peace. Regardless of season they carried on great struggles with one another.

The isolation and lack of a worthy shepherd rendered the males menaces indeed. Oddly, there were not many sheep there. For there was abundant year-round grass upon the island's dome, probably a full hide, or nearly so. Yet there were barely a dozen ewes, and nearly as many rams.

My first stone fence in my approaching new career was to enclose the ewes, to protect them from the rams, who did their best to get at them. Stinky, obnoxious bastards—God forgive me for disdaining their natural ways—I drove them off. After the first several years, I allowed only two to remain, and they mended their ways with proper guidance.

It was painful generosity to have given up Samson. The narrow paths up from the two beaches were steep, but tenable for a sure-footed mule. Without an animal, I had to haul most rocks up from the beach upon a sling fashioned so, and I was kept sinew and muscle and little else with the labors.

During the first few springs, Gyrth the Elder would offer to return Samson, but I resisted. Finally, good Gyrth died of the ague, and Samson of plain old age. Thoughts of a beast to help me were forgotten.

In short, during those nearly ten years and five upon the Isle of Cod, I had no shortage of labors. In performing them, I had long, peaceful periods to contemplate all that had gone on before me. I did much with them.

My readings were modest. Eventually, well-doers provided me with a modest quantity of tapirs; I used them sparingly. I preferred natural light by which to read. Using old-style notched sticks, I kept the time of the week, and never worked on Sabbath. I practiced my contemplation, prayer, and readings in the fashion that God intended working folk to do.

Sometimes on Sabbaths during spring and summers, I perused the island, and I enjoyed looking upon the flock and feathered animals. Given shears and taught their use by fishermen knowledgeable, I was able to bundle what little wool my sheep yielded and give it as thanks for whatever materials they brought to fish camp for me.

These peaceful times on Cod Island were God's gift.

I kept building fences and gaining skills at doing so. I crisscrossed Cod Island with them, if for no other reason than I enjoyed working to keep my head clear. The fishermen were impressed with my work and in truth it was sometime towards the twentieth year that I left Cod Island and began building fences on the mainland. I think it was at that time I heard myself referred to as the Cuthwin-the-Fencebuilder. This simplicity pleased me more than Scribe.

It was this time when I stopped looking to sea and instead was able to face the land once again. It came to me that my purpose and work upon the island was served.

It was somewhere around now people mistakenly understood from their own thoughts that I received a great vision from Our Savior, or one of the Holy Saints who told me to make fences upon the Kernowek mainland. This is not true and is mistakenly but lovingly maintained by working folk and now holy men who abide it to reaffirm any standing as a Saint.

But there is considerable distance between a God-given vision and the dreams of ordinary souls. On the contrary, I dictate here that the idea and picture of fences stretching across the peaceful fields of Kernowek came in a dream, the sort ordinary folk have every week of their life. Are they not a God-given balm whose content is fortuitous as the weather? This I believe is true.

I often explain this dream to those who visit me. They proclaim respect, even veneration, and always kindnesses because of my alleged holy standing, and I know they are disappointed when I inform of the contrary.

I believe that one's decisions are one's own, and that God's greatest benefit is the free will of his children upon the earth. So, my resolve to depart my beloved, generous isle was made with love and good intentions. But above all, it was a decision I made myself.

But, thank God, I did not squander my gift there by forgetting my purpose, ever. My aim was not be become a crofter or shepherd—or fence builder, but to make sense of the incongruences my life festooned before me in confusing contrast with the teaching of Our Savior.

Without doubt, the foremost of these was the sorry, tragic, and cruel demise of Cwenburh and Matilda—both Matildas and Elesa. I discovered that I might ponder their memories best if I built a modest chapel to each on various locations upon the isle, actually in a semi-circle facing the rising sun.

But then came the lessons I must learn, and perhaps it was the years that it took to build those chapels that was part of it—part of the vast lengths of time unhindered to discover my finest teacher.

For it was the sea that was my greatest teacher, provided by God. This most spectacular creation he rendered from the dark abyss. "In what way did it teach you Cuthwin?"—many curious souls have asked. I can only respond that the lessons were slow, and being an ordinary soul, the learning was slower, but God showed patience to me on Cod Island.

After a half dozen years or thereabouts, I lived and heard the many moods of the sea. I began to know that the sea is so much mightier than mankind; yet it too, like men, is subject to sudden, inexplicable violence.

And like great men who struggle in battle, this changing sea sows death, famine, drought on all. My beloved villagers—providers and friends—were regularly swept away, deprived of food with all of the sense that the savage Norman sword did to Cwenburh and others.

"Cruelty is not my way, Cuthwin," God seemed to say in each swell that broke steadily on Cod Island's cragged-bound shores, "...and you must accept the presence of evil, how its very darkest nature is random and senseless."

Yet these lessons I found impossible to present to other souls in a way to save them the time, discomfort, and effort it has taken me, God be praised. It is all I can do but say it now; the rest is for after I am gone.

I believe that those who have visited violence and gross unfairness upon my loved ones and friends are not assured of forgiveness in this life or next. I just hope that God might search his vast heart and forgive me.

But seamless forgiveness can no more be given to unrepentant men than might unthinking stone cliffs forgive the sea pounding upon them ceaselessly, unthinkingly.

In this end, I declare that I believe in the One and only God, and that I am a common man, blessed in many ways. My highest mortal service was as husband to Cwenburh-of-Loe, and this is how I want to be remembered by those who come after me, God be praised.

IRVING WARNER, writer, harmonica artist, retired fish and game biologist, and college professor was born in Modesto, California in 1941. He moved to Alaska in 1964 where he stayed until 1996. During that time, he worked in fisheries research, with a brief tenure in sea bird studies. Switching careers at the age of 40, he taught at Kodiak College and University of Alaska until 1996 when he took early retirement to become a full time writer in Washington, where he has lived ever since, minus a stint in Hawaii.

warnerlifetravel.blogspot.com/

OTHER BOOKS *by* WARNER
from PLEASURE BOAT STUDIO:

In Memory of Hawks, and Other Stories from Alaska
Wagner, Descending: The Wrath of the Salmon Queen
The War Journal of Lila Ann Smith
Crossing the Water: The Hawaii-Alaska Trilogies

BEHIND THE SCENES

"Writers must believe what they write," says Warner; "otherwise, they don't write at top form. When something devastating happens to one of my main characters, it is almost akin to having it happen to a living person in my life."

Warner was inspired to write THE LIFE & TRAVELS OF SAINT CUTHWIN by his love of medieval literature and history. "The 11th century was so central to the changes and impact on our language," says Warner. The novel took Irving Warner seven years of arduous research and six years to write. It was no small task. His research included many handwritten notes, which he then transferred to his computer files. It was his objective to remain faithful to the texture and ambience of the 11th century Saxon world of his fictional character, Cuthwin, and to that end he has written an extraordinary novel. I hope you will consider reviewing this outstanding literary achievement.

Vetted by medieval scholars for historical detail and authenticity, the reader is thoroughly immersed in the medieval period, experiencing in one's imagination along with the narrator, what it was like for an ordinary person living in the 11th century. For the common folk, life was filled with hardship and constant struggle: most importantly the struggle just to stay alive. Famine and poverty were rampant as well as lawlessness. One's life was always at risk from marauding bandits. The only safe havens were the abbeys and, living under the of auspices of the clergy, one was subject to their avarice and their corruption, and their often ruthless and hypocritical behavior, as young Cuthwin learned as a young boy, when he ran away to escape being brutally flogged for imitating the untoward behavior of one of the abbey's guardians.

CURIOSITIES REVEALED

If you are interested in delving into a more in-depth understanding of these medieval times, or would like to discover the motives behind plot development, engage in character analysis, or unmask reasons for religious commentary conveyed throughout the telling of this tale...or finally, if you have any curiosity as to why N.W. author Irving Warner felt compelled to write this book in general, please visit his website:

www.CUTHWINandCWENBURH.com

THE MAKING OF "CUTHWIN" ITS GENESIS

THE SOCIETY OF IT ALL

At the start of "Cuthwin", I was certain I wanted the reader to 'hear' a narrative from the common everyday person—from the so termed 'third' layer of society, meaning "Those who worked". Feudal society was made up of the three estates: The first estate being the church and its many offices; the second estate were the nobles, or those who ruled and fought; the third estate being those who worked.

There was mobility between the first and second estates, but less between the third and other two. I look at it this way: There were those who raised food and worked to earn a living and who directly or indirectly fed, clothed or equipped society. Then those who ate the food and were often embroiled in power and/or land issues. During these conflicts they killed each other, including anyone who got in the way, too often those who raised and prepared the food and were non-combatants.

This is how our protagonist Cuthwin views events around him, and he was right. So, he avoided all the power players in every way he could. This is an important and intelligent component of Cuthwin the person and character. Almost every time in my novel when Cuthwin becomes associated directly or indirectly with "power players" in the first or second estates, very bad things happen.

A commonly held concept was that, "Life (i.e for ordinary workers) on the medieval manor was perhaps dull and uninspiring...there must have been little time left over for things of an intellectual or cultural nature." (Kries, 2001).

This, of course, wasn't wholly true, and a challenge to a storyteller.

One of the main problems was little was written about this "third estate" or common worker. This continued for the first seven hundred years of the medieval period. (In schools of my time, they termed them the "dark ages", which was more appropriate for teachers and fellow students than a historical period.)

Much more was written about the second estate (those who fought and ruled) and the first estate, those who prayed. In fact, much was written about both of the foregoing in verse and prose history. So, then and later a great burgeoning of verse and prose fiction had a foundation to built upon around activities of war and conflict between the two estates. Meaning, the two often were complicit in wars and scourges and during them dealt out plentiful 'collateral damage' of the time.

LANGUAGE AND SOURCES

In the 11th century England people spoke a hodgepodge of languages if they got around at all. In fact, most who traveled on business or such were distinctly polyglot—able to speak in local Saxon dialects, and the language spoken in "Daneslaw", that area which is roughly north of the Umber river. In the north they spoke a mixture of Old East Norse and Old English, which supposedly were mutually comprehensible.

However, much of the population lived on farms either as thanes/freemen, serfs/cottars or slaves, and didn't travel far from home their entire lives. These people would speak the language of their area (say, Saxon, which was beginning to be called 'Anglish') but a regional dialect of Saxon; therefore, just listening to a person speak you could make like Henry Higgins and know where they were from.

The most dramatic and lasting development in the beginnings of our language was the Anglo-Saxon Chronicles, kept concurrently at different monastic locales between 871-1154. It began at the time of Alfred the Great (849-899) who had a great vision to have many documents and books written in the vernacular. In fact, he made some of these translations himself. In Alfred's view, literacy should be spread everywhere; hence, the language of the common people should be the language of the realm. This way, all people would have access, especially to religious works, not the least being the Gospels.

I would need to get all historical information for "Cuthwin" via translations. These must be respectful to their sources; hence, my previous scholarship did come in handy. I had learned some basic ways to discern a lousy translation from a better one, and a better one from an outstanding rendition.

My objective was single-minded, to not commit anachronisms that would destroy the texture and ambience of the eleventh century Saxon world of my fictional "Cuthwin's", and indeed he was fictional.

Yet, things and places I wanted to be real, unless I had no other alternative: I could not have doors opening and closing that were not there; people buttoning up clothing when there were no buttons. Nor could I have children of common people going to schools that didn't exist, evil-doers going to jails that were not there. And finally, contrary to many movies, common people sitting down to even the most festive meals with 'boards' festooned with fatted calves, pigs, lambs, poultry and just about fatted everything.

No, in the eleventh century common board, eating fare, was basically vegetable for animals were expensive to eat. In brief—kill an animal and eat it, it's gone! "Poultry were considered a luxury food and it was also recognized as a therapeutic diet for invalids particularly in broth form. (Lacey, Danziger, The Year 1000, p.58).

Oh, yes—boards were boards because there were few if any tables. Boards were kept along the side of the domicile, and moved out and set up during meal times—or, people just sat and ate from plain wooden bowls or trenchers. And, there were no chairs—an occasional stool, and that was it.

Move over to the monastery or church, or into the great hall either 'burh" or not (walled or unwalled) there were some of those human comforts, but not amongst the common folk, unless they were not common or struggling to be not common. I look at it this way about those who worked, and "the others": The difference in material means between an Archbishop or land owning Lord of a manor was wider than it is today between a C.E.O. and the janitor cleaning out the corporate offices, and today the janitor is free and not a slave or serf.

Making a very general statement about a complicated system, human beings could be slaves, serfs/villains or free. Serfdom was more common in European feudalism, but was present in Saxon and Daneslaw England. Slavery was common in England, "Slavery and the recruitment of slaves was an integral part of Anglo-Saxon society. The institution of slavery was never questioned by contemporary moralists" (Slavery in Early Mediaeval England: From the reign of Alfred until the Twelfth Century, David Pelteret).

Cwenburh, Cuthwin's wife, was a slave; Cuthwin was not, but owed money to (first) the manor he was raised upon, then Peterborough Monastery. Slavery/Serfdom/Free born in my view, was one of the hardest "nuts" to crack in understanding 11th century society. I don't think I'm clear on it now and trying to learn about the topic through readings is like counting eels bare-handed.

THE YEARS OF THE MEDIEVAL PERIOD

The medieval or middle ages is defined as: The history of Europe lasting from the 5th to the 15th century. It began with the fall of the Western Roman Empire and merged into the Renaissance and the Age of Discovery. The Middle Ages is the middle period of the three traditional divisions of Western history itself subdivided into the Early, High, and Late Middle Ages. The problem for me in researching was many authors just cast categories like the "Early, High and Late" divisions to the winds (I guess) and wrote on about the late Middle Ages as it were all one. This was way far from the facts as they were, and so their work was of little use to me. Seems unimportant here, but it sure wasn't to me.

In the case of a novel such as mine, we don't have to worry about if the events are real or not, for they are not; however, we (and "I" as an author) must make sure the entire human and physical surroundings of the novel/journal is spot on, or the result is genre fiction or a comic book.

Then there is the chronic problem in historical fiction. Just how much can we forgive a writer regards historical "warping" or outright omissions; or worse than all, historical facts and activities made up. So, if in our readings we run into a gay Henry VIIIth, Earl Marble at the Battle of Frostingbridge or Queen Carmen of Finland, as a reader how must we feel?!

If the writer is doing something humorous/comedic, that is, kicking history in the tail feathers, it works beautifully.

However, if you are writing a serious literary work and pull a fictional "who-haw" out of your pocket, then you —as an author—must deal with your audience's ability to suspend their belief for a bit. Now, with full disclosure, I have orphanages present in pre-Hastings England, but they were not. I just needed them to sufficiently bring out Cwenburh's nature, and the predicament it lands them both in. Well, I just put orphanages in. An author just must deal with their audience's suspension of belief—a little.

For more on this historical period, the making of 'Cuthwin', an author's journey, and book club questions, please visit:
CUTHWINANDCWENBURH.COM

CWENBURH'S CLASP, THE IMAGE:

AS SEEN ON THE COVER, A SYMBOL OF CUTHWIN AND CWENBURH'S LOVE, & ALSO REPRESENTING A LOCK TO OPEN THE BOOK'S ADVENTURE WITHIN. AQUIRED FROM THE BRITISH MUSEUM'S WEBSITE: BRITISHMUSEUM.ORG. THE INFO INCLUDED ON THIS PAGE CAN ALSO BE FOUND THERE.

A MASTERPIECE OF EARLY MEDIEVAL CRAFTSMANSHIP, made using over 400g of gold with an intricate decoration of intertwining creatures inlaid with niello (a black metal alloy). This type of animal ornament was popular with many Germanic-speaking peoples at the time.

Situated on either side of the boss at the tip of the buckle, two animals grip a smaller creature in their open jaws; on either side of the two, slightly smaller, upper bosses are two birds' heads with curved beaks. Between these is a circular plate which acts as a stop for the tongue of the buckle. This plate is decorated with a complex animal interlace; the tongue protruding from it is ridged and otherwise plain.

The internment of a ship at Sutton Hoo represents the most impressive medieval grave to be discovered in Europe. Inside the burial mound was the imprint of a decayed ship and a central chamber filled with treasures. But who was buried there and what did it reveal about this period in history?

Sue Brunning, Curator of Early Medieval European Collections, says the burial was the final resting place of someone who had died in the early seventh century, during the Anglo-Saxon period – a time before 'England' existed.

Ship burials were rare in Anglo-Saxon England – probably reserved for the most important people in society (possibly a King) – so it's likely that there was a huge funeral ceremony. She continues:

'It's this effort, coupled with the quality and the quantity of the grave goods from all over the known world at that time, that has made people think that an Anglo-Saxon king may have been buried here.

TO LEARN MORE ABOUT THE SHIPWRECK & GOLD BELT BUCKLE PLEASE VISIT BRITISHMUSEUM.ORG.

HOW WE GOT OUR NAME

...from Pleasure Boat Studio, an essay written by Ouyang Xiu, Song Dynasty poet, essayist, and scholar, on the twelfth day of the twelfth month in the renwu year (January 25, 1043):

"I have heard of men of antiquity who fled from the world to distant rivers and lakes and refused to their dying day to return. They must have found some source of pleasure there. If one is not anxious for profit, even at the risk of danger, or is not convicted of a crime and forced to embark; rather, if one has a favorable breeze and gentle seas and is able to rest comfortably on a pillow and mat, sailing several hundred miles in a single day, then is boat travel not enjoyable? Of course, I have no time for such diversions. But since 'pleasure boat' is the designation of boats used for such pastimes, I have now adopted it as the name of my studio. Is there anything wrong with that?"

-Translated by Ronald Egan